Palgrave Macmillan Studies in Family and Intimate Life

Series Editors
Lynn Jamieson
University of Edinburgh
Edinburgh, UK

Jacqui Gabb
Faculty of Arts & Social Sciences
Open University
Milton Keynes, UK

Sara Eldén
Lund University
Lund, Sweden

Chiara Bertone
University of Eastern Piedmont
Alessandria, Italy

Vida Česnuitytė
Mykolas Romeris University
Vilnius, Lithuania

'The *Palgrave Macmillan Studies in Family and Intimate Life* series is impressive and contemporary in its themes and approaches'
– Professor Deborah Chambers, Newcastle University, UK, and author of *New Social Ties* .

The remit of the *Palgrave Macmillan Studies in Family and Intimate Life* series is to publish major texts, monographs and edited collections focusing broadly on the sociological exploration of intimate relationships and family life. The series encourages robust theoretical and methodologically diverse approaches. Publications cover a wide range of topics, spanning micro, meso and macro analyses, to investigate the ways that people live, love and care in diverse contexts. The series includes works by early career scholars and leading internationally acknowledged figures in the field while featuring influential and prize-winning research.

This series was originally edited by David H.J. Morgan and Graham Allan.

Sally Savage

Musical Mothering

Intergenerational Strategies Amongst
the Middle Classes

Sally Savage ⓘD
Queensland University of Technology
Brisbane, QLD, Australia

ISSN 2731-6440   ISSN 2731-6459   (electronic)
Palgrave Macmillan Studies in Family and Intimate Life
ISBN 978-3-031-65156-4   ISBN 978-3-031-65157-1   (eBook)
https://doi.org/10.1007/978-3-031-65157-1

This Palgrave Macmillan imprint is published by the registered company Springer Nature Switzerland AG.
The registered company address is: Gewerbestrasse 11, 6330 Cham, Switzerland

If disposing of this product, please recycle the paper.

ACKNOWLEDGEMENTS

I am deeply grateful to have the opportunity to write this book from my doctoral thesis. Music has been such a large and important part of my life, and it has shaped many of my life decisions, including career directions and mothering experiences. I have found solace in music in challenging times and felt its warm embrace. Even as a very young child, I was drawn to its magic and beauty. I was determined to make music part of my children's lives and for them to have opportunities to be able to play instruments and enjoy music, more than I had. I was always going to be a musical mother.

I am very thankful to the mothers who took part in my study and who are the basis for this book. Seeing how musical mothering is enacted and navigated in various ways demonstrates and celebrates our diversity, and I sincerely thank all the women who generously shared their stories with me. I have experienced the depth of meaning that music, in its many forms, has for them and what a positive contribution music brings to all of their lives.

Thank you to the editorial team at Palgrave Macmillan, in particular Professor Chiara Bertone, the editor of the Family and Intimate Life Series for her meticulous feedback and helpful suggestions to strengthen the book. Thank you to the book reviewers for their initial encouragement and feedback on my proposal and for taking a chance on the manuscript.

Many thanks also go to my doctoral supervisors, without whom this book would never have got started. Thank you to Dr Clare Hall for allowing me to use the term 'musical mother' that you first coined in your work and to Dr Howard Prosser for his ongoing support and encouragement. Both of you have continued to take an interest in my work. Thanks also to my doctoral examiners—Professor Beatriz Ilari and Dr Anna Bull for their sage advice on my thesis and encouragement to turn my thesis into a monograph.

Special thank you to Professor Joanne Lunn and Professor Susan Danby who encouraged and assisted me to write my book proposal. They, too, have continued to support and take an interest in this work and have provided valuable feedback throughout the developing chapters. Many thanks to my sister-in-law, Carol Savage, who checked my writing for grammatical errors and sense-making. As a self-professed, non-musical mother, it was good to have her insightful input. I also want to thank Dr Abbe Winter and Dr Christine Yates for their keen eyes and generous feedback on the manuscript.

Finally, to my family. I am so very proud of my daughters and their achievements. I love that they enjoy music and that music is an important part of their lives. They are my biggest supporters, along with my husband, Bill. Huge thank you to you three especially—I love you all to bits … and more.

CONTENTS

CHAPTER 1

Introduction

INTRODUCTION

Music pervades everyday life. In Australia, you would be hard pressed to find a family that does not have music as some part of its fabric, being listened to incidentally via radio, television or other media, or more deliberately selected through streaming services. Digitalisation of music is changing the way people listen to music from a collective experience to a more individualised approach. Catchy tunes, however, may be shared and sung almost unconsciously within the everyday lives of family members. For some families, music is more than a casual engagement and is a particular and active choice that is made for specific reasons (De Nora, 2000), and involvement can have significant consequences for the mothers who are predominantly the primary carers and drivers of this engagement in their children (Savage, 2015a, 2015b, 2019; Savage & Hall, 2017). This context is the warrant for this book which stems from my PhD study where I explored the relationship between music and women's mothering practices, with sub-questions around what this means for the women in the study and how they mother their children, the intergenerational influences of musical mothering and how gender and class influence musical mothering (Savage, 2019).

© The Author(s), under exclusive license to Springer Nature Switzerland AG 2024
S. Savage, *Musical Mothering*, Palgrave Macmillan Studies in Family and Intimate Life,
https://Doi.org/10.1007/978-3-031-65157-1_1

Throughout my life, I have met many mothers for whom music was important, if not essential, and they made it a priority for themselves and their children. Encompassing family members, friends, work colleagues, music teachers, volunteer committee member-mothers, clients of my music teaching business and research participants, these women are all musical mothers. Without exception, active music participation was an imperative for their children's education and life more broadly. And it was important for these women to produce musical children.

Even before music was part of my parenting, music had been part of my teaching. As an early year's teacher, I recall when I left a nursery school in London where I had been teaching for several years, they played ABBA's *Thank you for the music* to thank me for all the musical times we shared. Music was valued by the teaching college I attended, where all students had to study guitar or keyboard and left with enough skills to accompany a small cache of songs to use with young children. We all learnt a repertoire of singing games and musical activities. Sadly, current early childhood courses do not have enough time allocated to such pursuits and students lack the confidence to utilise music in their teaching when they leave university (Bautista & Ho, 2021). I always found music to be a valuable tool in my teaching but also something that I enjoyed doing along with the children.

For many years upon my return to Australia after living overseas, I ran a music teaching business where children under five years of age would come each week with their parent or carer—mostly mothers, but some fathers and grandmothers. The mothers were largely stay-at-home mothers or working part-time, and some were music teachers themselves. For a majority, music had been part of their lives, and they wanted the same for their children. For others, they were denied the music tuition they wanted in childhood and sought it for their children. A few came along because their friends did, and it was a way of keeping up appearances. These people did not stay long citing the need to give their children exposure to a wide range of extra-curricular activities, enabling them to choose and become 'well-rounded' in their interests—and their resumes (Vincent & Ball, 2007).

It was through my teaching that I became interested in the motivations behind why mothers were sending their children to these early childhood music classes. This became the impetus for my Master's study which found that mothers utilised such classes to nurture confidence and arts appreciation and to accumulate cultural capital for their children which enabled them to gain enrolment to elite schools and gave them advantages in educational spaces (Savage, 2015a, 2015b). Not only that, but the participating mothers also enjoyed making friends with like-minded women and learnt parenting techniques through their involvement in the class.

Music is a practice that is often passed down through generations as 'something we do'. French sociologist, Pierre Bourdieu, labelled this unconscious routine behaviour as 'habitus'. Habitus is "a system of lasting and transposable dispositions which, integrating past experiences, functions at every moment as a matrix of perceptions, appreciations and actions and makes possible the achievement of infinitely diversified tasks" (Bourdieu & Wacquant, 1992, p. 18). In other words, habitus is ways of being that are enacted without thought as part of everyday life—those actions we take for granted. As individuals, and as families, we continue to do certain practices because they reward us in some way. As unconscious and conscious dispositions, habitus, through practices, enables us to achieve our aims and is subsequently passed down through generations (Bourdieu, 1990). In Chap. 3, I elaborate on Bourdieu's toolkit—his 'thinking tools' (Wacquant, 1989, p. 50) and how they intersect to show how practices are enacted and reproduced—and where I explore social and classed practices of musical motherhood through the lens of Bourdieu's theory and justify the inclusion of other theories to complement Bourdieu. As Bourdieu says very little about gender, I utilised feminist theories, most notably feminist mothering theory, to critique gender-based issues I encountered within the women's mothering practices.

There has been increased pressure on mothers to intensively mother children as worthy and moral citizens of the future and to adhere to dominant neoliberal ideals (Gillies, 2007, 2010; Goodwin & Huppatz, 2010). Further exploration of these ideals, and motherhood more broadly, within the Australian context is investigated in Chap. 2. Participation in music is seen as one way to gain advantages in educational and workplace institutions, achieve mothers' desires for their children and consequently be acknowledged as 'good' mothers. Through my research, I could see that for many mothers, music was a means to achieve their aspirations for their children (Savage, 2015a, 2015b; Savage & Hall, 2017). Music developed favoured dispositions that helped to set their children apart from others and gave them advantages of accrued cultural capital when seeking enrolment at prestigious schools.

It was with this in mind that I formulated the guiding research question for this book which was to explore the relationship between music and mothering as I wanted to understand what music meant to the middle-class mothers I interviewed and how involvement in music influenced their mothering. I wanted to examine the intergenerational influences on musical mothering and to investigate the role of class and gender in musical mothering. In this introduction, I set the scene for the book by outlining the overall conceptual framework and then examine music as family practice. I explore how family cultures develop, maintain and evolve over generations, what this looks like in families and the extraordinary efforts that some mothers go to develop their children's musical skills. I begin to show how the women's nurturing of certain dispositions in their children is influenced by gender and class to gain privileges and advantages in educational institutions and workplaces.

Defining Musical Motherhood

Many mothers sing, rock and soothe their children with music as part of their caring work (Mackinlay, 2009). Informal musical experiences are part of everyday life (Savage, 2015b; Savage & Hall, 2017). My definition of musical mothering is the deliberate and incidental work that mothers do through music with their children. It might be that music informs the strategies mothers use to transition children from dinner to bedtime with calmness (de Nora, 2000), to get them to pack away their toys (Savage, 2015a) or to learn cognitive skills such as rote learning of mathematical tables and the alphabet (de Vries, 2007). Clare Hall first coined the term 'musical mother' when exploring the lives of choirboys and the extensive work their mothers did to promote, nurture and facilitate their sons' musical development (Hall, 2018). Hall's ethnographic study illuminates the extensive emotional labour in mothers' work and the concurrent contradictions when guiding their sons' musical trajectories.

It is important to emphasise that mothering as a social practice is afforded very little value and power in everyday Australian society (Goodwin & Huppatz, 2010). Currently, motherhood is seen with ambivalence, and as detrimental to women's career paths, as recently and very publicly attested in a Radio Times podcast by famous pop diva Lily Allen who espoused that motherhood ruined her career (Lambert, 2024). Conversely, motherhood is celebrated as a special time, valorised for its significance in bringing up the future generation of moral citizens (Skeggs, 2004). It is a pursuit supposedly filled with self-sacrifice and nurturing of others. Mothers who raise children who are successful, capable, independent and 'useful' are admired, yet those whose children who become welfare-dependent, or live without aspiration, are deemed problematic (Gillies, 2007). Those mothers with high levels of economic resources, and with male partners, remain the most powerful within their field, although even some of these women slip between the hegemonic cultural narratives and lose their shine, struggling to be recognised. For these mothers, music can become a means to legitimacy and acceptance and a way to show that they are indeed 'good' mothers.

'Good' mothers are culturally defined as "white, middle-class, married, stay-at-home moms, while 'good' mothers from a politic of maternal empowerment are drawn from all maternal identities and include lesbian, non-custodial, poor, single, older, and 'working' mothers" (O'Reilly, 2010, p. 7). Maternal identities are diversified by social distinctions which are often used to marginalise mothers who inhabit those spaces outside the perceived and dominant norm (Crenshaw, 1991).

WHOSE STORIES I TELL

Ethics was approved by the university where I was enrolled for my doctoral study. Recruitment for the study was via purposive sampling, meaning that personal contacts established the initial contact with people who felt they may be interested in talking to me about their music experiences. These people acted as mediators and could vouch for my integrity and character (Kristensen & Ravn, 2015). This had a 'snowball' effect (Lewis-Beck et al., 2004), and potential participants then contacted me directly to be involved in the study. I invited mothers to be part of the study if they were engaging in regular music activities either themselves or with their child/ren. The mothers also had to ensure that their mothers would be willing to participate in the study as well. There was one exception where the mother did not disclose until the interview had started that her mother had passed away when she was a teenager. I decided to continue with this participant's story as she effectively became the mother for her siblings after her mother's passing which offered another view of musical motherhood.

Another point you may notice is the multiculturalism of the participants of the study. Australia has a rich history of Indigenous culture dating back many thousands of years. Indigenous populations in Australia only make up 3.8% of its current population (Australian Bureau of Statistics [ABS], 2021). Australia was colonised by the British in 1770, and since then there have been waves of immigrants who have made their home in Australia, mostly from Europe, initiated by settlement programmes or significant world and humanitarian events. According to the ABS (2022) since the end of WWII, there has been a steady increase in the number of overseas-born and second-generation migrants. In 2021, 27.6% of the Australian population were born overseas (ABS, 2022). Changes to Australia's immigration policies since 2006 have also seen an increased intake of skilled migrants to bolster the workforce (ABS, 2022). The countries represented as the countries of birth for most of these migrants are England and India representing 3.6% and 2.6% respectively of the overall population (ABS, 2022).

CREATING NARRATIVES OF MUSICAL MOTHERHOOD

The stories in this book are co-constructions between narrator and listener, and my own interpretation and our subjectivities are interwoven to create the mothers' stories (Squire, 2008). I met with the mothers over a seven-month period at various locations. This included their homes, cafes, and libraries as I ensured the interviews were convenient to them and where they felt at ease. Written consent was given to audio record the interviews, which ranged from one to two hours each. The semi-structured interviews were conversational in style, with guiding questions aimed to answer the research questions, in line with feminist principles. Feminist interview methods propose that the interviewer finds common ground with the interviewee and advocates for an open exchange to develop rapport (Lawler, 2000). Feminist methods seek to raise awareness of the complex relational dynamics that exist between identities and power which are inherent in cultural constructions of similarities and differences, and the research process reflects this (De Vault & Gross, 2012). Having shared subjectivities, as middle-class musical mothers, provided some common ground with which to share understandings; however, I was also cognisant that our experiences may not have been similar and that no two experiences are the same.

I had intended to interview mothers in each pair first; however, my first interview was with a grandmother. All subsequent interviews were with the mother first. Through the interview process, I could see how the women's subjectivities altered between daughter, mother and grandmother which meant that the order of the interview became less significant. Interviews were audio-recorded and transcribed verbatim by me as

soon as practicable after the interview. Reflective notes were taken immediately after each interview. I aimed to complete the transcription of the
mother prior to interviewing the grandmother.

I decided to interview mothers and grandmothers separately. This was
deliberate so that each could feel comfortable to share their experiences
freely as I felt they may otherwise be constrained by the other person
being there. The mothers and grandmothers were indeed frank in their
stories, and tensions within relationships were mentioned and explored.
Consent to be interviewed was freely given by all the women, and each
was given a copy of their transcript after the interview to check for accu-
racy. At this point, the women were given the opportunity to delete or add
anything to their transcripts, and some did this. A summary of the study
was given to all the women at the conclusion.

There is always a risk that in research such as this that the participants
will not agree or like the researcher's interpretation of the stories. Lareau
(2003/2011), in the later edition of her book, commented that her participants were quite angry and felt betrayed about being portrayed in the
way they were. In my study, some of the women were highly cognisant
that the other family member would read their comments in the write-up
of the study, but it was felt that the information would not be revelatory
but rather an affirmation of what they already knew. One such discussion
was in my interview with participant, Penelope:

Sally: So, as a mother, have you sort of felt compelled to mother in
            a particular way? Have you felt there's been pressure on you
            to do certain things?
Penelope: *Yes, I feel … you're not going to tell my mother about this … I've
            felt a lot of pressure from my mother to mother in a particular
            way … yeah*
Sally: Can you talk to me about that?
Penelope: *Yeah I can* (laughs)
Sally: She won't find out about it … unless she reads my thesis …
            but she won't know which one's you …
Penelope: *Ooooooh! She will though, exactly!!! Ah dear … um … it's inter-
            esting because …* (and she goes on to tell her story)

I did not share any parts of the mothers' interview with the grandmothers and vice-versa. Lareau (2003/2011) maintains that researchers need
to explicitly forewarn participants of the possibilities of such tensions while

maintaining control over the project and "the critical analytic framework necessary to undergird an argument" (p. 313). At the end of her second edition, Lareau writes extensively about the participants' reactions to her book and includes their comments, many of which are not complementary. The emotional work of research that examines lived experiences, for participant and researcher, should be acknowledged and addressed as an ethical and moral responsibility (Lareau, 2003/2011). I have actively tried to present the mothers' stories accurately and fairly, and all participants have been given pseudonyms and identifying features have been deidentified to protect the confidentiality of the women. Some aspects of their stories have been changed to protect the anonymity of the research participants.

Utilising Brannen et al.'s (2004) generational work, I analysed the individual transcripts first, guided by Riessman's (2002) and Squire's (2008) approaches. I looked at themes pertaining to the research questions, but also additional themes that became evident. Reading and rereading the transcripts also revealed the differing subjectivities experienced by the participants. The narratives were arranged into chronological life-stage order to show important times of change within the lifespan (Brannen et al., 2004). If historical events were mentioned, these were considered within the context of social norms at those specific times.

In the second stage of analysis, I made comparisons between the family members to look for similarities and differences, intergenerational changes and maintenances, and to infer family habitus structures, relations and patterns (McLeod & Thomson, 2011). The third stage was to look at mothers and grandmothers respectively to see if life stage was a factor in their decision-making and perspectives. Multiple perspectives were gathered through the narratives of both mothers and grandmothers. Throughout all the stages, continuous referral was made to the research literature and the data to inform my thinking.

I deliberately did not seek to include any fathers in the study, choosing to focus on the role of mothers. I acknowledge that fathers play an important role in families and some are 'musical fathers' (see Scarlato, 2021, for work in this area); however, my interest, and acknowledgement that it is mothers who usually do the work on fostering musical development in children, meant that I did not want to include fathers' perspectives for this book.

As interviews are socially constructed, it is important for the researcher to demonstrate reflexivity on their own positioning and how that influences the interview process. As Riessman (2015) points out, "all narrators [make] ... choices about what to include, what to emphasise, what to ignore—and as a narrative analyst, I recognise that these choices are significant ones" (p. 1056). As the narrator for the mothers' stories, it was imperative that I was transparent about my own background and experiences, and how they influenced my interpretations.

ADDING MY OWN STORY OF MUSICAL MOTHERHOOD

The idea for the work came from my own experiences as a musician, mother, and teacher of music and my interactions with other mothers over the years in various contexts. I have incorporated some of my own stories with the stories of the mothers I interviewed to be transparent about my own experience and the influence this had on my interpretation of the mothers' narratives, consistent with feminist research principles. As an insider in this research, my imagination of the mothers' stories is connected to my own lifelong bond with this art form and represents another example of musical motherhood. Prominent feminist theorists such as mothering theorist Andrea O'Reilly, write about their own experiences as examples of practice and points of reference. I acknowledge that all women's voices have the right to be heard and that includes my own, and which I assert was often silenced or ignored at various points in my life as being not worthy. Miller (2017) has argued that women's voices over time have been "essentialised and taken-for-granted or invisible in public or political contexts" (p. 59); however, this work has enabled me to reflect upon my experiences of middle-class musical motherhood, which has been imbued with desires of acceptability, respectability, heightened emotion, anxieties and meaning-making.

INTRODUCING THE GRANDMOTHERS AND MOTHERS IN THIS BOOK

Susan and Jessica

Susan
Susan referred to herself as an artist of many genres, not just music. Born in the mid-1950s, Susan grew up in an outer regional area of Australia on a farm. She was one of five children, all of whom learnt at least one

instrument. Susan is proficient in two instruments—piano (which she taught privately for many years), and the oboe (which she studied at Conservatorium-level). Divorced, Susan had three children, all of whom learnt music. Susan continues her musical creativities and involves herself in festival productions and other artistic pursuits, latterly taking up the treble recorder. She continues to find new music to explore and enjoy, and music is a way for Susan to make new connections.

Jessica

Jessica was born in 1985 in an outer regional area of Australia and is the daughter of Susan. She is the youngest of three siblings—all of whom learnt music. Jessica initially played the flute before picking up the cello[1] and teaching herself to play. Jessica works as a professional musician. She also teaches private students. Jessica is partnered in a same-sex relationship and has one child. Jessica is not the birth mother. Jessica enjoys Asian and contemporary music.

Sangeeta, Hema and Aarshia

Sangeeta

Sangeeta is the mother of Aarshia. Born in the early 1960s in India, Sangeeta has two children of whom Aarshia is the eldest. As a teacher, Sangeeta prioritises academic study before music, although she says that music has always been an important part of her life. Sangeeta has travelled a great deal in her married life, as her husband was often posted in different locations as a naval officer. Sangeeta and her young children were sometimes living in areas where it was not acceptable for women to go out unaccompanied. This meant that Sangeeta was housebound for extended periods of time. Sangeeta arranged the marriage of her daughter Aarshia to Hema's son in India. It was important for both Sangeeta and Hema that the marriage was suitable according to their caste system.

---

[1] This is the accepted abbreviation for the violoncello. The word cello will be used throughout the book for this instrument.

Hema

Hema is Aarshia's mother-in-law, a visual artist, and was born in 1955 in India. In Aarshia's family culture in India, the new bride must live with the son's family. In this respect, I felt it important to include Hema in this study, and fortuitously, she was in Australia at the time of the interviews. Hema once worked as an art and drama teacher so has sympathies with the arts. She recalled how, as a young married woman, her husband's family would only allow her to paint when she had completed all her domestic chores for the household (she too had to live with her husband's family when she was first married). Needless to say, she rarely had time to practice her art. Aarshia commented that Hema has always been a tremendous support to her and is just like her mother.

Aarshia

At 32, Aarshia is the mother of one daughter and is completing her PhD study full-time in Australia where she hopes to live after her studies are complete. Like her father, her husband works in a similar occupation and often works away from home. Fortunately, Aarshia can remain in the same location and has the support of her mother and mother-in-law when caring for her daughter. The grandmothers alternate coming over to Australia for three months at a time to share the caring responsibilities and to support Aarshia's young family. Aarshia mentioned that she attended playgroup and other extra-curricular activities with her young daughter so she could learn Australian parenting techniques, which she commented were vastly different to those she had seen in India.

Kelele

Kelele

Kelele is a Tongan-born woman who is married to an Australian man. She mentioned in her interview that she always wanted to marry a foreigner, preferring them to Tongan men. She has three children. Kelele was born in 1980 and at the time of the study was studying to be a teacher aide. After leaving school, Kelele worked in hospitality in Tonga. Much of Kelele's musical experience was from her attendance at church. Only men were allowed to play the instruments in church, but Kelele enjoyed the singing which she labels as singing in 'tone'. Sadly, Kelele's mother died when Kelele was a teenager. It was only when she had begun her interview that this information was revealed. Although the study was for mothers and grandmothers, I felt Kelele's experience, where she became the 'mother' for siblings, offered another perspective.

Rosemary and Penelope

Rosemary

Rosemary, born in 1942, is a trained primary teacher; however, as was the law in Australia at that time, once she was married, she was no longer able to teach and was therefore financially dependent on her husband, who was also a schoolteacher, and later school principal. They travelled to various locations in the Australian state where he taught. Rosemary's primary musical love is singing; however, she also learnt the piano from the local nuns when she was a child. Rosemary has three adult children and several grandchildren.

Penelope

Penelope, Rosemary's eldest child, had lessons in piano and violin as a child. She also played the guitar. In her early 20s, she played in bands and other groups, both in Australia and overseas. Penelope studied to be a primary teacher and now prefers to do relief teaching where she integrates her musical creativity with her teaching. Born in 1967, married, Penelope has one daughter.

Linda and Ashley

Linda

Linda was born in England in 1961. She attended international boarding schools throughout her childhood. Linda learnt several instruments as a child—piano, violin and flute. She played in orchestras and bands at school. After leaving school, Linda trained and worked as a nurse before the family relocated to Australia. Once Linda had children, she stopped work to care for her children. Linda has four children. Linda has resumed work now that her children are adults. Linda enjoys looking after her grandchildren.

Ashley

Ashley is Linda's eldest child. Ashley was born in 1993 and studied the violin from a very young age. Ashley achieved outstanding results in playing the violin when she was still in her early teens. She participated in orchestras and music competitions regularly. After later rejecting the instrument, she studied to become a nurse. Ashley is married and has one son.

The intergenerational stories in this book have been generated through interviews with mothers and their mothers, to see how music has been passed down through generations, how music has influenced the women's mothering practices and to explore the meaning music has for these women. Not all families practiced music to the same degree, but for all, music was important in their family life and was part of their family culture. Families are indeed all different and this book offers a small sample of Australian families, with mothers and grandmothers telling their stories of how engagement with music influenced their mothering practices and influenced their lives and the lives of their families.

OVERVIEW OF THE CHAPTERS

In Chap. 2, I explore various broader societal influences on mothering from neoliberal expectations and ideologies to notions of class and gender within the Australian context. I explain current and historical constructions of mothers in and out of the paid workforce. I then turn to looking at mothers, particularly stay-at-home mothers or those who do not work full-time in paid employment, who assume the role as the family CEO. This connects with mothers' aspirations for their children and how mothers' successes and children's successes become one. For some stay-at-home mothers, volunteering enables them to fulfil roles and exhibit the skills that they may have in the workplace. This can provide advantages for mothers and their children as I illustrate.

Mothers explain how important it is to 'be there' for their children, and I show the compromises they make to their careers and their lives to invest in their children. Some mothers believe in essentialist views that position biological mothers as the only and best carers for their children which often causes increased stress and unreasonable expectations on women. Mothers who work in paid employment are demonised by other mothers, while new generations of women express how working and mothering offers them a more balanced life. The mothers in this book vary in the amount of support they receive from extended family and in how they negotiate the tricky path of work and motherhood and how they navigate involvement in music when that is thrown into the mix.

Through mothers' decision-making, we begin to see how constructions of gender and class play out and form a rationale for this book, as the gendered and classed practices of women's involvement in music have rarely been examined in the wider literature. Exploration of music as a family cultural practice and subsequent transmission to future generations are considered.

In Chap. 3, I launch into what it is to be a musical mother using Bourdieu's theoretical toolkit as my theoretical framework to investigate the social and classed practice of music. I define Bourdieu's key terms and their relevance to the topic at hand. I begin to look at mothers' practices as intensive and investigate how they seek opportunities for their children in the field of music in their social and classed practices using a Bourdieusian lens. Conceptualisations of taste and distinction are argued, and we see how middle-class mothers make decisions for children's futures based on the exchange value of their accumulated capitals. Using Bourdieu's analogy of playing a game, I show how some mothers know and exploit the rules and how others withdraw when they realise they cannot compete.

To complement Bourdieu's toolkit, I include feminist theories to enhance understanding of musical motherhood. Considerations of the emotional labour, care work, intensive mothering, concerted cultivation, mental load and affective recognition that are entwined in mothers' work in developing musical children are theorised. Feminist mothering theory is articulated to show how mothers participate in the logic of 'good' motherhood.

In concert with these theories, I use narrative inquiry to generate the data for this book. I justify my use of feminist principles and methods when interviewing the mothers and discuss the relational nature of the interviews. While many stories adhere to the dominant cultural narratives of the day, the women also told counter-narratives—stories of resistance—and I explain how I explored the performative and relational aspects of the interactions with the mothers and how they conform—or not—to society's master narratives.

Chap. 4 includes a story of my own musical development. While much of the book is about mothers' encouragement and labour to produce musical children, my story is quite the opposite. It was through the nurturing of others and my own self-determination that my musical development and associated opportunities occurred. However, the broader literature in this field overwhelmingly supports the notion that most successful musicians have parents who fostered and encouraged their children's musical development. In this chapter, I discuss whether musical talent is an acquired skill or a matter of genetics. The cycle of "affective recognition" (Atkinson, 2016, p. 84) is defined and explored. I look at how the support of musical development is uneven in families, with some siblings receiving more attention than others, how mothers make decisions about who to nurture musically and who misses out and how this creates tensions within families.

Practices of intensive mothering and concerted cultivation are examined in Chap. 5. I explore how mothers strive to be perceived as 'good' by adhering to neoliberal tropes and middle-class social expectations. The 'good' mother is one who is self-sacrificing and child-centred. Mothers make investments in their children to create advantages that will maintain or improve their children's social standing. These investments are only successful when there is a full commitment to making them work. Mothers who are not prepared to do this drop out of the game. I show how middle-class mothers work hard to make their efforts look natural rather than 'pushy' like other mothers they openly demonise. Mothers judge each other and compete for middle-class respectability and recognition. Intensive mothering forms a continuum of practice in mothers. The amount of concerted cultivation enacted varies according to available financial, cultural and emotional resources.

Continuing the theme of intensive mothering and concerted cultivation, in Chap. 6, I examine the dispositions that mothers nurture to create moral and worthy citizens of value. Mothers are criticised when their children are not 'good' which reflects on them and their mothering. Through music, mothers foster the dispositions that are seen as morally right and valorised within our society. The chapter looks at the ways that mothers control, monitor and survey their children's behaviour. This ensures mothers and their children are seen as worthy, thereby maintaining their moral superiority over mothers who are less aspirational.

The cost of mothering intensively often comes with an emotional price. In Chap. 7, I investigate the emotional labour of musical motherhood. Drawing on Hochschild's research in this area, I look at how mothers modify the behaviour of themselves and others, again to maintain that persona of middle-class self-control and respectability, often through music. I also demonstrate how mothers utilise music as a resource for themselves to do their emotional work. The case study of Jessica highlights the exhausting emotional labour of being a mother, teacher, partner and professional musician and how she navigates her multiple roles.

In Chap. 8, I discuss the importance of music for the mothers, and how music acts as a social connection and creates a sense of family belonging. I return to the notion of "family feeling" (Atkinson, 2014, p. 340; Bourdieu, 1998, p. 68) that is engendered when families participate in music together. This thoroughly human activity is a means to generate family bonding and love, and to transmit cultural heritage and intergenerational traditions. I show not only how grandmothers and mothers transmit music to children, but how children influence the musical choices and repertoires of families too. Mothers' achievements are acknowledged through their children's engagement and love of music that they share.

In the Conclusion, the themes of the book are brought together to highlight the importance of music for the mothers intergenerationally.

References

Atkinson, W. (2014). A sketch of 'family' as a field: From realized category to space of struggle. *Acta Sociologica, 57*(3), 223–235. https://doi.org/10.1177/0001699313511114

Atkinson, W. (2016). *Beyond Bourdieu*. Polity.

Australian Bureau of Statistics [ABS]. (2021). *Aboriginal and Torres Strait Islander Australians*. https://www.abs.gov.au/statistics/people/aboriginal-and-torres-strait-islander-peoples/estimates-aboriginal-and-torres-strait-islander-australians/latest-release

Australian Bureau of Statistics [ABS]. (2022). *Cultural diversity*. https://www.abs.gov.au/articles/cultural-diversity-australia

Bautista, A., & Ho, Y. L. (2021). Music and movement teacher professional development: An interview study with Hong Kong kindergarten teachers. *Australasian Journal of Early Childhood, 46*(3), 276–290. https://doi.org/10.1177/18369391211014759

Bourdieu, P. (1990). *The logic of practice*. Polity.

Bourdieu, P. (1998). *Practical reason*. Polity.

Bourdieu, P., & Wacquant, L. (1992). *An invitation to reflexive sociology*. University of Chicago Press.

Brannen, J., Moss, P., & Mooney, A. (2004). *Work and caring over the twentieth century: Change and continuity in four-generation families*. Palgrave Macmillan.

Crenshaw, K. (1991). Mapping the margins: Intersectionality, identity politics, and violence against women of color. *Stanford Law Review, 43*, 1241–1299. https://doi.org/10.2307/1229039

De Nora, T. (2000). *Music in everyday life.* Cambridge University Press.

De Vault, M. L., & Gross, G. (2012). Feminist qualitative interviewing: Experience, talk, and knowledge. In S. N. Hesse-Biber (Ed.), *Handbook of feminist research: Theory and praxis* (pp. 188–206). Sage.

De Vries, P. (2007). I do music with my children because… Proceedings of the XXIXth Annual Conference: 2–4 July 2007. *Music Education Research, Values and Initiatives* (pp. 39–46).

Gillies, V. (2007). *Marginalised mothers: Exploring working-class experiences of parenting.* Routledge.

Gillies, V. (2010). Is poor parenting a class issue? Contextualising anti-social behaviour and family life. In M. Klett-Davies (Ed.), *Is parenting a class issue?* (pp. 44–61). The Nuffield Press.

Goodwin, S., & Huppatz, K. (2010). The good mother in theory and research: An overview. In S. Goodwin & K. Huppatz (Eds.), *The good mother: Contemporary motherhoods in Australia* (pp. 1–24). Sydney University Press.

Hall, C. (2018). *Masculinity, class and music education: Boys performing middle-class masculinities through music.* Palgrave Macmillan.

Kristensen, G. K., & Ravn, M. N. (2015). The voices heard and the voices silenced: Recruitment processes in qualitative interview studies. *Qualitative Research, 15*(6), 722–737. https://doi.org/10.1177/1468794114567496

Lambert, T. (2024). Lily Allen says motherhood ruined her career. The system failed her. https://womensagenda.com.au/latest/soapbox/lily-allen-says-motherhood-ruined-her-career-the-system-failedher/#:~:text=%E2%80%9CI%20never%20really%20had%20a,’t%2C%E2%80%9D%20she%20added.

Lareau, A. (2003/2011). *Unequal childhoods: Class, race, and family life.* University of California Press.

Lawler, S. (2000). *Mothering the self: Mothers, daughters, subjects.* Routledge.

Lewis-Beck, M. S., Bryman, A., & Futing Liao, T. (2004). *The SAGE encyclopaedia of social science research methods.* Sage.

Mackinlay, E. (2009). Singing maternity through autoethnography: Making visible the musical world of myself as a mother. *Early Child Development and Care, 179*(6), 717–731. https://doi.org/10.1080/03004430902944320

McLeod, J., & Thomson, R. (2011). Generation. In J. McLeod & R. Thomson (Eds.), *Researching social change* (pp. 107–124). Sage.

Miller, T. (2017). *Making sense of parenthood: Caring, gender and family lives.* Cambridge University Press.

O'Reilly, A. (2010). *Twenty-first-century motherhood: Experience, identity, policy, agency.* Columbia University Press.

Riessman, C. K. (2002). Analysis of personal narratives. In J. F. Gubrium & J. A. Holstein (Eds.), *Handbook of interview research: Context and method* (pp. 695–710). Sage.

Riessman, C. K. (2015). Ruptures and sutures: Time, audience and identity in an illness narrative. *Sociology of Health & Illness, 37*(7), 1055–1071.

Savage, S. (2015a). *Intensive mothering through music in early childhood education.* Unpublished Masters' Minor Thesis, Monash University.

Savage, S. (2015b). Understanding mothers' perspectives on early childhood music programmes. *Australian Journal of Music Education, 2*, 127–139.

Savage, S. (2019). *Musical mothering: Middle-class strategies and affect across generations.* Unpublished PhD thesis, Monash University.

Savage, S., & Hall, C. (2017). Thinking about and beyond the cultural contradictions of motherhood through musical mothering. In M. J. Rose, L. Ross, & J. Hartmann (Eds.), *The music of motherhood* (pp. 32–50). Demeter Press.

Scarlato, M. K. M. (2021). Musical fatherhood: A phenomenological study. *Journal of Research in Childhood Education, 35*(3), 373–388. https://doi.org/10.1080/02568543.2020.1728445

Skeggs, B. (2004). *Class, self, culture.* Routledge.

Squire, C. (2008). Experience-centred to socioculturally-oriented approaches to narrative. In M. Andrews, C. Squire, & M. Tamboukou (Eds.), *Doing narrative research* (pp. 42–64). Sage.

Vincent, C., & Ball, S. J. (2007). 'Making up' the middle-class child: Families, activities and class dispositions. *Sociology, 41*(6), 1061–1077. https://doi.org/10.1177/0038038507082315

Wacquant, L. (1989). Towards a reflexive sociology: A workshop with Pierre Bourdieu. *Sociological Theory, 7*(1), 26–63. https://doi.org/10.2307/202061

CHAPTER 2

Musical Motherhood in Everyday Australian Middle-Class Family Life

INTRODUCTION

Research about music in family life has predominately focused on participation and outcomes for children. Similarly, when studies have looked at music in the home, or musical play in various situations, it is the children's perspectives that are front and foremost. When parental perspectives are considered, there is rarely a focus on which parent is doing most of the work when it comes to involvement in musical activities. This book takes the view that music is a cultural practice and that meaning-making is produced and reproduced in families over generations and that it is primarily mothers that do this work. Social pressures to mother in particular ways have been exacerbated by neoliberal ideals over recent decades. While this book will not give a history of neoliberalism in Australia, I will extrapolate on contemporary notions of the neoliberal phase of capitalism and its influence on parenting, specifically mothering, in Australia.

NEOLIBERALISM IN AUSTRALIA AND ITS INFLUENCE ON MOTHERING

Neoliberalism is understood by many to be a complex array of varying practices centred around ideals of competition, choice, investment in the self, entrepreneurialism and self-responsibility (Oyarzún et al., 2022).

Neoliberalism is demonstrated by public services being privatised and preference for and deregulation of a free-market economy where competition reigns (Hamer & Tranter, 2021). Since the 1990s, neoliberal thinking has demonised those dependent upon welfare, contributing to a rise in the number of programmes to make people job-ready and demonstrated through increased accountability in workers through often unrealistic key performance targets (Bottrell, 2013). There has been a rise in programmes to foster better parenting, particularly aimed at surveillance of the working classes. Recent attention on the current cost-of-living crisis particularly impacting low and middle-income Australian families has evidenced Australian families seeking more housing support, with many families, particularly single mothers, experiencing homelessness (Warren & Barnes, 2023) and increasing child safety concerns due to previous neoliberal government policies and increasing social and economic inequity (see Warren & Barnes, 2023). A two-tier system within education and health exists in Australia with the gap between the haves and have-nots growing incrementally wider and with social welfare being increasingly inaccessible (Threadgold & Gerrard, 2022).

The influence of neoliberal ideology on parenting cannot be underplayed and is highly significant when considering the motivations behind such practices. Under neoliberalism, responsibility for outcomes is positioned directly with individuals who supposedly have an array of choices with which to develop economic, social and cultural capitals, perpetuated by aspiration, consumerism, competition and the so-called advantages of globalisation (Ball, 2003; Bok, 2010; Gale & Parker, 2015; Simpson et al., 2015). With fluctuating economic conditions, and the current cost-of-living crisis, along with increased choices in educational markets, parents have become increasingly anxious to make the 'right' decisions with regards to their children's schooling to ensure future success and maintain their position in the social hierarchy (Reeves, 2015), a position that is currently highly precarious. In step with other capitalist nations, the next generation of Australians is likely to be less well-off than their parents (Threadgold & Gerrard, 2022). Similarly, individualistic approaches to parenting, and the recent Covid-19 pandemic which immediately preceded the current cost-of-living crisis, have meant that parents are burnt out and demonstrating higher levels of stress (Wiemer & Clarkson, 2023), exacerbated by economic and social pressures.

Neoliberal ideology suggests that improving one's skills can reduce life's risks, with an emphasis on self-help initiatives to build resilience and prop up lives rather than relying on communities to support individuals (Bottrell, 2013; Threadgold & Gerrard, 2022). This translates to parents being deemed responsible for how their children turn out (Sanders, 2020) and, as Macvarish and Martin (2021) assert, form a basis for the "early politicisation of 'parenting'" (p. 473). Parenting practices that do not fit the hegemonic norm are labelled deficient by the dominant classes where poor parenting is blamed for society's problems (Gillies, 2007, 2010; Goodwin & Huppatz, 2010). Mothers, in particular, are seen as role models for their children, shaping their life trajectories and career paths. A plethora of reality television programmes have promoted optimal parenting; programmes such as 'Supernanny' and 'Parental Guidance' all judge parenting styles and rely on so-called parenting experts to guide parents on best practice.

In recent years, parenting has become a consumer-driven activity where many parents seek the services of experts to promote children's achievement (Colvin & Knight, 2023; Macvarish & Martin, 2021; Vincent & Ball, 2007). Parenting has been professionalised where it is considered necessary to outsource help in order to parent effectively (Macvarish & Martin, 2021) and to get ahead of the game, and issues with parenting are often judged in relation to class. Parenting programmes have been established to overcome this deficit model to improve outcomes for children and are intended to enhance social mobility (Bok, 2010; Gale & Parker, 2015; Hartas, 2016). Parents make investments in their children as a type of social capital (Sanders, 2020) which demands intensive parenting to enact. As Sims et al. (2022) posit, investments in children increase the likelihood of developing citizens who are employable and whose labour can be effectively utilised and potentially exploited in the future through ongoing control and surveillance (Gerrard, 2014).

Practices like intensive mothering, that are on the rise globally and that I look at more extensively in Chap. 5, are equated with good mothering. Atkinson (2016) articulates that 'good mothering' is locally specific:

> The dominant definition of 'good mothering', for instance, tends to represent the practices of the dominant ethnicity and the dominant class or at least the cultural faction thereof, possible only with the possession of certain resources. In many instances, therefore, it produces shame and guilt amongst those who, with less symbolic capital within the ethno-national space (Hage, 1998) and/or economic and cultural capital and drawing on local, practical models and methods of coping rather than the latest 'official' advice, are unable to provide the forms of interaction, pedagogy and support demanded. (p. 51)

Atkinson (2016) identifies the classed nature of 'good mothering' which he states is readily available to resourced mothers, that is, those with economic and cultural capital. For musical mothers, seeking tuition, the right teachers, instrument choice, ensembles and future-oriented opportunities are imperative for success. This takes time, substantial economic resources and cultural know-how to achieve and is therefore predominantly available to elites and the upper middle classes. However, intensive mothering practices cross class boundaries too, where "marginalised mothers do not have a choice as to how to mother, as it is imposed on them by society's views and expectations of them" (Ennis, 2014, p. 20). Working-class women do make similar investments in their children as middle-class women; however, they have less return on their investments due to the exchange value of their existing capitals (Reay, 1995, 1997; Skeggs, 2004b). Working-class mothers want their children to be successful and happy and, however, often apply a 'natural growth' (Lareau, 2003, p. 3) approach to their mothering where adult intervention in children's lives is minimal.

Within neoliberalism, the raising of aspirations has emerged as a legitimate policy domain, particularly targeted at low-income families, aiming to change intergenerational disadvantage (Hartas, 2016). There are policies aimed at decreasing welfare dependency and converting the poor into entrepreneurs within the competitive market space (Hamer & Tranter, 2021). Parents with low educational achievement are assumed to have "little or no aspiration … [and are] framed within a deficit model" (Bok, 2010, p. 83). Middle-class mothers aspire for their children to be unique and stand out from the crowd, whereas working-class mothers want their children to fit in (Gillies, 2007). Gillies' (2007) work is based on two studies in the UK, a small-scale qualitative case study of five white, working-class, lone mothers and another based on findings from a national survey study of parents with children 8–12 years, where the experiences of 25 working-class mothers and 11 fathers were subsequently documented from in-depth interviews. Working-class mothers work hard to promote resilience in their children, aiming to provide security and coping skills when life was filled with 'disappointment, frustration and vulnerability' (Gillies, 2007, p. 146), while middle-class mothers pass on privilege and feelings of entitlement. Threadgold and Gerrard (2022) assert that there is an overriding "domination of middle-class morals, values and tastes [which are] normalised as 'the way things are'" (p. 4). Responsibility to create moral and worthy citizens of the future is laid squarely with parents

(Oyarzún et al., 2022), predominately mothers. Middle-class mothers strategically utilise music tuition to foster the dispositions and future goals they hold for their children.

Mothers do not wish to be conspicuous; however, as neoliberal subjects, they work hard to develop individual traits in their children that will put them above everyone else. As I will also show in this book, middle-class mothers disavow any overtly concerted efforts to develop musical dispositions in their children and be perceived as forcing their children to do something they do not wish to do. This would be antithetical to 'good' mothering practice. However, mothers exercise judgement on other mothers to determine their moral worthiness and value.

Discussions on neoliberalism cannot exist without talking about class. It is in this next section that I will define how class is considered in this book.

CLASS IN AUSTRALIA

Class is a very slippery subject, and many in Australian society believe Australia to be a meritocracy. Class is not always about economic status and levels of cultural capital. It is something that pervades our everyday life, affecting opportunities and human interactions in families, education, the workplace and other institutions where class inequalities abound (Germov, 2004). As Skeggs (2004a) writes, social class is fought through symbolic conflict where "cultural privilege and power are seen as ascribed rather than achieved ... 'the self' (or the subject) and ... concepts of personhood make class" (pp. 4–5). Lawler (2005) explains class as:

> dynamic; as a system of inequality which is continually being re-made in the large and small-scale processes of social life: through the workings of global capital and the search for new markets, but also through claims for entitlement (and non-entitlement), through symbols and representations, and in the emotional and affective dimensions of life. (p. 797)

Class is tricky to define and is interwoven with issues of superiority and othering, marginalisation and prejudice, and, of course, power (Gillies, 2007; Skeggs, 2004a). Class is often defined by employment status, occupation, levels of education and income (Hays, 1996; Lareau, 2003/2011). Hays questioned whether it was accurate to define stay-at-home mothers by their partner's status, thereby complicating class definitions in existing frameworks. Just because women have partners who may be financially comfortable does not mean that they have access to these funds. I think of women in my mother's generation when, like my mother, women were not allowed to work, and in my mother's case at my father's insistence. My father wanted to be perceived as the provider, and keeper of the purse. It was an expression of power. In her recent book which explored middle-class mothers leaving high-status professional jobs to become stay-at-home mothers, Orgad (2019) interviewed husbands of these women. While professing to be egalitarian about their relationships, husbands were highly cognisant of their wives' financial dependence and saw their respective roles as female caregiver and male breadwinner as normative. In Australia, women who are now in their 50s and above are the fastest-growing group of homeless people, suggesting that years at home caring for children have severely penalised women in the economic stakes (Enticott et al., 2022).

Sheppard and Biddle (2015) undertook a quantitative study of 1200 Australian adults based on Bourdieu's theory of class and cultural capital and utilised a five-category system, and a latent class analysis. Class was calculated via six measures inclusive of household income and property value/ownership, social capital in the form of social contacts and occupational status, and cultural capital in the form of attendance at 'highbrow' (attending the opera/theatre, listening to classical music) and 'emerging' (watching sport, going to the gym) activities (Sheppard & Biddle, 2015). Gender differences associated with class membership were not factored although age disparities were evident where some of the youngest participants (18–24 years) and the oldest participants (55+ years) attributed themselves to be middle-class when they were working-class (Sheppard & Biddle, 2015). The perception of class among the participants of the Sheppard and Biddle (2015) study is contradictory; many of whom labelled themselves as working-class but were in fact identified as being middle-class and similarly those who were identified as being affluent-class perceived themselves as middle-class. The implications for how people identify themselves, what attributes they consider to be related to class and how class taxonomies demonstrate some fluidity. Bourdieu (1990) astutely points out "nothing classifies somebody more than the way he or she classifies" (pp. 19–20). While this may give information about the participants' subjectivities and the way they perceive themselves, it also has implications for the researcher. This is relevant in my research when looking at the classed practices of the women and the intergenerational influences on mothering to reflect upon the durable and changing class statuses within family groups.

For the purposes of this book and to be consistent with other class-based analyses in sociology, and the wider reading for this book, class will be defined into two categories—working-class and middle-class—where middle-class describes families with one or more parents possessing a tertiary education degree, higher than average income and higher cultural capital inclusive of educational and social capital (Hays, 1996; Lareau, 2003; Skeggs, 2004a). Whilst sociological research has predominantly centred on middle-class mothering with regards to intensive mothering practices (Ennis, 2014; Hays, 1996; Lareau, 2003), or when discussing mothering and extracurricular activities (Lareau, 2003; Savage, 2015a, 2015b; Vincent & Ball, 2007), music education research has rarely acknowledged classed differences in musical families. In this book, I focus on the classed practices of musical mothers, highlighting the similarities and differences in their experiences.

Gender and Class in Musical Motherhood

Issues of gender and class play a role in musical mothering from a cultural perspective. Mothers primarily do the transmitting of musical cultures in families. In musical families, mothers' labour extends to scheduling lessons, finding expert teachers, transporting children to lessons, rehearsals and camps, supervising practise, finding and maintaining instruments and organising family life around such activities and commitments (Savage, 2015a; Savage & Hall, 2017). Women remain the primary carers and assume most of the domestic labour in heterosexual two-parent homes and are increasingly active in the workforce (Goodwin & Huppatz, 2010). Mothers are still considered as 'natural' carers for children, and fathers are thought to be not as inherently capable (Doucet, 2006). This can be brought on by women themselves who act as 'maternal gatekeepers' when they restrict fathers' involvement with children and make them feel inadequate in their parenting (Miller, 2017, p. 46). Similarly, as Ishizuka (2019) points out, fathers who do care for their children are valorised for their efforts while women who do the same tasks are not noticed. The term parenting is often used to describe child-rearing within families and is used to denote an equality in this work; however, the reality is that women still do most of this work (Australian Institute of Family Studies [AIFS], 2021). Reay (1995) has always maintained that using this "universalising theme of discourse not only renders invisible the inequalities between the sexes, but also those existing between mothers" (p. 338). This is a theme that will be discussed further throughout the book.

MOTHERS IN AND OUT OF THE PAID WORKFORCE

In Australia, the number of registered heterosexual marriages was higher in 2023 than ever before—after declining during the Covid-19 pandemic (ABS, 2023)—and these are still considered the gold standard of committed relationships, and the most stable, appropriate and respectable foundation for children to be raised within. Some women utilise their femininity as an investment in respectability, to accrue profits in the marriage stakes, and to gain emotional and financial security (Skeggs, 1997). Many women who rely on their partner's income often come unstuck if the relationship breaks down. This reliance has contributed to an increasingly growing number of women being financially destitute, leading to homelessness and children being taken into care (HAAG, Social Ventures Australia, 2022). Successive Australian governments of both political leanings have actively encouraged women to get back into the workforce to meet workforce shortages (Australian Government Department of Education, Skills and Employment, 2020). The Covid-19 pandemic added further complexity and stress to the lives of mothers (Hand et al., 2020). Mothers' care work shouldered the bulk of this responsibility, with many having to juggle work and family commitments simultaneously.

For the many of the grandmothers in my study, working in paid employment was not an option. Prior to 1966 in Australia, married women in the public service had to leave the workforce. Rosemary, who was a teacher, commented that she had to leave the profession once she got married; however, her husband, also a teacher, was able to remain employed as a teacher. He subsequently went on to senior roles while Rosemary never returned to the paid workforce, like many women of her generation (AIFS, 2020). Susan, being separated from her husband, was ostracised by her local community for being a working mother when her peers were all stay-at-home mothers, yet she had little choice. For others such as Sangeeta,

Hema and Linda, being in paid employment was not acceptable on cultural or moral grounds. Or, like my own mother, my father forbade my mother from working in paid employment as he wanted to be perceived as the provider, and head of the household.

Most of the 'younger' mothers in the study were working or studying, except for Ashley, who was looking for work. Even now, when many women work, there is anxiety as to when the best time to have children is or whether to have children at all, a decision which is still culturally contentious. There is also debate about care arrangements which I discuss later in this chapter, about mothers' perceived obligations of 'being there' for their children.

Much has been written about stay-at-home mothers who have opted out of the paid workforce to become the family CEO. Some women state this is a deliberate choice, while other mothers leave the paid workforce when their lives become unmanageable, and husband's careers are prioritised (Orgad, 2019). The discourse around mothers and their parenting is complex and contradictory. Mothers of all classes are both valorised and demonised for working in paid employment, not working in paid employment, or working part-time in an effort to incorporate both. Yet, this is a choice afforded only to those with the privilege to be able to make this choice. And even then, for those financially buoyant families, the 'choice' is not as clear as it might appear (Orgad, 2019).

Mothers' aspirations for their children are often entangled within their personal, social and cultural desires, which are played out through their children's musical activities (Savage & Hall, 2017). Children's successes are seen as "a reflection and enhancement of their own" (Hays, 1996, p. 159). The connection between learning, fun and emotional closeness creates what Stefansen and Aarseth (2011, p. 392) label as 'enriching intimacy' with a blurring of the lines between sharing activities together and pedagogy enacted in the home environment. For many mothers, musical mothering and concerted cultivation through an intensive mothering practice echoes their organised life as successful career women in the workforce, where women experienced a positive sense of self and were respected for their capacity to do their job well. One way mothers try to redeem their sense of self and demonstrate their capabilities after 'choosing' to spend less time in paid employment to raise children is to volunteer.

MOTHERS VOLUNTEERING

Volunteering offers an opportunity to be with like-minded others and a chance to 'work' and show competency of skills that are valued within the workforce. People with accountancy skills, for example, may volunteer to 'do the books' for charitable organisations. Volunteers often work hard fundraising for groups that they support or that their children are involved with. There can be advantages for those who volunteer, but it can become competitive. However, this type of work is perceived as morally worthy and of value and is often the domain of those who are not in paid employment because of the time commitment involved.

Many years ago, I was chairing a session at a motherhood conference. I can't remember what the theme of the session was; however, what I do remember is the heated argument that ensued towards the end of the session. The discussion was about mothers volunteering, and there were two distinct camps—women who thought that volunteering was exploitation and that mothers filled a gap for what should be paid employees, and the other that volunteering provided opportunities for social connection.

In the first camp, the women argued that their work was not valued in the same way as if paid workers did it and that it took a great deal of labour. There is a view that this work only benefits the organisations rather than the women themselves (Orgad, 2019). Orgad, citing Arlie Hochschild's work, comments that women's volunteering roles offer the women a vision of what they might become in the future, in a way that doesn't impede on their husband's career, with one foot remaining firmly in the domestic space. My participant Linda mentions in her narrative how she volunteers at a prestigious orchestra where her children play every weekend. Volunteering offered Linda several advantages, particularly for her son, who tagged along to the orchestra rehearsal each week, attending with her other children who had earned their places through a rigorous audition process. Incidentally, Linda excused her husband who was out '*studying and whatever*', and I wondered why he did not care for the son at that time. Linda capitalised on this serendipitous opportunity,

Because (son) was doing violin when he, you know, with the school so he … I thought I'm just going to slip him in. He didn't do an interview. … so the conductor said, well if he plays, sit him in at the back … three of them … all day Saturday … who else is going to babysit him … (husband) was out doing you know, studying and whatever you know … but I loved (the orchestra) … I did but it was it took a lot, a lot of time because I was … helping out as the librarian.

Linda's voluntary music librarian's role provided an opportunity for her son that many aspiring musicians would love to have had. Her volunteer role gave Linda a purpose and power within the organisation, above that of other parents whose children also attended. She had a position of responsibility. Linda would argue that she enjoyed listening to her children play; however, it was also important for her to survey what was happening—monitor her children's instrumental playing and monitor who her children were socialising with—which I discuss later in Chap. 6.

Back to the other side of the argument at the conference was that volunteering created community—that without mothers doing much of this work, organisations would have to pay someone to do it and fees would increase. Volunteering connected people, nurtured positive relationships and enriched lives, and we needed more of this in the world. The discussion was hard to contain, and it spilled beyond the session and into the tea break, with passions high on each side.

I volunteered at my children's schools for the music support groups. It was a good way to meet people and that was partially why I joined my first group at my children's primary school. Similarly, when my children moved to secondary school, I joined the music support group there. When I enquired about the group, a staff member from the school whispered to me "I hope you survive the music support group". I was a little unsure what she meant at first, but after attending those first few meetings, it was obvious that the group consisted of some very formidable women, most of whom worked or had worked in the corporate world. The president of the group at the time had ostracised so many people that the group got smaller and smaller. This woman eventually left as her child left the school, and I and few others remained. The group dynamic changed, and more people joined. I was also told when I started that joining the group was a good way to find out what was going on the school and a means to become familiar with staff. Over the years I was part of this group, I could see how this had advantages for some families.

For some women in these groups, there was competition, and a sense of one-upmanship. However, Orgad (2019) argues that many mothers who volunteer on school committees, fundraising and similar activities mitigate the loneliness and isolation of stay-at-home motherhood. It gives these women an opportunity to use some of the skills they had when they were engaged in the workforce and a chance to reclaim their sense of self (Orgad, 2019). It may seem contradictory to experience loneliness when mothers are with their children, yet 'emptiness' (Stone, 2007, p. 17), lack of adult connection (Savage, 2015a) and 'loss of identity' (Stone, 2007, p. 19) are commonly felt by mothers. This feeling is exacerbated when mothers have given up their careers while their partners' lives remain largely the same (Orgad, 2019; Stone, 2007). While many mothers state the decision to give up work to care for the children was a deliberate choice, this is ultimately decided by the circumstances in which they find themselves and often to accommodate the work lives of partners (Crabb, 2014; Orgad, 2019). In my experience, volunteering did afford some close relationships with other parents and staff at the schools my children attended. School staff who get to know you, and find you share similar interests and values, do tend to give your children the benefit of the doubt if there are ever any issues. Middle-class parents are more likely to have greater involvement in their children's schooling; however, sometimes, that familiarity leads to expecting favourable treatment (Lilliedahl, 2021). This can extend to parent associations being quite powerful groups where parents can lobby regarding school matters to 'collectively dispute the school's authority' having the capacity to utilise their own resources and personal connections against the school (Lilliedahl, 2021, p. 247). This is exacerbated when parents donate large sums of money to schools.

On the flip side for me personally, volunteering in the music support groups was often time-consuming and financially expensive. While there was no obligation to purchase items in the campaigns for fundraising, there was a tacit understanding that music parents would 'support' each activity. I spent a great deal of time organising and picking up goods, meeting with people and managing events, so much so that the group generated more income than I did in my part-time music business. As a musical mother, I wanted to be seen as supporting my children, both of whom were heavily involved in the school's music programme, and seen as 'giving something back'. Music was something that I valued, and I wanted that to be seen.

Many stay-at-home mothers involve themselves in running volunteer groups like mini corporations, working intensively in these groups, which is matched only by their intensive mothering within the home. These women make a commitment to sacrifice their own careers for their children's development, musical development in these cases, by shunning neoliberal capitalist expectations to participate in the paid workforce yet working tirelessly on developing cultural capital for their children's secure middle-class futures (Orgad, 2019). In this way, Orgad states that children have become "human capital—investing in them is a way of increasing good returns in the future" (2019, p. 103).

INVESTING IN CHILDREN TO INCREASE FAMILY CULTURAL CAPITAL

Women who work in paid employment and who manage the domestic space, including childcare, are said to perform a double shift. Arguably, a 'third shift' includes the continuous mental load mothers carry to facilitate the smooth running of family life and wider familial obligations (DeGroot & Vik, 2020); mothers in paid employment must also be 'good mothers' and 'good' employees (Stone, 2007). The Australian Government Workplace Gender Equality Agency (WGEA) recently cited the gender pay gap to be 14.2%, showing that women's domestic arrangements mean that they still earn significantly less than men (WGEA, 2021). The years that women spend looking after children also means that their superannuation is also significantly less than their male counterparts. Women tend to work in more part-time employment and in sectors where wages remain low, such as early childhood education, aged care and disability services (Goodwin & Huppatz, 2010), and are still underrepresented in top professional and corporate positions. The sacrifices women make for their families contribute to growing numbers of women living in poverty as they reach their later years (Commonwealth of Australia, 2016; World Economic Forum, 2022).

The emotional work that mothers do is rendered invisible yet is crucial. There is no recognition for mother's work or payment for the hours of labour as there is for other work; however, there is an acknowledgement that this work is important when it does not work out as it 'should'. That is, mothers are judged based on the outcomes of their children (Williamson et al., 2023). Mothers are bound to their children very differently from how fathers are seen to be connected to their children (Miller, 2017). Workplace environments can be so toxic for women that their unrealistic expectations make motherhood and working life impossible (Orgad, 2019).

Mothers utilise music as an investment to accumulate cultural capital for their children, through developing children's culturally valued skills and dispositions, aimed at increasing their success in educational and workplace arenas. Within the family space where children's potentials are nurtured, and mothers are still the primary caregivers of children (AIFS, 2021), it is their 'moral responsibility' to cater to children's needs, or else be vilified as neglectful and selfish (Miller, 2017, p. 36; Oyarzún et al., 2022). Bourdieu (1986) has always acknowledged mothers' roles in the development of children's cultural capital:

It is because the cultural capital that is effectively transmitted within the family itself depends not only on the quantity of cultural capital, itself accumulated by spending time, that the domestic group possess, but also on the usable time (particularly in the form of mother's free time) available to it. (p. 253)

Mothers are often torn between wanting to or needing to work in paid employment and their desire to stay at home to be with their children. I recall a mother commenting to me once, as I was setting up to run a music class, that her children did not attend early childhood music classes because she worked, insinuating that the two were mutually exclusive. Many extra-curricular activities are scheduled during the day and are aimed at stay-at-home mothers who have time during the day to attend such classes. This can be a dilemma for mothers who might want their children to participate in these activities to develop desired dispositions in their children.

Compromising Paid Employment to 'Be There' for Children's Music

Engagement in formal music creates tensions within the fields of employment and family life for some of the women in this study. Unlike other extracurricular endeavours, musicking (Small, 1998) often takes place within the family home as part of everyday family life. Participation in music tuition also penetrates the domestic space where practise occurs, and sometimes teaching too for musician mothers. Mothering through music can be considered even more intensive than other extracurricular activities because of the temporal and spatial fluidity that can disrupt and pervade all areas of family life. There is emotional labour to juggle work and home commitments simultaneously. This tension was exacerbated by the Covid-19 pandemic.

Participant Susan worked as a piano teacher, and her working hours were often after school with private lessons, but also preparing and performing at concerts, music competitions and other school functions where music was required. She states, "*I was working ridiculous hours—all the prime times when you should have been spending time with your kids*". Being there for children is complicated when your home is also your workplace. This became usual practice for many women during the pandemic but is often commonplace for musician mothers. Referring to Bourdieu (1984), children need time with a parent whether it is from a mother, father or significant other, and Susan acknowledges this:

I wouldn't have worked. I would just want to be with the kids, all the time because I think that's really important. In a perfect world [pause], I firmly believe the parents are the key to children's education and, if they're demanding of their children ... encouraging them to articulate, giving them the patience and the time that's needed to make a child feel valued. I think my kids missed out on that—a lot—but other friends' children, of course, got it in spades.

Susan makes comparisons with her family life to those of her peers and feels she is dealt a weaker hand. However, Susan was restricted in her ideal because she had to work. As an unpartnered parent, Susan faced added emotional stress because the children's father was not always around, and her peers were mostly stay-at-home mothers without the responsibility of work commitments—"*I was always working, and none of my friends were ... they all had stable marriages and families where I was only one parent, worked ... I was often isolated because of that*". Working mothers are often considered selfish for putting their own needs before their children's, and media reports that focus on the negative impacts of working parents on children's development have exacerbated these perceptions (Guendouzi, 2006). This stigmatising of working mothers as 'bad' mothers denies the necessity for them to work to house and feed their children.

Experiencing guilt in motherhood has become a normative experience, with mothers demonised for working, sending their children into early education and care settings, and seen to be putting their own self-interest before that of their children (Guendouzi, 2006). This is despite the recent government initiatives to entice more women into the workforce (Australian Government Department of Education, Skills and Employment, 2020). This vilification usually comes from those who are not mothers and feel entitled to judge and where they "lay the primary responsibility for child-rearing and the production of 'good' future citizens at the feet of women (ie: mothers) ... [with] little appreciation of the motherwork that mothers do" (Raith, 2015, p. 166). Susan articulates the emotional work involved in parenting—making children feel valued, listening and giving them time; she knows they need attention. Embodying the 'imperfect mother' subjectivity, there is a sense of guilt, as Susan feels unable to give her children the full attention she feels they need. Although difficult, Susan tries to give voice to this feeling, "*I was working a lot [pause]I think [pause] the kids [pause] would [pause] have suffered [pause] through not having a one-on-one parenting and lots and lots of attention, but I said to them, they've grown up beautifully*", she stuttered. This is hard for Susan to reconcile as denoted by her punctuated and staggered speech. Susan's time was maximised to its fullest, and she often relied on the support of local babysitters to fill the gaps. She mentions how she went 'with the flow'—an adaptive parenting style—and tried to imply a casual logic to her mothering that defies the intensity with which she maintained the pedagogical labour of musical standards of her children and herself, and her indomitable work ethic, not to mention her adept utilisation of her cultural capital, which will be seen throughout the book. Her counternarrative articulates how she would like to be there for her children; however, she mitigates her guilt and reconciles her absence by acknowledging they do not appear to be adversely affected by having a working mother.

Penelope, Rosemary's daughter, on the other hand, decided to work casually before she had children. Employment for Penelope was eclectic with travel, playing in bands, other casual work over the years and then finally completing a teaching degree when she was 30. She prioritised playing in various bands over teaching in a full-time position:

> *The year I started teaching, you had to put your name down to say you'd be available to go all over the state and I didn't want to, because I wanted to have fun in this band … We had two break-off bands at the side with two members doing a few solo projects … As a result, I only ever did contract work—supply teaching … for the last twenty years … 'cause I prefer it and what I've done … I didn't want to move away from the band and then I got married and had my daughter.*

In Australia, newly qualified teachers are encouraged to take contracts in rural and remote schools—sometimes referred to as 'country service'. This is then seen favourably if teachers subsequently apply for urban positions. Penelope did not wish to travel to a remote location and so decided to work casually, enabling her to continue her music performances with her band and stay at her family home. In some ways, Penelope could be seen as defying 'good mothering logic' by meeting her own needs first. However, there are financial compromises that Penelope made in order to do this. In being there for your children, women who choose part-time or flexible work or no participation in paid employment have less superannuation and are often paid lower salaries (Manne, 2018). Similarly, women are less likely to be selected for employment because it is assumed that children will impact their workability (Manne, 2018) despite workplace legislation forbidding this discrimination. Penelope has chosen part-time teaching work over a full-time appointment, which means she is able to help in her daughter's class at school and play in her bands. Unlike Susan, she is fortunate to have the financial support of her partner, but this does not negate the full-time unpaid emotional labour exercised within family life and the financial reliance on her partner.

Aarshia is a married mother with a six-year-old child. She moved to Australia from India to study and hopes to remain here after her post-graduate study is completed. Many years before, her mother, Sangeeta, also moved to a new area when she had a young child due to her husband's work, although Aarshia enjoys many more freedoms than Sangeeta did as a young mother in India in the 1980s. Aarshia found that she and her husband could not afford childcare when their daughter was small due to their limited family budget, so Aarshia, Sangeeta and Aarshia's mother-in-law, Hema, devised a plan to assist with caring responsibilities. Aarshia's husband regularly worked away from home. Sangeeta and Hema visit Aarshia's family on rotation for three months at a time to assist with childcare and household duties. In the first instance, it was suggested that Aarshia's daughter return to India to be brought up by her grandmother; however, Aarshia was not happy about this:

There were phases that my dad was not there, and I know that (my daughter's) dad is not going to be there because he's sailing, and my point was my mum was always there ... my anchor was my mum ... what will happen to the kid if she doesn't have an anchor? So, I want to be with her always as a support ... I had an irrational fear ... that I felt that if I leave her in India, she will not want to come back to me, she will want to stay with them.

I was fortunate to meet both grandmothers during the time I was interviewing, and this was important to see the influence of each on Aarshia. Hema, Aarshia's mother-in-law, expressed the value in having other family members mothering Aarshia's daughter and how it was important to be present for children when they were growing up:

Practically we can give her some knowledge, this is good for you, this is bad for you ... whatever she take from school or from the other side, we can polish her ... we [can] give her suggestion. Day by day, this will give her right to good way ... Aarshia has her own way, and her mother has her own way because we all have our own way ... we just suggest, and this depends on Aarshia ... the last decision must be for her.

The analogy of 'polishing', as if the granddaughter was a diamond, shows the careful attention each family member gives to guide Aarshia's daughter and shape her personhood to become a radiant gem. The inter-generational cultivation is evidenced here in concert with their combined domestic labour. Together, these women have developed a workable strategy for caring for each other and enabling Aarshia to fulfil her study commitments. The grandmothers are there for Aarshia as part of their enduring mothering even when children become adults and mothers themselves.

Linda instead made a very deliberate decision not to mother as she had been. As the child of parents who did missionary work throughout Asia, she only saw her parents during the long school holidays. In contrast, Linda wanted to be there for her children. Interestingly, Linda's parents had a similar upbringing to Linda, where her mother attended boarding school, and her father was brought up by a nanny. Linda states:

> *Because of my background, I was very, very protective I think, and I had to kind of hold back because I didn't have my parents around for all, all of my younger years ... they were there. They loved us and I knew that, but I had nobody to talk to ... to tell me what to do ... reprimand me when I needed it (laughs) so I, I think, motherhood ... I'm gonna stay in one spot and I'm gonna love my kids, not that my parents didn't.*

Linda's narrative is full of contradictions and mixed emotions. She spoke of how other children at the boarding school she attended were very bitter about their childhoods when speaking about them in later years; however, she stated that she was not, despite her feelings of loneliness and solitude (See Pollock, & Van Reken, 2009). Linda repeated several times that her mother was "*the best mother in the world. If you put it into context, she did the best job*" yet it seems she is trying to convince herself rather than me when speaking these words. Linda's strongly held Christian views compounded her ambivalence as she reconciled that her parents were doing '*God's work*', which she considered the ultimate raison d'etre. However, she was also critical of her upbringing and resolute that her children would experience always having their mother there for them. It was important for Linda to be physically present, to give them '*aspirations*', '*opportunities*' and '*probably a good education* (laughs) *that was a bit more consistent than mine*'. She also mentions being there to '*reprimand them*' which speaks to her desire to develop a particular kind of child and to control their behaviour. Her daughter Ashley concurred, stating they would not have become *"the musicians [we] they are today"* without Linda's dedication and constant presence. Ashley also says this with some reservations about Linda's mothering style, which has been challenging for Ashley and impacted her mental wellbeing.

When Ashley accidentally became pregnant with her boyfriend, there were consternations from her mother because she was not married; this did not align with her strict religious and traditional views. In addition, Linda had made her views clear to Ashley, that once women had children, they shouldn't go back to work. Ashley remarked, *"I kinda thought when I was pregnant my life was over, like that's it, I'm just going to be a mother for the rest of my life"*.

Linda had framed Ashley's intention to work and not always 'being there' as missing out on her son's development. Linda had enjoyed her time at home with her children. Teaching them and organising their schedules gave her purpose. Linda stated, *"I did love teaching. I mean you have to be a teacher when you're a mother … I wasn't very good at it, but I did love seeing the outcomes"*. Linda knows she was good at it because this was validated by her children's outstanding outcomes in the musical field. Her good motherhood is embodied in her children. However, there is also a sense of missing out. Linda may be concerned about who will pass on the family's religious and musical capital if Ashley is not there? Ashley's partner did not share the same values as her parents, so who will reinvest the family cultural capital? As a stay-at-home mother, Linda was able to focus fully on her children. She created value as a 'good' self-sacrificing mother:

> *I just wanted to be the best mother really … nothing against people wanting to work … that was my career, being a mother. That was the career that I wanted … I looked after the kids for 17 years and then I thought, oh better find another job.*

'Being there' has become synonymous with the "'mental work' and '24/7 thinking responsibility' taken on (mostly) by mothers" with "moral associations with 'good' and intensified parenting" (Miller, 2017, pp. 100–101), and where 'bad' mothering equates to absence, selfishness and children who are unruly (Adkins, 2002). At the time of my interviews, Ashley was at home with her infant son; however, she was actively looking for work. She is keen to get back to nursing—a job she enjoys and where she feels she is giving to the community. Ashley does not want to be *'just a mother'*, suggesting that she feels there is more to life, including time for herself and her partner.

MUSIC AS FAMILY CULTURAL PRACTICE

Families develop their own musical cultures. I remember during long car rides, my brother and I would start singing the '*Mahna mahna*' song from the Muppets, and my father would assume a lead role, while my brother and I would take on the backing vocals. Usually, I would have had little to do with my brother; however, family memories have been forged through this joint musical experience. It is experiences like this that are the foundation of a 'family feeling' (Atkinson, 2011, p. 340; Bourdieu, 1998, p. 68) that reinforces the family habitus and how families develop certain ways of being. It is through such everyday experiences that family cultures are born and enacted.

Music scholarship has often looked at culture from a hierarchical perspective of high or low culture; however, Williams' (1989) notion that 'culture is ordinary' with Small's (1998) idea of 'musicking' demonstrates that music:

> instead of being merely a transcendental, aesthetic object, should be viewed as a variety of acts—including making music, performing music, listening to music, and dancing to music—as well as the everyday usage of popular music and media culture. In that case one might begin to appreciate the craft of musical as more than the traditional skills, and rather understand it as the full spectrum of producing, practicing, perceiving, and debating all aspects of music. (Dyndahl, 2013, p. 10)

Williams (1989), when discussing culture, asserts that "an interest in learning or the arts is simple, pleasant and natural" (p. 5) rather than only for elites. Arts-based activities are everyday practices for peoples of any demographic. Different activities form part of wider cultures, which may not be arts-based but perhaps sports or other interests. More broadly, culture is a system of shared beliefs and values that are performed by members of a society.

Cultural communities, such as families, are dynamic and are places where traditions are shared, enacted and constantly reappraised (Conkling, 2018). Culture can be considered a contentious term, as according to Skeggs (2004a), culture is not only "symbolic, but also (as) a resource in the practices and relationships we engage in daily" (p. 174). In this way, culture can be seen as a form of privilege, where particular types of culture become a resource that is ripe for exchange (Skeggs, 2004a). Dyndahl (2013) agrees by stating,

A cultural view of music indicates that musical activities and actions, including music education always already take place *in* culture; there is no other place or space for them. Likewise, these phenomena and practices inevitably also construct culture; i.e. they should be regarded *as* culture. (p. 11)

In Custodero's (2006) mixed-methods study, mothers were found to use music to assist with routine tasks at home which became part of their family culture, illustrated by the actions of one mother "modelling for her children what her parents had done—she uses the same parenting strategies, updated with contemporary musical material and her personal style" (p. 44). Here, such routines were passed on, or new ways of being were created and maintained, serving to strengthen family relationships. Decisions around music were based on intergenerational considerations and past knowledges of how music can mediate mood and comfort and provide learning opportunities. Fancourt and Perkins (2017), in their quantitative study of 391 new mothers, found that singing to their newborns improved mothers' wellbeing and enhanced the bonding between mother and child. In Barrett's (2009) study, participation in an early years music class gave one mother "encouragement and confidence to interact and play with my baby" (p. 123) and helped her to cope with the everyday demands of domestic life and establish a positive relationship with her infant. Similarly, Mackinlay and Baker's (2005) study showed lullaby singing was a preventative strategy for post-natal depression. Singing releases oxytocin, serotonin and dopamine which assists in building connections with others because it feels good (Keeler et al., 2015).

The family is the predominant site where musical values and tastes are transmitted (Bourdieu, 1984). Mothers who have been involved in music themselves as children are more likely to encourage their children to participate in musical activities due to "familial identity and because they perceive their children (and themselves) to be musical" (Reeves, 2015, p. 20). I recall a mother who I interviewed as part of my Master's study stating that when she met her now husband, she was astounded that he had never learnt a musical instrument as a child and had had very few musical experiences. For this woman, this was something that she had never encountered before, and she felt it very strange. The decisions made regarding musical involvement are made within cultural practices that are often influenced by class and gender, and these connections will be explored in more depth throughout the book. Everyday musical experiences, through musical practices, routines and rituals, form culture and develop the self (Conkling, 2018).

As Dyndahl (2013) and Campbell (1998) state, the cultural transmission of music within family lives can be through everyday engagements of performing, listening and perceiving, with repertoires often chosen by the transmitters for a variety of reasons and to their preference. Campbell applies an interactionalist perspective when discussing children's musical cultures to describe how children become integrated into the musical cultures of their families, schools and communities. Children are embedded into 'big' cultures when they are joined through experience with their peers of the same developmental stages, and 'small' cultures in their engagement with smaller friendships groups, family and teams. According to Campbell's (1998) paper looking at how children use music and the enculturation-education interface, she remarks, "cultural transmission occurs through children's engagement in games, stories, songs and other lore that have been selected (whether consciously or not) by adults as 'the best' standard or most representative ideas of people" (p. 45). While children have many influences and belong to many cultural groups, mothers are the dominant transmitters of culture within families, usually within the home. Musical practices within families form family cultures and ways of being. Later I will show the strategies some middle-class mothers employ to gain social advantages through the dispositions their children learn through engagement with music. This is indeed the culture that mothers pass onto their children and that is passed down through generations.

THE TRANSMISSION OF FAMILY CULTURE THROUGH INTERGENERATIONAL MUSICAL PRACTICES

The family is the primary site where musical values and tastes are established and transmitted (Bourdieu, 1984) and can also be conceived as intergenerational. Transmission is what people do in their everyday practices and their relations with others (Brannen, 2019). Bourdieu (1990) spoke of a 'family habitus', a concept I will delve into in more detail in Chap. 3, but it is defined as dispositions and patterns of behaviour that have been passed down through generations.

In Gracio's (2016) study of 59 white Portuguese women, family bonding, memory work and music education were all embraced when these women nurtured a specific style of music—in this case, rock music—in their family life. Parental preferences for rock music align with daughter's interests in rock music but not son's (Bogt et al., 2011). These findings align with Morgan et al.'s (2015) study that mothers often share musical tastes with their daughters and not their sons, who are more likely to resist their mothers' desires.

Susan, the first mother I interviewed as part of my study (mother to Jessica and a grandmother to many), comes from a family where the expectation to play music has been passed down through generations. Early in her interview, she articulated a story from her childhood, *"we all did one instrument, minimum, I did two, three of us did two instruments and the youngest just did just one"*. Susan was born in regional Australia in the mid-1950s and was from a family of five children. She gives the analogy of her father driving his tractor up and down the paddocks as his children's fingers played up and down the keys of the piano, describing her family's musical history, as a *'cultural inheritance'*. Susan explains why she was considered musical:

> *I had no aspirations whatsoever—none. I didn't know what I was doing ... it's not even that I enjoyed it incredibly much (laughs). Apparently, I was good. I don't think so. We just did AMEB[1] exams, and that was the criteria, and if you did well in exams and competitions and things, they thought you were a good musician ... So, I think I'm musical but not a musician ... I see other musicians and how they compose and how they arrange and how they can harmonise, and I just didn't have any of that. I was a bit of a parrot.*

Music was fundamental to Susan's family life and something she felt skilled in without having to put in much effort. Music was *"so much a big part of our lives that they just did it automatically because it was culturally what you did"*, she stated. It was an expected practice, and as such, there was no question about continued participation in music on some level.

This is contrary to my own experience where it was teachers throughout my education who took an interest in my musical development, drawing my mother's attention to my potential. However, my parents only supported this to a degree. For me as a growing musician, further involvement was constrained by my parent's lack of financial resources and their expectations for my future which did not include music as a major factor. They did not see music as a suitable career as it was considered unpredictable and salacious. Unfortunately, my mother believed the gossip magazines where famous musicians' lives were embroiled by affairs and substance abuse. The world of classical musicians was largely foreign to them, despite both my parents learning classical piano when they were younger. While my grandmother enjoyed performing in amateur musical shows, this was frowned upon by her increasingly conservative husband, and she stopped performing. Music training offered to my parents was squandered due to their lack of interest and perseverance.

In this chapter, I have discussed how neoliberalism and capitalism have influenced mothering practices in recent decades. Government policies have been focused on improving workforce participation and minimising welfare dependency. Mothers must be seen to be developing moral citizens of the future and be aspirational in their objectives by continually seeking to improve their status. One way that mothers do this is through music, where I have begun to show how mothers utilise music to develop favourable dispositions in their children. In this chapter, I explored how mothers navigate motherhood and paid work along with those who opt out of paid employment, including some who volunteer. I argue that volunteering is a contentious issue within women's groups. Also contentious is the essentialist view that 'good' mothers need to be there for their children, a notion that is very pervasive in current Australian society but juxtaposes with increased workforce participation. Finally, music as family culture and family habitus was considered as an intergenerational practice that evolves over time.

In the next chapter, the study's theoretical framework will be explained. I delve into Bourdieu's tool kit and how habitus, capital and field are useful in looking at the mothers' practices. I argue that issues of gender are limited within Bourdieu's conceptualisations and add feminist theories to interrogate the work that mothers do. I also discuss the use of narrative inquiry to generate the mothers' stories and show that the mothers also tell counternarratives that resist the dominant cultural norms they encounter.

References

Adkins, L. (2002). *Revisions: Gender and sexuality in late modernity.* Open University Press.

Atkinson, W. (2011). From sociological fictions to social fictions: Some Bourdieusian reflections on the concepts of 'institutional habitus' and 'family habitus'. *British Journal of Sociology of Education, 32*(3), 331–347. https://doi.org/10.1080/01425692.2011.559337

Atkinson, W. (2016). *Beyond Bourdieu.* Polity.

Australian Bureau of Statistics [ABS]. (2023). *Marriages and divorces.* https://www.abs.gov.au/statistics/people/people-and-communities/marriages-and-divorces-australia/latest-release

Australian Government Department of Education, Skills and Employment. (2020). *Increasing women's workforce participation with Career Revive.* https://www.employment.gov.au/newsroom/increasing-women-s-workforce-participation-career-revive

Australian Government Workplace Gender Equality Agency [WGEA]. (2021). *Parental leave and gender equality.* https://www.wgea.gove.au/sites/default/files/documents/Parental-leave-and-gender-equality.pdf

Australian Institute of Family Studies [AIFS]. (2020). *Families then and now: How we worked.* Research Report. https://aifs.gov.au/research/research-reports/families-then-now-how-we-worked

Australian Institute of Family Studies [AIFS]. (2021). *Work and family.* https://aifs.gov.au/facts-and-figures/work-and-family

Ball, S. J. (2003). The risks of social reproduction: The middle class and educational markets. *London Review of Education, 1*(3), 163–175. https://doi.org/10.1080/1474846032000146730

Barrett, M. S. (2009). Sounding lives in and through music – A narrative inquiry of the everyday musical engagement of a young child. *Journal of Early Childhood Research, 7*(2), 115–134. https://doi.org/10.1177/1476718X09102645

Bogt, T. F. M., Delsing, M. J. M. H., van Zalk, M., Christenson, P. G., & Meeus, W. H. J. (2011). Intergenerational continuity of taste: Parental and adolescent music preferences. *Social Forces, 90*(1), 297–319. https://doi.org/10.1093/sf/90.1.297

Bok, J. (2010). The capacity to aspire to higher education: 'It's like making them do a play without a script'. *Critical Studies in Education, 51*(2), 163–178.

Bottrell, D. (2013). Responsibilised resilience? Reworking neoliberal social policy texts. *M/C Journal, 16*(5). https://doi.org/10.5204/mcj.708

Bourdieu, P. (1984). *Distinction: A social critique of the judgement of taste.* Routledge and Kegan Paul.

Bourdieu, P. (1986). The forms of capital. In J. Richardson (Ed.), *Handbook of theory and research for the sociology of education* (pp. 241–258). Greenwood.

Bourdieu, P. (1990). *The logic of practice.* Polity.

Bourdieu, P. (1998). *Practical reason.* Polity.

Brannen, J. (2019). *Social research matters: A life in family sociology.* Bristol University Press.

Campbell, P. S. (1998). The musical cultures of children. *Research Studies in Music Education, 11*(1), 42–51. https://doi.org/10.1177/1321103X9801100105

Colvin, E., & Knight, E. (2023). The development of career-related early intentions in the home. In I. E. Colvin & E. Knight (Eds.), *Young people and parenting obligations of the state: Implications for higher education in Australia* (1st ed., pp. 61–87). Springer International Publishing. https://doi.org/10.1007/978-3-031-38285-7

Commonwealth of Australia. (2016). *'A husband is not a retirement plan': Achieving economic security for women in retirement.* The Senate: Economics

References Committee. https://www.aph.gove.au/Parliamentary_Business/ Committees/Senate/Economics/Economic_security_for_women_in_retirement/Report

Conkling, S. W. (2018). Socialization in the family: Implications for music education. *Update, 36*(3), 29–37. https://doi.org/10.1177/8755123317732969

Crabb, A. (2014). *The wife drought*. Random House Australia.

Custodero, L. A. (2006). Singing practices in 10 families with young children. *Journal of Research in Music Education, 54*(1), 37–56. https://doi.org/10.1177/00242940605400104

DeGroot, J. M., & Vik, T. A. (2020). 'The Weight of our household rests on my shoulders': Inequity in family work. *Journal of Family Issues, 41*(8), 1258–1281. https://doi.org/10.1177/0192513X19887767

Doucet, A. (2006). 'Estrogen-filled worlds': Fathers as primary caregivers and embodiment. *The Sociological Review, 54*(4), 696–716. https://doi.org/10.1111/j.1467-954X.2006.00667.x

Dyndahl, P. (2013). Towards a cultural study of music in performance, education, and society? In P. Dyndahl (Ed.), *Intersection and interplay. Contributions to the cultural study of music in performance, education, and society* (pp. 7–20). Lund University.

Ennis, L. R. (2014). Intensive mothering: Revisting the issue today. In L. R. Ennis (Ed.), *Intensive mothering: The cultural contradictions of modern motherhood* (pp. 1–23). Demeter Press.

Enticott, J., Callander, E., Garad, R., & Teede, H. (2022). Women, work and the poverty trap: Time for a fair go to support health and wellbeing for Australian women. *Monash University: Lens.* https://lens.monash.edu/@medicine-health/2022/04/06/1384563/womens-reverse-wealth-trajectory-leads-to-poverty-in-older-age

Fancourt, D., & Perkins, R. (2017). Associations between singing to babies and symptoms of postnatal depression, wellbeing, self-esteem and mother-infant bond. *Public Health, 145*, 149–152. https://doi.org/10.1016/j.puhe.2017.01.016

Gale, T., & Parker, S. (2015). Calculating student aspiration: Bourdieu, spatiality and the politics of recognition. *Cambridge Journal of Education, 45*(1), 81–96. https://doi.org/10.1080/0305764X.2014.988685

Germov, J. (2004). What class do you teach? Education and the reproduction of class inequality. In J. Allen (Ed.), *Sociology of education: Possibilities and practices* (pp. 250–269). Cengage Learning Australia.

Gerrard, J. (2014). All that is solid melts into work: Self-work, the 'learning ethic' and the work ethic. *The Sociological Review, 62*, 862–879. https://doi.org/10.1111/1467-954X.12208

Gillies, V. (2007). *Marginalised mothers: Exploring working-class experiences of parenting*. Routledge.

Gillies, V. (2010). Is poor parenting a class issue? Contextualising anti-social behaviour and family life. In M. Klett-Davies (Ed.), *Is parenting a class issue?* (pp. 44–61). The Nuffield Press.

Goodwin, S., & Huppatz, K. (2010). The good mother in theory and research: An overview. In S. Goodwin & K. Huppatz (Eds.), *The good mother: Contemporary motherhoods in Australia* (pp. 1–24). Sydney University Press.

Gracio, R. (2016). Daughters of rock and moms who rock: Rock music as a medium for family relationships in Portugal. *Revista Crítica de Ciências Sociais, 109*, 83–104. https://doi.org/10.4000/rccs.6229

Guendouzi, J. (2006). "The guilt thing": Balancing domestic and professional roles. *Journal of Marriage and Family, 68*(4), 901–909. https://doi.org/10.1111/j.1741-3737.2006.00303.x

Hamer, L., & Tranter, K. (2021). Parents...Next: The ongoing neoliberalising of Australian social security. *Griffith Journal of Law and Human Dignity, 9*(1), 29–55.

Hand, K., Baxter, J., Carroll, M., & Budinski, M. (2020). *Families in Australia survey: Life during COVID-19 Report no. 1: Early findings.* Australian Institute of Family Studies.

Hartas, D. (2016). Young people's educational aspirations: Psychosocial factors and the home environment. *Journal of Youth Studies, 19*(9), 1148–1163.

Hays, S. (1996). *The cultural contradictions of motherhood.* Yale University Press.

Housing for the Aged Action Group [HAAG], Social Ventures Group. (2022). https://www.oldertenants.org.au/resource-author/social-ventures-australia

Ishizuka, P. (2019). Social class, gender, and contemporary parenting standards in the United States: Evidence from a National Survey Experiment. *Social Forces, 98*(1), 31–58. https://doi.org/10.1093/sf/soy107

Keeler, J. R., Roth, E. A., Neuser, B. L., Spitsbergen, J. M., Waters, D. J. M., & Vianney, J.-M. (2015). The neurochemistry and social flow of singing: Bonding and oxytocin. *Frontiers in Human Neuroscience, 9*, 518–518. https://doi.org/10.3389/fnhum.2015.00518

Lareau, A. (2003/2011). *Unequal childhoods: Class, race, and family life.* University of California Press.

Lawler, S. (2005). Introduction: Class, culture and identity. *Sociology, 39*(5), 797–806. https://doi.org/10.1177/0038038505058365

Lilliedahl, J. (2021). Class, capital, and school culture: Parental involvement in public schools with specialised music programmes. *British Journal of Sociology of Education, 42*(2), 245–259. https://doi.org/10.1080/01425692.2021.1875198

Mackinlay, E., & Baker, F. (2005). Nurturing herself, nurturing her baby: Creating positive experiences for first-time mothers through lullaby singing. *Women and Music: A Journal of Gender and Culture, 9*, 69–89. https://doi.org/10.1353/wam.2005.0010

Macvarish, J., & Martin, C. (2021). Towards a 'parenting regime': Globalising tendencies and localised variation. In A. M. Castrén et al. (Eds.), *The Palgrave handbook of family sociology in Europe*. Palgrave Macmillan. https://doi.org/10.1007/978-3-030-73306-3_22

Manne, A. (2018). Mothers and the quest for social justice. In C. Nelson & R. Robertson (Eds.), *Dangerous ideas about mothers* (pp. 17–34). UWA Publishing.

Miller, T. (2017). *Making sense of parenthood: Caring, gender and family lives*. Cambridge University Press.

Morgan, J. P., MacDonald, R. A. R., & Pitts, S. E. (2015). "Caught between a scream and a hug": Women's perspectives on music listening and interaction with teenagers in the family unit. *Psychology of Music, 43*(5), 611–626. https://doi.org/10.1177/0305735613517411

Orgad, S. (2019). *Heading home: Motherhood, work, and the failed promise of equality*. Columbia University Press.

Oyarzún, J. d. D., Gerrard, J., & Savage, G. C. (2022). Ethics in neoliberalism?: Parental responsibility and education policy in Chile and Australia. *Journal of Sociology (Melbourne, Vic.), 58*(3), 285–303. https://doi.org/10.1177/14407833211029694

Pollock, D. C., & Van Reken, R. E. (2009). *Third culture kids: Growing up among worlds*. Nicholas Brealy Publishing.

Raith, L. (2015). Support, judgement, and marginality: The shifting terrains of the mother country. In L. Raith, J. Jones, & M. Porter (Eds.), *Mothers at the margins: Stories of challenge, resistance and love* (pp. 157–171). Cambridge Scholars.

Reay, D. (1995). A silent majority? Mothers in parental involvement. *Women's Studies International Forum, 18*(3), 337–348. https://doi.org/10.1016/0277-5395(95)00029-C

Reay, D. (1997). Feminist theory, habitus, and social class: Disrupting notions of classlessness. *Women's Studies International Forum, 20*(2), 225–233.

Reeves, A. (2015). 'Music's a family thing': Cultural socialisation and parental transference. *Cultural Sociology, 9*(4), 493–514. https://doi.org/10.1177/1749975515576941

Sanders, R. (2020). The impact of capitalist-led neoliberal agendas on parents and their children. *Children Australia, 45*(2), 101–108. https://doi.org/10.1017/chn.2020.1

Savage, S. (2015a). *Intensive mothering through music in early childhood education*. Unpublished Masters' Minor Thesis, Monash University.

Savage, S. (2015b). Understanding mothers' perspectives on early childhood music programmes. *Australian Journal of Music Education, 2*, 127–139.

Savage, S., & Hall, C. (2017). Thinking about and beyond the cultural contradictions of motherhood through musical mothering. In M. J. Rose, L. Ross, & J. Hartmann (Eds.), *The music of motherhood* (pp. 32–50). Demeter Press.

Sheppard, J., & Biddle, N. (2015). *ANU Poll 19 Social class*. [Computer file]. Australian Data Archive, The Australian National University.

Simpson, D., Lumsden, E., & Clark, R. M. (2015). Neoliberalism, global poverty policy and early childhood education and care: A critique of local uptake in England. *Early Years: An International Journal of Research and Development, 35*(1), 96–109. https://doi.org/10.1080/09575146.2014.969199

Sims, M., Calder, P., Moloney, M., Rothe, A., Rogers, M., Doan, L., Kakana, D., & Georgiadou, S. (2022). Neoliberalism and government responses to Covid-19: Ramifications for early childhood education and care. *Issues in Educational Research, 32*(3), 1174–1195.

Skeggs, B. (1997). *Formations of class and gender*. Sage.

Skeggs, B. (2004a). *Class, self, culture*. Routledge.

Skeggs, B. (2004b). Exchange, value and affect: Bourdieu and the 'self'. In L. Adkins & B. Skeggs (Eds.), *Feminism after Bourdieu* (pp. 75–96). Blackwell.

Small, C. (1998). *Musicking: The meanings of performing and listening*. The University Press of New England.

Stefansen, K., & Aarseth, H. (2011). Enriching intimacy: The role of the emotional in the 'resourcing' of middle-class children. *British Journal of Sociology of Education, 32*(3), 389–405. https://doi.org/10.1080/0142569 2.2011.559340

Stone, P. (2007). The rhetoric and reality of "opting out". *Contexts, 6*(4), 14–19. https://doi.org/10.1525/ctx.2007.6.4.14

Threadgold, S., & Gerrard, J. (Eds.). (2022). *Class in Australia*. Monash University Publishing.

Vincent, C., & Ball, S. J. (2007). 'Making up' the middle-class child: Families, activities and class dispositions. *Sociology, 41*(6), 1061–1077. https://doi.org/10.1177/0038038507082315

Warren, S., & Barnes, A. (2023). *"I've never seen it as bad as this": Community sector family homelessness research priorities in the current housing and homelessness crisis*. QUT, Centre for Justice Briefing Paper, 35.

Wiemer, S., & Clarkson, L. (2023). "Spread too thin": Parents' experiences of burnout during COVID-19 in Australia. *Family Relations, 72*(1), 40–59. https://doi.org/10.1111/fare.12773

Williams, R. (1989). *Resources of hope: culture, democracy, socialism*. Verso.

Williamson, T., Wagstaff, D. L., Goodwin, J., & Smith, N. (2023). Mothering ideology: A qualitative exploration of mothers' perceptions of navigating motherhood pressures and partner relationships. *Sex Roles, 88*(1–2), 101–117. https://doi.org/10.1007/s11199-022-01345-7

World Economic Forum. (2022). *Global gender gap report 2022*. Insight Report 2022. https://www3.weforum.org/docs/WEF_GGGR_2022.pdf

CHAPTER 3

Making Time in Motherhood to Invest in Children's Music

INTRODUCTION

A core objective of neoliberal-intensive mothers is to maintain or improve the standard of living of their children compared to themselves (Milkie & Warner, 2014). Mothers make investments in their children to develop attributes that will be advantageous in the future. Involvement in some forms of music, specifically classical forms of music, is largely a middle-class practice aimed at social reproduction and accrual of cultural capital. These practices are investments aimed at developing specialised dispositions that will have exchange value in the future at prestigious educational institutions and workplaces and have been passed down in families through generations and form part of who they are. Bourdieu's toolkit provides one way to explore these practices.

BOURDIEU'S TOOLKIT

Bourdieu (1984) developed a useful formula for examining practices based on relations between habitus, capitals and field. These entities are considered 'thinking tools', and the way they intersect shows how practices are produced and reproduced (Wacquant, 1989, p. 50). As Reay (2015) articulates, a "Bourdieusian analysis demands a recognition of power, struggle and hierarchy" (p. xvii). Through Bourdieu's theory, a view of social structures and how they regulate and constrain individuals and reproduce social norms is provided (Bourdieu & Passeron, 1977). This explains the constraints and structures that impact the everyday lives of mothers and their aspirations and highlights the practices in which they take action without thinking.

Firstly, I present a brief overview of Bourdieu's theory of practice. *Habitus*, or the classed self, displays embodied dispositions unconsciously. Bourdieu has labelled such tendencies as having "a feel for the game" (Bourdieu, 1990, p. 66) where learning how to 'be' in a classed way is the product of inculcation through experience, history and circumstances (Gillies, 2007). In other words, habitus is ways of being that are enacted without thought as part of everyday life. *Capitals*, as Bourdieu (1984, 1990) explains usually in economic terms, are expressed in accordance with their potential for exchange. There are four categories of capitals: *economic* (money and assets); *cultural* (tastes, appreciations, preferences, knowledges and collections—also known as objective capital), embodied (posture, deportment and language use) and educational level (institutional capital); *social* (family, religious or cultural background, social connections and affiliations) and *symbolic* (which includes all other things that may be exchanged such as credentials). To be valuable, others must recognise the capital's value—sometimes thought of as a struggle for distinction—otherwise, it is worthless and has no exchange power, thereby indicating the intersubjective nature of capitals as relational (Bourdieu, 1990). Finally comes Bourdieu's concept of *field*, which are the social spaces where the struggles for distinction play out. As Bourdieu explains, field is where capital is exchanged. Positions in any given field are determined by one's power or legitimacy within that field (Bourdieu & Wacquant, 1992).

Bourdieu (1984) developed a formula for interrogating practices based on relations between habitus, capitals and field: [(habitus) (capital)] + field = practice. By looking at how the individual's habitus interacts within the field, by the position they hold, and what capitals are being utilised, one's practices become apparent (Maton, 2012). The field structures the habitus just as the habitus feeds back into the field, thereby producing an interactive relationship "as a meaningful world ... with sense and value, in which it is worth investing one's energy" (Bourdieu & Wacquant, 1992, p. 127). In this way, the reproduction of those structures becomes evident. Mobilising Bourdieu's concept of habitus, I explore family and musical dispositions, some of which will be classed, and how that has influenced future generations. In considering habitus, I look for the values and dispositions that are privileged. I examine the women's mothering practices to see the structures that impact their everyday experiences to establish links between the mothers' desires and cultural norms.

The transmission of cultural capital via practices, such as classical music lessons, reproduces classed positions, where maternal practices of cultural cultivation in the past are evident in the future through their children's on-going engagement (Reeves, 2015). Within the field of classical music education, a relationship exists between cultural capital, class, educational achievement and parental involvement to create practices that maintain classical music's elite membership (Bourdieu & Passeron, 1977).

THE SOCIAL AND CLASSED PRACTICE OF MUSIC AND MOTHERING THROUGH A BOURDIEUSIAN LENS

Bourdieu does not consider the function of music as creative agency, but rather as an accumulation of capital. Engagement with classical music, or Western art music as it is sometimes called, has long been seen as an elitist pursuit and a means to accrue cultural capital (Bourdieu, 1984). Bourdieu states that music is a status symbol, delineating social classes, with classical music being the prime marker of 'taste' and 'affirmation of class' (1984, p. 26). Those from working-class backgrounds also participate in formal music tuition, but this has often been in different streams, such as playing brass band instruments (Scharff, 2017). Programmes such as *El Sistema* in Venezuela (Bull, 2014) and numerous similar programmes enlist partici-pant children from low socioeconomic backgrounds and give scholarships to students who show an aptitude for music but do not have the financial resources needed to continue. Many public schools in some Australian states offer tuition in music at reduced rates to make these classes more accessible. There is growing evidence of how music enhances learning and non-musical skills, known colloquially as 'the musician's advantage'. Musical engagement, when practiced for over two years, is understood to provide enhanced neural connections and improved self-regulation, lead-ing to improved learning outcomes (Williams et al., 2023). A plethora of organisations and schools now promote and support tuition in music for disadvantaged populations. However, middle-class parents' choices regarding music tuition are often connected to seeking these advantages in a social and economic sense. Music tuition, particularly in classical music, remains largely the domain of the privileged (Savage, 2015).

Bourdieu's (1984) theory cites the family and the home as the places where social reproduction occurs and posits mothers as the primary transmitters of cultural capital. Practices such as concerted cultivation can only be successfully transmitted by mothers who have the recognised cultural capital (Gillies, 2007). Bourdieu makes many references to music in his seminal work on class—*Distinction* (1984). Music is the epitome of class distinction—"nothing more clearly affirms one's 'class', nothing more infallibly classifies, than tastes in music" (Bourdieu, 1984, p. 18). He states that this is not just an aesthetic choice but rather an outcome of privileged social circumstances. Speaking the language of classical music, understanding the genre and showing an appreciation denote cultural capital that has been nurtured over successive generations. Classical music is a signifier of self-regulation, self-discipline and self-development (Bull, 2014) which are dispositions valued in society and educational institutions. Consumption of middle-brow types of classical music such as musical theatre has been adopted by the lower middle classes to claim a space in this field; however, the working classes have remained absent, preferring not to enter a space where they feel they do not belong (Bourdieu & Passeron, 1977).

Bourdieu's taste theories have been challenged in recent years with protagonists arguing that middle-class tastes now encompass a broader range. Peterson and Simkus (1992) proposed the omnivore/univore binary, stating that those with broader tastes in music demonstrated higher education and trajectories of upward mobility. It is more advantageous to be a cultural omnivore, that is, fluent in all genres of music, rather than a cultural univore with narrow tastes (Prior, 2013). Being a cultural omnivore demonstrates a cosmopolitanism which shows social and cultural superiority, particularly a sensibility to know what music to play when and an aesthetic sensitivity and knowledge of its effect (Chan & Goldthorpe, 2007). Eclectic tastes, according to Atkinson (2011), are divided by gender, class and age, while Coulangeon (2015) includes education in the mix, stating that popular music is consumed primarily by younger people. In addition, Bennett et al. (1999) posit that social value in Australia is not always consistent with being 'cultured' and that there is often an incongruence with those seen as fiscally privileged which is sometimes equated with conspicuous consumption rather than having refined tastes. In Australia, the vision of the 'cashed-up bogan' prevails, where those from the working classes who come into money spend it on a range of lavish but tasteless items to exhibit their success and aspirations.

Another marker of privilege in music tuition is the instrument that is selected for study. Learning 'noble' instruments such as piano or violin is "already accumulating nascent mastery over legitimate musical culture" (Prior, 2013, p. 183). Not only this, the quality of the instrument, and the status of the instrumental tutor and groups the student belong to are highly significant. Aspirational Asian parents desire for their children to learn Western instruments rather than indigenous instruments as the exchange currency is more valuable when applying for positions in Western educational institutions. Independent schools in Australia often advertise the fact that they offer music—tuition and instrument—to all children within their first three years of starting school, and this has become a popular marketing tool. Violin is often the instrument of choice as it caters for small fingers. Piano is also popular for young children's private tuition. These form part of legitimate culture, and middle-class children are schooled early to recognise and exploit this within cultural and educational settings. Playing by ear or teaching oneself from the internet does not carry that same gravitas (or potential opportunities) as learning from a high-status professional teacher (Savage, 2019). However, one may argue that platforms such as TikTok and Instagram can offer performance opportunities that supersede traditional forms, yet the legitimacy of these platforms for creating durable success is still undecided (Tiggermann & Anderberg, 2020).

Bourdieu (1990) labels the family as a 'structuring structure' (p. 53) and a site of reproduction, meaning that it is considered as both a construction and social body. Specific practices are aligned with certain classes which vie for position within a field. In the home, children have their first social interactions which are usually constructed around social norms. Families behave in certain ways, and these ways become family practices— routines and ways of being. As Atkinson (2014) explains:

> [the family] is united by interest in a particular mode of *recognition* and a cluster of taken-for-granted assumptions about 'what one does' revolving around it (or doxa), yet dispersed by unequal possession of the powers (or capitals) necessary to garner that recognition and spurred to engage in various *struggles* and *strategies* to gain them. (p. 224, original emphasis)

Bourdieu labels this as 'doxa' which is "a particular point of view, the point of view of the dominant, which presents and imposes itself as a universal point of view" (1998, p. 57). As an example of doxa I referred to the 'proper way' to learn an instrument which is via lessons from a master coach—someone who was or is a professional in the field—and where other ways of becoming proficient are seen as deficient. This creates the illusion of just one legitimate path to develop skill mastery and become a professional musician. Those with privilege like to maintain these illusions because they can maintain their positions of power. Of course, we can all cite highly successful musicians who cannot read music or who play by ear; however, these are always posited as the exception or perhaps just had that 'lucky break'.

Many middle-class mothers spend a vast amount of time researching what are the best courses of action to achieve advantages for their children. Mothers assess the requirements to succeed, such as how to gain entry to elite schools, then make clear plans and strategies on how best to achieve their goals for their children based on existing capitals and a cost/benefit analysis of what they judge to be viable. Using Bourdieu's (1984) analogy, middle-class mothers demonstrate a 'feel for the game', knowing what is needed to be successful. Some mothers make significant investments in their children's futures without guarantees that their investments will be successful. Bourdieu labels this as 'illusio'. He states that mothers become so invested in the game—in this case, the pursuit of cultural capital through music—that they lose the capacity to think logically about the game itself. These mothers tell themselves that the investment is worth it because they convince themselves that success is real and achievable (Bourdieu, 1998), although arguably there is still some anxiety about whether this is indeed guaranteed (Perrier, 2013). Mothers participate in the game through intensive mothering and concerted cultivation which I explore in detail in Chap. 5.

The learning of a musical instrument in some families is an expected pastime and an activity that all members engage in. Susan, as an experienced musician and music teacher, was able to utilise her cultural capital and insider knowledge in the field to assist her daughter Jessica to get a head start on the road to music as a career. Susan found "*one of the best cello teachers ever*", and through her contacts was able to negotiate early entry for her daughter into the conservatorium. Susan is an active player of 'the game'—she knows how to play it well from her previous experience. However, the game is always biased, with Bourdieu calling it "a competition resembl[es]ing a handicap race that has lasted for generations, in which each player has ... the cumulated scores of his ancestors" (2000, p. 215).

And at some juncture, mothers decide whether they will continue to play the game based on the returns, or exclude themselves from the game, therefore perpetuating the dominant norms (Bourdieu, 1984). Staying in the game is easier for those with the requisite resources to fund continued involvement. When mothers are unable to compete, or rationalise from the outset that their children may not be successful (such as not having the funds needed, or time for lessons, or their children do not wish to practise, or mothers assume that their children will not make the same progress as others), they exclude themselves by saying the game is not for the likes of them. According to Bourdieu (1990), "agents shape their aspirations according to concrete indices of the accessible and the inaccessible, of what is not 'for us'" (p. 62). Bourdieu and Passeron (1977) posit "the level of aspiration of individuals is essentially determined by the probability (judged intuitively by means of previous successes or failures) of achieving the desired goal" (p. 111). This explains why some mothers may choose not to enrol in music tuition for their children. Middle-class mothers' work around 'playing the game' is time-consuming. Many middle-class mothers leave the paid workforce so they can focus on managing their children's lives and supporting their partner's careers. Children become projects to be worked on and managed (Vincent & Ball, 2007) and much of this investment into children is done through music.

Enhancing Understanding of Musical Mothering Through the Integration of Feminist Theories

Motherhood is a social construction which encompasses issues of gender, morality and social values, just as music does. Feminist scholarship has largely ignored the concerns of mothering and motherhood (O'Reilly, 2016). Second-wave feminists linked motherhood to women's oppression, and so entrenched was this idea that a feminist anthology of essays around the family published in 1971 stated, "we are not against love, against men and women living together, against having children. What we are against is the role women play once they become wives and mothers" (Babcox & Belkin, 1971, p. 106). Over time, feminism has worked hard for women's rights to vote, work and for other facets of social life such as ready access to contraception. Many women are ambivalent about becoming mothers, with concerns over career trajectories and the impact on women's lives as being limiting, often described as the 'motherhood penalty' (the cost of raising children while mothers are in the workforce either by taking time out or working shorter hours to care for children); however, it is also valorised as one of life's greatest achievements. O'Reilly (2016) coined the term 'matricentric feminism' (p. 25) which is concerned not with how mothers will fit with society but how society will fit with and meet the needs of mothers. O'Reilly (2008) has spent a lifetime advocating for matricentric feminism:

> A theory of feminist mothering begins with the recognition that mothers *and children* benefit when a mother lives her life, and practices mothering from a position of agency, authority, authenticity, and autonomy ... Likewise, from this standpoint, a women's race, age, sexuality, or marital status do not determine her capacity to mother. (p. 11, *emphasis in original*)

Feminist mothering theory, as promoted by O'Reilly, has provided concrete suggestions for improving the lives of women through affordable and readily accessible childcare and parental leave, aiming to enhance agency through collective bargaining power. Such efforts can assist marginalised groups to achieve their aims; however, this requires interrogation on the enablers and barriers of such pursuits (Appadurai, 2004).

Feminist mothering theory advocates for maternal agency, authority, autonomy and authenticity (Middleton, 2006). Middleton's (2006) definitions of these aspects are such: maternal agency is demonstrated by mothers' ability to mother as they choose and resist the demands of patriarchal motherhood. This might include raising children or arranging domestic lives that may not adhere to social norms. Having authority relates to being listened to within the family, being part of equal partnerships, and being able to make decisions on behalf of the family when dealing with outside institutions such as schools. Autonomy in this instance refers to mothers being financially independent and being able to make choices about staying at home to raise their children or to work and pay for care. Finally, authenticity is mothers asserting and having their needs and interests met outside of motherhood. This supports a realisation that mothers' desires may not always be fulfilled by motherhood alone. As Middleton (2006) writes, these disrupt the dominant discourse of 'good' mothering.

Feminist mothering theory is also cognisant of the relentless emotional and mental work involved in mothering and how pervasive it is within the mothering experience. This aligns with other feminist scholars' work and conceptualisations such as Hochschild's emotional labour (1983; Chap. 7), Hays' intensive mothering (1996; Chap. 5), and Lareau's concerted cultivation (2003/2011; Chap. 5) which are utilised within this book to analyse the mothers' experiences. In addition, I will utilise Atkinson's (2014, 2016; Chap. 4) thinking around affective recognition, or love, to interrogate the affective dimensions within family dynamics created through musical motherhood.

In agreement with O'Reilly's (2016) theory, I acknowledge that the experience of mothering and motherhood is different for every mother. There may be similarities, but no two experiences will be identical. I also argue that not all women wish to be mothers and that being a mother does not always fulfil and meet the needs of every woman and mother. Within families, there is constant negotiation and navigation of everchanging systems of privilege and affordances, costs and constraints that shape how mothering is enacted (Few-Demo et al., 2014). Intersectionality is the interconnection of social categories where race, class and gender overlap to create varying affordances and discriminations and explains how the experiences of two women, even those from the same social class for example, may be completely different. Motherhood is performed differently by and within different classes and societies. McLeod (2005) states that exploring motherhood through habitus and field enables us to reimagine the social and cultural practices of gender. Dominant discourses of motherhood are culturally significant and culturally sanctioned and are interwoven with and performed around constructions of femininity, beliefs around respectability and patriarchal constructions of what it means to be a 'good' mother (Lawler, 2000; Skeggs, 1997; Stahl, 2015). In analysing the constraints and processes that differentiate lived experiences, the distinctions between mothers can be made explicit. Skeggs (1997) states:

(T)he explanatory power of feminist theory develops from interrogating the production of categories, their applicability, the experiences of them and from assessing their explanatory adequacy for different groups of women in different relations of power at historically specific times and places. This is how knowledge becomes situated. (p. 21)

Feminist theory is suitable for interrogating motherhood and the work that mothers do in creating musical children and musical selves because it is mothers who do this work. Feminist theory acknowledges that experience is key to subjectivity which is enacted through practice and discourse

(Skeggs, 1997). These processes evolve through continuous evaluations in line with current thinking and theories. O'Reilly champions the work that mothers do but challenges any notions of gender essentialism. Motherhood is framed as a cultural practice rather than a natural biological function (O'Reilly, 2004).

O'Reilly (2008) lobbies for a feminist mothering that manifests as activism, where child-rearing can become a 'social-political act' (p. 19), and mothers can utilise their positions to advocate for change in and outside of the domestic space. This theory also uncovers the use-value of music and its aesthetic and functional value in women's lives, and how it encapsulates meaning (Frith, 1996). Bourdieu has articulated his view of the world through economic analogies of accumulated capitals and their potential for exchange in relation to habitus, field and capitals. Rather than only viewing engagement with music to accumulate capital ripe for exchange, music is understood to be a resource for women, acknowledged for its inherent beauty and ethereal quality, its ability to enhance wellbeing, and a means for creating culture and a sense of belonging within families.

Middleton, like the previous work of Skeggs (1997), critiques feminist mothering theory to espouse that current frameworks fail to recognise the challenges faced by working-class mothers and how enactment of feminist mothering is constrained through the intersections of class, race, ethnicity and gender and that recent feminist motherhood studies have only explored the experiences of middle- and upper-class mothers. Similarly, 'good' mothers, as O'Reilly (2010) states, are perceived as "white, middle-class, married, stay-at-home moms" (p. 7), thereby excluding mothers who do not identify with this definition.

Using feminist mothering theory to interrogate the mothers' stories, I will show to what degree the mothers participate in the logic of 'good' motherhood and the power they feel they have in disrupting the manifestations of patriarchal motherhood in their domestic and paid work lives. The personal accounts given in this type of qualitative study convey the meaning to the participants' broader lives and that of their families, through the rich and thick descriptions of their contextual experiences (Geertz, 1973). The stories also implicate the participants' subjectivities as mothers, performers, partners and members of communities and their places within in it.

Throughout the book, I show the varying subjectivities the mothers inhabit at different times in their stories. The mother-daughter relationship is explored from the past and in the present, looking at the different subjectivities the women inhabit over time (Bueskens, 2018; Kenway & McLeod, 2004). The mothers illustrate how they felt as daughters, as workers, as mothers, as partners, as musicians and sometimes as grandmothers with each offering a different perspective of their story at that point in time. Feminist mothering theory helps to explore how mothers' work in families creates a sense of family belonging through music and showing 'who we are' through habitus, which is integral to the intergenerational transmission of culture and social reproduction.

LISTENING TO THE STORIES OF MATERNAL EXPERIENCE WITH MUSIC

Narrative inquiry was chosen as the method of generating data for the study because such methods enabled me to delve into the participants' stories to show how, through musical habitus, practices have been passed down through generations. Storytelling as a social practice links with Bourdieu's 'habitus' due to its relational nature of bringing the past into the present and future (Bourdieu, 1984). Fleetwood (2016) labels story as "connection to a life lived in a particular time" (p. 174). The narrators can describe past and present events as a re-telling and re-imagining of everything up until that time point (Andrews, 2014; Bourdieu, 1990). This reveals habitus as part of history but also within new contexts (Bourdieu, 1990). Similarly, there is a very real connection to habitus when the mothers tell their stories from the past but as shaping their present which "generate perceptions, appreciations and practices" in a future-oriented view (Bourdieu, 1990, p. 53).

Within the study, I utilised experience-centred narrative to share the mothers' stories. The narratives are not linear but rather "representative of human reality where our recollections navigate between past, present and future, with the meaning of words altering upon each retelling and re-experiencing" (Savage, 2019, p. 56). I was particularly interested in how participants portrayed themselves, and as Phoenix and Brannen (2014) explain, storytellers "clarify(ing) what they believe their audiences need to know in order to understand … placing limits on what they say … deploying emphasis, repetition and direct appeals to the audience's attention and judgement" (p. 13). With Riessman's (2002) suggestions, I looked at the use of language, such as pauses, silences and emphases, and paralinguistic elements, such as gestures, sighs, utterances, and finally posture and body movements to reveal how the narrator places themselves within their stories.

Stories are the 'social act of remembering' (Murakumi, 2004, p. 49) and are performed by storytellers in a way that meets the perceived relationship between themselves and the listener. Stories are constructed by individuals and their interpretation of their relationship with their own subjectivities (Stahl, 2015). Participants choose which stories to tell and how they tell them, adjusting them for different audiences to receive differing responses. There were many times I felt the mothers mentioned things to me because they assumed I felt the same or had had a similar experience. It is why such stories are collaborative constructions (Squire, 2008). Narratives are habitus set to words, as linguistic representations of 'who we are', where agents integrate stories from their pasts to perceive present contexts, to make projections about the future (Bourdieu & Wacquant, 1992).

The stories of mothers and grandmothers may have slightly differing emphases as each tells the story from their own perspective. It is also interesting to see how participants may speak of past events through the lens of the present, particularly when mothers may be cognisant that practices that were ordinary are now seen to be outdated or even outlawed (Andrews et al., 2008). Riessman (2002) also comments that it does not matter if stories are not the 'truth'. Any story is only ever a partial representation of an event that is influenced by cultural practices, social views, perceptions of the listener and personal viewpoints. The stories told by the mothers in their interviews were made via the choices that were currently available to them, their existing contexts and past experiences (Calhoun, 2013; Maton, 2012). The mothers' stories are 'socially and historically specific' (Lawler, 2000, p. 14) and reveal how they position themselves in contrast to others and their perceptions of the fields they occupy.

In line with feminist methodologies, I reflected upon my own experiences when involved in the study. There were clearly times within the interviews when there were moments of shared meaning, almost so that the mothers did not need to articulate their thoughts but could give a non-verbal gesture to indicate what they were feeling. Skeggs (1997) states, "recognition is one of the means by which experiences are interpreted … positionality is understood and responded to" (p. 29). If participants asked me questions about my experience, I exchanged stories and views with them. Such open exchanges are encouraged to develop ease and rapport in feminist approaches as means to redress any power imbalances (Lawler, 2000). Even though my own interjections are brief, they position me. Similarly, I have put parts of my own story throughout the book as another example of musical motherhood, offering another standpoint and demonstrating my experience and background. Feminist principles suggest finding common ground with participants to develop empathy but also to be mindful of the complexity of research relations and issues of power. As a white, middle-class, heterosexual, tertiary-educated woman, I am considered a stereotype of the mothers who utilise music in the educational care of their children (Lareau, 2003/2011; Savage, 2015). Having this shared subjectivity allows me some common ground with the women I interviewed, although I acknowledge that we are also very different in many other aspects of our lives. The women in this study come from different locations within Australia, are of various life stages and ages, varying ethnicities and are partnered in different ways. Therefore, even though our gender, class status and interest in music for our children and ourselves may be similar, I do not assume that we are the same nor that generalisations about middle-class musical mothering can be forged from such a small sample. However, experiences presented throughout this book may resonate with readers.

In addition to the stories of the mothers I interviewed, and my own story, I have included some more general information about women in Australia particularly in relation to paid employment. My rationale for this was for the reader to be able to contrast these broader views with the stories presented. Similarly, I have sometimes included views from popular culture and blogs to offer further perspectives on the issue at hand. While some of these support the narratives being presented, they also offer counter-narratives and differing outlooks.

Telling a Different Story: Counter-Narratives of Musical Motherhood

Normative discourses of motherhood and mothering are based on essential notions of motherhood as being easy, natural and something that women are made to do, and that raising children is equally as intuitive and fulfilling (Miller, 2005). I was interested to see if any of the women in my study offered alternative viewpoints and counter-narratives to this dominant trope. Counter-narratives are "stories which people tell and live which offer resistance, either implicitly or explicitly, to dominant cultural narratives" (Andrews, 2004, p. 1). Counter-narratives tell of power dynamics and resistance (Bamberg, 2004), and I was keen to see what stories were offered and why the participants may choose to tell the stories they did, in the way that they did. Rather than seeing the mothers' narratives as only life stories, I was interested in seeing how the women perceived themselves at particular times in their lives, how they demonstrated their various subjectivities and what this revealed about their identities. This provided valuable insight into how the women positioned themselves in relationship to dominant cultural norms and their justifications for doing so (Bamberg, 2004).

I also explored how the mothers I interviewed worked hard to perform their narratives in certain ways, to be perceived as 'good' mothers or, perhaps at times, to justify the decisions they made that may reveal them as not so good. I looked for inconsistencies within their stories that may counter how they may wish to be perceived—not to catch them out but to reveal the performative and relational aspect of the interaction and how mothers negotiate the presentation of themselves with society's master narratives (Bamberg, 2004). It is through these small stories, as Bamberg (2004) calls them, that we can see the resistances and compliances to the dominant stories of the times which may or may not align.

A narrative approach connects neatly to Bourdieu's concept of habitus because stories of lived experience within history and social structures are essentially habitus set to words (Fraser & Hagedorn, 2016). As such, these linguistic representations are about who the women were, are and about to become (Bourdieu & Wacquant, 1992). The stories presented are reimaginings of past events that have been reassessed with knowledge from the present where "both the possibility of history and of a tomorrow … revisiting our pasts, in light of changing circumstances of the present, and in so doing, our vision for the future is reconstituted" (Andrews, 2014, p. 3). Here is the synergy between narrative and habitus which are both unconsciously presented but also performative and generative.

REFERENCES

Andrews, M. (2004). Memories of mother: Counter-narratives of early maternal influence. In M. Bamberg & M. Andrews (Eds.), *Considering counter narratives: Narrating, resisting, making sense* (pp. 7–26). John Benjamins Publishing.
Andrews, M. (2014). *Narrative imagination and everyday life*. Oxford University Press.

Andrews, M., Squire, C., & Tamboukou, M. (Eds.). (2008). *Doing narrative research*. Sage.

Appadurai, A. (2004). The capacity to aspire: Culture and the terms of recognition. In V. Rao & M. Walton (Eds.), *Culture and public action* (pp. 59–84). Stanford University Press.

Atkinson, W. (2011). From sociological fictions to social fictions: Some Bourdieusian reflections on the concepts of 'institutional habitus' and 'family habitus'. *British Journal of Sociology of Education, 32*(3), 331–347. https://doi.org/10.1080/01425692.2011.559337

Atkinson, W. (2014). A sketch of 'family' as a field: From realized category to space of struggle. *Acta Sociologica, 57*(3), 223–235. https://doi.org/10.1177/00016993135114

Atkinson, W. (2016). *Beyond Bourdieu*. Polity.

Babcox, D., & Belkin, M. (1971). *Liberation now! Writings from the women's liberation movement*. Dell.

Bamberg, M. (2004). Considering counter narratives. In M. Bamberg & M. Andrews (Eds.), *Considering counter narratives: Narrating, resisting, making sense* (pp. 351–372). John Benjamins Publishing.

Bennett, T., Emmison, M., & Frow, J. (1999). Music tastes and music knowledge. In T. Bennett, M. Emmison, & J. Frow (Eds.), *Accounting for tastes: Australian everyday cultures* (pp. 170–200). Cambridge University Press.

Bourdieu, P. (1984). *Distinction: A social critique of the judgement of taste*. Routledge and Kegan Paul.

Bourdieu, P. (1990). *The logic of practice*. Polity.

Bourdieu, P. (1998). *Practical reason*. Polity.

Bourdieu, P. (2000). *Pascalian meditations*. Polity.

Bourdieu, P., & Passeron, J. C. (1977). *Reproduction in education, society and culture*. Sage.

Bourdieu, P., & Wacquant, L. (1992). *An invitation to reflexive sociology*. University of Chicago Press.

Bueskens, P. (2018). From containing to creating. In C. Nelson & R. Robertson (Eds.), *Dangerous ideas about mothers* (pp. 197–210). UWAP Press.

Bull, A. (2014). *The musical body: How gender and class are reproduced among young people playing classical music in England*. Unpublished doctoral thesis, Goldsmiths University.

Calhoun, C. (2013). For the social history of the present: Bourdieu as historical sociologist. In P. S. Gorski (Ed.), *Bourdieu and historical analysis* (pp. 36–66). Duke University Press.

Chan, T. W., & Goldthorpe, J. H. (2007). Social stratification and cultural consumption: Music in England. *European Sociological Review, 23*(1), 1–19. https://doi.org/10.1093/esr/jcl016

Coulangeon, P. (2015). Social mobility and musical tastes: A reappraisal of the social meaning of taste eclecticism. *Poetics, 51*, 54–68. https://doi.org/10.1016/j.poetic.2015.05.002

Few-Demo, A. L., Lloyd, S. A., & Allen, K. R. (2014). It's all about power: Integrating feminist family studies and family communication. *Journal of Family Communication, 14*(2), 85–94. https://doi.org/10.1080/1526743 1.2013.864295

Fleetwood, J. (2016). Narrative habitus: Thinking through structure/agency in the narratives of offenders. *Crime Media Culture, 12*(2), 173–192. https://doi.org/10.1177/1741659016653643

Fraser, A., & Hagedorn, J. M. (2016). Gangs and a global sociological imagination. *Theoretical Criminology*, 1–21.

Frith, S. (1996). Music and identity. In S. Hall & P. du Gay (Eds.), *Questions of cultural identity* (pp. 108–127). Sage.

Geertz, C. (1973). *The interpretation of cultures: Selected essays*. Basic Books.

Gillies, V. (2007). *Marginalised mothers: Exploring working-class experiences of parenting*. Routledge.

Hays, S. (1996). *The cultural contradictions of motherhood*. Yale University Press.

Hochschild, A. R. (1983). *The managed heart: The commercialization of human feeling*. University of California Press.

Kenway, J., & McLeod, J. (2004). Bourdieu's reflexive sociology and 'spaces of points of view': Whose reflexivity, which perspective? *British Journal of Sociology of Education, 25*(4), 525–544.

Lareau, A. (2003/2011). *Unequal childhoods: Class, race, and family life*. University of California Press.

Lawler, S. (2000). *Mothering the self: Mothers, daughters, subjects*. Routledge.

Maton, K. (2012). Habitus. In M. Grenfell (Ed.), *Pierre Bourdieu: Key concepts* (2nd ed., pp. 48–64). Acumen.

McLeod, J. (2005). Feminists re-reading Bourdieu. *Theory and Research in Education, 3*(1), 11–30.

Middleton, A. (2006). Mothering under duress: Examining the inclusiveness of feminist mothering theory. *Journal of the Association for Research on Mothering, 8*(1–2), 72–82.

Milkie, M., & Warner, C. H. (2014). Status safeguarding: Mothers' work to secure children's place in the social hierarchy. In L. R. Ennis (Ed.), *Intensive mothering: The cultural contradictions of modern motherhood* (pp. 66–85). Demeter Press.

Miller, T. (2005). *Making sense of motherhood: A narrative approach*. Cambridge University Press.

Murakumi, K. (2004). Socially organised use of memories of mother in narrative re-construction of problematic pasts. In M. Bamberg & M. Andrews (Eds.),

Considering counter narratives: Narrating, resisting, making sense (pp. 351–372). John Benjamins Publishing.

O'Reilly, A. (2004). *From motherhood to mothering: The legacy of Adrienne Rich's of woman born*. SUNY Press.

O'Reilly, A. (2008). Introduction. In A. O'Reilly (Ed.), *Feminist mothering* (pp. 1–24). SUNY Press.

O'Reilly, A. (2010). *Twenty-first-century motherhood: Experience, identity, policy, agency*. Columbia University Press.

O'Reilly, A. (2016). *Matricentric feminism: Theory, activism, practice*. Demeter Press.

Perrier, M. (2013). Middle-class mothers' moralities and concerted cultivation. *Sociology, 47*(4), 655–670. https://doi.org/10.1177/0038038512453789

Peterson, R. A., & Simkus, A. (1992). How musical tastes mark occupational status groups. In M. Lamont & M. Fournier (Eds.), *Cultivating differences: Symbolic boundaries and the making of inequality* (pp. 152–168). The University of Chicago Press.

Phoenix, A., & Brannen, J. (2014). Researching family practices in everyday life: Methodological reflections from two studies. *International Journal of Social Research Methodology, 17*(1), 11–26. https://doi.org/10.1080/1364557 9.2014.854001

Prior, N. (2013). Bourdieu and the sociology of music consumption: A critical assessment of recent developments. *Sociology Compass, 7*(3), 181–193. https://doi.org/10.1111/soc4.12020

Reay, D. (2015). Foreword. In P. Burnard, Y. Hofvander Trulsson, & J. Söderman (Eds.), *Bourdieu and the sociology of music education* (pp. 43–59). Ashgate.

Reeves, A. (2015). 'Music's a family thing': Cultural socialisation and parental transference. *Cultural Sociology, 9*(4), 493–514. https://doi.org/10.1177/1749975515576941

Riessman, C. K. (2002). Analysis of personal narratives. In J. F. Gubrium & J. A. Holstein (Eds.), *Handbook of interview research: Context and method* (pp. 695–710). Sage.

Savage, S. (2015). *Intensive mothering through music in early childhood education*. Unpublished Masters' Minor Thesis, Monash University.

Savage, S. (2019). *Musical mothering: Middle-class strategies and affect across generations*. Unpublished PhD thesis, Monash University.

Scharff, C. (2017). *Gender, subjectivity, and cultural work: The classical music profession* (1st ed.). Taylor & Francis Group.

Skeggs, B. (1997). *Formations of class and gender*. Sage.

Squire, C. (2008). Experience-centred to socioculturally-oriented approaches to narrative. In M. Andrews, C. Squire, & M. Tamboukou (Eds.), *Doing narrative research* (pp. 42–64). Sage.

Stahl, G. (2015). *Identity, neoliberalism and aspiration: Educating white working-class boys.* Routledge.

Tiggermann, M., & Anderberg, I. (2020). Social media is not real: The effect of 'Instagram vs reality' images on women's social comparison and body image. *New Media & Society, 22*(12), 2183–2199. https://doi.org/10.1177/1461444819888720

Vincent, C., & Ball, S. J. (2007). 'Making up' the middle-class child: Families, activities and class dispositions. *Sociology, 41*(6), 1061–1077. https://doi.org/10.1177/0038038507082315

Wacquant, L. (1989). Towards a reflexive sociology: A workshop with Pierre Bourdieu. *Sociological Theory, 7*(1), 26–63. https://doi.org/10.2307/202061

Williams, K. E., Bentley, L. A., Savage, S., Eager, R., & Nielson, C. (2023). Rhythm and movement delivered by teachers supports self-regulation skills of preschool-aged children in disadvantaged communities: A clustered RCT. *Early Childhood Research Quarterly, 65*, 115–128. https://doi.org/10.1016/j.ecresq.2023.05.008

CHAPTER 4

Being Musical: Nature or Nurture?

INTRODUCTION

In Western society, the idea that musicality is innate is widespread, and children are labelled as musical or non-musical very early on in their lives. Parental perceptions of children's musicality directly correlate with children's participation in instrumental tuition and engagement with arts-based activities (Nagel, 2010). Parents and music teachers alike are complicit in making these judgements, labelling children as "'unmusical', a perception that will most likely be carried into adulthood" (Dwyer, 2016, p. 23). A plethora of television talent programmes ridicule people who audition with a less-than-perfect pitch and tone, which suggests that only people with good singing voices should sing in public. This is in stark contrast to many non-Western nations where music and song are part of the very fabric of their everyday lives, which is where I start the chapter.

Many mothers who perceive their children to be musical, that is, to demonstrate an interest early on, often enrol their children in early childhood music classes (Savage, 2015). Here, young children learn the basics of music but also develop non-musical skills in a deliberate strategy by mothers to nurture cognitive and social skills to get 'ahead of the game' and accrue cultural capital for themselves and the family (Savage 2015; Vincent & Ball, 2007).

© The Author(s), under exclusive license to Springer Nature
Switzerland AG 2024
S. Savage, *Musical Mothering*, Palgrave Macmillan Studies
in Family and Intimate Life,
https://doi.org/10.1007/978-3-031-65157-1_4

This chapter has four sections. Firstly, I explore what it means to be considered musical and, secondly, how this feeds into notions of talent or acquired skill. I share a story of my own musical development, which, unlike most others in this book, was not encouraged by my parents but by 'non-parental others' (Atkinson, 2016, p. 96). Using the idea of affective recognition as a cycle of positive reinforcement, a reason why mothers and their children engage with music in the first instance is explored. Finally, I look at who makes this subjective call that shapes future musical engagement and self-perceptions about musical ability and argue that it is mothers who are the primary determiners of whether children should receive music tuition or not. I show how these decisions are made over generations and implicate lives and musical trajectories.

Engagement with music can be a casual pursuit, and this is true of some of the musical families in this book who engage in music in various ways—listening to and singing along to songs on the radio, singing in church, sharing songs with young children. For many cultures, music is fundamental and a way of life, not something that is only for the 'talented' or privileged. For the musical mothers in this book, I begin to show how important their children's musicality is to them, and how the perceptions of being musical are passed down through generations.

BEING MUSICAL

For many cultures, music is integral to what they do every day—song and dance for working, family times, putting children to sleep and for social occasions. Music and dance are integral to cultural identity and important for children's overall development (Mapana, 2011). In Tanzania, the Wagogo peoples sing, dance and drum every day fostering cultural identity and belonging (Mapana, 2011). Song conveys culture to future generations. Indigenous peoples in Australia utilise music and song to tell stories and for communicating culture, to reconcile the effects of colonisation and as a form of 'cultural resilience' (Bracknell, 2020a, p. 140). Bracknell (2020b) writes that the performance of song in Aboriginal culture "is to create a feeling of being in the moment—with kin, in Country" (p. 221). Ibarra's (2017) study of the Araquio in the Philippines tells how music begins in the wombs of mothers, as embedded practices in a type of theatre-ritual to transmit customs and cultural practices. Dwyer's (2016) work found that throughout many cultures around the world, the idea that people were not able to actively participate in musical activities was inconceivable. Differences in abilities were evident, but this did not preclude anyone from participating. Music and dance were integral to life, and everyone joined in.

In contrast to non-Western cultures, people in Western cultures seem to hold a view that participation in music is only for those who demonstrate a certain level of ability (Dwyer, 2016). Classical music, also called Western art music, is seen as elitist and not for the consumption of the masses (Dwyer, 2016). According to Dwyer (2016), music can be viewed as presentational or participatory, with a clear divide between audience members and performers. In some Western families, music can also be used to transmit family cultures and can be seen as 'something we do'. Families and individual family members are considered 'musical' or not. This is something I explore in the next section of the book. But even if children are perceived as 'musical', mothers may choose not to develop these skills in their children due to having other aspirations for their children or being constrained by the financial costs of tuition or lack of time to take children to lessons. My own musical development was not something that was nurtured by my parents nor was part of our everyday family practice.

My first public performance from memory was when I was in my first year of formal schooling. I remember our class stood on the wooden stage at the front of another first-year class. We were singing *Twinkle twinkle little star*, a familiar childhood song in the repertoire of most Australian young children, especially back then when Australia was not so culturally diverse. I am not sure if I was singing a little too loudly or too enthusiastically; however, at the end of our rendition, my teacher asked if I would sing the song in front of the other class by myself. As an obedient child, I did so.

I always loved singing. My parents listened to music on the radio and enjoyed popular artists of the day, although they were not concert goers, did not play musical instruments and only occasionally went to the local amateur musical theatre productions. In my primary schooling, I looked forward to music sessions in class which consisted of singing along to a radio broadcast. It was the highlight of my week. In early secondary school, we had a student drama teacher who encouraged us to put on a musical. We did an *a capella* version of *Joseph and the amazing technicolour dreamcoat*, and I played Joseph. There were mostly girls in the cast, and only one boy. Musicals were not seen as very masculine, and this was important in 1970s Australia. At the end of the two-night run of performances in the packed school hall, the student teacher spoke to my mother, suggesting I should have singing lessons.

Singing lessons did not occur until I had the opportunity at my next secondary school for group lessons. These were heavily subsidised, and so after my request to attend, my parents allowed me to go. This school opened many musical possibilities, and I joined choirs and *a capella* groups and continued to have singing lessons for the next 20 or so years, way beyond my school days. My parents did not allow me to join the local musical theatre group until after I had finished my high schooling for fear it would interfere with my studies. Once finished, I began doing musicals with this local amateur group that my parents used to go to occasionally, and landed small, then larger roles. I joined more theatre groups and did more roles, competitions and guest performances, and much later in my life, I travelled overseas and worked in professional musical theatre and opera for several years much to the dismay of my parents. They did not understand the thrill I received from singing and performance.

The point of this story is that my musical journey was driven by me and encouraged by my teachers—'non-parental others' (Atkinson, 2016, p. 96)—not my parents, who would not allow me to attend university to do a music degree because they felt a job in the music industry would not offer job security. I completed an early childhood teaching degree because it was considered a suitable job for a young woman whose parental expectations were that I marry, have children and become a home maker for the rest of my life. My parents believed the musical world to be 'false', and they didn't want me to be a part of that.

I have continued my interest in music, singing in choirs in my later years, running a music teaching business, and researching musical parenting as part of my academic work. My own children were given the opportunity and support to learn music and participate in musical activities, and we enjoy engaging in music together as a family. We are considered a 'musical family'; however, it is something that I have intentionally worked on as a mother. It is this intentionality that I will now explore further in the next few chapters where I investigate the decisions mothers make when investing in their children musically, the cycle of affective recognition that establishes that musical and personal bond.

TALENT AND GENETICS OR ACQUIRED SKILL?

There is a cultural myth that music is a genetic trait that runs in families (Howe et al., 1998; Scripp et al., 2013). Rosemary staunchly stated in her interview,

> *there's a bit of a stream that runs through the family. Dad's just always been musical. Mum is musical ... but the music has come down through me ... my side, because Penelope's father hasn't got a musical bone (laughs) ... my side are very musical.*

Rosemary's comment suggests an inherited nature to this disposition, and she was very proud of her supposed role in transmitting this proclivity to her daughter and one of her sons.

The notion that musical talent is inherited is pervasive as Koza (2001) explains,

> The belief that musical talent is innate ... divides children into the 'haves' and 'have nots', effectively prohibiting the 'have nots' from ever becoming 'haves'... Today, most music educators advocate music for every child, regardless of perceived ability, but few have considered the possibility that musical talent may be a social and cultural construct. (p. 249)

Considering Bourdieu's concept of habitus, Hall (2015) gives an example of the professional musician who "by learning and practising a range of skills over many years, musicality becomes so deeply ingrained that it becomes 'automatic', giving the appearance of an 'innate talent'" (p. 47). Psychologists such as Dweck (2006) state that through application of a 'growth mindset' (p. 16), her famous term, any skill can be enhanced through practise. In many families, such as Rosemary, Susan and Linda, the formal learning of music over generations has been, and continues to be, an expected practice, as part of their habitus.

And yet there are variations of this expected practice within families and between siblings. Rosemary retold a discussion she had with her son. "*You didn't have me taught music!*" her son exclaimed, "*But you didn't want to*", she replied. At this point, she laughed when she reported this and then continued, "*He didn't want to ... He is not very musical, in my opinion*". Here, Rosemary had judged her son to be not musical, and so he was not afforded the same music lessons as his sister Penelope. Rosemary mediated this by saying her son still had opportunities to pursue music at school. It was significant that Penelope also mentioned her 'non-musical' father and brother in her interview:

> *My father cannot sing to save his life … born in the '30s, you can't play the horn, you're not good at it, you're useless. So never tried. Never did anything … so can't sing … couldn't sing. And I've got another brother who's like that as well and another brother who is very musical. We love singing together, yeah, it's great. It's really good.*

From Rosemary and Penelope's comment, you might infer that they had a closer relationship with their similarly musical family member. It was difficult to tell if her son's comments showed resentment of the fact that he was not given the same chances or merely tongue-in-cheek.

In Penelope's interview, she spoke of an *'inner expectation'* that her child would be musical. She made this assumption prior to her child's birth. As a pregnant woman, she had imaginings of sharing musical experiences with her child, just as she had shared such moments with her mother, Rosemary. Penelope said, *"all I wanted, okay, was to be able to sing in the car with my daughter and sing in harmony"*. She described not being able to do this would equate to a *'loss'* and a *'disappointment'*. These are intense emotions and illustrate the depth of meaning this has for Penelope. Singing together and sharing music is interwoven with layered meanings and affective relations. As Hall (2018, p. 12) writes, "the performativity of the singing voice is concentrated by the fact that the performer's body is the instrument", and engagement in such activities releases the body's feel-good hormones, adding to the experience. As humans, we gain pleasure from interacting in activities we enjoy with others who we like and who exhibit enjoyment doing these activities too. This feeling is enhanced when you love the person, like your child. In Penelope, this feeling was arguably more intense because she only had one child—*"if I'd had three kids and one couldn't sing then maybe there's another one … but I've just got one"*. In retrospect, I wondered if this is what Rosemary felt about her son. Penelope envisioned sharing her musicality with her daughter to strengthen their emotional connection, and the burden of expectation was huge.

Wanting to share music, or perform music together with your child, is a common phenomenon. Recently, a colleague was playing in a concert with a group she regularly plays with. This time, however, her teenage son was joining the group to play for the concert. The joy and pride in the mother's Facebook post was palpable, and responses from musical friends were equally ebullient—with one friend suggesting it was like a dream come true for this musical mother. It was like the intergenerational transmission of musical mothering was complete in this one action.

Returning to notions of talent, Koza (2001) states these assumptions have elitist underpinnings and can be divisive because it separates those who can and those who cannot. Classical musicians who are trained to perform music are considered competent with high status, in the same realm as elite sportspeople, which generates admiration and respect (Dwyer, 2016). The hours of practise to achieve such ability are rarely acknowledged. It is also suggested that music-rich environments will nurture musical children by way of osmosis, as was the case with my colleague and her son. Bourdieu (1984) states that such inculcation is a form of 'domestic cultural training' (p. 46) where mothers carefully design the home environment to provide opportunities to develop the traits, abilities and dispositions they value. Renowned music pedagogues, Kodály and Suzuki both advocate for the role of providing musically rich environments to foster musical skills. Kodály famously stated, "music education should begin nine months before the mother's birth" (Kokas, 1970, p. 53). Suzuki (1978) similarly refutes the notion that talent is innate by maintaining it is through providing the right environment from the beginning of a child's life that is crucial. "Talent is no accident of birth", Suzuki (1978, p. 10) states that, however, such abilities appear to be genetic because they have been nurtured from the very start of a child's life, or before as Kodály and other music educators advocate (Ilari et al., 2013; Savage & Hall, 2017). Bourdieu (1990) states "the silence of prerequisites for the acquisition of art competence is self-serving for the privileged classes because it makes it possible to pretend that it is a gift of nature" (p. 211) when in reality it is the result of years of inculcation, training, practise, and opportunities to perform and been seen in the right arenas by the right people. When a skill or interest has been nurtured from the very genesis of life, through osmosis in the family setting, it is easy for this skill to be perceived as innate.

It is the middle classes who often have the resources needed to develop such attributes in their children through access to expert tuition, quality instruments, and time to take their children to rehearsals, concerts and lessons. The idea that musical ability is innate is refuted by Burland and Davidson (2002) who posit that it is not only practise and the support of significant others that implicates success in the musical field, but the importance for young musicians to also have well-developed coping strategies to transition from early musical training to later success. In their earlier studies, Davidson et al. (1996) over a period of four years found that the contexts in which aspiring musicians grew up in were critical for success in children's musical development. Having parents who attended lessons with their child, high levels of support from family and others, first teachers who were personable, later teachers who were role models, and those who practised more were more likely to achieve musical success (Davidson et al., 1996; Kamin et al., 2007). To be musically successful, a range of affordances need to be presented, inclusive of whether musical aptitude is also evident.

The opportunity to play musical instruments is not afforded to all children due to structural constraints rather than their parents' wishes. Even if you are very capable musically or show a proclivity for music, there may be limitations to the continuation of musical development due to a range of reasons, as I showed in the example of my own experience. While school programmes can offer some opportunities, there are still fees to pay, and support is limited. Once children reach a certain level, they need individualised training which is expensive. Linda grew up with music as a large part of her life. All of her siblings showed musical skills from a young age and music was something they enjoyed as part of their family life when they got together in the school holidays when they returned from boarding school. Unfortunately, Linda's parents could only afford for one of their children to continue playing the piano and chose her sibling, something Linda still regrets. Linda had played piano, flute and violin. Music had been a large part of Linda's parents' lives, too—her mother a pianist and her father a chorister. Linda was determined that her children would not miss out on learning their chosen musical instrument, as she had done. Linda tells a story of the musical childhoods she provided. Singing songs in the garden, banging on improvised household equipment and sound-making on their simple percussion instruments, Linda encouraged musical play with her children from an early age. As her children were about to start school, she bought them all recorders and taught them how to play. From a conservative Christian family, Linda said that her husband "*let me be the parent*" where she aimed to be "*the best mother*" she could be. She qualified this by saying:

Being there for them, being a Godly woman and (pause) giving them aspirations, opportunities, probably more than I had, probably a good education (laughs) that was a bit more consistent than mine. I wanted not only music, it was sport, to do bits of everything. I think music gives you a little bit of an enjoyment and if you didn't want to go, pursue it, it's such a wonderful hobby to have at the end.

Linda did not work in paid employment when her children were still at home, devoting her time to developing and nurturing their musical futures, stating she considered music to be a '*wonderful hobby*'. Linda valued balance, so by having experience in sporting activities too, her children would become 'all-rounders', a common aspiration among middle-class parents where experience in a range of activities presents well on resumes (Vincent & Ball, 2007). In their first year of formal schooling at a private Christian school, Linda's children were offered the chance to learn the violin. "*They just picked it up so quickly*", Linda exclaimed. Linda's work to immerse her children in music in their preschool years had begun to work its magic, and they were on their way.

Studies have shown that the positive contribution of parents towards music and music tuition increases the chances that children will continue with their musical practice and build positive relationships with their teachers; parents must believe that their children will be successful for this to occur (McPherson, 2009; McPherson & Davidson, 2002). Furthermore, this impacts children's motivation, self-efficacy and perception of the music lessons (Creech, 2010). A positive parent-teacher-pupil dynamic is also considered pivotal for music tuition to be successful. Suzuki's approach to music tuition insists that a parent also participates in lessons with their young child (Suzuki, 1978). However, most studies do not acknowledge that it is mothers who do the majority of this work.

Musical ability is a skill that is developed through practise and exposure to music. Middle-class mothers can provide greater opportunities for children to learn culturally sanctioned forms of music, afford quality instruments and tuition, attend concerts and have time to supervise practise, drive children to lessons and rehearsals, and encourage children's musical development. If music has been part of family culture, then musical ways of being are embedded into family life. Deeper connections are formed when music is shared between family members who love and value music as something that defines them as a 'musical family'.

AFFECTIVE RECOGNITION

Shared music-making in the home affirms that doxa, or taken-for-granted, 'family feeling' as a form of affective recognition. Affective recognition, as defined by Atkinson (2016), is love. Atkinson writes about this in the family field where he argues that "*love* and *care* constitute forms of (mis) recognition and thus symbolic power" (*original emphasis*, p. 12). He argues that the family is a 'category' of "expectations and practices of everyday life which, [is] pregnant with unarticulated assumptions, implicit definitions and pedagogy" (Atkinson, 2016, p. 49). Not limited to those rebellious periods in adolescence, resistance in family fields can take many forms such as struggles for autonomy and agency, disputes about tastes and preferences, and, as Atkinson (2016) argues, can present as children being the dominant players.

Engagement with music exemplifies the familial struggles for power within the family field. Music is something that 'we do', that is, certain families do as part of their family life, accepting it as 'normal' or 'usual'. Mothers who love music themselves enjoy participating in informal musicking with their children and encourage their children's involvement in musical activities. Children who see that their mother is experiencing joy when they engage in music, and who receive attention and love for this involvement, are likely to pursue it further. It becomes a cycle of positive reinforcement, as the effects of engaging and enjoying music contribute to the construction of family doxa, that is the perception that music is integral to family life and is the family's social reality (Savage, 2019). This is no different from any parent encouraging an activity that they too are invested in, such as sporting activities and other leisure pursuits, and is a common phenomenon.

Mutual affective recognition is evident in the relationships between Penelope and Rosemary and also between Susan and Jessica. Here, Rosemary celebrates Penelope's musical ability,

Rosemary: *It was really easy and just chords (sings) John B, Grandpappy and me … I wasn't good at it. I couldn't do that. Penelope just picks it up and plucks with two fingers ... And then ... used a finger to change the chords all the way up (laughs)*

Penelope: *That's what you do*

Rosemary: *That's what you do (laughs and mimics disparagingly) ... you didn't get that from me—the singing you did—I'm not that talented.*

Sally: *I'm just a three-chord person*

Penelope: *Most songs are just three chords anyway (laughs).*

Rosemary: *Don't you believe it. She's very, very good—very good.*

Penelope is valorised for her musical prowess. It is something Rosemary values, and in her praise of Penelope, she is also praising herself for passing on this ability. There is a misrecognition that their musical skill is inherited, and a self-deprecation that acknowledges their sometimes-fractious affective relationship. Atkinson (2016) notes,

> ... the development of practical and symbolic mastery are forged in the quest for recognition from those we misrecognise, that is to say, love and esteem from those we love and esteem, which is ultimately symbolic power in the eyes of those possessing symbolic capital in the field. (p. 92)

Within the family, it is the mother who holds the symbolic capital, according to Bourdieu. It is through mothers' reputation and honour that families are seen as respectable or not which I will explore later in Chap. 6. As the predominant primary carer, the mother is the one from whom the child seeks recognition and love, although this soon becomes a mutual need. When mother and child participate in music, the love of music is inextricably interwoven with their love for each other. The intense emotional feeling one gets when engaging with music, especially with one you love, deepens the feeling. Frith (2008) comments that as social beings, it is these shared empathic experiences that make us human. Through mothers' praise and acknowledgement, encouragement and affirmation, the need for love and recognition is sated. It fulfils our desire to continue and perpetuates a cycle of affective recognition (Sayer, 2005b). There is a need within Rosemary to have Penelope's love and appreciation (even if Penelope feels that Rosemary is sometimes critical of her) as shown by her comment:

Penelope's the musical one in the family ... but I keep telling her it's come through my side of the family ... as long as she knows that

Penelope reciprocates and acknowledges the gift of music that Rosemary has given. Their affective recognition is affirmed and is mutually agreeable. However, familial tensions are also present, as Penelope recalls to me,

She never likes any of the music I liked. She never liked modern stuff. She liked a lot of old-fashioned stuff and then when you were a teenager, you depart. Whereas with your age group and my age group, with our kids we know all that pop music and we don't really depart ... or we'll say, "Oh, that's quite a good song" or "that's crap", but she would go ... "Oh, I don't know that" (in a caricatured 'old person' tone).

The tone in which Penelope 'mimics' her mother's voice is dismissive, where she suggests that parents of her mother's era would belittle children's musical tastes as inferior, positioning children as inferior and of unequal status. Parenting over generations has changed from being adult-centred when Penelope and I were children, to being child-centred as it is now. Mothering is very focused on children's needs and developing skills and dispositions and goes beyond the care work that was the core work of parenting during the time of my childhood. Contemporary mothers, like Penelope, make a point to know their children's listening repertoires, which can be related to surveying their children's music consumption as part of moral parenting, which is discussed further in Chap. 6 and connected to mothers wanting to be seen as good mothers and morally worthy. Cho and Ilari's (2021) study of 19 mothers of children 18 months to five years in the US showed that all mothers used recorded music as part of their mothering. They stated that the choice of music was varied; however, they rarely shared their own musical tastes with their children, preferring children's music to dominate their children's listening repertoires. The exceptions to this were classical and religious music which were shared to children by a small percentage of the mothers. Koops' (2018) study to look at the perceptions and beliefs of tweens and parents on their musical experiences, interests and aspirations showed that both children and parents chose family listening repertoire. In contrast to Cho and Ilari, Koops commented that children initiated interest in listening to their parents' music.

For many mothers and daughters, relationships can be peppered with resistance and struggle over the lifespan, particularly when expectations differ or decisions regarding children and family matters must be made and justified (Bourdieu, 1999; Harrigan & Miller-Ott, 2013). Tensions can arise when,

> the expectations of the parents, constituted in a prior social world, are in some way out of touch or out of sync with the present world, to which the children's expectations, which have been constituted in different conditions of socialisation, are better adjusted. (Bourdieu, 1999, p. 508)

In Penelope and Rosemary's relationship, cohesion is most evident when they are connected musically. Music becomes the glue that binds them. Their narratives point to differences in parenting styles and beliefs, yet their affective recognition is based on their mutual relationship with music.

Mothers of Rosemary's generation were not as demonstrative as contemporary mothers. Parenting, as I said before, was very adult-centred rather than child-centred. In the 1960s and early 1970s, mothers were advised by experts not to 'spoil' their children with praise and affection (Warner, 2006). I recall Susan's comments in her interview when speaking of her childhood, "*I cannot remember a single hug from my mother, all my life*". Being of a similar generation, I have similar recollections. While this is an indicator of mothering at that time, this dearth of affection has remained foremost in Susan's mind and influenced her own mothering where Susan stated she was "*pretty tactile with my children*".

Susan felt unable to give her children the time she would have liked due to paid work commitments and her status as a single parent. In families where parents might be unsupportive, absent or unable to give the requisite affective recognition desired, children may seek affective recognition from 'non-parental others' (Atkinson, 2016, p. 96). Susan's daughter, Jessica, spoke of other family members and friends who were instrumental in encouraging her musical development,

My sister brought a cello home from the school storeroom just to have a go at it over the weekend, and I picked it up and loved it … the other thing I was thinking about down there [in the rural town where she lived] was [the] amazing kind of network of people who were just willing to have a jam. So, I taught myself cello by playing with a group of people who used to do this open mic night … like my aunty and some other friends … and they were really into their bush music and Irish music … and it's been this sort of focus, you know, this sort of thing that drives your life along in a particular direction ... through something you love, and you're interested in.

Open mic nights afforded Jessica the opportunity to play and practise her music, supported by her extended family and friends. Developing proficiency was also a way to gain her mother's love by being involved in music which she knew was one of her mother's passions. Traditionally, open mic nights are held in local venues—bars and cafes—to give aspiring soloists and seasoned others who love to play, an opportunity to play in front of an audience, test out new material, or simply enjoy playing together in a relaxed and non-competitive environment. For amateur musicians, this kind of practice helps to "develop individual confidence, individual techniques and the ability to negotiate the organisation of staged behaviour" (Aldredge, 2006, p. 112). Kamin et al. (2007) explored the talent development of non-classical musicians to assess whether the lack of structure within the learning environment mattered. They also wanted to investigate if an individual's psychological characteristics of developing excellence were necessary in talent development in non-classical musicians, as well as the influence of peers and other external factors. It was found that extreme internal motivation and other innate qualities such as confidence and commitment are essential for non-classical musicians to succeed without the support of parents. Dispositions consistent with a middle-class habitus act as enablers to be successful when other supports, such as immediate family, are not available. Middle-class families, often nuclear in composition, have moved away from wider family connections in pursuit of employment opportunities and therefore must rely on others for the types of support that might usually have been provided via the family. The influence of peers was also seen as highly significant to continued success and involvement. Jessica's pursuit of music was nurtured not only by her mother but by others with the requisite cultural capital, which enabled Jessica to receive the affective recognition and support she desired.

Affective recognition from her mother was not as easy for Linda who spent much of her childhood away at international boarding schools. Linda made several comments about her parents' absence in her interview, with positive remarks such as the important missionary work her parents were doing, and the negative remarks where she felt alone without guidance from her mother. Linda was involved in many music groups while at school, providing her with enjoyment; she still found boarding school challenging, however reframing this by saying it gave her a '*stronger char-acter*'. Linda was determined to create a sense of belonging in her own family, and music became integral to her care work, to give her children the affective recognition that she felt she had missed out on.

Linda had wanted six children, and her husband only two, so they compromised at four. Linda's relationship with her children was always intense to compensate for the lack of attention she received from her own parents which Villalobos (2015) calls 'compensatory connection' (pp. 1931–1932). Linda mentioned the 'non-parental others' influencing her life at that stage, "*we had so many different influences (laughs) not only my mother but teachers and sisters*". Through music, Linda was able to form connections with boarding-school peers, fostering "*a sense of community, a sense of friendship*", as they became like family to help mediate the affective recognition she wanted and was missing from her parents. Linda was able to utilise her cultural and emotional capital at school to make the necessary connections to succeed, providing her with a positive identity and purpose.

Engaging with music was how Linda connected with her own children but also her parents in those infrequent times they shared throughout her formative years. As illustrated throughout this book, Linda delighted in being an intensive mother because it meant that she could be with her children as much as possible, fulfilling her need for love and connection. Linda's daughter, Ashley, reflected on the structured parenting she had received, which was punctuated with appreciation,

She definitely helped me and everyone with music. She would literally sit down with you and help you practise for the full hour. Like, what she did for us kids is amazing and I really take my hat off to her. She has been honestly an incredible mother and she, she's given us every single thing we've needed to help and paid and everything.

Ashley's words appeared difficult to say as she had often been critical of her mother's parenting approach throughout the interview, but there was an underlying guilt that she was being uncharitable. Perhaps it was the scope of what her mother had done for them more keenly felt now that Ashley is now a mother herself, or that she felt obliged to say something positive to me, when that was not always the case. Later, Ashley stated, "*she's just meant to be a mum her whole life. She's so maternal … She's just meant to do this*". Despite the tensions in their relationship, Linda would be pleased to hear this affirmation of her mothering from Ashley. What was also evident was the need for Ashley to receive affective recognition from her mother through showing Linda what a good mother and wife she is and will continue to be.

Interactions between mothers and children are in constant flux incurring adjustments and alterations which shape the actions of both mother and child. In children's earliest years, habitus is formed and ways of being, as raced, classed and gendered selves are imitated, tested and developed (Atkinson, 2016). Affective relations are intrinsically bound up between the interactions of mother and child. These dynamic relationships are under continual processes of revision and renewal over generations. For musical mothers, the intense commitment to music makes them vulnerable to disappointment, shame and guilt when their aspirations are not realised (Sayer, 2005a). While it may seem that mothers are in a position of power within these family relationships, this is tenuous because of the desire for reciprocity. Villalobos (2015) states that mothers desire affective recognition from their children as much as children want it from them, perhaps even more.

Siblings and the Inequity of Maternal Affect

As the mother of an only child, Penelope cast all her hopes and dreams regarding music onto her daughter. Penelope wanted her daughter to share her passion for music so they could share music together, just as she had with her mother. Penelope did not have the same degree of expectation thrust upon her as she had two brothers. Rosemary stated numerous times that Penelope was the most musical one in her family. Sosniak (1995) states that it is unusual for only one child in a family to receive extra attention from parents; however, first-born children do get the unrivalled attention of their parents prior to the birth of their siblings.

Individual family members may struggle to gain attention from those whom they would like it most. Davidson and Borthwick's (2002) study provides an example of maternal affective recognition in supporting musical endeavours and the influence this had on each of the children in the family. The study shows how each child thrives musically at different times in their lives when they are given the attention of their mother who was a keen musician. This may seem obvious; however, initially only one child was given musical attention and thrived until he decided he did not want to do music. The attention then moved to the other child who then excelled in this space after originally choosing another field of interest.

Rosemary tells a related story about her son. As mentioned previously, both Rosemary and Penelope have labelled this son 'unmusical'. Regardless of this, the son still actively participates in music, particularly listening to his preferred music, and music is a large part of his life. Rosemary shared an anecdote from when her son was a teenager:

> *He loves all that rock stuff—Billy Bragg. He would try to play music for me. He put every single record on one day. "Mum you'll love this, you'll love it", and he put on this horrible, "Like that?" "No, no love" and [he] tried something else, "You'll like this one, mum". So, this went on for a few more times, "Look, mum, I'm trying to please you". So, of course you are, you poor thing. So eventually, "Ah, that ones' not too bad" (laughs). I mean I didn't like it. (laughs) So, they all loved music. They had it on—the stuff I don't like.*

Rosemary's story illustrates how her son tried hard to connect their mutual love of music, seeking her approval. Rosemary shares this story in a playful way, chiding her son for his musical tastes that she did not share. As mentioned earlier in this chapter, Rosemary considered her son 'not musical', and as such, he was not afforded the same opportunities and became what Davidson and Borthwick (2002, p. 135) describe as 'prophecies to fulfil'. Conversely, this story could be reframed as an example of Rosemary's patient motherhood, listening to music she didn't like, demonstrating the emotional labour of musical motherhood. Family doxa may not be homogeneous with factions struggling for recognition within the family field (Atkinson, 2014). However, between Rosemary and her son, like the relationship between Rosemary and Penelope, there is a mutual valuing of music, and a valuing of each other, with music being the binding factor. Music as affective recognition in Rosemary's family is differentiated and afforded varying levels of acknowledgement with Rosemary, as the family matriarch, holding the position of power within their family field.

In Linda's family, Ashley was cognisant of her perceived position where she never felt like she reached the heights that her sister had,

> *I was always kinda known as the black egg [sic] in the family … it was just something I had to learn to feel like … the judgement and disappointment will be there, and I knew that but, I just had to do my best to keep going*

I remember when I passed my AMusA,[1] [my younger sister and I] we did it at the same time. And she passed hers, even though I was 13 and she was 10. So, it didn't matter how old I was (laughs), she was always one step ahead of me. No, honestly, she was a prodigy. She was so good.

Ashley yearned for her mother's love and approval and always felt that she was in her younger sister's shadow. Although Linda wanted to encourage and support her children's musical development, she was never keen for them to pursue music as a career. Over time, this became problematic for Linda and Ashley, as Ashley attained mastery of her instrument and sought a place at the conservatorium. Linda had doggedly fostered Ashley's musical development from an early age (which I will explore further in Chaps. 5 and 6), and while initially delighted, Linda's acceptance of Ashley following a career in music changed when she saw how challenging Ashley found study at the conservatorium. Ashley withdrew from her studies, left home, went through a rebellious period and then forged a career in nursing—her mother's training was in nursing—to achieve her mother's approval. Ashley's sister kept up her instrumental playing but decided on an alternative career path, playing music for enjoyment, just as Linda had wanted:

She's at uni and went on and did cello at the [university] orchestra. Without doing music and she was like first cellist and she wasn't even doing music! In the first two years and then she went [overseas] for her placement, and then went back and she was still up the front. But she adored it ... She never wanted to do music as a degree because ... she said "I don't want to change the way I play"

Linda's pride is obvious, particularly when she remarks that her daughter took the first cellist's desk over and above the students who were studying cello as part of their music degree to become professional solo artists. And Ashley remains the 'black egg', demonstrating that relations, interactions and expectations between mother, child and music are not always

---

[1] The Associate in Music, Australia (AMusA) is one of the highest-level practical examinations in the Australian Music Examination Board syllabus. It is conducted by two examiners. Musicians perform repertoire from prescribed lists of pieces for 30–40 minutes, with an additional ten minutes to test the candidate's general musical knowledge of the prescribed pieces. Achieving this award is indicative of a high-performance standard. Grade 5 theory must also be passed to achieve the AMusA award. See www.ameb.edu.au.

positive or aligned. Bourdieu (1999) explains this is a common experience, stating "a great many people are *long-term* sufferers from the gap between their accomplishments and the parental expectations they can neither satisfy nor repudiate" (p. 508, original emphasis). Ashley, as a 'long-term sufferer', continues to seek approval from Linda through her music, her career and now in motherhood; however, she has reconciled that she would like to do some things differently. Her partner has very different views to those of her family, and so she is adjusting her beliefs, values and ways of being accordingly. Nevertheless, the need for love and affective recognition from our mothers remains a powerful structural force in the family space (Atkinson, 2016; Bourdieu, 1999).

Susan and Jessica acknowledge the positive contribution that each has made to the lives of the other. Susan celebrates Jessica by introducing her to more diverse music styles and valorises her musicianship: "*I think I'm musical but not a musician, in that if I see what Jessica does now, and how she can sidestep into Tibetan and into Indian [music] … her ears are really switched on*"—and Susan also applauds her parenting—"*it's very, very communicative … they're both [partners] very good communicators and terrifically engaged*". And Jessica is grateful for the opportunities that Susan has afforded her. It is through their mutual acknowledgement that I recall Susan's comments about her eldest daughter, who is also musical. Susan recounted that this older daughter did not achieve the same accolades as Jessica because of Susan's 'relaxed' parenting style, where she did not force her children to do anything. More on this later when I illustrate how Susan's parenting is not quite as casual as she claims it to be and how she disavows, like many middle-class mothers, the effort involved in her musical mothering practices. Most of Susan's energies and musical foci were poured into Jessica although she does speak favourably of her other daughter's musical ability. However, it is Jessica who seems to relish her sister's casual, non-competitive musical life, rather than her own as a professional musician,

In her family, music is just this lovely, joyous, easy-going part of their life and it's got no pressure. It's just pure fun—like they go to folk festivals all the time and they go, they sit in the pub and they jam, and she plays the piano accordion, and the kids are all fantastic singers and they're all really into it but there's no aspiration in it. It's just for life and woven into their daily life and their daily fun … I love that …

Jessica recognises her sister's mothering as an exemplar of good musical mothering. Jessica's sister is the recipient of affective recognition from her family as they acknowledge the wonderful musical experiences that are part of their family culture.

The unequal attention given to siblings within families regarding their musical development shows how the cycle of affective recognition manifests. It illustrates how important it can be for musical development to flourish or how detrimental it can be for those siblings who miss out and who foster connections with their significant others in different ways—those 'compensatory connections' (Villalobos, 2015, pp. 1931–1932). The need for love and acceptance from our mothers and their need for children's love and acceptance means that both can be considered 'long-term sufferers', as Bourdieu (1999, p. 508) attests. Both are playing for power and recognition within the family field; however, early in children's lives, it is mothers who make judgements about who is considered musical and who warrants further investment. Musical talent is a learned skill and, however, often has the appearance of being innate due to the ways in which musical development is enculturated and encouraged through everyday engagement and involvement via family musical activities in the home. These early activities in children's lives enable children to be ahead of the game when first starting school music, for example, because they have been exposed to music before formal training begins. For those whose parents do not or cannot support their children's musical development, for whatever reason, encouragement may come from 'non-parental others' who take on the role of mentor and supporter of children's intrinsic motivation for music to continue and persevere. This is only successful if children have the requisite cultural and emotional capital to seek and recognise the support of those able to assist.

REFERENCES

Aldredge, M. (2006). Negotiating and practicing performance: An ethnographic study of a musical Open Mic in Brooklyn, New York. *Symbolic Interaction, 29*(1), 109–117. https://doi.org/10.1525/si.2006.29.1.109

Atkinson, W. (2014). A sketch of 'family' as a field: From realized category to space of struggle. *Acta Sociologica, 57*(3), 223–235. https://doi.org/10.1177/0001699313513114

Atkinson, W. (2016). *Beyond Bourdieu*. Polity.

Bourdieu, P. (1984). *Distinction: A social critique of the judgement of taste.* Routledge and Kegan Paul.

Bourdieu, P. (1990). *The logic of practice.* Polity.

Bourdieu, P. (1999). The contradictions of inheritance. In P. Bourdieu, A. Accardo, & P. P. Ferguson (Eds.), *The weight of the world: Social suffering in contemporary society.* Polity.

Bracknell, C. (2020a). The emotional business of Noongar song. *Journal of Australian Studies, 44*(2), 140–153. https://doi.org/10.1080/1444305 8.2020.1752284

Bracknell, C. (2020b). Rebuilding as research: Noongar song, language and ways of knowing. *Journal of Australian Studies, 44*(2), 210–223. https://doi.org/1 0.1080/14443058.2020.1746380

Burland, K., & Davidson, J. (2002). Training the talented. *Music Education Research, 4*(1), 121–139.

Cho, E., & Ilari, B. S. (2021). Mothers as home DJs: Recorded music and young children's well-being during the COVID-18 pandemic. *Frontiers in Psychology, 12.* https://doi.org/10.3389/fpsyg.2021.637569

Creech, A. (2010). Learning a musical instrument: The case for parental support. *Music Education Research, 12*(1), 13–32. https://doi.org/10.1080/14613800903569237

Davidson, J. W., & Borthwick, S. J. (2002). Family dynamics and family scripts: A case study of musical development. *Psychology of Music, 30,* 121–136. https://doi.org/10.1177/0305735602301009

Davidson, J. W., Howe, M. J. A., Moore, D. G., & Sloboda, J. A. (1996). The role of parental influences in the development of musical performance. *British Journal of Developmental Psychology, 14*(4), 399–412. https://doi.org/10.1111/j.2044-835X.1996.tb00714.x

Dweck, C. (2006). *Mindset: The new psychology of success.* Random House.

Dwyer, R. (2016). *Music teachers' values and beliefs.* Routledge.

Frith, S. (2008). Why music matters. *Critical Quarterly, 50*(1–2), 165–179. https://doi.org/10.1111/j.1467-8705.2008.00811.x

Hall, C. (2015). Singing gender and class: Understanding choirboys' musical habitus. In P. Burnard, Y. Hofvander Trulsson, & J. Söderman (Eds.), *Bourdieu and the sociology of music education* (pp. 43–59). Routledge.

Hall, C. (2018). *Masculinity, class and music education: Boys performing middle-class masculinities through music.* Palgrave Macmillan.

Harrigan, M. M., & Miller-Ott, A. E. (2013). The multivocality of meaning making: An exploration of the discourses college-aged daughters voice in talk about their mothers. *Journal of Family Communication, 13*(2), 114–131. https://doi.org/10.1080/15267431.2013.768249

Howe, M. J. A., Davidson, J. W., & Sloboda, J. A. (1998). Innate talents: Reality or myth? *Behavioural and Brain Sciences, 21*(3), 399–407. https://doi.org/10.1017/S0140525X9800123X

Ibarra, F. P. (2017). Transmission of Araquio music, songs and movement conventions: Learning, experience and meaning in devotional theatre. *The Qualitative Report, 22*(4), 1031–1049. https://doi.org/10.46743/2160-3715/2017.2699

Ilari, B., Hafteck-Chen, L., & Crawford, L. (2013). Singing and cultural understanding: A music education perspective. *International Journal of Music Education, 31*(2), 202–216. https://doi.org/10.1080/1461380 8.2011.553277

Kamin, S., Richards, H., & Collins, D. (2007). Influences on the talent development process of non-classical musicians: Psychological, social and environmental influences. *Music Education Research, 9*(3), 449–468. https://doi.org/10.1080/14613800701587860

Kokas, K. (1970). Kodaly's concept of music education. *Bulletin of the Council for Research in Music Education, 22*(Fall), 49–56.

Koops, L. H. (2018). Musical tweens: Child and parent views on musical engagement in middle childhood. *Music Education Research, 20*(4), 412–426. https://doi.org/10.1080/14613808.2018.1491541

Koza, J. (2001). Multicultural approaches to music education. In C. A. Grant & M. L. Gomez (Eds.), *Campus and classroom: Making schooling multicultural.* Prentice-Hall.

Mapana, K. (2011). The musical enculturation and education of Wagogo children. *British Journal of Music Education, 28*(3), 339–351. https://doi.org/10.1017/S0265051711000234

McPherson, G. E. (2009). The role of parents in children's musical development. *Psychology of Music, 37*(1), 91–110. https://doi.org/10.1177/0305735607086049

McPherson, G. E., & Davidson, J. W. (2002). Musical practice: Mother and child interactions during the first year of learning an instrument. *Music Education Research, 4*(1), 141–156. https://doi.org/10.1080/14613800220119822

Nagel, I. (2010). Cultural participation between the ages of 14 and 24: Intergenerational transmission or cultural mobility? *European Sociological Review, 26*(5), 541–556. https://doi.org/10.1093/esr/jcp037

Savage, S. (2015). Understanding mothers' perspectives on early childhood music programmes. *Australian Journal of Music Education, 2*, 127–139.

Savage, S. (2019). *Musical mothering: Middle-class strategies and affect across generations.* Unpublished PhD thesis, Monash University.

Savage, S., & Hall, C. (2017). Thinking about and beyond the cultural contradictions of motherhood through musical mothering. In M. J. Rose, L. Ross, & J. Hartmann (Eds.), *The music of motherhood* (pp. 32–50). Demeter Press.

Sayer, A. (2005a). *The moral significance of class.* Cambridge University Press.

Sayer, A. (2005b). Class, moral worth and recognition. *Sociology, 39*(5), 947–963. https://doi.org/10.1177/0038038505058376

Scripp, L., Ulibarri, D., & Flax, R. (2013). Thinking beyond the myths and misconceptions of talent: Creating music education policy that advances music's essential contribution to twenty-first-century teaching and learning. *Arts Education Policy Review, 114*(2), 54–102. https://doi.org/10.1080/1063291 3.2013.769825

Sosniak, L. A. (1995). Learning to be a concert pianist. In B. S. Bloom (Ed.), *Developing talent in young people* (pp. 19–67). Ballantine.

Suzuki, S. (1978). *Nurtured by love*. Centre Publications.

Villalobos, A. (2015). Compensatory connection: Mothers' own stakes in an intensive mother-child relationship. *Journal of Family Issues, 36*(14), 1928–1956. https://doi.org/10.1177/0192513X13520157

Vincent, C., & Ball, S. J. (2007). 'Making up' the middle-class child: Families, activities and class dispositions. *Sociology, 41*(6), 1061–1077. https://doi.org/10.1177/0038038507082315

Warner, J. (2006). *Perfect madness: Motherhood in the age of anxiety*. Vermilion.

CHAPTER 5

Intensive Mothering, Concerted Cultivation and Good Mothering

Introduction

Recent research coming out of the United States has found that intensive parenting now constitutes a norm in parenting, not only within the middle classes but in all classes (Bennett et al., 2012; Chin & Phillips, 2004; Ishizuka, 2019). Mothers' determinations to involve their children in music, to develop skills and the dispositions associated with music, can become an intensive practice. Opportunities to experience music in the home and to attend concerts, have lessons, and receive encouragement and support, combine to nurture and enhance interest in music. This forms part of the work that musical mothers do which takes on various levels of intensity depending on the advantages mothers perceive may be gained from such involvement.

Sharon Hays (1996) famously coined the term 'intensive mothering' to describe mothering practices that are "child-centred, expert-guided, emotionally absorbing, labour intensive, and financially expensive" (p. 8). There has been a plethora of literature around intensive mothering which is largely understood to be detrimental to women's mental health and wellbeing (Arnold, 2014; Atkinson, 2016; Golden & Erdreich, 2014; Hays, 1996; Lareau, 2003/2011; Reay, 1998; Shirani et al., 2012). Despite Hays' research being nearly 30 years old, intensive mothering

© The Author(s), under exclusive license to Springer Nature Switzerland AG 2024
S. Savage, *Musical Mothering*, Palgrave Macmillan Studies in Family and Intimate Life,
https://doi.org/10.1007/978-3-031-65157-1_5

continues to be the dominant and normative form of middle-class mothering practiced in Western countries (Vincent & Maxwell, 2015).

Intensive mothering equates to 'good' mothering, and everything else is seen within a deficit model. Conforming neatly into neoliberal tropes where the individual is responsible for their own success, the 'good mother' has myriad choices readily available with which to accumulate capitals and is driven by competition, consumerism, aspiration and the opportunities afforded by globalisation (Gale & Parker, 2015). The 'good mother', as portrayed in the media and public discourse, is both a mother and a successful worker, aligning with the idea that women have 'choice and female liberation' and can do it all (Orgad, 2019, p. 31). However, in her book, Orgad reveals that the notion of 'choice' is a cruel paradox where "barriers, constraints, regrets, or broader implications" (p. 31) are evident within the everyday lives of the middle-class mothers she interviews.

In this chapter, the mothers' practices are scrutinised to show the varying degrees of intensive mothering enacted as part of children's musical development. A continuum of intensive mothering is evident. The mothers' work shows how they cultivate their children's dispositions to provide advantages and opportunities for capital exchange in the future. These future-oriented investments are perceived as being worth the huge amount of effort exercised due to the affordances they will acquire later. There are slippages where to be too intense can go against the logic of good mothering and position mothers as having unrealistic expectations of their children and diminishing their childhoods. Judgements are made by society on mothers' mothering performances and from within middle-class musical mothering itself. The fine line between such perceptions of good and bad mothering is demonstrated through children's musical practice. It is not just mothers who concertedly cultivate their children's musical development but also the grandmothers who perform this intergenerational musical nurturing.

INVESTMENTS IN CHILDREN'S FUTURES, FUTURE-ORIENTED PRACTICES

Intensive mothering is driven by consumer demands; parents seek expert tuition and activities that will enhance children's abilities and set their children apart from the crowd (Vincent & Ball, 2007). These enrichment pursuits, such as music tuition, are only accessible to those mothers with expendable resources in the form of economic and cultural capital. When playing this game, middle-class mothers make investments to develop their children's abilities to secure their futures. To play the game, one must have a notion that they will win or that participation will be useful on some level. If you are not part of the game, you inevitably miss out on opportunities; however, it is not until you begin to play the game that all the rules of the game become clear (Bourdieu, 1977). And often, it is those in power that make the rules, changing them to suit their own needs, while everyone else follows along, trying to keep up. To be ahead of the game, Bourdieu (1998) states that one must already have an embodied understanding of the game, through habitus, where deliberate strategies inform mothers' decision-making. Through habitus, middle-class mothers already know what to do—they have insider knowledge emanating from experience.

Intensive mothers perform a commitment to their children that appears selfless, while simultaneously cultivating their child-projects to compete in a competitive world (Vincent & Ball, 2007). With constant expectations to make the 'right' choices, mothers live with continual concern about "getting things wrong, about failing the child" (Ball, 2003, p. 171). As Milkie and Warner (2014) argue, this is all about 'status safeguarding', where mothers "create a thriving child who is distinguished as unique, more fundamentally, over the many long years to adulthood, set to achieve a similar better place in the social hierarchy compared with his parents" (p. 68). This intensive mothering work is about social reproduction and the astute investments needed for this to be successful.

In some respects, one must be willing to sacrifice their investment if things do not work out. Investments in children's futures are a value-exchange calculation, that is, there is a tacit understanding that something of value will come from the investment for either the person doing the investing, the person being invested in or perhaps both (Jaeger, 2022; Skeggs, 2004). However, Lareau (2000) argues that "possession of high-status cultural resources does not ... automatically lead to a social invest-ment. Rather, these cultural resources must be effectively activated by individuals, in and through their own actions and decisions" (p. 178). There is a precarity around status maintenance that feeds into middle-class mothers' anxieties and adds to the pressure to get things 'right'. Throughout this book, we see the investments and results of those investments.

While this intensive type of parenting was considered stressful for mothers, for many families, decisions regarding schooling were also perceived as stressful and anxiety-provoking. There is a movement towards privileged parents resisting neoliberal tropes of competitiveness and constant one-upmanship, to embrace meditation and wellbeing and trying to consider social justice issues in their choice-making (Debs et al., 2023). Crozier et al. (2011) found that some middle-class parents chose to send their children to local state schools rather than elite independent schools. This was seen as enabling middle-class children to access the scarce resources within these local schools because they have the knowledge, social and cultural capacity to navigate and dominate these spaces, as well as having access to high levels of resources at the elite schools they usually inhabit. Debs et al. (2023) cite a change in recent parenting manuals that promote less scheduling for children and a return to greater child autonomy and freedom. However, this could be targeted at parents whose status within the classed hierarchies is secure. Many of these 'happiness-oriented parents' (Debs et al., 2023, p. 1) are choosing home-schooling as an alternate, less-pressured schooling for their children. However, there are underlying mechanisms at play when parents home-school their children, as I investigate in Chap. 6.

I suggest that intensive mothering is a continuum that is not linear. Middle-class mothers adjust the intensity of their mothering to suit their circumstances and influences at the time. For example, a mother might enrol her children in an intensive course of swimming lessons or for tuition in a particular subject to assist them to pass a test. Once the child has reached an acceptable standard, then the mother may stop lessons. Sometimes, mothers would enrol in my music classes if their friend had enrolled, and there are many such classes that are considered fashionable to do, and to not participate would be to miss out; many of these mothers have a fear of missing out. They might then move to the next popular activity after a term or two. The intensity of the mothering is directly related to the available time, and labour the mother wants to expend, and the resources needed to participate (Bennett et al., 2012; Chin & Phillips, 2004). Some mothers pay for others to take their children to classes when they are not free due to work commitments (Reay, 2010).

'Good' mothers make significant investments into their children's futures (Savage, 2015, 2019) and significant sacrifices to their own careers and ambitions (Orgad, 2019). Music is a means by which mothers nurture their children's proclivities and create opportunities for music-making, often forsaking large amounts of money and time in doing so. Mothers are developing their children's portfolios (Vincent & Ball, 2007) through cultural visits to the art gallery, the theatre and the museum. Concerts feature regularly as an outing where children learn how to become a good audience member and how not to clap between orchestral movements. This intentional work that mothers do, often through an intensive practice, is aimed at achieving advantages in life and is known as concerted cultivation.

CONCERTED CULTIVATION THROUGH INTENSIVE MOTHERING IN MUSICAL MOTHERING

The deliberate management and investment of children's futures which takes substantial time, economic resources and cultural know-how to achieve successfully is also known as 'concerted cultivation'. 'Concerted cultivation' is a term coined by Annette Lareau (2003/2011) from her seminal work on how parents of different classes raise their children. Lareau defines this as parents' work to deliberately "cultivate (their children's) talents in a concerted fashion" (p. 1). Part of this work is to seek out experts to guide children and nurture their skills that will be advantageous in the future, particularly when children enter the workplace. For some musical mothers, this is done in an intensive way, which consumes a great deal of time and financial and emotional resources, while others take a more casual approach where their children may only attend one or two extra-curricular activities, for example, and children may have autonomy to spend most of their leisure time as they wish. In a previous study, I interviewed mothers and spoke with them about how many extra-curricular activities their children did each week. For most, it was around two; however, I did have one parent who stated her children attended 14 extra-curricular activities each week. So, while both sets of mothers enacted concerted cultivation in a sense, the latter mother was doing it in a particularly intensive way where children had no leisure time to themselves, and their lives were constantly scheduled. It is not only attendance at activities but also an intentional parenting style that encompasses "talking to children, developing their educational interests, and playing an active role in their schooling ... reasoning with children and teaching them to solve problems through negotiation rather than physical force" (Lareau, 2003/2011, p. 4). Hence, there is a difference between intensive mothering concerning the amount mothers' time, energy, and financial and emotional resources to enact concerted cultivation, and about the strategies employed to achieve advantages. Middle-class mothers show a proclivity for this behaviour as they search for the best tutors, instruments, ensembles and the most strategic opportunities to promote their children in future educational and workplace arenas. For the mothers in this book, music is the vehicle used to gain advantages in their children through the practice of concerted cultivation. This deliberate and 'intentional parenting style' (Lareau, 2003, pp. 346–347) is largely the domain of the middle classes who institutionalise their children's leisure time to seek expert tuition (Perrier, 2013). Lareau's (2003/2011) antithesis to concerted cultivation is the 'accomplishment of natural growth' (p. 3) which Lareau states is the predominant strategy utilised by the working classes where parents allow children to develop in their own way. While middle-class parents want their children to rise above others and be unique, Gillies (2007) argues that for working-class parents, fitting in and being inconspicuous is preferable. Gillies' (2007) interview study shows that working-class mothers aim to promote resilience in their children, fostering coping skills and providing security, to compensate for the 'disappointment, frustration and vulnerability' often experienced in their children's lives (Gillies, 2007, p. 146). This contrasts with middle-class mothers who transfer entitlement and privilege to their children.

There has been some push-back against the vilifying of working-class mothers from those who claim that parenting is different rather than deficient (Cooper, 2021). Cooper (2021), citing the expansive amount of work Val Gillies has done in this area, states that parenting can be extremely challenging. Demonisation of such parents, particularly mothers, for trying to find money to meet the basic needs of the family, is unjustified because often their parenting was rated as 'ideal' (Cooper, 2021). Two of the mothers I interviewed spoke of times when money was scarce and how they managed, with 'family time' being important. Linda relayed how her family had very little money when her children were young. Musical games were improvised on household equipment, and later, she tells how they had no money to pay repetiteurs and accompanists for examinations and concerts, recruiting family members where she could. Similarly, Kelele tells of idyllic childhoods where, on her island home in Tonga, they had no money to speak of, yet always had enough to eat, a roof over their heads, and they spent a great deal of time as an extended family. Dermott and Pomati's (2016) study revealed that economically poorer parents tend to spend more of their leisure time with their children. Being together in this way, that is, having 'family time', is often considered a benchmark of 'good' parenting (Cooper, 2021; Dermott & Pomati, 2016) and is therefore in contrast with the deficit view of working-class parenting.

Critiques of Lareau's work have cited other reasons apart from seeking cultural capital for participation in extra-curricular music tuition, such as mothers' child-rearing beliefs, the children's gender, and available economic resources and contest that this is solely a middle-class phenomenon. In Sweden, Sjödin and Roman (2018) found that working-class families' lower levels of concerted cultivation were due to the lack of flexibility in their working hours in addition to cultural and economic considerations. The children of working-class parents attended extra-curricular activities often because they wanted to, rather than being directed to by their parents (Sjödin & Roman, 2018). Economic limitations were also not as prevalent in Sweden due to many extra-curricular activities being run by volunteer organisations that keep costs low or free. However, in a large-scale quantitative study by Cheadle and Amato (2011), children from blended families, children with single mothers, children attending long day care prior to preschool, parents with boys and those with 'low educational expectations' were reported to demonstrate lower levels of concerted cultivation (p. 700). This is not to say that those former groups have low expectations for their children; however, it does correlate with the view that concerted cultivation occurs mostly with mothers who are perceived as 'good mothers by O'Reilly's (2010) definition, that is "white, heterosexual, middle-class, able-bodied, married, thirty-something in a nuclear family with usually one or two children, and ideally, a full-time mother" (p. 7). Cheadle and Amato (2011) noted that girls were more likely to participate in extra-curricular activities, particularly in families where parents had high expectations of achievement. Again, this speaks to the pathologising of working-class families who may not necessarily have low expectations for their children but are limited in their choices due to economic and time constraints.

Concerted cultivation is considered primarily a middle-class phenomenon; it is also a global phenomenon. Cho's (2015) study of mothers in South Korea showed a prevalence of concerted cultivation practices among middle-class mothers, where music tuition was a way to flaunt their status and exploit their children's impressive resumes to access elite schools. In Hong Kong, Choi (2015) found middle-class mothers worked hard to create learning opportunities out of everyday activities. Ilari et al. (2011) found that in Brazil, early childhood music programmes were sought for developing socialisation and "affirmation and reproduction of their social standing" (p. 62). Parents from China, Korea and Japan utilise music for admission into elite American schools (Wang, 2015). Wang (2015) tells of 'music moms' who are extreme in their self-sacrificing, often giving up their high-profile careers and moving away from the family home to assist their children to follow their musical aspirations. Gudmundsdottir and Gudmundsdottir (2010) studied mothers in Iceland who were all cognisant of the value of music for children's development and who all enjoyed singing with their children. They found that older mothers had more preconceived ideas about their children's futures than younger mothers. In pursuing music lessons, the younger mothers said they would wait until their child showed an interest in music before providing lessons, whereas older mothers were determined to make music a part of their children's lives no matter what. This finding is corroborated by Cheadle and Amato (2011) who also found higher levels of concerted cultivation in older mothers.

Families from the Netherlands, Greece, Denmark, Spain, Kenya, England, Taiwan, the United States and Israel participated in Ilari's (2013) study, and all showed evidence of concerted cultivation in varying degrees. For some families, music classes assisted with childcare for working families (Ilari, 2013) as they utilised extra-curricular classes and rehearsals as another means to occupy their children within safe environments when they were having to work long hours (Sjödin & Roman, 2018). Immigrant families in Sweden also utilised music for social reproduction to counter any downward mobility (Hofvander Trulsson, 2013). It can be said that all of these countries have been influenced by Western cultures and have embraced neoliberalism. Ilari (2013) suggests that while middle-class families in these countries may have more available resources, it is imperative to consider that "parenting continues to be influenced by local realities and contexts" (p. 193).

Other such contexts include culturally diverse locations. Mukherjee and Barn (2021) theorise how concerted cultivation acts as a means for minority ethnic parents to "comprehend processes of racialisation and racism" (p. 523) and how to navigate parenting by aiming to instil positive ethnic and racial identities in their children and overcome endemic racism within our societies. Their study of 18 British Indian middle-class parents found that ethnically specific tuition developed their children's understanding of their heritage and languages to open up possibilities in wider employment spheres, and to teach self-defence, for example, as mechanisms to combat racism.

Concerted cultivation often takes on an intensity because of the amount of labour and expense required to enact it. Like the continuum of intensive mothering, concerted cultivation too is on a continuum, where middle-class mothers will jump on the latest trend and become obsessed for a while before moving to the next big thing. I recall when mothers would come to my early childhood music classes for one or two terms with a close friend, and then they would go and try yoga or robotics or coding, or the next thing that supposedly everyone was doing. These mothers cited giving their children a range of experiences, to be 'well-rounded' (Wardman et al., 2010, p. 251) and capable of later making up their own minds about what they would like to spend more time doing. Music researchers state it takes two years to develop any sort of proficiency when playing an instrument and advise parents to sign their children up for a commitment of at least two years. After this initial period, it is thought that the novice instrumentalist can play well enough to make a half-decent sound which encourages them and probably their parents as well, to persevere with more lessons. Furthermore, the benefit for brain development is also optimal if tuition has been longer than two years (Tierney et al., 2015). There are debates around whether discourses around parenting and neuroscience (and music in this instance) are just another thing for mothers to be anxious about and for society to judge mothers on. Macvarish (2016) cites this as invasive of family life and adding pressure on families to constantly stimulate babies' brains during critical periods of development rather than enjoy the intimacy and privacy that can be attributed to family life. Macvarish argues that parents know their children best and are better placed to know what is right for their children rather than experts or government authorities (See Macvarish (2016) for further critique in this area). Many mothers attending my early years music classes only attended two extra-curricular classes a week with their children (Savage, 2015), usually music and swimming (In Australia, learning to swim is seen as a safety imperative). Sometimes, during the winter months, when swimming lessons were not on, another 'indoor' type activity might replace it or that would be when they attended music.

Concerted cultivation is aligned with anxiety, tiredness and parental regret for their choices (Vincent & Maxwell, 2015). This is particularly so when enacted with intensive mothering (Hays, 1996). During the

Covid-19 pandemic, when many extra-curricular classes were closed due to lockdowns and periods of isolation, some mothers re-evaluated their children's extra-curricular activities. When extra-curricular activities started up again, they cut down the number of activities their children were involved, which they state saved them money and time (Savage, 2021). It took the pandemic to alert them to the fact they were spending hours in their cars ferrying their children around from one activity to another, particularly when some of these activities could be done at school. Weinshenker and Kim (2023) investigated the impact of concerted cultivation on parental wellbeing linked to overall satisfaction with partner relationships and life satisfaction. According to Weinshenker and Kim, increased wellbeing in parents is associated with "parents having a low propensity to mistreat their children" (p. 2). However, as Golden et al. (2021) note, mothers' concerted cultivation is deeply embedded with care, love and concern for children's futures and a desire for the best life outcomes for their children and their wellbeing. In this next section, I will illustrate the 'fine line' between encouragement and coercion in concerted cultivation and intensive mothering through music.

THE 'FINE LINE' OF CONCERTED CULTIVATION AND INTENSIVE MOTHERING THROUGH MUSICAL PRACTISE

Musical mothers keenly demonstrate their concerted cultivation of children's musical skills through varying degrees of intensive mothering, as seen through their work in encouraging their children to practise. A continuum of intensity is observed from relaxed and informal approaches to rigorously scheduled timetables of structured practise, lessons and rehearsals. When children are engaged in formal music tuition, mothers spend hours driving to lessons, rehearsals, examinations and performances. They spend exorbitant amounts of money on instruments, music, and uniforms. They are often willing to give up their own leisure time to volunteer as administrators, such as music librarians, or fundraisers for schools and musical organisations, such as youth orchestras. Without such support and unpaid labour, many of these organisations would cease to function. Through extensive research, mothers select the teachers and classes that meet the perceived needs of their children. All of these are intended to make mothers appear 'good' (VanderValk, 2010) and committed to the cause through social sanctioning and support for their actions by peers and society more broadly.

It is widely agreed upon that practise is necessary to gain mastery. To become a professional musician, the expectation is to practise for many hours each day. The expectation to practise is closely aligned with mothers' expectations and assumptions of success and purpose for involvement in music. Both of my parents were afforded the opportunity for piano lessons when they were young; however, neither practised and gave up lessons after a short while. Neither continued playing music in their adult lives. Through their own unwillingness to practise, they had an assumption that I would not practise (despite being a good student and enjoying school, unlike my parents), and therefore, I was not allowed to learn the piano. I also equate this with an unwillingness to devote the time to encourage me to practise which is fundamental for young musicians to keep motivated (McPherson, 2009).

The mothers I interviewed illustrated the continuum of concerted cultivation through intensive mothering. What is startling in the women's narratives is the deliberate articulation of not wanting to 'force' their children to practice or to coerce them into doing something they did not wish to do. Forcing children to practise is antithetical to child-centred mothering and 'good' mothering logic—a practice some of my participant mothers openly denigrate in other mothers' behaviour. However, it is through Linda, Rosemary and Susan's stories that we see the intensity and contradictions of musical mothering.

Linda

As a stay-at-home mother, Linda was conservative and traditional in her views regarding the roles of husbands and wives, mothers and fathers, in that she did not engage in paid employment once she had children. She did all the unpaid domestic work and believed it was her job to raise the children and encourage their musical practice. Linda stated, "*I had nobody telling me to practise … I think you need a mother to tell you to practise. I think you do need that*". Linda lived in boarding schools from the age of five and missed having her mother around to encourage her to practise. Research in music education agrees with Linda, stating that parental support is crucial for providing motivation and encouragement to practise which has substantial results in whether children continue to study music (McPherson, 2009; Witte et al., 2015).

Linda had always an intention for her children's musical futures. This was borne from her own musical experiences when she was young, *"[at school] we were in the orchestra and the bands and absolutely loved it and I think it's the sense of community, the sense of friendship, the sense of competition"*; however, experiences with her own children suggested she did not like the extreme competitiveness of other musical parents. Linda acknowledges the competitiveness of parents whose children strive for one of the limited places in prestigious orchestras and participate in classical music competitions. Linda comments, *"it's the parents though … [she imitates those parents' voices] 'My child should have won, yours shouldn't have'"*. Yet Linda staunchly maintains that her intentions for her children's formal musical training were never about pursuing music as a career, but rather to develop skills to be competent enough to join an ensemble if her children so wished. It was part of their accrual of cultural capital.

> *I did tell them they had to practise (laughs). I don't know if they were grateful. I think I said to them 'at least half an hour'. I always said I want you all to get to grade six in whatever instrument and if you want to continue you can, but grade six will enable you to have a hobby in the end and will enable you to play in an orchestra and high school you can do anything you like, so if you want to pursue that, and do that then you'll have to practise a bit more than that.*

Proficiency in music, Linda believed, opened up multiple choices and possibilities: through music, you could do *'anything you like'*. Developing skills in music was part of her investment in her children's cultural capital. Linda could see the profit from her investment—socially and educationally. Her own values and self-worth were also entangled in her comment, inferring that without putting in the effort, choices would be limited and that they should be grateful to her for this advice. Linda's admission that she made them practise suggests she realises the contradiction in her logic. While playing music was about enjoyment, it was also about appearances, ability and opportunity.

With more investment comes greater profit, Bourdieu (1986) claims. Here, the accumulation of capital is an embodiment of labour. Linda is creating persons of distinction, where habitus encapsulates their cultural capital in the form of preferred values and dispositions (Moore, 2012). An investment in the field of music is an economic privilege, states Bourdieu (1984), "to play the games of culture with the playful seriousness … a seriousness without the 'spirit of seriousness'" (p. 54). According to

Linda, music was only going to be a hobby after all. At times, this assertion does not seem to ring true for Linda, who tells of having a house in disrepair, not being able to afford to continue attending their private school and having to ask family members to accompany her children on the piano when doing exams, instead of paying an accompanist. Linda's family was far from comfortable financially at that point. But there was much more to why musical excellence for her children was important to Linda, which will be revealed throughout this book.

Returning to practice, Linda did not wish to appear that she made her children practise by framing this as family time—a time she maintains was mutually enjoyable.

> *I actually had it all scheduled ... You have to make them practise but I don't think anyone enjoys practise. My kids loved you just sitting there with them. So, I used to sit there with them and that made them enjoy their practise a little bit more. So sometimes I would be sitting there doing my work and listening, even though they were doing it again and again and again, just having someone there.*

For Linda, this time was a shared pleasant experience. She was with her children, experiencing music, all that she loved, seeing their progress and the fruits of her labour. However, Linda's daughter, Ashley, recalls their rigorous daily schedule of practise, with Linda's constant monitoring, offering a perspective that contradicts Linda's opinion of the experience being enjoyable:

> *She [Linda] always wanted to do it professionally that's why she really pushed us a lot. She pushed us a lot when we were kids. We had to practise one hour before school, we had to wake up at 6, 7, 8 to practise, have all our homework done the night before and practise when we got home. So, we were very much on a schedule at a very young age.*

Ashley recalled the hours she had spent practising and her mother's powerful insistence on maintaining a very regimented routine. Several times, she mentioned being controlled and restricted. I will delve into this further when I discuss intensive mothering and morality in the next chapter; however, it is clear that Linda spent a huge amount of emotional and cognitive labour on her children's musical development, particularly around practise and the concurrent organising of their lives.

I must confess that I, too, often sat in on my children's music lessons and their subsequent practise, making sure they were practising the way they had been taught, using the correct fingerings, and playing the correct notes. I loved seeing them play for they were far better musicians than I had been, and it was emotionally gratifying to see them master a piece. Like Linda, I loved my children, and I loved music and music-making. And like Linda, I didn't see how my children disliked the time it stole from them, the pressure to perform it caused, the competitiveness with their friends, and the heightened expectations, until much later.

I wondered how Ashley's childhood musical experiences had influenced her musical intentions for her own child as she had expressed reflexivity regarding her upbringing and articulated the social restrictions she endured. As a mother of a young child herself now, Ashley commented:

> I see that we're going to be good parents because we are just both open-minded. I've been brought up very close-minded, right and wrong, black and white. I now have a bit of grey in my life which I think is good because you get to see a little bit more of the world and you see a bit more love in the world as well. I want to be able to stand up for myself. I want to be able to say what I want and make my own decisions. That's a big one for me 'cause I haven't had that. ... Obviously, I've been quite musical my whole life. I want [my son] to enjoy that, you know. [Music's] been like a negative and a positive thing for me in my life. So, I feel like I really want to bring back that positive music to [my son].

In some ways, I feel this is a little harsh on Linda whose love for her children and music was palpable. There are multiple possibilities as to why Linda may have behaved the way she did. Music was part of Linda's family habitus, and in her childhood family, engaging in music together was how they shared their love for each other. It speaks to Stefansen and Aarseth's (2011) notion of 'enriching intimacy' (p. 390) because Linda sees "an intimacy based on shared enjoyment of enriching activities in the broad sense" (p. 400) but also how shared enjoyment of activities also leads to cultural capital accrual. Other reasons for Linda's intensive involvement in her children's music were entangled in her desire to be present with her children because her own parents were not always there, to create the musical opportunties she was not afforded, and to satisfy her need to be perceived as a respectable and 'good' mother.

Away from the immediate family, Ashley was able to construct her own musical mothering narrative. She re-evaluated how she wanted to mother

her son in comparison to her own upbringing. The family doxa she once accepted had now become foreign. Bourdieu describes this as a habitus *clivé*—a divided habitus (Bourdieu, 2007). Ashley is grateful for her musical training; however, she asserts that her musical mothering will not take the same strict format as her own childhood experience.

Linda told a story of Ashley's brother in her interview. At an eisteddfod, a competition for musicians, her son chose not to compete. Linda did not say why although it was clear throughout her story that his musical ability was not as proficient as that of his sisters. Instead, he asked the judges if he could play an instrumental piece to the audience when the judges were doing their adjudication—a break in the proceedings. Linda tells,

> He just performed while they were (laughs) trying to find out who was the winner, you know—and he was so happy—oh I love it—and he did so well. He just did a jazzy piece and you know, it didn't have to be a concerto. So, I was really happy with that. I want them to enjoy, not be pressurised into doing things. It's a fine line.

Linda's son shows a high degree of audacity to secure a performance spot at the competition, where he would be noticed but not judged. This sense of entitlement is consistent with Lareau's (2003/2011) assessment of middle-class children and their confidence to speak with people in authority and assert their needs. Linda was complicit in this by allowing her son to do this, as it reflects on her success as a musical mother. I wonder if he had not been so proficient whether he would have been encouraged to perform. What if everyone attending wanted their child to perform just for the experience? I also wonder if her son was able to dictate his own rules with Linda more than Ashley.

In some ways, Linda's son's performance reiterates her desire for them to enjoy music without forcing them to do something they did not wish to do, in the 'fine line' between getting things right and terribly wrong. Traversing this line is what Hays (1996) calls the mothering contradiction:

> Mothers are ... endeavouring to maximise their social assets and to organise their lives in efficient ways ... they generally do not make a self-conscious decision to oppose the system that values competitive individualism and material advantage ... They act as members of a culture that maintains two

contradictory ideologies, and their actions take place in the context of a social hierarchy that gives women primary responsibility for creating and maintaining nurturing ties. (pp. 172–173)

Those contrasting ideologies are to be a 'good' mother; mothers must be self-sacrificing of their own desires and totally committed to their children, selflessly nurturing their children, while simultaneously living up to the social expectation to create successful and independent citizens who will thrive in the competitive workplace (Hays, 1996). Linda was committed to this task—it was her raison d'etre—however, she crossed the 'fine line' with Ashley, whom she 'pushed' into going to the conservatorium to study music.

> ... when they played ... I didn't want to push it. I did feel like I pushed her (Ashley) into going to the con—only because she was so good and that was all that I thought, something that she really loved doing but she really didn't. But that wasn't for her—just wasn't.

As Linda spoke about this, her voice faltered; it was as if her own insistence that her daughter loved playing was not the complete truth and her role in coercing her to play, practise and perform was indeed crossing that 'fine line' she mentioned earlier. In Chap. 4, I discussed how children and mothers operate on a cycle of affective recognition and how this feeds into itself to maintain a need for love and acceptance. In addition, in Chap. 7, I discuss the emotional labour mothers expend in their chase to accrue cultural capital and the affordances and costs of this.

Susan

Turning now to Susan. Susan articulates a different story, yet in many ways, it presents as being quite similar. Susan maintains that her musical mothering was more 'casual' in its approach, and she openly stigmatised those with more deliberate intentions, such as some of the mothers of her piano students:

> I didn't set out to say thou shalt be brilliant, thou shalt practise. But some of the parents—I hesitate to say this—Asian parents that we deal with are just on the children's case 24/7. So, that's an extreme example of what I was not. I say I had a much more casual approach ... I didn't actually have aspirations, I

think I let the kids create those. If I had aspirations for [eldest daughter] I'm sure she would have achieved a lot more highly and a lot more things, had I been a more directive parent.

A stereotype of Asian mothers, known as 'Tiger mothers' after Chua's famous book in 2011, as 'grim-faced and single-minded' (p. 141) in their determination to accrue cultural capital for their children through severe punishment and gruelling schedules (Wang, 2011). And yet, concerted cultivation is practiced all over the world in Western countries and those influenced by them, with varying intensities. Kong (2021) quotes a Chinese proverb 'beating and scolding are emblems of love' (p. 290), stating that Chinese parents demonstrate their parental involvement and care through showing their children that certain attributes are important, and they want to motivate their children to achieve high academic, behavioural, and moral standards. Showing harsh parenting is an indication of love and care and that your children are worth making an effort for (Kong, 2021). Kong maintains that this parenting style is practiced in parents from all socio-economic backgrounds. As Wang (2015) states, the "traits of sacrifice, pushiness and determination embodied in the 'music mom' have increasingly become associated with being Asian" (p. 29). Wang states that these Asian mothers resist the racist marginalisation they experience by utilising their cultural capital. They deliberately inhabit subjectivities as the "rightful inheritors of this field of high culture and resignify(ing) the pursuit of classical music as an implicit means of preserving 'Asian' identity" (Wang, 2009, p. 899). Such Asian mothering, with its connotations of excessive pressure and demands, continues to be demonised as 'bad'.

Susan realises her comment is racist as indicated by her hesitation; however, she takes a chance in articulating these thoughts by thinking that I might share similar ideas as a non-Asian, white middle-class woman like her. She acknowledges that there may be perceptions that her mothering is the same as that of such Asian mothers (Wang, 2015) and wants to offer a point of difference. Susan does not wish to appear 'pushy' like Tiger mothers, which she knows is against 'good' mothering ideology and something she openly disapproves of (Perrier, 2013). These moral judgements within middle-class mothering will be explored further in Chap. 6.

Mirroring Asian Tiger mothering, Susan had her own strategies for encouraging her daughter, Jessica, to practise, demonstrating her concerted cultivation was hardly 'casual'. Susan revealed "*when she decided at thirteen or so that she wanted a cello, the deal was that she had to get grade five Honours on the flute, and I would buy her a cello*". There were provisos to be followed before Jessica could have what she wanted. Jessica had learnt the flute initially at her mother's suggestion; however, in later years, she decided it was the cello that she wanted to play. Susan argues here that she is enabling her daughter to play her instrument of choice rather than forcing her to play:

> *I was gobsmacked when she came home and said she wanted to be a classical cellist. And then because she had that sense of direction and because she didn't get her Honours for grade five and prove that she could practise—she was really naughty—I pulled out all the stops to make it work for her.*

While Jessica did not meet Susan's prerequisite, she was given a cello anyway. Susan seemingly enjoyed this rebellious side of Jessica and commented in her interview how she also liked those piano students who had a bit of 'character'. This may be a retrospective viewpoint, rather than how she felt at the time, as Susan was keen to send Jessica to the conservatorium, far away from her influential peers and possible distractions. Susan maintains she was nurturing Jessica's dream, rather than forcing her to play, thereby differentiating herself from those pushy Tiger mothers. Susan's self-professed 'casual' parenting style contrasted with her role in making things happen for Jessica. For white middle-class musical mothers, their efforts to make their children's 'talent' seem natural and not a product of their intense labour is arguably more strategic and more labour-intensive than Asian mothers who are overt about their intentions for their children's development. Like Linda, Susan had been fostering Jessica's musical proclivity since birth, if not before. Susan had come from a musical family where learning an instrument was expected, and music had always been an embodied family practice. Unsurprisingly, Jessica had shown an interest in music, and Susan was happy to encourage it, giving Susan the appearance of being child-centred and responsive. Susan, like Linda, is aware of the 'fine-line' and how easy it is to cross, but she believes that she practices within those parameters as stated in her earlier comment about her eldest daughter and her achievement, or lack thereof.

Rosemary

While Susan might appear to be less intensive in her concerted cultivation than Linda, stay-at-home mother Rosemary is even less so. Rosemary trained as a primary teacher and worked in the state education system in the 1960s; however, once she married, she was forced to give up her career. Rosemary's narrative tells of a less intensive approach to mothering, in line with parental expectations of the day, where the lives of adults and children were often quite separate. Children of this generation were expected to go out and play without the constant guidance and supervision of adults. Rosemary's approach to her first daughter Penelope's musical development demonstrates the boundaries she placed on her cultivating efforts, particularly when music was not going to be a career. Penelope studied music in and outside of school but recalls learning to play by ear and not practising. In her interview, she performed a parody of the conversations she would have with her mother around this issue:

Rosemary: *Have you practised?*
Penelope: *Yes (said in a feeble voice)*
Rosemary: *I didn't hear you!*
Penelope: *I did!*

Rosemary did not sit in during practise sessions, like Linda and me (and incidentally the Chinese parents Kong (2021) talks about), although it appears she may have been listening from a distance. Rosemary was happy to leave the teaching to the nuns, who taught Penelope piano, just as they had taught Rosemary when she was a child. Interestingly, Rosemary states that she didn't enjoy her lessons, stating, "*I didn't enjoy it at all. I did do all these exam pieces and that's no fun ... learning from the nuns and if I played wrong notes, she'd hit me, hit me with a stick*". With such punitive teaching methods, one might wonder why Rosemary wanted Penelope to receive the same fate, which she apparently did:

I had a beautiful nun when I started. She was kind and musical and sweet ... and then she left and then I got a crabby old meany who did that (slapped wrist) and I stopped in Year 10 because I couldn't handle the formality of it ... because I played by ear and I didn't do any practise.

As far as Rosemary was concerned, she didn't need to enforce practise as this was the job of the nuns. Parents of Rosemary's generation, like that of my own mother, left the role of teaching and education to those who were enlisted for the job, and even though Rosemary was a teacher, this was not her domain. This compares starkly to many current middle-class mothers who intervene in their children's education, feeling compelled to advise teachers how to best teach their children (Lareau, 2003/2011). Rosemary didn't need to worry because she believed that music was already in their bones.

Later, with three children in tow, Rosemary explained how the labour of following all their extra-curricular pursuits became too much. Rosemary decided after her third child that she was not going to support their musical endeavours further, and they could only do what was provided at school. She states how fortunate Penelope was '*to have all the music*'. I wonder if Penelope had been more invested in practise and if Rosemary would have supported her children's musical development further. Studies suggest that mothers sometimes discourage their children from continuing activities like music if it requires additional labour on their part, and they can no longer see value in the investment (Lareau, 2003/2011). Rosemary explained:

> *The reality was, I ran around with them, mainly with the boys with sport—five days a week. Their father did anything with them on the weekend that they needed to do. I was always taking them to something—gymnastics, or swimming, or something, or music. Penelope had all the music. And by the time it got to [third child], they only did it at school. It was too bad. I'd had it!*

Rosemary was satisfied that she had given her children a musical start. Rosemary had never concertedly cultivated her children in the same way as Linda or Susan; however, she was confident that their musical habitus was in progress. Rosemary's attitude is typical of many within her generation and is representative of mothers who invest in their children's training in any number of activities but as children's motivations change and friendships, study commitments or the desire for freedom away from the family overtake, mothers are no longer willing to commit to this additional labour.

The continuum of concerted cultivation of children's musical development through intensive mothering is highlighted in these examples of rigid schedules to self-regulated approaches. It is also pertinent that not all siblings receive the same level of cultivation as I mentioned earlier. The tensions are evident when encouraging practise, revealing mothers' dilemmas in supporting current trends in neoliberal competitiveness and individualism compared with the good mothering logic of maternal self-sacrifice, and a more caring, nurturing approach.

MISRECOGNISING CONCERTED CULTIVATION

'Disinterest' is a term used by Bourdieu (1998) to describe the disavowal that middle-class mothers demonstrate when they deny concertedly culti-vating their children's musical abilities. Bourdieu's (1977) analogy of the gift exchange shows disinterestedness at work. A person gives a gift to another, knowing that this person will like the gift but also feel the need to return the favour by giving a gift to reciprocate, and feigning surprise when this happens. Bourdieu explains the symbolic labour in this exchange and the labour involved in the process, also labelled as 'misrecognition', where there is an appearance of no calculation or effort, when in fact, the opposite is true (Bourdieu, 1977, p. 171). For those who belong to the middle classes or elite, that is those who play by these rules continuously, the labour appears minimal because it is already part of the fabric or every-day life.

Part of being a mother and parent is to do the routine caring of your children but also to teach your children about life, values and culture. It can be tricky if you are a teacher to separate the care and educational work you do as a mother. Walkerdine and Lucey (1989) label pedagogical mothering as 'sensitive mothering' (p. 17) where mothers make the edu-cational processes they implement, particularly in the domestic space, seem natural and spontaneous rather than deliberate and strategic. It is not only teachers who engage in sensitive mothering as Linda demon-strated. Linda was adept at making every opportunity a chance to learn something, and she prided herself on her ability to do this, describing herself as a '*Montessori mother*' meaning that she was "*hands on, teaching them how to write ... I was very music involved in doing things all the time (laughs) yeah, so I was a Montessori mum, I think*". Here, teaching is natu-ralised, as part of everyday life, and the pursuit of advantage and the stra-tegic development of proclivities is hidden.

Susan, who was a teacher, albeit a music teacher rather than a generalist teacher, provided many examples of how she adopted a 'sensitive mother' subjectivity. Susan made a point of saying how her parenting was far from dictatorial, implying a disinterestedness in her approach. This is highlighted in an example she gave of her daughter playing in a piano competition,

> *I thought it was perfectly normal for a three-year-old to play two-part Bach ... she had already done her first performance on a grand piano which was 'Mary had a little lamb' where the left hand was too strong from the right, and then something else she played, where out of twenty-eight children she came fourth in the eight-years-and-under [aged section of the music competition] and ... her fourth birthday was like two weeks before.*

While Susan claims that her daughter's musical ability was 'normal', she knows it is extraordinary, and a result of her pedagogical labour. She concedes this when she comments on the age bracket her daughter is competing in where she is much younger than her rivals, yet still manages to place fourth. And Susan would know that most children who come to her for piano lessons would not be at that level at that age, even if they started learning at three. In my experience, most piano teachers will begin lessons for children at five or six years old, after their first year of schooling. Similarly, the attention to detail of her daughter's performance and its critique demonstrates Susan's delight at her daughter's potential, and a sign of her mothering and teaching success made visible (and audible). Not only were Susan's daughters learning to play instruments well, but they were also learning to perform, to overcome any nerves and to compete against other children with similar abilities and parental aspirations. Participating in music competitions was something that Susan did as a child and is engrained as part of her family's cultural inculcation and capital accumulation.

For another of Susan's daughters, Jessica, her musical habitus was developed well before she had chosen to do music as a career. Starting at school, Jessica was playing in small music groups organised by her mother; music was an important part of family life. Jessica explains, "*it wasn't a hectic kind of childhood ... we were just always kind of musically on that spectrum ... I did a little bit of sport ... did a lot of music*". Support for Jessica's musical development came from other family members as well as her mother. While the desire to play the cello came from Jessica, Susan did all she could to ensure that she was able to do this. Utilising her cultural capital, Susan was able to organise for Jessica to start at the conservatorium early. Most aspiring conservatorium students enter after Year 12 through a competitive audition process; however, Jessica was able to start after Year 10.

When discussing Jessica's early arrival at the conservatorium, Susan recounted the story of Jessica's musical development, beginning with the physical toll to get Jessica to lessons—travelling hours each way—to attend lessons with '*one of the best cello teachers ever*'. Susan extrapolated, "*she left school after Year 10 to go straight to tertiary study which may or may not have been sane ... but it did short circuit the study time and she coped very well*". Here is evidence of Susan's value exchange on her cultural capital and Susan's acknowledgement of her labour in making this happen. Susan, as a single mother, time-poor, steals the time to find an expert tutor and take Jessica to her lessons. There were reasons other than the pursuit of a musical career that also influenced Susan's decision-making, and this will be explored further in Chap. 6.

Throughout this book, there will be countless examples of such behaviour. Middle-class mothers want their children's abilities to appear natural and innate rather than a product of their intense labour. These mothers want their effort to appear minimal and effortless. The idea of disinterestedness is pertinent in this case because it denies musical habitus and the idea of habitus as strategising to produce classed practices. Bourdieu (1984) explains,

> Culture is the site, par excellence, of misrecognition, because, in generating strategies objectively adapted to the objective chances of profit of which it is the product, the sense of investment secures profits which do not need to be pursued as profits; and so it brings to those who have legitimate culture as a second nature the supplementary profit of being seen (and seeing themselves) as perfectly disinterested, unblemished by any cynical or mercenary use of culture. (p. 86)

Just as the 'sensitive mother' ensures every experience becomes a learning opportunity, musical mothers actively seek ways to stimulate their children through play-based and child-centred approaches so that their pedagogies are enacted in socially acceptable ways and, therefore, become invisible. It becomes simply 'what we do'. Misrecognition, as cultural inculcation, in the field of music is evident when learning an instrument, for example, which is very financially, physically and emotionally demanding; however, it is made to look like an innate talent. Susan maintained that Jessica's interest in the cello was initiated by Jessica, and while this may be true, music was an integral part of family life from Jessica's conception, just as it had been for Susan. Cultural capital accumulated by Susan through her family background, and her own musical journey as student, teacher and mother, was actioned to help Jessica's musical trajectory. Despite Susan's denial of her aspirations for her children's musical journeys—"*I didn't actually have aspirations, I think that I let the kids create those*"—she demonstrated an intentional 'facilitation' for Jessica's development in this field; music was a big part of Susan's family life and part of her 'cultural inheritance'. Bourdieu (1990) writes:

> This disposition, always marked by its (social) conditions of acquisition and realisation, tends to adjust to the objective chances of satisfying need or desire, inclining agents to 'cut their coats according to their cloth', and so to become the accomplices of the processes that tend to make the probable a reality. (p. 65)

For Jessica, and Ashley as we saw earlier, the chances of becoming a professional musician would have been most likely.

Middle-class musical mothers mediate discourses of intensive mothering and concerted cultivation in complex ways (Perrier, 2013). Susan wants to be perceived as a caring and nurturing mother in contrast to the mothering she received in her own childhood. She views her musical mothering as child-centred rather than 'directive'—a term she baulks at—however, her mothering philosophy belies her underlying belief that by being directive in the form of making children practise, getting good teachers, playing at competitions, playing in ensembles, gets results in the musical field. Jessica's success as a professional musician is now concrete evidence of Susan's musical mothering, par excellence, where she has created a person of distinction that reflects her middle-class tastes (Vincent & Maxwell, 2015). Not only must she be a good mother but also a good teacher, as her performance is assessed against her daughter's success.

Like Susan, Linda wanted to give her children '*a nudge*'; Linda could see their potential, misrecognising their abilities as natural talent even though she had proactively fostered their musicianship from birth or perhaps in utero. Adding complexity to Linda's cultivation of her children's musical development was that she believed their ability was a gift from

God. Denying her daughter's assertions that Linda only wanted her children to pursue music because she had missed out on doing it herself, Linda states,

> *You have to have the dream … not your parents. You have to have the passion, you have to feel God's call, I believe … and it's a gift and you feel … you know, you're there … bless others with it …*

Linda aligns her children's musical ability as their calling from God. God has given them a gift which they are obliged to fulfil on moral grounds as part of God's plan for them. This then negates any intentional strategising on Linda's part, demonstrating another form of misrecognition.

CULTIVATING THE NEXT GENERATION

The grandchildren of Rosemary, Susan, and Linda, all continue to be involved in music. Their mothers are actively developing their children's musical dispositions in 'natural' ways rather than what they would consider as a deliberate action. Jessica's narrative shows that the disavowal of concerted cultivation continues.

Jessica comments that her daughter, who is four years of age, is experiencing music '*just through doing and having fun*'. She makes a point of saying her musical efforts are unprompted. There are no intentions for her to have formal lessons at this juncture, even though Jessica is a professional musician herself. Jessica is also cognisant that this is the correct thing to say, having previously mentioned that she was not looking forward to her child starting her first year of formal schooling and not having a play-based learning approach as she had in kindergarten. In saying that, Jessica's daughter gets to see her mother teaching the cello in the home environment and often sees her mother play at concerts. Jessica maintains that she is keeping everything low key, although she admits buying her daughter a small viola and other instruments—"*really nice, sort of sounding ones … like a good chromatic glockenspiel and those sorts of things*". Jessica also provided additional examples of how her daughter engages with music:

She sits and she watches while I practise. She's interested in the cello and I think that she knows it's kinda this special, exciting thing, you know, people come to concerts and they dress up ...

Just let her play, let her have fun ... and I think that partially, 'cause I didn't really start formal lessons until I was a bit older but I just had it around me all the time, so it was a bit nice. So, partially it's reflecting the way I learnt ... but it's also a bit of a reaction against the music profession, as job, and pressure and that kind of stuff ... I don't want to have that sort of intention with her musical development at the moment ... I feel if she wants it later, we'll know, and we'll support her. Definitely ...

Jessica rejects the dominant discourse of classical music tuition as not for her daughter at this stage; however, she is cultivating her daughter's musical habitus through informal inculcation—those 'things we do'—watching her mother practise, playing good quality instruments and going along to concerts. Jessica embraces the 'sensitive mother' mother subjectivity by being responsive in her parenting. She will 'know' when the time is right for more formal learning because they will 'feel' it. This adheres to 'good' mothering logic and Jessica can be seen as not 'pushy'. However, there is some forward thinking in Jessica's logic in her co-opting of Susan regarding a suitable birthday gift for Jessica's daughter, Susan's grandchild, as Susan tells:

I came up for her [granddaughter's] birthday party and everybody else is giving her little kiddie toys so, Jessica asked if I could give her some of my teaching materials. So, I bought her a whiteboard and some instructions to draw. I drew a couple of staves with a lot of magnets because when I'm teaching, I use magnets to do sol-fa and all of this sort of stuff and all the coloured pens. Jessica said from 2 o'clock until 8 o'clock at night she didn't put it down and here I was worrying that she'd say, "It's not Frozen" or it's not something like that! (Laughs) ... so, they can just be introduced to music through play rather than formal lessons.

Social reproduction of musical habitus is evident through this interaction. Jessica wondered if she should be taking her daughter to early music classes but then realised that she probably didn't have time and reconciled this by stating that they did lots of music at preschool. Although music was introduced in a less formal way, there is clear intention in the processes of Jessica and Susan—what Bourdieu would call 'disinterested interest' (Bourdieu, 1977, p. 177)—and Jessica's daughter was already hooked.

Middle-class mothers invest in children's musical development for many reasons. As Skeggs (2004) writes, "[I]investments ... must be about a projection into the future of a self/space/body with value. We only make investments in order to accrue value when we can conceive of a future in which that value can have a use" (p. 146). Investments are a calculation of value exchange. Cultural capital accrual is seen as a means to gain advantages in educational and workplace arenas. This form of social reproduction requires 'an active and constructed process' (Kaufman, 2005, p. 247) or else 'face the very real prospect of generational decline' (Parkin, 1979, p. 63).

Linda's investment in Ashley, as intensive mothering and concerted cultivation, did not lead to Ashley having a successful career in music. However, Susan was able to capitalise on her utilisation of cultural resources to benefit Jessica's transition to the conservatorium. There was a dilemma for mothers who acknowledge that practise is essential for skill development yet did not wish to be seen as forcing their children to play. The fine line between competitive individualism and nurturing interest was evident and problematic. Mothers try to make their work look natural, but in doing so, their efforts are arguably more tactical, strategic and labour-intensive. Middle-class musical mothers frame their parenting as 'good' or 'bad' in their pursuit for cultural capital. White, middle-class mothers feel pressure to ensure their investments are successful, as they increasingly see 'other' mothers taking up places in privileged institutions that are usually reserved for them. Mothers who perform musical mothering differently can be pathologised as 'bad' even when their practices are not dissimilar to those making the accusations. Both intensive mothering and concerted cultivation are on a continuum that mothers dance along as required.

References

Arnold, L. B. (2014). I don't know where I end and you begin: Challenging boundaries of the self and intensive mothering. In L. R. Ennis (Ed.), *Intensive mothering: The cultural contradictions of modern motherhood* (pp. 47–65). Demeter Press.

Atkinson, W. (2016). *Beyond Bourdieu*. Polity.

Ball, S. J. (2003). The risks of social reproduction: The middle class and educational markets. *London Review of Education, 1*(3), 163–175. https://doi.org/10.1080/1474846032000146730

Bennett, P. R., Lutz, A. C., & Jayaram, L. (2012). Beyond the schoolyard: The role of parenting logics, financial resources, and social institutions in the social class gap in structured activity participation. *Sociology of Education, 85*(2), 131–157. https://doi.org/10.1177/0038040711431585

Bourdieu, P. (1977). *Outline of a theory of practice.* Cambridge University Press.

Bourdieu, P. (1984). *Distinction: A social critique of the judgement of taste.* Routledge and Kegan Paul.

Bourdieu, P. (1986). The forms of capital. In J. Richardson (Ed.), *Handbook of theory and research for the sociology of education* (pp. 241–258). Greenwood.

Bourdieu, P. (1990). *The logic of practice.* Polity.

Bourdieu, P. (1998). *Practical reason.* Polity.

Bourdieu, P. (2007). *Sketch for a self-analysis.* Polity.

Cheadle, J. E., & Amato, P. R. (2011). A quantitative assessment of Lareau's qualitative conclusions about class, race, and parenting. *Journal of Family Issues, 32*(5), 679–706. https://doi.org/10.1177/0192513X10386305

Chin, T., & Phillips, M. (2004). Social reproduction and child-rearing practices: Social class, children's agency, and the summer activity gap. *Sociology of Education, 77*, 185–210. https://doi.org/10.1177/003804070407700301

Cho, E. (2015). What do mothers say? Korean mothers' perceptions of children's participation in extra-curricular musical activities. *Music Education Research, 17*(2), 162–178. https://doi.org/10.1080/14613808.2014.895313

Choi, K. W. Y. (2015). On the fast track to a head start: A visual ethnographic study of parental consumption of children's play and learning activities in Hong Kong. *Childhood, 1*, 1–17. https://doi.org/10.1177/0907568215586838

Cooper, K. (2021). Are poor parents poor parents? The relationship between poverty and parenting among mothers in the UK. *Sociology (Oxford), 55*(2), 349–383. https://doi.org/10.1177/0038038520939397

Crozier, G., Reay, D., & David James, D. (2011). Making it work for their children: White middle-class parents and working-class schools. *International Studies in Sociology of Education, 21*(3), 199–216. https://doi.org/10.108 0/09620214.2011.616343

Debs, M., Kafka, J., Makris, M. V., & Roda, A. (2023). Happiness-oriented parents: An alternative perspective on privilege and choosing schools. *American Journal of Education, 129*(2), 145–176. https://doi.org/10.1086/723066

Dermott, E., & Pomati, M. (2016). "Good" parenting practices: How important are poverty, education and time pressure? *Sociology (Oxford), 50*(1), 125–142. https://doi.org/10.1177/0038038514560260

Gale, T., & Parker, S. (2015). Calculating student aspiration: Bourdieu, spatiality and the politics of recognition. *Cambridge Journal of Education, 45*(1), 81–96. https://doi.org/10.1080/0305764X.2014.988685

Gillies, V. (2007). *Marginalised mothers: Exploring working-class experiences of parenting.* Routledge.

Golden, D., & Erdreich, L. (2014). Mothering and the work of educational care – An integrative approach. *British Journal of Sociology of Education, 35*(2), 263–277. https://doi.org/10.1080/01425692.2012.747589

Golden, D., Erdreich, L., Stefansen, K., & Smette, I. (2021). Class, education and parenting: Cross-cultural perspectives. *British Journal of Sociology of Education, 42*(4), 453–459. https://doi.org/10.1080/01425692.2021.1946301

Gudmundsdottir, H. R., & Gudmundsdottir, D. G. (2010). Parent-infant music courses in Iceland: Perceived benefits and mental well-being of mothers. *Music Education Research, 12*(3), 299–309. https://doi.org/10.1080/1461380 8.2010.505644

Hays, S. (1996). *The cultural contradictions of motherhood.* Yale University Press.

Hofvander Trulsson, Y. (2013). Chasing children's fortunes. Cases of parents' strategies in Sweden, the UK and Korea. In P. Dyndahl (Ed.), *Intersection and interplay. Contributions to the cultural study of music in performance, education, and society* (pp. 125–140). Lund University.

Ilari, B. (2013). Concerted cultivation and music learning. *Research Studies in Music Education, 35*(2), 179–196. https://doi.org/10.1177/132110 3X13509348

Ilari, B., Moura, A., & Bourscheidt, L. (2011). Music education research between interactions and commodities: Musical parenting of infants and toddlers in Brazil. *Music Education Research, 13*(1), 51–67.

Ishizuka, P. (2019). Social class, gender, and contemporary parenting standards in the United States: Evidence from a National Survey Experiment. *Social Forces, 98*(1), 31–58. https://doi.org/10.1093/sf/soy107

Jaeger, M. M. (2022). Cultural capital and educational inequality: An assessment of the state of the art. In K. Gërxhani, N. D. de Graaf, & W. Raub (Eds.), *Handbook of sociological science: Contributions to rigorous sociology.* Edward Elgar Publishing.

Kaufman, P. (2005). Middle-class social reproduction: The activation and negotiation of structural advantages. *Sociological Forum, 20*(2), 245–270. https://doi.org/10.1007/s11206-005-4099-x

Kong, S. H. (2021). A study of students' perceptions of parental influence on students' musical instrument learning in Beijing, China. *Music Education Research, 23*(3), 287–299. https://doi.org/10.1080/14613808.2020. 1832978

Lareau, A. (2000). *Home advantage: Social class and parental intervention in elementary education.* Rowman & Littlefield.

Lareau, A. (2003/2011). *Unequal childhoods: Class, race, and family life.* University of California Press.

Macvarish, J. (2016). *Neuroparenting: The expert invasion of family life.* Palgrave Macmillan. https://doi.org/10.1057/978-1-137-54733-0

McPherson, G. E. (2009). The role of parents in children's musical development. *Psychology of Music, 37*(1), 91–110. https://doi.org/10.1177/03057356 07086049

Milkie, M., & Warner, C. H. (2014). Status safeguarding: Mothers' work to secure children's place in the social hierarchy. In L. R. Ennis (Ed.), *Intensive mothering: The cultural contradictions of modern motherhood* (pp. 66–85). Demeter Press.

Moore, R. (2012). Capital. In M. Grenfell (Ed.), *Pierre Bourdieu: Key concepts* (2nd ed., pp. 98–113). Acumen.

Mukherjee, U., & Barn, R. (2021). Concerted cultivation as a racial parenting strategy: Race, ethnicity and middle-class Indian parents in Britain. *British Journal of Sociology of Education, 42*(4), 521–536. https://doi.org/10.108 0/01425692.2021.1872365

O'Reilly, A. (2010). *Twenty-first-century motherhood: Experience, identity, policy, agency.* Columbia University Press.

Orgad, S. (2019). *Heading home: Motherhood, work, and the failed promise of equality.* Columbia University Press.

Parkin, F. (1979). *Marxism and class theory: A bourgeois critique.* Tavistock.

Perrier, M. (2013). Middle-class mothers' moralities and concerted cultivation. *Sociology, 47*(4), 655–670. https://doi.org/10.1177/0038038512453789

Reay, D. (1998). *Class work: Mothers' involvement in their children's primary schooling.* Routledge.

Reay, D. (2010). Class acts: Parental involvement in schooling. In M. Klett-Davies (Ed.), *Is parenting a class issue?* (pp. 31–43). The Nuffield Press.

Savage, S. (2015). *Intensive mothering through music in early childhood education* (Unpublished Masters' Minor Thesis), Monash University.

Savage, S. (2019). *Musical mothering: Middle-class strategies and affect across generations.* Unpublished PhD thesis, Monash University.

Savage, S. (2021). The experience of mothers as university students and pre-service teachers during Covid-19: Recommendations for ongoing support. *Studies in Continuing Education, 45*(1), 71–85. https://doi.org/10.108 0/0158037X.2021.1994938

Shirani, F., Henwood, K., & Coltart, C. (2012). Meeting the challenges of intensive parenting culture. *Sociology, 46*(1), 25–40. https://doi.org/10.1177/ 0038038511416169

Sjödin, D., & Roman, C. (2018). Family practises among Swedish parents: Extracurricular activities and social class. *European Societies, 20*(5), 764. https://doi.org/10.1080/14616696.2018.1473622

Skeggs, B. (2004). *Class, self, culture.* Routledge.

Stefansen, K., & Aarseth, H. (2011). Enriching intimacy: The role of the emotional in the 'resourcing' of middle-class children. *British Journal of Sociology of Education, 32*(3), 389–405. https://doi.org/10.1080/0142569 2.2011.559340

Tierney, A. T., Krizman, J., & Kraus, N. (2015). Music training alters the course of adolescent auditory development. *Proceedings of the National Academy of Sciences, 112*(32), 10062–10067. https://doi.org/10.1073/pnas.1505114112

VanderValk, D. H. (2010). Sensitive mothering (Walkerdine and Lucey). In A. O'Reilly (Ed.), *Encyclopaedia of motherhood* (pp. 1112–1113). Sage.

Vincent, C., & Ball, S. J. (2007). 'Making up' the middle-class child: Families, activities and class dispositions. *Sociology, 41*(6), 1061–1077. https://doi.org/10.1177/0038038507082315

Vincent, C., & Maxwell, C. (2015). Parenting priorities and pressures: Furthering understanding of 'concerted cultivation'. *Discourse: Studies in the Cultural Politics of Education, 37*(2), 269–281. https://doi.org/10.1080/0159630 6.2015.1014880

Walkerdine, V., & Lucey, H. (1989). *Democracy in the kitchen: Regulating mothers and socialising daughters*. Virago.

Wang, G. (2009). Interlopers in the realm of high culture: "Music Moms" and the performance of Asian and Asian American identities. *American Quarterly, 61*(4), 881–903. https://doi.org/10.1353/aq.0.0114

Wang, G. (2011). On tiger mothers and music moms. *Amerasia Journal, 37*(2), 130–136. https://doi.org/10.17953/amer.37.2.v5127j0371807341

Wang, G. (2015). *Soundtracks of Asian America: Navigating race through musical performance*. Duke University Press.

Wardman, N., Hutchesson, R., Gottschall, K., Drew, C., & Saltmarsh, S. (2010). Starry eyes and subservient selves: Portraits of "well-rounded" girlhood in the prospectuses of all-girl elite private schools. *The Australian Journal of Education, 54*(3), 249–261. https://doi.org/10.1177/000494411005400303

Weinshenker, M., & Kim, S.-K. (2023). Concerted cultivation and parental satisfaction: A profile analysis via principal component analysis. *Journal of Family Studies, 29*(3), 1249–1269. https://doi.org/10.1080/13229400.2022.2040574

Witte, A. L., Kiewra, K. A., Kasson, S. C., & Perry, K. R. (2015). Parenting talent: A qualitative investigation of the roles parents play in talent development. *Roeper Review, 37*(2), 84–96. https://doi.org/10.1080/02783193.2015.1008091

CHAPTER 6

Mothers' Moral Responsibility to Produce Worthy Children Through Socially Valued Dispositions and Behaviours

INTRODUCTION

Living a life of value is embroiled in classed values (Sayer, 2005b; Skeggs, 2011). A 'moral authority' (Skeggs, 2004, p. 76) is generated by middle-class mothers, who decide what is considered and judged as 'good' mothering (Perrier, 2013). Mothers carefully researched decision-making in consumption of food, clothes, education and leisure pursuits determine what is considered 'best' and what will afford future opportunities. They assume superiority over working-class mothers for whom choices are limited.

Through music, mothers want their children to develop attributes that will hold them in good stead for the future. Mothers feel a moral responsibility to produce children who will be seen as moral and worthy citizens, valued members of society with positive contributions to offer, in comparison to mothers whose children are a drain on the welfare system (Gillies, 2007). Constantly developing oneself fits neatly into neoliberal tropes of self-improvement and always trying to better one's circumstances, with the responsibility for this being squarely with the self (and mothers, in this instance). Mothers often develop such attributes in their children through music. To become proficient in music requires practise, perseverance and commitment over the long term, thereby demonstrating

S. Savage, *Musical Mothering*, Palgrave Macmillan Studies in Family and Intimate Life, https://doi.org/10.1007/978-3-031-65157-1_6

123

an ongoing determination for improvement. This aligns with the desired 'work ethic' under capitalism where a well-developed work ethic and commitment to lifelong learning is considered a life of value (Gerrard, 2014). People who do not live up to this are simply not realising their potential (Weeks, 2011), and this is imperative in neoliberal society and neatly tied into discourses around social mobility and understanding of classed practices (Gerrard, 2014) as discussed in Chap. 2. In addition, involvement in music provides a way to maintain control over children so that mothers manage and sculpt their children's behaviour in ways that are deemed legitimate and acceptable. This is also about mothers avoiding judgements from others through the strict management of their children to maintain respectable selves. Sometimes this goes awry. Mothers can lose control of the children they worked so hard to rein in over time.

SELFISH SELFLESSNESS

When mothers seek to gain cultural and social capital through investing in their children, the investment in the children can also become an investment in the self, in what I call 'selfish selflessness'. In many ways, this is antithetical to moral mothering because 'good' mothers are expected to be self-sacrificing. I reiterate the comment made by Linda who discusses missing out on her own musical ambitions as a child, and her musical mothering practice:

You can't live through your children … you know how you dream big and then you, 'cause your dreams don't work, you go and put your dreams on your kids. I didn't, no, I don't feel like I ever did that. I saw potential in my kids, and I thought … ah … look … nudge a bit.

In this instance, mothers negate their self-interest in such practice as a form of disinterestedness. Mothers' aspirations for their children are interwoven into their own personal desires (Savage & Hall, 2017) where children's successes become an indication of mothers' success (Hays, 1996). This becomes integral to their sense of purpose and their identities as 'good' mothers (Savage, 2015a).

To enact moral superiority, mothers develop a code where they seem to sacrifice themselves for their children in a way that is altruistic rather than competitive (Sanghera, 2016). Skeggs (2011, p. 507) writes that there is often a moral cost to middle-class mothering that is seen as "evidence of self-centredness, conceit, pretentiousness and exploitation". I showed this through the pathologising of Tiger mothers due to their relentless pressure on children to achieve as discussed in Chap. 5. Much of the work that middle-class mothers do is to inculcate desired dispositions in their children that will be useful in the future. These dispositions will have exchange value in arenas such as schools and workplaces, where children will have a better position in society than their parents, or at the very least, social status is maintained.

INCULCATING DISPOSITIONS

Part of mother's work to nurture moral citizens is to develop socially valued personal dispositions and behaviours in their children from the outset. Formal music education is said to develop the 'musician's advantage', a phenomenon where not only musical skills are developed but non-musical skills such as self-regulation, confidence, perseverance and resilience (Savage, 2015b). Such dispositions are important for middle-class mothers who know these have value in job markets and in educational spheres.

Susan's story provides an example of nurturing a desired disposition and is related to developing a positive work ethic, but also a redemption of her 'immoral' status to claim their moral worth. Susan holds herself to high standards and expectations, despite being vilified by her community for being a single mother when her children were young. Susan used the word 'demanding' several times throughout her interview to speak about her own subjectivity and as a quality she sought for her daughter's music tutors. Through music, Susan was providing Jessica with training and strategies to cope with challenges she might confront in the future.

The demanding flute choir—she was only about six and she was playing with high school kids and keeping up with them very nicely ... her flute teacher at the time was one of the most esteemed flute players and teachers in Australia ... he was cool as a button but really demanding as a teacher.

I still think [her teacher] was one of the best cello teachers ever ... she was very demanding of Jessica, even though Jessica did in about 18 months more than people do in ten years. I'd go to pick her up and Jessica would be white and [her teacher] would be red! (laughs) ... Yeah, but you know it's good training.

As Bull (2014, p. 3) writes, participation in classical music develops 'an ethic of correction' in (re)producing a form of disciplined body and bodily excellence. Engagement in classical music promotes self-regulation through perseverance, resilience-building and having to be fully committed to the task-at-hand. Working in an ensemble requires teamwork, acute listening and an intense form of attunement to your fellow players. Self-regulation is a key attribute of the controlled middle-class self to maintain appearances and acceptable ways of behaving. Susan continued:

> *By engaging with the kids but by being demanding and being tough as a teacher, I somehow think that that sinks into their minds. It comes out in their … ability to bring up their kids a certain way.*

Susan foresees the longevity in the inculcation of these dispositions in her students' behavioural development. She is not only teaching music but also fostering a particular type of person who is committed, resilient and works hard, just like she is as a mother and teacher. Through music, self-development and character improvement are creating a person of worth (Vincent & Maxwell, 2015) and nourishing the classed selves to carry on with determination—'good training' for life ahead (Stefansen & Aarseth, 2011). It is likely that Susan is selected as a music teacher for some children because of her demanding expectations and the emotional capital she fosters to positively shape classed relations (Skeggs, 2004). This created a juxtaposition with her social standing as a single mother in her local community where she was perceived as morally contemptuous according to the married stay-at-home mothers that predominated her community.

The labour in producing a demanding work ethic is recognised by Susan's daughter, Jessica. Jessica applauds Susan's work as a 'good' mother which is evidenced in her role in (re)creating children of value and in social reproduction:

> *I've got this thing, and it's from my mum, 'cause she was a bit tough and it's don't drop out at the point where it starts to get hard … and it definitely comes from music and I think from her teaching and just from her family … if you're working towards a goal and at some point, it starts to get difficult, because it's going to … you don't give up at that stage. Give up when you've plateaued … like with kids who are prepping for exams and they've chosen to do it and it all seems very nice at the beginning but at that bit where they have to practise every*

day, and it feels a bit tough and they're a bit tired ... that's the moment to keep pushing through you know, that's definitely part of my teaching and my approach to music ... and is very present in my kinda parenting as well.

Jessica transfers the broader teachings from her music education into her parenting, thereby ensuring she is perceived as a 'good' mother who has made the 'right' choices. Koops et al. (2017), in their study of a young mother, found that the mother "identified three principles from her piano lessons that she applied to other areas of her life: 'focus and attention, small and do-able, and quality over quantity'" (p. 209). Both young mothers have translated the skills developed in music education into their parenting, with perceived positive benefits to their families, and also for Jessica in her teaching.

Learning ethic, as a form of work ethic and development of the neoliberal subject, is part of the pursuit of continual self-improvement. According to Gerrard (2014), the responsibility for learning has shifted from provider to student, meaning "*to learn* demonstrates social participation ... [and] represents a performative demonstration of an effort to better oneself and one's social position" (p. 869, original emphasis). We are in a constant state of becoming with a moral imperative to continually seek to improve ourselves and our status, and accrue value, while separating ourselves from those who do not do this (Skeggs, 2004). Lifelong learning is a mandated activity and demonstrates not only middle-class struggles for moral worthiness and distinction (Skeggs, 2004) but also alignment with consumer capitalism that maintains a reliance on market capitalism for training and future education (Gerrard, 2014).

Studying a musical instrument connects to this learning ethic as many years of continuous hard work and practise are necessary to achieve mastery. When a level of mastery is acquired, practise, coaching and ongoing tuition are needed to maintain that proficiency, as Susan recalls,

The frustration is that the pieces that I really like to play are now too hard, so, you have to accept a lesser level ... Well, I just don't have time to practise. There's just not any time for anything. I am a realist—just a realist. So, I enjoy listening to playing. I'm quite happy playing soupy, easy to play stuff. I'm not a musical snob. As much as I love Beethoven, Shostakovich, Prelude 24 out of Book 2 and Fugue—that was probably the ultimate thing I loved playing, but I just can't play it anymore. So, I just accept and enjoy.

The logic of perpetual 'becoming' and never being quite good enough is pervasive in our current society, shared with a notion that success will always come to those who work hard (Gerrard, 2014). This remains true for adults, even in their later years, where these neoliberal tropes continue to pervade everyday lives. Susan has decided that she does not have time to practise, and as such has opted out of the need to compare herself to others—almost. Susan told a story of how she wanted to be part of a small group of friends who met to enjoy music together. She waited sometime before an invitation to join the group appeared from them:

I've got a friend up here actually, and she's always been a mover and a shaker— into all sorts of mischief … she's finally took me in into accompanying and playing here at her place with a whole lot of other people and it was just such fun because there was no pressure. Some performances were full of holes and people falling off keys and others were very confident, but they were all honest and fun and really intelligent wonderful people … so that's doable.

Susan continues with her 'self-improvement', her 'becoming'. She is constantly learning. In her interview, she mentioned that she had recently taken up the treble recorder as something to do. Learning music continues to be part of the process of her development of personhood and consolidation of her worthy self (Gerrard, 2014).

The dispositions learned through involvement with music are consistent with societal values that are considered worthy. Mothers utilised music as a means to teach their children skills such as perseverance, resilience and the value of hard work. To be good at something takes practise and time; however, pervasive neoliberal social themes remind us that this ongoing self-development is the responsibility of individuals to continually strive to do their best. This self-improvement is a lifelong pursuit as individuals are in a perpetual state of becoming and never quite complete. The advice of experts is needed to procure this improvement. Engagement in classical music is one space where these practices play out and where children develop these valued dispositions such as a positive work ethic. Mothers make choices about the values they wish to nurture in their children, and there is overwhelming pressure to get this right or face condemnation.

Facing Judgements to Make the 'Right' Choices

Pressure to make the 'right choices' is a constant task for mothers, as mothers are held accountable for the way their children turn out (Gillies, 2007; McRobbie, 2004; Skeggs, 2004).

McRobbie (2004) writes,

> Middle-class women have played a key role in the reproduction of class society, not just through their exemplary role as wives and mothers but also as standard-bearers for middle-class family values, for certain norms of citizenship and also for safeguarding the valuable cultural capital accruing to them and their families through access to education, refinement and other privileges. (p. 101)

This is a huge pressure to bear for middle-class mothers, where they are judged on the outcomes of their children and there is an overwhelming judgement from societal structures and from within middle-class motherhood itself. Middle-class mothers live with a constant eye for assessment of current trends, making value judgements and rationalising for what is right for them and their children and how these might be perceived and capitalised.

Mothers are judged by everyone, including themselves. There is no respite from the criticism, critique and scrutiny. It is this constant pressure to adhere to the demands to create worthy children and always maintain respectability that can become overwhelming. Sayer (2005a) writes:

> Actors use moral and other evaluative distinctions not only to draw boundaries between themselves and others but to discriminate among behaviours across and within class and other social divisions for they can hardly fail to notice that they can be well or badly treated members of any group, including their own. (p. 141)

I have already discussed some areas of interclass adjudication between middle-class musical mothers and their disapproval of intensive practice regimes in Chap. 5. Benhabib (1992) states "moral judgement is what we 'always already' exercise in virtue of being immersed in a network of human relationships that constitute our life together" (pp. 125–126). To judge is to be human. As relational and social beings, we crave acceptance and recognition for our work and decision-making (Sayer, 2005b). But there is always a binary judgement that pervades—good versus bad, positive versus negative.

We have seen evidence of judgement by others through some of the women's narratives around musical practise, Ashley's enrolment at the conservatorium, and Susan's inability to connect with other mothers in her community due to her status as a single, working mother. Mothers are 'sign-bearing, sign-wearing' (Bourdieu, 1984, p. 192), that is 'on show' displaying their abilities as mothers and moral citizens, facing intense calls for accountability. Mothering children is a 'self-conscious moral enterprise' (Hays, 1996, p. 32) and an indicator of mothers' desire to participate and comply with the rules of current society and make a valuable contribution (Skeggs, 2004). What is considered appropriate is culturally sanctioned, classed and gendered. Strong emotions including shame and guilt are often experienced concurrently with perceptions around sense of belonging and self-worth (Ignatow, 2009); these emotions are deeply entrenched in mothering practice. One way that mothers try to mitigate judgements from others is to carefully monitor and control their children's lives, so they are perceived as 'good' mothers. Engagement in music is a means to do this.

SURVEILLANCE AND CONTROL

The first social field that humans encounter is that of the family, and through these relationships, we begin to form understandings of interaction, others and behaviour. As we grow up, our interactions extend beyond the family, and we meet others who may possess different values, beliefs and ways of being than we are used to. These contribute to our developing identities and creating self. As humans, we tend to gravitate towards people that have similar interests and values, and those with similar cultural capital (Atkinson, 2016). These trends are enduring, even when children leave the family home, thereby maintaining society's classed divisions (Atkinson, 2016).

Research has shown that participation in music is one way that mothers maintain control over the friendships and social connections that their children make (Conkling, 2018). In my previous study, some mothers commented that one of the reasons they enrolled their children in extracurricular music groups was so their children would make 'like-minded' friends and their time would be spent playing music rather than being unoccupied, which they felt would lead to delinquent behaviour especially when they reached adolescence (Savage & Hall, 2017). Involvement in music, particularly the more classical streams, was a sign of good taste and class, and of academic endeavour. Music was seen to promote skills for the future (Ilari, 2016) and keep children off the streets (Lareau, 2003/2011).

There are various mechanisms of surveillance and control that mothers utilise to manage their children's behaviour through music. I recall my mother tried to restrict my childhood friendships by telling me who I could and could not play with at school. Managing children's social relationships is one way that mothers aim to maintain their status as 'good' and respectable mothers by ensuring their children are also 'good'. Mothers also monitor their children by being involved in their leisure activities, as we saw with Linda and her work at the orchestra her children belonged to, and through restricting their children's listening repertoires.

Restricting Music Repertoires

Children's consumption of music that is condoned by parents reveals parental values, beliefs and their views on childhood. Childhood can be viewed as preparation for adulthood or as a special time in its own right. Children are often symbolic markers of their mothers' choices and preferences, aligning with their position within social spaces (Atkinson, 2016). In the process of integrating their children within these spaces, mothers keep watch on the way their children perform. In children's earliest years, mothers have unique powers to influence children's music listening repertoires which are guided by their habitus and cultural attitudes as to what is deemed appropriate.

Lullabies and children's play-songs are often chosen for young children as age-appropriate repertoire (Cho & Ilari, 2021; Ilari, 2005). Migrant mothers often sing to their children in their first language to nurture connections to their ethnic identities (Ilari, 2005). Similarly, the mothers whom I interviewed also described how they curated their children's listening libraries. Kelele, a Tongan-Australian woman, stated how she is very careful in selecting music for her children to listen to. She is particularly mindful not to choose music with offensive lyrics, "*sometimes I play music, any ... sort of music that does not have those bad words in it, I not really like*". She did not want her children hearing these words and accidentally repeating them as it would potentially reflect badly on her. In another example, Sangeeta, the mother of Aarshia, tells how she would not allow Aarshia to listen to Hindi music when she was growing up. Growing up in India, Sangeeta explains, *"Hindi music is basically those romantic songs. I didn't want to expose them to that culture … I didn't want them to deviate from the path, like do study, enjoy music, play yourself, play games—but not do that—no!"* Sangeeta did not want her daughter distracted from her academic studies, and there was plenty of time for romantic love stories later. Mothers pass on their cultural values through music (Ilari et al., 2013), and these beliefs are deeply embedded in their care work (Gracio, 2016). Like Kelele, Sangeeta censored her children's music choices as part of her mothering.

These notions were also discussed by Penelope in her narrative. As children grow up and meet others outside the family domain, they are exposed to a 'wider typology of class relations' (Atkinson, 2016, p. 97) and begin to make their own judgements on what is appropriate or not. Penelope spoke about her own childhood experience, *"Lizzie and I used to play records—Alex Hood, 'Yellow dog dingo' (she sings) 'how old are you?' When children had age-appropriate songs … unlike now where they all twerk"*. As a teacher and mother, Penelope voices her concerns more broadly, about children's music:

> *I'll say—'what's your favourite song?' and I won't know any of the names of the songs … it's the latest tuneless piece of music. None of them say anything that's age-appropriate anymore. I find that very sad. I try to teach children's songs to children and that's the good thing about [the state] music program too, they teach a lot of traditional stuff and a lot of age-appropriate stuff within their music system, and I think, thank god they still do. I wonder when that's going to change, when some millennial gets up there and says we gotta make it more contemporary and they'll start twerking. I think that's terrible.*

Being 'age-appropriate' was a concern for Penelope and something she reiterated several times. She aims to provide her students with *"children's songs for children"*, composing the songs herself with input from the students:

> *We would write a song about what's in the curriculum at that particular time … I wrote all sorts of things, science, maths, anything you can think of … stuff for little kids about … we are taking turns, that sort of stuff that's important for socialising and everything.*

Here, the songs are considered 'good' because they teach children about things that integrate curriculum content and socially sanctioned behaviours that are deemed important for creating 'good' children. Penelope has revealed her values through her music work, aiming to preserve childhood innocence through cultural and moral gatekeeping, in a similar way to Kelele and Sangeeta.

Penelope continued the conversation to include her opinions about the internet and its lack of regulation. She comments that having people livestream music via various platforms from their bedrooms '*creeps her out*'. Parental vigilance surrounding internet and social media use is not unlike parental censorship of television viewing decades ago. Linda, Ashley, Penelope and Susan all made remarks about how television viewing was either banned or restricted when they or their children were young. Susan commented that her children were much more productive, academically and musically, when the distraction of television was gone. Television viewing is seen as a classed practice, where working-class families have the television constantly on with little discretion as to the programmes watched (Lareau, 2003/2011; Perrier, 2013). This unfettered television viewing is considered 'bad' parenting (Perrier, 2013). Ashley stated, "*I think my early childhood [was] all good memories, all family-oriented ... We had no television back then. We weren't allowed to go on the computer or anything like that*". Linda was providing the 'right choice' by encouraging active involvement in other activities and not the passive stimulation of television or the potential exposure to inappropriate content on the internet. Rather, like other middle-class mothers, time was spent engaged in musical pursuits (Lareau, 2003/2011).

Parental values can sometimes be assessed through children's listening repertoires. Linda's daughter, Ashley, mentioned at one point that she found it difficult to relate to peers at school—"*I didn't know the hip-hop*". This could be because Linda was protecting her from hip-hop's often misogynist and graphic sexual and violent themes, or that Linda herself was unaware of this music, or that she focused their listening on the classical repertoire which her children were playing on their instruments. Childhood can be seen as preparation for adult life, or as an innocent time where children need protecting from adult themes (Ilari, 2016). These notions can pervade mothering choices around music selection for children's consumption. Mothers' surveillance and control over listening repertoires is not the only area where musical mothers exercise their management of children to maintain middle-class respectability. Curation of their friendship groups so that children only socialise with those considered acceptable, with similar values and standards of behaviour, is also imperative. Home-schooling and engagement with music are ways that mothers can control their children's social relationships.

Control and Surveillance over Social Relationships

Linda's children all attended a private Christian school. Her four children were all bright academically and often won bursaries and scholarships which helped with the fees. Although Linda shared the school's philosophy and Christian values, she was disparaging about some of the students at the school who she saw as '*mucking around*' and not taking their studies seriously. Linda's moral judgement of other students suggests that she did not feel they were suitable peers for her children. This aligns with literature around mothers' decision-making regarding suitable schools and the students that attend these schools (Jamal Al-deen, 2018) and middle-class mothers' anxieties around finding suitable institutions for their children.

As a teenager, Linda's daughter Ashley recalls that she was having some issues socially at school. She felt ostracised because she was not like the other students, and she was never allowed to go to the cinema or out with friends on weekends because they had to practise or go to church. It was during this time that Linda decided to home-school her children, although Linda maintains that it was because they were having difficulty paying the school fees.

Linda had not had traditional schooling herself, attending an international boarding school with her siblings from a young age. Parents who have diverse schooling experiences are more likely to choose non-traditional options for their own children (Neuman & Guterman, 2019). Linda only got to see her parents in the long school holidays, and over her childhood and adolescence, Linda lived in several different countries, labelling herself a 'third culture kid' (Pollock & Van Reken, 2009). It would be understandable that Linda's boarding school experience and being isolated from her parents would manifest in wanting her own children to remain close.

According to Lois' (2012) book, *Home Is Where the School Is: The Logic of Homeschooling and the Emotional Labour of Motherhood*, Linda had all the attributes of the stereotypical home-schooling mother. She did not work in paid employment, rigidly managed her children's daily schedules with the goal of strengthening her relationships with her children and wanted to be perceived as a 'good' mother who relished the experience of being a mother. Home-schooling was the perfect vehicle for Linda—"*I loved it … They went back to school, and they were ahead of everybody. They read all the time—it was amazing—and practised*". This phrase is very telling. Linda's first response is that *she* loved it—not the children—but she loved being with her children all the time. It gave her purpose and control. And then, "*they were ahead of everybody else*" which reiterates that competitiveness she felt with other mothers (and the school), what a great job she felt she did (because mothers have to applaud themselves because rarely do others do this) and they '*practised*' (all that concerted cultivation would pay off eventually). Choosing to home-school the children for a few years, Linda tells how this escalated their musicianship, academic abilities and promoted their self-directed learning.

Interestingly, her children were not all home-schooled simultaneously, with the girls mainly being home-schooled. Girls are more likely to be cultivated than boys (Cheadle & Amato, 2011) with mothers being more concerned about their daughters' moral upbringing and school choices. This reflects traditional gender stereotypes regarding respectability (Jamal Al-deen, 2018) and aligns with Linda's conservative religious values. Linda's daughter, Ashley, stated that her brothers resisted their mother's insistence on music tuition in their later years, citing wanting to do team sports. There is some research which suggests that sons are less likely to listen to their mothers' opinions and conform to mothers' desires than daughters (Morgan et al., 2015).

Research suggests that parents choose to home-school their children for two main reasons: pedagogical decisions and ideological purposes (Nichols, 2005). Nichols (2005) writes that,

> The transmission of a distinct set of beliefs and values to children, close family relationships, controlled and positive peer social interactions, quality academics, alternative approaches to teaching and learning, and the safety of children and youth. (p. 28)

Jackson and Allan (2010) found that most parents choose to home-school their children because they are discontented with the current school system and environment where their children attend and have the perception that they can do a better job. Anecdotally I had heard that some parents chose to home-school their children so they could practise their instruments for hours each day in preparation for lives as potential professional musicians. The parents were often professional musicians themselves. Blog sites such as Violinist.com (2008a) cite examples of such practice as the comment by one online participant on this site shows:

> scheduling of orchestra, lessons, sessions with a pianist, and chamber rehearsals was much easier once we started homeschooling. There was a lot more time for practicing ... homeschooling gave Bobby time to spend one afternoon with his piano teacher, working on music theory, musicianship (with his violin), and piano lessons. We travelled a distance for violin lessons, and that was only possible with the flexibility homeschooling gave us.

There are numerous such examples. Literature suggests that home-schooling parents believe that educating their children at home will strengthen family relationships and children will be able to develop and practice their abilities (Hanna, 2012; Lois, 2017). The latter is certainly true for Linda and her family; however, Ashley shared a counter-narrative about this point:

> We wouldn't be the musicians we are today which is what I think is the reason why she did what she did, but it was very, very difficult like practise, school, practise, homework, every single day. Weekends we had to practise, we had orchestra, then we had sport in the afternoon, and then Sundays we had church. We'd play a bit at church too so from a very young age it was 7 days a week, it was quite intense ... we were very much, not controlled but in a structured kinda household ... I was very much in a bubble my whole life—in a rule book as well—just the parenting ways, which is fine. I respect that. Both mum and dad were brought up with very strict faith. Coming from that I can see now why I was brought up the way I was, and I'm gonna learn from that. And there's some positives from that, don't get me wrong, but there's some things I would definitely change to suit my children.

Ashley was reticent to say she had been controlled and stumbled on those words to say that her childhood was 'structured' instead. She struggled and did not wish to be critical of her mother, not wanting to appear disrespectful, but her apparent bitterness at the restrictions imposed on her was evident. She knew it was not how she was going to mother. Ashley has previously told of freedoms in her early childhood—"we were very much outdoor kids, you know, made cubby houses with cardboard boxes. Very simple life which I absolutely loved. Didn't have the coolest toys but we always had fun"—however, Ashley spoke of a lack of agency in her later years was challenging—"*when you're young and want to go out with your friends to the movies, we weren't able to do that [because] we had to practise*". Linda and Ashley's representations of these events are very different as perspectives and recollections often are between mother and child. Linda saw her actions as protective and loving while Ashley viewed them as too limiting at the time.

Linda's labour is demonstrated through her home-schooling, her volunteering at the orchestra her children belonged to, and her 'babysitting' of her son, every Saturday, as he was not yet a member of the orchestra. Linda used this term when she was talking about how she had to take her youngest child along as well, stating "*Who else is going to babysit him? [husband] was out doing, you know, studying or whatever*". Linda utilised this to her advantage as her son, after attending many weeks and waiting on the sidelines, was invited to play alongside the orchestra for something to do. Linda's husband, however, had free rein to do what he wanted—"*studying or whatever*" highlighting the genderedness of parenting in this family. Even when it was only the girls being home-schooled, Linda scheduled her time in the evening for the boys. Linda did most of the childrearing; however, she did acknowledge that she found her children's teenage years more difficult to cope with, leaving some of this work to her husband:

> *I was not good when they were teenagers. I'm alright when they're twenties now but teenagers, I left that to [husband]. [He] was better. (Laughs) I think I like the control. (Laughs). I think I like knowing exactly what I was going to do, you know.*

Through music, Linda could control her children via their rigorous schedule.

Significant costs and affordances arise when children are home-schooled. Home-schooling is growing in popularity in Western countries in recent times (Neuman & Guterman, 2019), and for many during the Covid-19 pandemic, it was a mandatory requirement. Mothers shouldered most of this added responsibility during the pandemic (Savage, 2021) in addition to added caring responsibilities and catching up with paid employment or study demands once children were in bed (Hand et al., 2020). This had notable impacts on mothers' mental health and wellbeing (Evans et al., 2020). The benefits of home-schooling are reported as having flexibility to accommodate children's individual needs and ways of learning and, as we have seen with Linda, additional time to practise instrumental skills. The costs are documented as being an added burden and acts to minimise leisure time for the parent facilitating the schooling, and for the children, a potential lack of socialisation (Neuman & Guterman, 2019). It is this latter point that was most strongly felt by Ashley who found returning to school challenging after her home-schooling period:

> *Home-schooling was really good in some ways but making friends when I came back, I found extremely difficult. It was very [hard] socially adjusting talking to people. I had really just talked to my mum and, and older people. I didn't know the cool things.*

While Ashley's dispositions as a classical musician, bright student and Christian are valued within the 'family-forged' community she is connected to (Atkinson, 2016, p. 99), appreciation of these does not always translate to the broader field where life experience and local knowledges are culturally sanctioned, particularly with others of her own age. Having an affiliation with her church group and orchestra friends, these 'networks of sociality' (Vincent & Maxwell, 2015, p. 9) do not always transfer to other domains despite Ashley's burgeoning levels of cultural capital in the field of classical music.

Notions about home-schooling as being socially isolating for students are purported to be outdated (Conejeros-Solar & Smith, 2021). However, Ashley does not ascribe to this view—"*I think we did miss out on a lot of the social and doing what we want to do*"—and states how she would like to have furthered her contact with peers rather than with the extensive contact with adults which concurs with research in this area (Allan & Jackson, 2010). Ashley described how her social contacts were mostly from the same small groups—"*I really had just talked to my mum … and older people*". 'Intergenerational closure' is when parents know the parents of their children's friends, and these often-homogenous groups replicate social norms such as the Christian community all bringing up their children with the same values (Glanville et al., 2008; Vincent & Maxwell, 2015). The limitation on Ashley's social contacts was keenly felt by her. Despite this, Linda's desire for her children to keep with children of families of similar values was actioned—the church groups, the home-schooling and her music friends—as a means of control over Ashley's friendships and social interactions.

When Control Is Lost

Control of children is arguably easier when they are younger; however, once Ashley was older and no longer educated at home, her perspectives were widened, and she was exposed to new things. Linda was no longer able to manage everything that was happening in Ashley's life, but there was always hope that Ashley had been inculcated with the 'right' ways of being and that her own choices would be based on the moral upbringing she had been exposed to. Ashley was continuing her studies in the field of music and that brought confidence to Linda.

Linda's ability to make the 'right choices' in her parenting was realised when Ashley was offered a position at a conservatorium of music. Most capital cities in Australia have such institutions which are usually affiliated with universities and offer degrees in varying aspects of music, from performance to composition, theory to conducting. Conservatoriums are considered the peak of musical respectability and prestige where places are highly sought after, and entrance is by audition. Students of conservatoriums are afforded the best teachers in their field, are provided with extensive performance opportunities and the chance to form influential connections with industry partners. Acceptance to this kind of institution is associated with symbolic capital that primes aspiring musicians for a career in the professional music industry.

Institutions such as conservatoriums typically encourage individuality for those wishing to be soloists, which is consistent with developing artists to find their point of difference and aligning with the neoliberal capitalist notion of developing the individualised self and choice-making (Gerrard, 2014; Skeggs, 2004). Many people struggle with the competitiveness of the conservatorium experience to 'maximise their position' (Maton, 2005, p. 689; Perkins, 2013). This acts in concert with the ability to play seamlessly as an ensemble, blending in a sea of respectable bodies (Bull, 2014). In a field where all are excellent at their craft, developing that extra something sets some above the rest and increases market appeal (Juuti & Littleton, 2010). An example of this is musician Nigel Kennedy whose appearance as a flamboyant punk rocker was positioned paradoxically with his skill as a virtuoso violinist. Yet, those who have looked at his pedigree would not be surprised as his mother was a piano teacher and his father a professional cellist with a leading orchestra in Europe. Kennedy's musical habitus and high levels of cultural capital almost guaranteed his celebrity position.

I recall when Linda began talking about how things started to go awry when Ashley went to the conservatorium. She was not able to clearly articulate what occurred during this time or I suspect she chose not to. Her narrative was spluttered with sounds that suggested I knew what she was meaning. No longer was Linda able to contain Ashley's contacts. Connections, meetings and influential conversations were often negotiated in the pub over a beer or two. Ashley was exposed to alcohol for the first time. People were diverse. Ashley talks about her first meeting with openly gay people—people she had been sheltered from her whole life and discussed this in a deficit way:

> *I didn't know really what I wanted to do except for music, and I applied for and auditioned for the conservatorium of music, and I got in which was kind of amazing and such a surprise and my mum was over the moon and so the next year I travelled back and forth doing my classes and performances. I was so anxious to make new friends. They are very different type of people in my mind. I came in there ... it was very open to different types of people and the way they wore their clothes, and they spoke, and I got influenced like ... I think that's the first time I'd kinda witnessed gay people and those types of different opinions and judgements ... It was quite a raw thing because I had never been in that world before, but I was very much wanting to fit in as much as I could.*

To use Bourdieu's analogy, Ashley felt like a 'fish-out-of-water' (Interestingly, this perception was also held by Susan when she attended the conservatorium in her youth—"*I was a little kiddie wearing my Indian dress and my brown sandals, so wondering what on earth I was doing at the conservatorium in the first place*" and also by Susan's daughter, Jessica—"*regional kids—you can't live at home, you're paying rent and I had to work ... it [the Con[1]] kinda belongs to people of resource*"). Pecen et al. (2018) articulate the challenges of students entering institutions like the conservatorium as being "marked by severe psychological challenges, disorders and trauma" (p. 1) and offer a range of strategies to meet the constant demands of training and competitiveness to be a professional musician. Despite Ashley's high levels of cultural capital reflected in her musical ability and knowledge of classical music, she felt dislocated from her peers and did not possess the social capital needed to feel comfortable in that space. Christina Scharff's (2017) work discusses the perspectives of

---

[1] The Con is a colloquial term for the conservatorium.

classical musicians from working-class backgrounds in music colleges, noting how accents and appearance separate those with a sense of belonging and those without. With exorbitant fees and scant chances of getting full-time employment in the field of music at the end of the degree, the conservatorium domain is perceived as being only for children of wealthy backgrounds, where parents pay for their children's lifestyles and classical music becomes an expensive 'hobby'—interestingly a term that both Scharff and Linda use.

Ashley had enjoyed playing the violin immensely; however, it was the constant demands to practise and compete, particularly exacerbated once she entered the conservatorium, that made her shun the violin.

I knew that my mum wanted me to keep studying and focus on the violin but that just wasn't my focus. I didn't want to practise any more—it wasn't my hobby. It was something I struggled every day to get up and do, and at the very last semester I remember thinking, is this for me? Maybe, maybe I shouldn't do this … I think another part of the reason … I didn't actually think I was good at anything else other than music. I'm not saying my mum said that to me in that way, but she did as well … my mum thought that this was the career for me, and this was it. And I really didn't have a plan B … so when I decided to leave the conservatorium, that was a very dark day for me because I didn't know what to do with my life because that was it and I had just failed.

Ashley's powerful admission illustrates how the tensions she experienced in trying to live up to her mother's expectations and trying to summon up the courage to continue despite knowing she no longer wanted to play the violin. Linda, like many middle-class parents, desires for their children to become good 'all-rounders'. Ashley was involved in sporting activities as well as music. The literature also tells us that many students with higher-than-average abilities in music are generally very capable academically (Holochwost et al., 2017). Ashley was torn between her own desires for freedom and her loyalty to her mother who had nurtured her musical development for years. The rawness of Ashley's narrative was heart-breaking. In some ways, it raises feelings of guilt within me for making my own daughter continue studying and playing the cello when she clearly wanted to stop towards the end of her formal schooling. The messiness of expectations, and pressure from the school and her teacher made the decision emotionally difficult for me. Like Linda, our emotional, temporal and financial investments in our daughters' musical educations meant more to us than perhaps it did to our daughters. Even though Linda had been excited by Ashley's acceptance into the conservatorium, she quickly realised that this was not 'right' for her:

> *I did feel like I pushed her into doing the Con, only because she was so good and that was all that I thought—something that she really loved doing but she really didn't. But that wasn't for her ... just wasn't. All the, I (pause), you know, the, some music students were a little (laughs) different (laughs).*

This was hard for Linda to say. Linda had to admit that narrowing down Ashley's choice to focus on music had perhaps narrowed her choices for other careers. Linda was about to say that music was all that she thought Ashley could do, and Ashley says this herself as shown earlier. Being a Christian woman, Linda also didn't want to deprecate the other students who were all musically talented, but who held differing values and were ostensibly unlike them. Linda reconciled her earlier decision:

> *You know everyone's got their gifting. We are all here to help each other and you have to find it and I think that's what mothering is. They're different. You know you can't treat each child the same ... but you're there to ... just make them ... give them choices, I think. To find out their identity, what they like. You can get it wrong. She's good at music, she must do music. If you're good at music, you don't have to do music. Yeah, that's what I found.*

The slippage in words from 'make them' to 'give them' demonstrates her complicity in this scenario. Linda then cited the example of her youngest daughter, who studied something other than music at university, even though she was equal in ability to Ashley on her instrument. She only played as a '*wonderful hobby*', and here Linda believes she got it 'right'.

Linda and Ashley's narratives made me consider how elite musicians and sportspeople, and their families, must feel when they have trained to such a high level, sacrificed so much socially, financially and emotionally, but fall short of making a successful career out of their ability. Research has shown that people who have elite status in their fields often experience depression after their career has ended, even if their decision was self-initiated (Chen & Wong, 2013). While many gifted musicians and sportspeople go on to other successful careers in aligned fields, many are resigned to living average lives after being seen as extraordinary which is often difficult (Ho et al., 2023). Young people, like Ashley, have been highly trained to become elite musicians, and as she articulated, believe that they are only capable of doing one thing. It is easy to see how they might struggle to cope when they decide or realise that this direction is not for them.

In a different example of losing control, Susan expedited her daughter Jessica's transition to the conservatorium to mediate issues that were occurring in Jessica's life. Jessica explained:

> *I was a bit drifty ... [where I lived] was a bit rough and ready ... troubled teenagers down there ... you know, lots of my friends had kids really young and dropped out of school ... there's a bit of culture down there of disestablishment ... so it probably came at a good time for me ... I was drifting around a bit and I found this one thing that I was really into ...*

Susan could see that Jessica was being negatively influenced by her peers, as Jessica now articulates herself. Having to move away from home and her social community to live close to the conservatorium, Jessica had to make new friends which was Susan's plan to get her away from those peers who were showing disaffection with schooling and life, more generally, and potentially influencing Jessica down a path she didn't want her to travel. Life at the conservatorium was something Susan was familiar and comfortable with, having had similar experiences in her own life. For Susan, control was regained.

Musical mothers feel under scrutiny from others to make the 'right' choices regarding their children's musical development and feel compelled to adhere to societal pressures to raise morally worthy citizens of the future. Involvement with music offers an opportunity to provide social interactions with like-minded peers. Mothers control their children through limiting their listening repertoires and tightly scheduling their lives. This is further exacerbated when children are home-schooled which further restricts their social relationships but offers affordances to practise their instruments to get ahead of the game. The control measures used also ensure mothers are seen as 'good' mothers, developing valued dispositions in their children which will have exchange value in the future. However, when children are free to make their own choices, disruption and tensions can occur when these choices do not align with mothers' expectations. This can engender complex feelings of guilt and disappointment in both mothers and their children. Musical mothering is emotional work. In the next chapter, I show the emotional work that mothers do as part of their musical mothering but also how music can become a resource for mothers to help mediate the pressures experienced as part of their role.

REFERENCES

Allan, S., & Jackson, G. (2010). The what, whys and wherefores of home education and its regulation in Australia. *International Journal of Law & Education, 15*(1), 55–77.

Atkinson, W. (2016). *Beyond Bourdieu.* Polity.

Benhabib, S. (1992). *Situating the self.* Polity.

Bourdieu, P. (1984). *Distinction: A social critique of the judgement of taste.* Routledge and Kegan Paul.

Bull, A. (2014). *The musical body: How gender and class are reproduced among young people playing classical music in England.* Unpublished doctoral thesis, Goldsmiths University.

Cheadle, J. E., & Amato, P. R. (2011). A quantitative assessment of Lareau's qualitative conclusions about class, race, and parenting. *Journal of Family Issues, 32*(5), 679–706. https://doi.org/10.1177/0192513X10386305

Chen, C. P., & Wong, J. (2013). Career counseling for gifted students. *Australian Journal of Career Development, 22*(3), 121–129. https://doi.org/10.1177/1038416213507909

Cho, E., & Ilari, B. S. (2021). Mothers as home DJs: Recorded music and young children's well-being during the COVID-18 pandemic. *Frontiers in Psychology, 12.* https://doi.org/10.3389/fpsyg.2021.637569

Conejeros-Solar, M. L., & Smith, S. R. (2021). Homeschooling gifted learners: An Australian experience. *Australasian Journal of Gifted Education, 30*(1), 23–48. https://doi.org/10.21505/AJGE.2021.0003

Conkling, S. W. (2018). Socialization in the family: Implications for music education. *Update, 36*(3), 29–37. https://doi.org/10.1177/8755123317732969

Evans, S., Mikocka-Walus, A., Klas, A., Olive, L., Sciberras, E., Karantzas, G., & Westrupp, E. M. (2020). From 'It has stopped our lives' to 'Spending more time together has strengthened bonds': The varied experiences of Australian families during COVID-19. *Frontiers in Psychology, 11,* 588667. https://doi.org/10.3389/fpsyg.2020.588667

Gerrard, J. (2014). All that is solid melts into work: Self-work, the 'learning ethic' and the work ethic. *The Sociological Review, 62,* 862–879. https://doi.org/10.1111/1467-954X.12208

Gillies, V. (2007). *Marginalised mothers: Exploring working-class experiences of parenting.* Routledge.

Glanville, J. L., Sikkink, D., & Hernández, E. I. (2008). Religious involvement and educational outcomes: The role of social capital and extracurricular participation. *The Sociological Quarterly, 49*(1), 105–137. https://doi.org/10.1111/j.1533-8525.2007.00108.x

Gracio, R. (2016). Daughters of rock and moms who rock: Rock music as a medium for family relationships in Portugal. *Revista Crítica de Ciências Sociais, 109*, 83–104. https://doi.org/10.4000/rccs.6229

Hand, K., Baxter, J., Carroll, M., & Budinski, M. (2020). *Families in Australia survey: Life during COVID-19 Report no. 1: Early findings.* Australian Institute of Family Studies.

Hanna, L. (2012). Homeschooling education: Longitudinal study of methods, materials, and curricula. *Education and Urban Society, 44*(5), 609–631. https://doi.org/10.1177/0013124511404886

Hays, S. (1996). *The cultural contradictions of motherhood.* Yale University Press.

Ho, C., Hu, W., & Griffin, B. (2023). Cultures of success: How elite students develop and realise aspirations to study medicine. *Australian Educational Researcher, 50*(4), 1127–1147. https://doi.org/10.1007/s13384-022-00548-x

Holochwost, S. J., Propper, C. B., Wolf, D. P., Willoughby, M. T., Fisher, K. R., Kolacz, J., Volpe, V. V., & Jaffee, S. R. (2017). Music education, academic achievement, and executive functions. *Psychology of Aesthetics, Creativity, and the Arts, 11*(2), 147–166. https://doi.org/10.1037/aca0000112

Ignatow, G. (2009). Why the sociology of morality needs Bourdieu's habitus. *Sociological Inquiry, 79*(1), 98–114. https://doi.org/10.1111/j.1475-682X.2008.00273.x

Ilari, B. (2005). On musical parenting of young children: Musical beliefs and behaviors of mothers and infants. *Early Child Development and Care, 175*(7–8), 647–660. https://doi.org/10.1080/0300443042000302573

Ilari, B. (2016). Middle-class musical childhoods: Autonomy, concerted cultivation, and consumer culture. In B. Ilari & S. Young (Eds.), *Children's home musical experiences: Across the world* (pp. 92–106). Indiana University Press.

Ilari, B., Hafteck-Chen, L., & Crawford, L. (2013). Singing and cultural understanding: A music education perspective. *International Journal of Music Education, 31*(2), 202–216. https://doi.org/10.1080/1461380 8.2011.553277

Jackson, G., & Allan, S. (2010). Fundamental elements in examining a child's right to education: A study of home education, research, and regulation in Australia. *International Electronic Journal of Elementary Education, 2*(3), 349–364.

Jamal Al-deen, T. (2018). Class, honour and reputation: Gendered school choice practices in a migrant community. *Australian Educational Researcher, 45*, 401–417. https://doi.org/10.1007/s13384-017-0255-6

Juuti, S., & Littleton, K. (2010). Musical identities in transition: Solo-piano students' accounts of entering the academy. *Psychology of Music, 38*(4), 481–497. https://doi.org/10.1177/0305735609351915

Koops, L. H., Kuebel, C., & Smith, S. S. A. (2017). Mama's turn: A mother's musical journey. *Research Studies in Music Education, 39*(2), 209–225. https://doi.org/10.1177/1321103X17711629

Lareau, A. (2003/2011). *Unequal childhoods: Class, race, and family life.* University of California Press.

Lois, J. (2012). *Home is where the school is: The logic of homeschooling and the emotional labor of mothering.* NYU Press.

Lois, J. (2017). Homeschooling motherhood. In M. Gaither (Ed.), *The Wiley handbook of home education* (1st ed., pp. 186–206). Wiley.

Maton, K. (2005). A question of autonomy: Bourdieu's field approach and higher education policy. *Journal of Education Policy, 20*(6), 687–704. https://doi.org/10.1080/02680930500238861

McRobbie, A. (2004). Notes on 'What not to wear' and post-feminist symbolic violence. In L. Adkins & B. Skeggs (Eds.), *Feminism after Bourdieu* (pp. 99–109). Blackwell.

Morgan, J. P., MacDonald, R. A. R., & Pitts, S. E. (2015). "Caught between a scream and a hug": Women's perspectives on music listening and interaction with teenagers in the family unit. *Psychology of Music, 43*(5), 611–626. https://doi.org/10.1177/0305735613517411

Neuman, A., & Guterman, O. (2019). How I started home schooling: Founding stories of mothers who home school their children. *Research Papers in Education, 34*(2), 192–207. https://doi.org/10.1080/02671522.2017.1420815

Nichols, J. (2005). Music education in homeschooling: A preliminary inquiry. *Bulletin of the Council for Research into Music Education, 166,* 27–42.

Pecen, E., Collins, D. J., & MacNamara, Á. (2018). "It's your problem. Deal with It." Performers' experiences of psychological challenges in music. *Frontiers in Psychology, 8,* 2374–2374. https://doi.org/10.3389/fpsyg.2017.02374

Perkins, R. (2013). Hierarchies and learning in the conservatoire: Exploring what students learn through the lens of Bourdieu. *Research Studies in Music Education, 35*(2), 197–212. https://doi.org/10.1177/1321103X13508060

Perrier, M. (2013). Middle-class mothers' moralities and concerted cultivation. *Sociology, 47*(4), 655–670. https://doi.org/10.1177/0038038512453789

Pollock, D. C., & Van Reken, R. E. (2009). *Third culture kids: Growing up among worlds.* Nicholas Brealy Publishing.

Sanghera, B. (2016). Charitable giving and lay morality: Understanding sympathy, moral evaluations and social positions. *The Sociological Review, 64,* 294–311. https://doi.org/10.1111/1467-954X.12332

Savage, S. (2015a). *Intensive mothering through music in early childhood education.* Unpublished Masters' Minor Thesis, Monash University.

Savage, S. (2015b). Understanding mothers' perspectives on early childhood music programmes. *Australian Journal of Music Education, 2,* 127–139.

Savage, S. (2021). The experience of mothers as university students and pre-service teachers during Covid-19: Recommendations for ongoing support. *Studies in Continuing Education, 45*(1), 71–85. https://doi.org/10.108 0/0158037X.2021.1994938

Savage, S., & Hall, C. (2017). Thinking about and beyond the cultural contradictions of motherhood through musical mothering. In M. J. Rose, L. Ross, & J. Hartmann (Eds.), *The music of motherhood* (pp. 32–50). Demeter Press.

Sayer, A. (2005a). *The moral significance of class.* Cambridge University Press.

Sayer, A. (2005b). Class, moral worth and recognition. *Sociology, 39*(5), 947–963. https://doi.org/10.1177/0038038505058376

Scharff, C. (2017). *Gender, subjectivity, and cultural work: The classical music profession* (1st ed.). Taylor & Francis Group.

Skeggs, B. (2004). *Class, self, culture.* Routledge.

Skeggs, B. (2011). Imagining personhood differently: Person value and autonomist working-class value practices. *The Sociological Review, 59*(3), 496–513. https://doi.org/10.1111/j.1467-954X.2011.02018.x

Stefansen, K., & Aarseth, H. (2011). Enriching intimacy: The role of the emotional in the 'resourcing' of middle-class children. *British Journal of Sociology of Education, 32*(3), 389–405. https://doi.org/10.1080/01425692.2011. 559340

Vincent, C., & Maxwell, C. (2015). Parenting priorities and pressures: Furthering understanding of 'concerted cultivation'. *Discourse: Studies in the Cultural Politics of Education, 37*(2), 269–281. https://doi.org/10.1080/0159630 6.2015.1014880

Violinist.com (2008a). https://www.violinist.com/discussion/archive/14196/

Weeks, K. (2011). *The problem with work: Feminist, Marxist, antiwork politics, and postwork imaginaries.* Duke University Press.

CHAPTER 7

The Emotional Labour of Musical Motherhood

INTRODUCTION

Middle-class mothers do emotional training work through engaging their children in music to develop valued dispositions. As I have discussed in earlier chapters, this work is labour-intensive and time-consuming, and is a drain on mothers' emotional resources. 'Emotional labour' is a term coined by Hochschild (1983) which refers to the work humans do in moderating their own behaviour and emotions, which in turn moderates the behaviour and emotions of others. For mothers, emotional labour includes caring for others, particularly within the family home environment and managing domestic duties. In addition, emotional labour concerns the management of feelings. Musical mothers may mediate anxieties around music performance and practise, assist children to cope with disappointment and frustration, help them when they must compete against their friends for competitive positions, and develop resilience and perseverance, while also keeping their own emotions in check. Zembylas (2007) also notes that emotional labour is the regulation and suppression of emotions to perform a specific way of being to others. According to Bourdieu (1998), "this work falls more particularly to women, who are responsible for maintaining relationships" (p. 68). Emotional labour is used and exchanged by others; however, emotional capital is "an asset that derives

© The Author(s), under exclusive license to Springer Nature Switzerland AG 2024
S. Savage, *Musical Mothering*, Palgrave Macmillan Studies in Family and Intimate Life,
https://doi.org/10.1007/978-3-031-65157-1_7

from personal abilities, connections and investments in and from the self" (Silva, 2007, p. 115). Emotional capital has a use and exchange value in some markets, such as the workplace, where soft skills are seen as crucial to many occupations.

The "commercialisation of human feeling" (Hochschild, 1983, p. 189), or soft skills, are sought after in work environments, particularly where employers connect social mobility to character. The development of 'soft skills' (hard work, self-control, self-direction and empathy) through formal and informal education makes clear the distinctions between successful (productive and socially mobile) and failing (unproductive) character traits (Gerrard, 2014, p. 870). In Chap. 6, I showed how Susan developed these soft skills with her children and her students—through being 'demanding'—and how this aligns with mothers' expectations for their children, and demonstrating how this work is commodified in this form of affective labour (Adkins, 2005). This emotional training becomes something that can be bought and exchanged as an economic capital or "work exchange value" (Adkins, 2005, p. 203). Having emotional competencies is increasingly more desirable in the workplace where they are seen as essential (Rivera, 2012). With the continued casualisation of the workforce, the rise of portfolio careers and the precarity of full-time ongoing positions, those who demonstrate socially valued dispositions and soft skills are privileged over those without such skills and are more likely to secure work (Castrillon, 2022). In this chapter, the case study of Jessica illustrates how flexibility and cosmopolitanism are advantageous in her working life as a professional musician but also brings together some of the themes already addressed separately in this book, that is, perspectives on control and agency in one's own life and in motherhood, the myth of work-life balance and the desire to be there for family. In addition, the emotional labour of musical motherhood and being a musician is explored. I reveal the tensions that can occur between parent, child and music teacher and how musical mothers navigate to seek the best outcomes for their children and themselves. However, even though involvement in music can be challenging and demanding, music can also be a welcome resource and a means to replenish oneself. For some mothers, these examples of nurturance through music have been passed down through generations.

NAVIGATING MUSICAL MOTHERHOOD AND MUSIC FOR THE SELF—THE CASE STUDY OF JESSICA

Jessica, Susan's daughter and mother of one, is a full-time professional musician. That said, being a full-time professional musician means that Jessica spends her time performing, rehearsing and also teaching. At the time of the interview, Jessica was also studying for a postgraduate degree. Her professional musician work was casual, and she said she prefers the autonomy of casual work, rather than being tied to a system:

> *I much prefer my hippie folk music learning, upbringing. My experience was very much driven by me and my own interests and I never felt like I needed to play music that I didn't want to play … I had complete control … I always had this sense that I could … make my own artistic choices.*

In describing the development of her musicianship, Jessica misrecognises the concerted cultivation that was very much a part of her development, perhaps just as she misrecognises the constraints that her casual work has on her life. She suggests that because her musical training was less rigid than those who may have taken a strictly classical path, it has enabled her to have self-direction and flexibility in her paid work, albeit with compromises regarding the stability of work and finances. Jessica has also done the 'hard yards' in the classical repertoire, and this has earned her an ongoing position in an elite orchestra. The hours of Jessica's work are variable and often antisocial—just as her mother experienced. The components of Jessica's work all fall within the after-school availability of her school-aged clients and the social lives of those she entertains. Jessica has what is known as a 'portfolio career', described as having diverse activities which can be a mixture of paid and unpaid labour, mainly encompassing freelance and part-time engagements, and very common amongst musicians (Bartleet et al., 2012, p. 35). So, while Jessica states she prefers a more flexible approach to work where she can maintain '*complete control*', her story as a working mother demonstrates that this is almost impossible to achieve. Jessica and her partner have established a routine where they share the care work, but this sometimes means they have little time with each other. Having working hours that are antisocial can negatively impact stress levels and strain partnerships.

Jessica showed some reticence in becoming a mother because of her unstable working life, particularly given the precarity of her casual work.

The interview with Jessica was prior to the Covid-19 pandemic, where musicians found themselves without work as concert halls shutdown and events were cancelled due to lockdowns. Again, this is another example of how 'complete control' is never possible. Returning to Jessica's unreliable working status, she commented:

> *To be a parent with absolutely no work stability whatsoever—and I still don't—I mean, who knows, if I hurt my hand, or if I piss somebody off, you don't know what's going to happen around the corner … money was part of it.*

Financial anxiety translated into Jessica feeling unprepared for motherhood—"*I wasn't quite ready mentally, or I don't know, I was just finding it a daunting idea*". However, when it did happen, she said, "*I didn't really fully appreciate that something could be the most wonderful thing and the most amount of hard work at the same time … (laughs)*". Jessica's partner, who is the birth mother of their child, previously financially supported the partnership as she worked in well-paid positions; however, she was now doing contract work,

> *We [Jessica and partner] were having a really nice time on less money actually, 'cause we've loved time as a family and were not so bothered if we're only earning 80 grand*[1]*—that's fine, we'll survive on that—keep everything simple and have a bit of time together. So that's sort of what we're working on at the moment, trying to engineer a situation where we're pretty stable in what we're earning, we know what's going to happen year to year.*

Although Jessica is enjoying this time now, she does not see it as a long-term prospect. Again, while she enjoys the flexibility and freedom that this new work arrangement has, it also has restrictions on what is possible. Eighty-thousand dollars could be considered a large amount for many people to live on. Her philosophical position does not reflect the challenges she mentions regarding her employment and parenting situation. Navigating the work-life tightrope to allow time to be together and time to earn money takes some 'engineering' for mothers. The emotional labour involved in managing and wrangling with these decisions, concertedly cultivating children's lives, and maintaining a reasonable income is often stressful and often comes at the cost of mothers' health and wellbeing.

---

[1] $83,000AUD represents the average annual wage in Australia in November, 2018. Retrieved from https://www.abs.gov.au/ausstats/abs@.nsf/mf/6302.0 on 14 March 2019.

Stress was mentioned a great deal by Jessica in her interview. The urgent need to have a reliable income was more apparent once her daughter had arrived, compromising the 'control' she wanted to have over her life and her decision-making. When I interviewed Jessica, she had secured a contract to play in the orchestra for a visiting musical theatre show at the city's arts centre. *"I'm enjoying it actually"*, she enthused, *"it's not killing me like I thought it would"*. This type of music is not Jessica's chosen genre, yet it is paid work. Here is another example of Jessica having to adjust what she would ideally like to do, to procure money for the family. Similarly, Jessica teaches at home to supplement her income:

I teach at home and so, [daughter and partner] often get home from work and childcare right at the end of that lesson, so I'll still be finishing off the lesson and they'll be coming through the door in our tiny flat. So, she [daughter] comes in and sits at my feet and watches …

This is a scenario that many music teachers will be familiar with. On the other side, as the mother of a child who had lessons at music teachers' homes, you often become familiar with the teacher's whole extended family. I explore this further in the next section of this chapter. There are challenges when teachers have small children, and I recall that part of the deal with one piano teacher was that I would look after her children while she taught my daughter. For Jessica, living in a small flat makes it tricky to have a dedicated space to teach. However, hiring space for teaching is costly, so teaching at home has financial affordances, even if it is inconvenient for other family members. Jessica's daughter sees this as a normal part of family life; learning music is what people do. Boyd (2002) explains the work/home dichotomy:

A mother at home may do some part-time work (and still define herself as a mother at home, ie: one who does not work…). Mothers who work are also mothers at home when they are not doing paid work and crucially, mothers do not cease to be mothers, or necessarily cease to do mothering work while "at work". (p. 465)

Jessica fulfils two roles by being there, that is, physically present for her daughter, and also teaching. She cannot appear to be attentionally 'there' for her daughter, as she is being paid to give her attention to her student. Like many other working mothers who bring their work home, there is an intense stress and emotional labour in juggling work and domestic responsibilities simultaneously (Rose, 2017). Being a musician mother teaching at home can be messy.

Stress was also mentioned when Jessica was talking about her work. The field of music is highly competitive and can be emotionally draining when having to perform at your best particularly in public view. Jessica tries very hard not to always speak about her work in a way that might connect her work in music with stress:

> *It's not the parenting itself, it's trying to make space for her and trying to provide for everybody, remain calm when I'm really stressed about work. Just trying to keep it chilled so I don't put all my worries in everybody in the household—that kinda stuff ... takes a lot of energy to rein it in ... She [daughter] sees me walking out the door with my face like freaking out if I've got a difficult concert, I do feel stressed... 'Mumma, where are you going? 'I've got to go and do a concert, but I'll be back in a minute'. And I think that has an impact on her perception of what music is.*

Jessica articulates the challenges of trying to meet the needs of all family members, including her own. For musician mothers, there is an added complexity where they must maintain their bodily aesthetics aligned with respectable middle-class motherhood, and a corporeal capacity primed for optimal musical performance. Jessica emphasises the exhaustive internal and embodied work of mediating the self to continue to present the musical body ripe for performance alongside the responsibilities and emotional work of mothering.

Musician's bodies are acutely sensitive and embody a bodily knowledge *par excellence*. Not dissimilar to elite athletes, professional musicians must maintain their bodies in peak form, mentally and physically (Williamon & Thompson, 2006). Musicians are primed to notice any small deviations within their body that may affect their performance. Complaints such as incorrect posture, muscle fatigue, poor fitness levels and having to transport heavy instruments and work extended hours are all experienced by professional musicians (Williamon & Thompson, 2006). Being in the public eye when they work, musicians must also demonstrate "skilled embodied labour in performance" (Pettinger, 2015, p. 283). What this means is that their bodily labour is interwoven with the whole aesthetic experience of the performance. That "body labour involves anticipation, understanding, awareness of self and others; it is sensory, aesthetic and affective as it engages with objects and human others" (Pettinger, 2015, p. 284). Pettinger's work describes the toll on bodies through sustained performance work. Through their live performances, musicians are often being viewed by the audience, and therefore, the emotion of the work is shown through their playing but also their body (Hofman, 2015). Hofman articulates this as "work intended to produce or modify people's emotional experiences" (p. 31), which is not unlike the work of mothers to appease family life by mediating emotions of others while regulating their own. In this way, the conceptualisation of musicians offered by Hofman is similar to my understanding of the emotional labour in mothering. The emotional work of the musician is visible, yet in our society, mothers' emotional work is rendered invisible (Gillies, 2006).

Jessica explains how relentless she finds mothering work, and yet she is still able to articulate how it has reshaped her in a positive way:

> *I'm much more resourceful and just ... [a] bit stronger in those moments of being frustrated and tired and you feel like you're at the end of your tether, but you need to keep it together because it's not about you, it's about someone else ... I think that's good.*

Becoming a mother has made her more focused and resourceful, more organised and less self-absorbed.

> *It's changed my focus, definitely not much more focused on myself, focused on family—much healthier for me. It's lovely and at the same time it's shrunk the amount of time that I have ... to work on my own things ... and when you don't have much time, you use it really well.*

Women who are artists sometimes comment that having constraints on their time limits their creativity, and this is true when they become mothers, although some state that having children has increased their creative spirits (Power, 2015). Jessica comments that there is pressure to use any free time productively which resonates with others in similar positions (Power, 2015; Rose, 2017). However, Jessica maintains that she uses this time well, and this is evidence of her emotional training passed down from her mother.

Travelling for work can also add to the tension in family relationships. Performing with local ensembles and teaching locally provide the most family-friendly work environments, whereas touring and working away offer the least appropriate work for family life (Teague & Smith, 2015):

*When I was overseas for five weeks last year ... [daughter] was still only three ...
it was great for me professionally and personally ... I really missed them, and it
had a huge impact on [my partner] at the time and on [my daughter] ... she
was really clingy a long time after that, and it really did affect us ... the nature
of my work sort of means that I miss out on lots of stuff.*

Here, the ramifications of working away are laid bare, citing the emotional toll it has on them all.

As a musical mother and professional musician, Jessica faces many competing demands as she works irregular and antisocial hours, juggling work to make money for the family and being present for her young daughter and her partner, while maintaining a positive sense of self. The dispositions Jessica has developed as part of her musical training have become strategies for coping with life and any challenges she may face, particularly the ongoing challenges of motherhood.

Mediating Tensions Within the Mother-Child-Music Teacher Relationship

The relationship between mother, child and music teacher can be one that is very close and lasts over many years. Music teachers and parents must work in partnership; parents play a significant role as supervisors of practise, transporters of lessons and providers of encouragement and support (Ang et al., 2021). The connections between stakeholders are "mutually and continually shape(d) (through) each other's roles through interaction"; however, these enduring connections are sometimes fraught with competing roles and expectations (Ang et al., 2021, p. 26). Musical mothers spend extensive time searching for suitable teachers who will fulfil their desires to create and maintain children's musical and non-musical development. As Jessica's narrative in the last section showed, the boundaries between home and work can become quite messy when teachers perform their work from and within the home environment.

As already discussed, the support of parents is often considered crucial for children's successful development through music tuition. Throughout this book, I have shown how this support is enacted through generations and where mothers and grandmothers support through encouragement of practice, find the best and most suitable teachers, pay for tuition, seek opportunities for performance and development, provide instruments and reorganise family schedules to meet the needs of their musical children.

The genesis, and I add, the ongoing effectiveness, of the relationships' productivity is directly related to the various roles that each stakeholder plays.

As shown through Susan's narrative, some mothers look for teachers who share similar values, such as being 'demanding', thereby ensuring consistency and a united front. Mothers choose teachers they can afford and ensure that schedules can be met. Expectations of children's musical futures are often discussed, so that teacher and parent can work towards similar goals. However, tensions can occur when the parameters of the relationship change, and mothers need to carefully manage these challenges sensitively to maintain the relationships of those involved. These parameters include when a change of teacher is desired for whatever reason; when the music teacher relies on the income generated by the children's lessons; when the teacher relies on the mother to ensure practise and commitment; and when there is over-familiarity within the relationship.

One of the predominant reasons for tensions within relationships is when mothers decide that a change of teacher is needed, and they no longer wish their child to learn from their current tutor. Sometimes, these conversations are initiated by the existing teacher who feels they have given the student all they can, and it is time to move to a more experienced teacher once the student has reached a particular level. This can occur when children are taught by older students. More often, however, these conversations are initiated by mothers. Tensions occur when younger or more inexperienced teachers lose more competent students to teachers with greater experience and expertise. Musician teachers may rely on their students' abilities as a form of advertising to acquire new students.

Numerous blog sites are available on the internet that are set up by music teachers and act like a community of practice (pianostreet.com; violinist.com as examples). These sites invite music teachers' comments on a range of topics, including when parents wish to change teachers. Music teachers can express surprise and incredulity when their impression was that the student was doing well and achieving high standards. For example:

A colleague of mine lost a student recently—an 11-year-old boy who has done exceptionally well with her since he started taking lessons 4 years ago. He works very hard, enjoys his lessons, has won several competitions etc … "we are changing to a teacher who will motivate and pressure him to work harder" … I just want to understand … what is it these parents want? … My friend hasn't heard this reason before and hasn't been teaching as long as I have and she's really upset, feels betrayed. She puts her all into this kid. (Lou, pianostreet.com, 2010)

Another example for changing teachers is illustrated in the following post,

I had a … very talented student. She was playing advanced Beethoven Sonatas within a year's time of beginning lessons. It was amazing. Her mother wanted her to test as well… Her mother was in medicine (naturally she knew nothing about music) wanted her daughter to do MORE. I did what I thought best, put her in several appropriate events. They dropped me because the mother's partner recommended a concert pianist for the teacher. I was so upset at the time … (mrsmusic, pianostreet.com, 2010)

Mothers choose teachers based on a range of factors—status, experience, affordability, location, accessibility and popularity. Music teachers will go in and out of favour with parents due to the teacher's own successes or that of their students. There is an expectation that teachers are competent teachers, knowing how to teach effectively, as well as being proficient on their instruments (Ballantyne et al., 2012). In the example above, the music teacher believes they are competent; however, the parent believes the student could be achieving more. The teacher is disparaging about the mother who they assume knows nothing about music, although this may not be the case. There appears to be a lack of mutual respect in this instance.

Other music-related blog sites mentioned that students may wish to discontinue musical tuition, so the mothers communicate to the teacher an excuse so that lessons cease. Reasons on Violinist.com (2008) include "our personalities clash" (Tasha), "Don't like the teacher's style" (Jodi B), wanting to play a different type of music (Anne) and moving further away. Ang et al. (2021) state that expectations between parents and teachers may align or be in tension, and often these need to be dynamically negotiated. It is mothers who predominantly must navigate this tricky emotional work. Studies have shown that teachers, like parents, have a huge influence on student motivation, capacity and confidence (Pitts, 2012) and can influence whether music is continued over the lifespan (Ang et al., 2021).

Blog sites can also be populated by mothers to give advice on "reasons to look for a new music teacher" which include inappropriate behaviours, unprofessionalism such as being late or distracted in lessons, having too far to travel, personality clashes, different teaching styles, and "your student has progressed to the limit of the teacher's abilities" (amusicmom.com, 2023). Such sites also offer advice on how to 'break up' with the music teacher. This is emotionally challenging work, particularly as many mother-child-teacher relationships have endured for many years, and over that time, friendships and strong connections have been established.

When teachers conduct music lessons in their home environment, the teaching domain becomes a messy space because the parent and/or student gets to see and be immersed in their teacher's home—arguably a private space—and where mothers and students can get to meet other members of the teacher's family, thereby disrupting the professionalism and privacy of the teacher and blurring of their professional boundaries. Parents and students may get to see how their teacher manages their own children or might make judgements about how they maintain their homes. These can influence how the teacher is perceived and yet may not be related to their ability to teach their instrument. As mentioned in Jessica's case, her daughter would sit at her feet and listen while she was still teaching after her partner brought their child home from kindergarten. I remember with my daughters' instrumental teachers, that our families got to know each other well. The fact that I was also a music teacher and either performed with them as a musical peer, or their children came to my classes, potentially put additional expectations on the relationship. This increased familiarity made it more difficult to cease lessons or change teachers because there was more to risk than just losing a music teacher.

With similar issues of tensions between school expectations and my children's, my own story of when my eldest daughter was in her last years of high school continues to plague my mind many years later. By the time my eldest daughter was in secondary school, she belonged to several different ensembles. This meant a great deal of organising of family routines to accommodate lessons in two instruments, rehearsals and concerts for five different ensembles, and fit in practise. Towards the end of my eldest daughter's schooling, the pressure of playing and singing in several ensembles plus the high expectations on academic excellence from the school became such that my daughter wanted to give up playing the cello. There was a school requirement that to play in the highest-level ensembles, students must be having private lessons, so she continued to play under strain, and we continued paying the tuition fees. She had also sustained a shoulder injury from carrying a heavy cello and a school bag full of books. My daughter received a half-scholarship for tuition fees at the school which certainly helped mitigate the exorbitant fees, particularly with two daughters attending the same school. The school wanted her to play because she was competent and reliable. I felt pressured to make her play, yet she was ambivalent about her involvement. At the end of her final year of high school, her cello went in its case and has only been taken out of its case once in twelve years. Several years later, I wonder what all the stress was for.

As a musical mother, I still feel guilty about my role in insisting my daughter continue to play the cello when she clearly did not wish to. I did not put such constraints on my younger daughter, who pursued music in a more leisurely way, and went on to do a music degree. I felt pressured to make my eldest daughter continue from both her music teacher and the school. The school used the musical ensembles as advertising for the school. As a devoted parent of the school at that time, and because I was on the music support committee, I felt obliged to engage and committed to these activities. This was additionally challenging because we lived a long way from the school, and I had to navigate this between work commitments, but also because the music staff at the school had become my friends, and I didn't want to let them down. Again, this blurring of roles made any decisions more difficult.

Similarly, the expectation to continue with private music lessons for all ensemble members was challenging from both an emotional and a financial perspective. Knowing that the music teacher was relying on the money from tuition for their existence, a moral dilemma developed when we wanted to cease lessons, and yet, we were also struggling financially. Due to the longevity of the relationship and the friendships developed, boundaries were crossed, and again, making decisions around finances was burdensome.

Through knowing students over long periods of time, teachers may be seen as role models (Ang et al., 2021). They might have been through some difficult times with the student, for example through adolescence, all adding to the complexity of the relationship and the smudging of the roles between teacher as professional to that of one of friendship. Such relationships may have enjoyed added privileges such as the teacher giving the student extra time and being flexible with lesson times, and on the other side, the teacher may have appreciated parents who encouraged practise, spruiked the teacher's ability to gain new clients, paid their fees on time, and who generally supported the student in achieving success.

I have also been on the other side of the parent-teacher tensions when I taught early years music classes. In my role as a music teacher of young children, I found that many of the mothers who attended the early years music classes with their children became so invested in the classes that they found it hard to leave. The children could only attend until they reached school age. Mothers would often cry in the last session as they said good-bye, because they would miss the friendship and ritual of the group while their child was undeterred, looking forward to their next adventure. Deep social connections were formed during these classes, with mothers sharing their parenting trials and other life experiences while participating in the music sessions (Savage, 2015a).

Although I am reticent about my mothering decisions taken at the time of my daughters' schooling, I am still pleased that I gave them the opportunity to have the gift of music. Even though my daughter no longer plays the cello, the instrument purchased by her late maternal great-grandfather remains in its case; when both my daughters are at home, they will take out their old piano music and tinkle. Their playing evokes pleasant memories; the words my daughters used to describe this experience include 'happiness', 'calm' and sometimes, 'challenge'. The fact that they still want to play fills me with joy.

I have shown another side to the emotional labour involved in musical motherhood through navigating the sometimes-tricky relationship with music teachers and revealed the complexity within such connections particularly when families have been with the same teacher for extended periods, or the relationship becomes more familiar. Having lessons within the home of the music teacher can additionally blur these boundaries, with mothers doing their best for their children but also themselves.

NURTURING THE SELF THROUGH MUSIC

Being a mother is emotionally challenging and draining work; however, music can provide mothers with an emotional resource. Jessica, Susan's daughter, demonstrates how she has utilised the emotional capital drawn from her experience of being mothered through music to strengthen her own family connection (Allatt, 1993; Gillies, 2006; Reay, 2004). Jessica's emotional capital, manifested as embodied resilience in the instance below, has been created from her mother's 'demanding' work ethic as part of Jessica's habitus (Reay, 2015). Mothers' bodies act as receptacles for capital accumulation for their families and themselves (Lovell, 2000). The dispositions learnt through Jessica's musical training are interwoven in her mothering and assist her to cope with everyday challenges:

We've [Jessica and partner] kind of been having little general conversations about our values and education and thinking what's important to us, and my thing is very much that that little bit of resilience in moments of difficulty, 'cause I think if you have that, if you're patient with yourself and you're kind to yourself when you're learning, you're gonna get through most difficult situations if you just accept that little moment of difficulty. Take a deep breath, you know, don't freak out, and be a bit soft on yourself and think about what the steps might be, break the steps down, try to work through it, just give it your best shot, be easy about it. I feel like those kind of internal skills are the most important thing for me.

If mothers' emotional resources are diminished, then they are less likely to be able to nourish their children emotionally. Middle-class mothers are more likely to be able to build emotional capital to strengthen family connection due to their financial security but also the social and contextual contexts in which they find themselves (Reay, 2004). It is these circumstances that dictate the efficacy of mothers' work in translating emotional capital to their children, as Illouz (1997) comments:

The ability to distance oneself from one's immediate emotional experience is the prerogative of those who have readily available a range of emotional options, who are not overwhelmed by emotional necessity and intensity and can approach their own self and emotions with the same detached mode that comes from accumulated emotional competence. (p. 56)

Returning to Bourdieu's notion of playing the game, middle-class mothers have the emotional capital to be able to tinker in fields where they may not be successful because they have other options; their eggs are rarely in one basket. They may facilitate children's desires to learn a skill, participate in an activity, and so forth, knowing that the outcome does not necessarily matter and that their lives will go on comfortably because they have the requisite economic and social capitals for this to happen (Reay, 2004). Children will find their groove in time. Mothers may encourage perseverance and resilience in their children and mitigate disappointments and failures, bolstering character building through a sense of entitlement but also through "visible … patient or prickly assistance with homework and discussion of behaviour" (p. 60). Atkinson (2016) states that a particular emotional style serves as another resource that can be passed from parent (specifically mother) to child via involvement in the latter's schooling to ensure educational success—it too therefore generates a 'profit' in so far as it is converted into cultural capital. (p. 60)

Atkinson further discusses how it is mothers' encouragement, support and high expectations that can generate positive outcomes for children, although Reay (2004) states that this can also mean emotional losses where wellbeing is compromised for educational success. Atkinson (2016) finds the term 'emotional capital' problematic, citing Gillies (2006), because it is closely aligned with schooling, whereas 'emotional investment' more broadly relates to all parental support in regard to children's wellbeing and development. Gillies (2006) notes that working-class mothers are more concerned with protecting their children from exploitation at school rather than academic success. In either classed scenario, mothers' work to mediate such circumstances requires substantial emotional labour to enact. In a Bourdieusian sense, this emotional work is seen as a form of struggle in the family field. However, rather than consider this in terms of emotional 'investment', Atkinson (2016) suggests this work needs to be understood as a struggle for love alongside the classed expectations that mothers have for their children and "all the emotional fallout that brings when aspirations go unfulfilled" (p. 60). Reay (1998) articulates how difficult it is for mothers whose experiences have been challenging, at school for example, to generate sympathetic encouragement for their children's schooling. However, in contrast, middle-class habitus provides an assuredness that their children will be successful; middle-class mothers envisage the long-term gain rather than any short-term discomforts (Reay, 2004). In the case of Jessica and Susan, we have seen the challenges they have both faced over time and the emotional training that Susan provided through music that has armed Jessica with an emotional resource to draw upon in her work and her mothering.

In another example of how music has become a resource for the self, Kelele, an Australian-Tongan woman whose mother passed away when she was a teenager, explains how music offered her peace and was a means to remember her mother and connect with family. Kelele was very close to her mother, and in her childhood years, Kelele would spend time weaving and cooking alongside her mother in their small island home off the mainland of Tonga. Kelele's parents had traditional roles where her father, considered the 'king' of his small island home, provided the food for the family, while her mother maintained the home. They were devout Christians and regularly attended church on Sundays. Kelele's mother made special grass skirts for her daughters to wear, expressing pride in how beautiful they looked. Church also provided Kelele with her early rich musical experiences.

Kelele moved to her aunt's house on a larger island to attend high school. It was during this time that her mother suddenly passed away:

> *When my mum passed away, my eldest sister didn't go to school after that. So, she stayed home washing our clothes, iron the clothes … In the morning, I'm the one that knows how to braid the hair … then after have to braid my own hair, walk them (siblings) to school. That's my life as a teenager, it was like a mother.*

Kelele maintains that she was the only sibling who knew how to braid hair, so that became her job. Life for Kelele changed dramatically after her mother's death, and the children moved to the mainland without their father, to finish their schooling. Kelele said she assumed the 'mother' role—the caring responsibilities for her siblings and the organisation of her sister to do the domestic chores. After Kelele finished her basic schooling, she got employment in the hospitality industry, not only providing for her family financially but emotionally. She later became pregnant to her Tongan boyfriend, from whom she had recently separated. Although he refused to support her or her unborn child, it was Kelele who was demonised by her community. However, she found peace through the songs her grandmother shared with her when she was a child:

> *My grandmother …*
> *she loved singing. …*
> *I grew up see her singing …*
> *it just like a Tongan word, but it was like putting it into a tone …*
> *when you translate it into English it sounds funny*
> *but in Tongan, it sounds good*
> *and if I translate it into English*
> *it sounds like sleep, sleep.*
> *When I see my grandma singing …*
> *she made up the words into it while she was moving together,*
> *like singing, holding …*
> *I have to put my kids in the pram or little rocking bed*

and sing from there,
but my grandma used to like,
and my mum,
I see her do it to my siblings and she had to rock them,
singing and rocking,
like that until they fall asleep
then put them in the bed.
I used to do that to my kids when they were really unsettled.
I would have their face close to my face
and sing slow-mo and they go slowly to sleep.
They're really calm, and they go to sleep.

This deeply personal account that Kelele shares describes the closeness of the bond between mother and child. She tells of the tender swaying of bodies to the beat of the song and the drone-like sounds that instil a sense of calm and peace. This song as a way of regulating tired and fractious bodies has been passed down through generations, and every time Kelele repeats these actions, she is transported back to her own childhood and the swaddle embrace of her mother. The practice of everyday singing has become a family tradition, created from memories. In many families, music forms the basis of memories and family rituals, requiring ongoing emotional commitment to maintain (Smit, 2011). This is often the work of mothers.

These precious moments are so much more than a simple song that has traversed the generations. It is a technique Kelele enacts for soothing her children, creating a durable bond of physical and emotional closeness, as a way of being (Fancourt & Perkins, 2017), of interpersonal synchrony and nurturing the self. Unspoken yet keenly felt, this cultural transference is deeper than class or economic considerations; it is about being human. It is habitus in action as embodied history where ways of being from the past are also integral to the present. So much of this work occurs in women's domestic spaces. Mackinlay (2009) argues "[s]inging to children is 'naturally' embedded in the social role of women as mothers and therefore has been afforded little importance within the higher order of 'culture'" (p. 724). Lullabies, as such, are rarely represented within the elite classical music field, the genre of legitimated music, adhering to the patriarchal tropes of classical music where women have not enjoyed the same musical credibility (Mackinlay, 2009). The importance of lullabies for children's early socialisation and musical beginnings cannot be dismissed (see Dissanayake, 2012, for work in this area). Importantly, the singing of lullabies can relieve the symptoms of anxiety and post-natal depression, improving mothers' subjective "wellbeing, self-esteem and perceived mother-infant bond" (Fancourt & Perkins, 2017, p. 151). Mackinlay and Baker (2005) agree, stating "by engaging in the singing of these songs mothers are, in effect, singing about their own feelings, and the very act of doing so allows them to release and let go of pent-up emotions" (p. 71). This aligns with Kelele's story—the emotional labour she expends calming her child also soothes her, and positions her as a 'good', nurturing mother.

While the benefits of singing and engagement in music for mothers are made clear, it is not always so straightforward. Penelope tells a story of how she wanted more children. "*I always wanted to be a mother*", she claimed, "*I just thought I'd have more children*". Penelope, consistent with her peers and my own background, was of a generation where many women were having their first babies in their mid to late thirties and early forties. There was an outward admission that mothering was challenging. Penelope commented on '*the constancy*' and the '*difficulty*', although she felt like she may have had more of an idea than some of her peers because she was a teacher. She says she "*did all the singing to bubby and playing music … not a lot, not overly, but sometimes, when she was in the tum*". Initially confident to go out with her new baby after the birth, Penelope developed post-natal depression when her baby was about ten months old, "*I distanced myself from everyone … that's when I got that depression so there weren't many opportunities to be out. Like two opposites*". I asked if music played a role in her life at that time and she replied, "*that's interesting (sigh)… I don't think I played as much music for her during that period of time*". I pursued this line of questioning to ask if she played any music for herself, and she responded,

I'll say not. This is interesting though. I did get to an age where instead of putting music on—and this is very odd—I wouldn't put any music on. I would prefer silence. That happened after, when I was about 28 and came back from Singapore teaching and whereas I would always have put on heaps of music on loudly, I didn't do it anymore. I didn't mean I didn't love music. I just loved being quiet instead and I've been like that ever since. Sometimes my husband will put music on and I'll say 'turn it down or turn it off'.

As typical in people with depression, activities that may have been enjoyable are no longer so.[2] Penelope withdrew from music. As she points out, it didn't mean she no longer liked music. I can empathise with her position as a lover of music but one who does not always like music 'on'. Unlike my children, I cannot study or work with music playing as I find it distracting. Perhaps it is because it is too important to be in the background. Or perhaps it is because there is often a soundtrack already playing in my head. Or perhaps, as De Nora (2000) might advocate, the music playing might not align with my current mood.

Penelope had high standards for herself as a performer of music. She had developed confidence as a performer slowly over time. She recalled her school experience, where clearly, she was an accomplished player but lacked the self-confidence to play in front of others, *"One year I got to go in the firsts, first violins … but I was too nervous, and I asked if I could be put back in the seconds … I couldn't cope"*. This trend continued in her early band-playing days, *"I was terribly shy, played at the back, didn't want to plug in … just quietly went der der der der … but I was also so afraid of performing, I would always stay at the back"*. This lack of confidence transferred to her teaching early in her career, *"I was too nervous to get in front of a class"*. Penelope enjoyed the social engagement of playing with a group and being with others to engage in music; however, it was the performative aspect she found confronting. Penelope has worked through this anxiety now and is happy to play in bands up front and is confident in her teaching; however, the positive benefits for wellbeing through engagement with music cannot always be drawn upon in all circumstances for all people.

Fancourt and Perkins (2017) posit that social engagement through music supports mothers' wellbeing. My previous study into the reasons why mothers enrol in early childhood music classes for their children concurs with their research findings, showing that one of the key reasons was to *be* with like-minded others, and to observe and share parenting tips (Savage, 2015b). Motherhood, in its very substance, is an interactive social relationship between two humans—mother and child—and yet many mothers cite times of loneliness and social isolation as part of this experience.

---

[2] According to the American Psychiatric Association (APA), depression can manifest this way. This information is based on the APA (2013) *Diagnostic and Statistical Manual of Mental Disorders (DSM-5)*, Fifth edition. See https://www.psychiatry.org/pateints-families/depression/what-is-depression.

While Penelope also highlighted the demanding nature of motherwork and how it can deplete mothers' emotional reserves, Sangeeta paints an alternate picture of personal growth and learning from her life as a supervised single woman to new opportunities as a married woman, albeit still limited. Sangeeta, Aarshia's mother, states, "*if you have music in your life, you will never be lonely*". She speaks from experience. As a young married mother, Sangeeta brought up her two children almost single-handedly as her family travelled around due to her husband's work. Her husband was away for months at sea. The family often moved to areas that were unfamiliar and sometimes hostile to Sangeeta, away from the support of extended family and friends. Sangeeta tells of her unplanned and '*tough*' first pregnancy, positively reflecting on what may have been a challenging time,

> *I was all alone. It was fine ... fine! (laughs). That was how you learn, and you grow up. Before your marriage, nothing—I wasn't even allowed to cross the road alone. I never travelled in a bus, and so when you are left—go ahead—so that was a big challenge.*

Throughout Sangeeta's narrative, she positions herself as a 'good' mother. Motherhood afforded her unrivalled satisfaction, and this was enhanced through her engagement with music. Contrary to common beliefs about her culture and its preference for male children, Sangeeta commented,

> *[Having a] daughter means you get the feeling that you're complete ... The feeling what I got ... so thrilled after having her ... Then singing lots of nursery rhymes to her ... singing all the time ... I used to play rhymes for her, sing with her, dance with her. I never left her alone, slept with her. When I am cooking, I used to make her sit next to me on the slab, see what I was doing. I used to keep talking to her, continuous talking, because it's the only way—for me also, to entertaining her because we don't have such paths as what you have here to go out and play. In those days it was not safe also—husband being in the defence services—it was not safe for me to go out.*

Sharing music with Aarshia became a way to amuse Sangeeta in the long days at home, to stave off loneliness, with her admission that her '*continuous talking*' was '*for me also*'. The constancy of the emotional labour in motherhood is illustrated as Sangeeta moderates her daughter's emotional wellbeing and her own. Sangeeta was also engaged in cultural training, and by sitting her child on the slab as she cooked, her daughter would learn vicariously the ways of domestic life.

New mothers often use music with their children to resource themselves, as Sangeeta has (Savage, 2015; Savage & Hall, 2017). Music mediates emotions as part of a 'care of the self' (De Nora, 1999, p. 37). Aarshia, Sangeeta's daughter, reflected how when she feels low, she will put on music that matches her frame of mind. "*I like music from the upbeat, and its mood. If I'm sad, I'll listen to the saddest, lowest, crankiest songs*" enabling the music as a "medium to work through moods" (De Nora, 1999, p. 40). De Nora (1999) labels this 'aesthetic reflexivity' (p. 36) where there is a deliberate acknowledgement of one's own feelings while using music to deepen that feeling.

Similarly, Ashley, Linda's daughter, puts on classical music each morning to set the mood for her family for the day,

> He [son] loves music, loves classical music, always have classical music in the car. It's a big part, guitar music and anything like that, acoustic … always have it in the mornings, instead of television, we have music … that's just the way I like to wake up in the mornings and he's always woken up in a good mood.

De Nora (1999) explains this as "self-conscious articulation work, thinking ahead about the music that will 'work' for the purpose at hand … made on the basis of what respondents perceive the music to afford" (p. 38). Cho and Ilari's (2021) study substantiates this sentiment with 81% of their participants reporting that music helped their young children maintain or improve a positive mood. Ashley makes a concerted effort to put on calming music that will engender a sense of peace. This may have been something that Ashley learnt from her mother, Linda. Although Linda did not comment much about how music made her feel, she did say, "*if you have nice music on it does affect you. And it calms everything down, especially when you have young kids, or even older kids*". Linda hints throughout her story how much labour she expended in her motherhood with 'nice' music to achieve desired states.

Mothers create emotional reserves in their children through their emotional capital which include love, attention, care and time (Allatt, 1993). But unlike other capitals, emotional capital does not have the same exchange value (Jamal Al-deen & Windle, 2017). Reay (2004) argues that building stocks of emotional capital may deplete existing emotional well-being due to diminished self-esteem and increased levels of anxiety in mother and child.

The vast amount of thinking work and navigating and mediating emotions that mothers do as part of their musical mothering is described as emotional labour. This maternal work intersects with broader cultural and social expectations and demands on the one hand and family desires on the other hand. This impacts mothers' wellbeing and self-identity and is exacerbated by involvement in music, which can be time-consuming, and emotionally draining. From encouragement to practise, maintenance of motivation and constant support, all the while moderating mothers' own emotions, feelings and reactions to keep a stable equilibrium in the family home.

When mothers struggle to cope with these expectations, some will draw upon music for support. Some mothers who are involved in music may still experience judgement and demands from their peers, which increases the pressure they feel on themselves. This sometimes-overwhelming pressure to appear 'good' or maintain appearances to be in control or manage their emotions can take a considerable toll on mothers. Conversely, mothers can take solace in music through intimate emotional interactions with their children. Musical connections are meaningful, joyful and loving. Music affords the women a soundtrack of their lives to nurture themselves, their moods, attitudes and relationships. Family musical interactions become family rituals and routines, memories that transcend judgements and considerations of class. Musical habitus is transmitted between mother and child, passing through generations and making the labour worthwhile for these women.

REFERENCES

Adkins, L. (2005). Social capital: The anatomy of a troubled concept. *Feminist Theory, 6*(2), 195–211.

Allatt, P. (1993). Becoming privileged: The role of family processes. In I. Bates & G. Risenborough (Eds.), *Youth and inequality* (pp. 139–159). Open University Press.

Amusicmom.com. (2023). https://amusicmom.com/changing-music-teachers/

Ang, K., Panebianco, C., & Odendaal, A. (2021). Viewing the parent-teacher relationship in music education through the lens of role theory: A literature review. *Update: Applications of Research in Music Education, 39*(2), 25–33. https://doi.org/10.1177/8755123320951994

Atkinson, W. (2016). *Beyond Bourdieu.* Polity.

Ballantyne, J., Kerchner, J. L., & Aróstegui, J. L. (2012). Developing music teacher identities: An international multi-site study. *International Journal of Music Education, 30*(3), 211–226. https://doi.org/10.1177/0255 761411433720

Bartleet, B.-L., Bennett, D., Bridgestock, R., Draper, P., Harrison, S., & Schippers, H. (2012). Preparing for portfolio careers in Australian music: Setting a research agenda. *Australian Journal of Music Education, 1*, 32–41.

Bourdieu, P. (1998). *Practical reason.* Polity.

Boyd, E. R. (2002). "Being there": Mothers who stay at home, gender and time. *Women's Studies International Forum, 25*(4), 463–470. https://doi.org/10.1016/S0277-5395(02)00283-2

Castrillon, C. (2022). *Why soft skills are more in demand than ever.* https://www.forbes.com/sites/carolinecastrillon/2022/09/18/why-soft-skills-are-more-in-demand-than-ever/?sh=45e3efde5c6f

Cho, E., & Ilari, B. S. (2021). Mothers as home DJs: Recorded music and young children's well-being during the COVID-18 pandemic. *Frontiers in Psychology, 12.* https://doi.org/10.3389/fpsyg.2021.637569

De Nora, T. (1999). Music as a technology of the self. *Poetics, 27*, 31–56. https://doi.org/10.1016/S0304-422X(99)00017-0

De Nora, T. (2000). *Music in everyday life.* Cambridge University Press.

Dissanayake, E. (2012). The earliest narratives were musical. *Research Studies in Music Education, 34*(1), 3–14.

Fancourt, D., & Perkins, R. (2017). Associations between singing to babies and symptoms of postnatal depression, wellbeing, self-esteem and mother-infant bond. *Public Health, 145*, 149–152. https://doi.org/10.1016/j.puhe.2017.01.016

Gerrard, J. (2014). All that is solid melts into work: Self-work, the 'learning ethic' and the work ethic. *The Sociological Review, 62*, 862–879. https://doi.org/10.1111/1467-954X.12208

Gillies, V. (2006). Working class mothers and school life: Exploring the role of emotional capital. *Gender and Education, 18*(3), 281–293. https://doi.org/10.1080/09540250600667876

Hochschild, A. R. (1983). *The managed heart: The commercialization of human feeling.* University of California Press.

Hofman, A. (2015). Music (as) labour: Professional musicianship, affective labour and gender in socialist Yugoslavia. *Ethnomusicology Forum, 24*(1), 28–50. https://doi.org/10.1080/17411912.2015.1009479

Illouz, E. (1997). Who will care for the caretaker's daughter? Toward a sociology of happiness in the era of reflexive modernity. *Theory, Culture and Society, 14*(4), 31–66. https://doi.org/10.1177/026327697014004002

Jamal Al-deen, T., & Windle, J. (2017). 'I feel sometimes I am a bad mother': The affective dimension of immigrant mothers' involvement in their children's schooling. *Journal of Sociology, 53*(1), 110–126. https://doi.org/10.1177/1440783316632604

Lovell, T. (2000). Thinking feminism with and against Bourdieu. *Feminist Theory, 1*(1), 11–32. https://doi.org/10.1177/14647000022229047

Mackinlay, E. (2009). Singing maternity through autoethnography: Making visible the musical world of myself as a mother. *Early Child Development and Care, 179*(6), 717–731. https://doi.org/10.1080/03004430902944320

Mackinlay, E., & Baker, F. (2005). Nurturing herself, nurturing her baby: Creating positive experiences for first-time mothers through lullaby singing. *Women and Music: A Journal of Gender and Culture, 9*, 69–89. https://doi.org/10.1353/wam.2005.0010

Pettinger, L. (2015). Embodied labour in music work. *The British Journal of Sociology, 66*(2), 282–300. https://doi.org/10.1111/1468-4446.12123

Pitts, S. (2012). *Chances and choices: Exploring the impact of music education.* Oxford University Press.

Reay, D. (1998). *Class work: Mothers' involvement in their children's primary schooling.* Routledge.

Power, R. (2015). *Motherhood and creativity: The divided heart.* Affirm Press.

Reay, D. (2004). Gendering Bourdieu's concept of capitals? Emotional capital, women and social class. In L. Adkins & B. Skeggs (Eds.), *Feminism after Bourdieu* (pp. 57–74). Blackwell Publishing.

Reay, D. (2015). Habitus and the psychosocial: Bourdieu with feelings. *Cambridge Journal of Education, 45*(1), 9–23. https://doi.org/10.1080/0305764X.2014.990420

Rivera, L. A. (2012). Hiring as cultural matching: The case of elite professional service firms. *American Sociological Review, 77*(6), 999–1022. https://doi.org/10.1177/0003122412463213

Rose, J. (2017). Never enough hours in the day: Employed mothers' perceptions of time pressure. *Australian Journal of Social Issues, 52*(2), 116–130. https://doi.org/10.1002/ajs4.2

Savage, S. (2015a). *Intensive mothering through music in early childhood education.* Unpublished Masters' Minor Thesis, Monash University.

Savage, S. (2015b). Understanding mothers' perspectives on early childhood music programmes. *Australian Journal of Music Education, 2*, 127–139.

Savage, S., & Hall, C. (2017). Thinking about and beyond the cultural contradictions of motherhood through musical mothering. In M. J. Rose, L. Ross, & J. Hartmann (Eds.), *The music of motherhood* (pp. 32–50). Demeter Press.

Silva, E. B. (2007). Gender, class, emotional capital and consumption in family life. In E. Casey & L. Martens (Eds.), *Gender and consumption: Domestic cultures and the commercialisation of everyday life* (pp. 141–162). Routledge.

Smit, R. (2011). Maintaining family memories through symbolic action: Young adults' perceptions of family rituals in their families of origin. *Journal of Comparative Family Studies, 42*(3), 355–367. https://doi.org/10.3138/jcfs.42.3.355

Teague, A., & Smith, G. D. (2015). Portfolio careers and work-life balance among musicians: An initial study into implications for higher music education. *British Journal of Music Education, 32*(2), 177–193. https://doi.org/10.1017/S0265051715000121

Violinist.com. (2008). https://www.violinist.com/discussion/archive/13037/

Williamon, A., & Thompson, S. (2006). Awareness and incidence of health problems among conservatoire students. *Psychology of Music, 34*(4), 411–430. https://doi.org/10.1177/0305735606067150

Zembylas, M. (2007). Emotional capital and education: Theoretical insights from Bourdieu. *British Journal of Educational Studies, 55*(4), 443–463. https://doi.org/10.1111/j.1467-8527.2007.00390.x

CHAPTER 8

Belonging and Family Connections Across Generations

INTRODUCTION

It is beyond impossible to explain the sense of joy, love, peace and over-whelmingly beautiful feeling of sharing music, particularly with those you love. I remember describing it to my doctoral supervisors as better than, or at least on par with (good) sex. Susan explained a similar feeling in her interview. She stated,

> there's heaps of music that just moves me to, to absolute distraction ... for instance, my poor computer fixer was ... in his shop, he's got a massive set of speakers, and he loves listening to Beethoven. Well, I said to him—you're not going to get any sense out of me whatsoever ... it was just the most exquisite sound, you know—oh oh—I was just going off! I couldn't give him no intelli-gent answers about anything—you just have to go with the music. So, if I hear it, I can't dismiss it. You've just got to go into it ... it's a very personal thing.

Frith (2008) attempts to articulate why music matters and aims to capture what it feels like to experience and 'do' music. He states:

Music may be useful psychologically, socially, politically or whatever. But that's not why people do it. Music matters because it is pleasurable—to do and to experience—and because it is a necessary part of what we are as

S. Savage, *Musical Mothering*, Palgrave Macmillan Studies in Family and Intimate Life, https://doi.org/10.1007/978-3-031-65157-1_8

175

humans, as feeling, empathetic beings, interested in and engaged with other people. To study music is to study what it is to be human—biologically, cognitively, culturally; to play music is to experience what it is to be human—physically, mentally, socially, in an aesthetic, playful, sensual context. Music matters, in short, because without it we wouldn't know who we are and what we are capable of being. (p. 178)

Intertwined with these strong emotions is also pride, happiness and a heady cocktail of other potent feelings that arguably any people who love each other share when participating in a mutually pleasurable activity. I agree with Frith that music is more than a means to something else but rather something of exquisite worth in its own right. It is these intense emotions that make it even more devastating when the relationship with music and its makers breaks down.

In this final chapter, I explore what music means for the mothers in this book. The ongoing intergenerational nature of music that is transmitted from mothers to children is articulated as well as the influence of children on the musical repertoires and experiences of mothers and grandmothers, creating family cultures and ways of being.

Music, Wellbeing, 'Family Feeling' and Love

I have written extensively about music in families as 'something we do', embedding that doxa of family belongingness like being in on an insider joke. Like sporting families, families that like hiking, trainspotting, or bee-keeping, involvement in music acts as a means of affective recognition (Atkinson, 2016). Atkinson describes this as an "evenly distributed product of the practical realisation of 'family'" (p. 58). In musical families, music is what we do. Mothers, as the drivers of capital accumulation in families through musical pursuits, encourage involvement and maintain motivation to engage in music with their children. From very early on in young children's lives, children learn ways to garner affection from those significant others. Infants tune in and seek emotional responses and connection from familiar others and learn how to react to unfamiliar happenings (Atkinson, 2016). Children's desire and need for love and recognition within the family are deeply embedded within the classed and gendered ideals and aspirations mothers have for their children. For the mothers in this book, their deep desire was to have music as part of their children's lives. Here Linda articulates, "*I think it's good they can enjoy concerts, then they can enjoy going out when they're adults. Because they know what music is all about, I think it's important"*. While Linda comments on the enjoyment aspect, the emphasis is on being able to understand music and explicate its value.

Mothers who are musical can experience joy through engagement with music for themselves and with their families. When mothers participate in music through performance, both in formal and informal settings, and experience profound joy, their children sense the meaning it has for their mother. A cycle of reinforcement is created when mothers listen to, engage with and perform music, and their children respond in a positive way because they see their mother's positive affectation. Similarly, mothers perceive that their children are enjoying music through listening, engagement and performing, perhaps because they want this to happen and they encourage it to happen. Children are being praised for their musicality and positive emotional cues from mothers, who in turn give them attention and love for being involved in something they too value and love (Clement & Dukes, 2017). Mothers are pivotal in driving children's interests and nurturing participation in the musical field (Atkinson, 2016; Savage & Hall, 2017). Music in this cycle of engagement creates the family doxa, that is, the perception that music is fundamental to the way some families function.

As humans and social beings, we have an innate need to feel love and a sense of belonging. Rosemary and Penelope demonstrate their family doxa and the recognition of this when they get together and perform music, usually singing. Both Rosemary and Penelope sang in their interviews with me, demonstrating their confidence and comfort in sharing this form of communication, which I consider to be very intimate. This act represented generosity and was a sign of their trust within our relationship. To me, singing is highly personal and demonstrates an allowance to feel vulnerable in a particular setting. Being able to sing freely and without self-consciousness is a rare thing in Western society as was mentioned earlier in Chap. 4, where I discussed singing as embedded with notions of talent and ability. Singing is seen as a performance rather than part of everyday experience (Ilari et al., 2013). But for Rosemary and Penelope, singing was part of everyday life. Rosemary never wished to sing professionally but says she *'never stopped singing'*. This remains a vivid recollection in memories of Penelope's childhood—*"yeah, she'd sing all the time which was nice. Yeah, I have all those lovely memories of lovely songs around the home which is great"*. Rosemary was the personification of the joy of song, and this was passed on to Penelope through their everyday experience as part of family life. This routine enculturation develops cultural capacity within the family home (Campbell, 2011). Cultural capital is accumulated and, in this instance, becomes an 'inheritance' (Bourdieu, 1999, p. 508).

The act of singing continues in Rosemary's extended family lives, even now when her children have grown and have children of their own. Rosemary shared anecdotes of their family holidays:

> *[Penelope] is brilliant, my brother's brilliant. He just sits at the piano and plays by ear. Penelope's the same. She plays guitar and violin; she prefers guitar. But we can sit some nights in holiday times, because no time otherwise, and whatever we ask Penelope to play, even songs she doesn't know, and we start singing it within a few bars, she can just join in.*

These musical get-togethers have become part of who they are as a family—a musical family—and as musical individuals. Through this practice, their children have been influenced as they experience that this is what they do when they all come together and share in the joy. Rosemary has passed on her musical interest which continues to be practiced on family holidays, reinforcing their family cultural capital and what it means to be part of their family. Rosemary is the good mother who has successfully transferred these musical leanings to her children and grandchildren. The joy of musical motherhood is narrated through vignettes provided throughout this book. There are numerous examples of musical interactions that are spontaneous, fun and easy-going, and just as many that show a deliberate, planned and meticulous attention to detail.

Earlier in Chap. 4, I discussed affective recognition and the mutual need for acceptance and love from significant others in our lives. Humans seek out these relationships. When discussing the role of music in people's lives, we need to divert from reductionist views that see people's motives as only for personal gain in a status or economic sense (Sayer, 1999). Indeed, Sayer (2005) critiques rationalising everything to "social position and influences, discourses, cultural norms or indeed habitus" (p. 949). While he acknowledges that humans are physically and economically dependent on others, we are also psychologically dependent on them too. Involvement with music can bring advantages and benefits, and this is why some parents choose music for their children (Savage, 2015b). But for many parents, this is not the predominant motive for having music as part of their lives. Music makes life happier, richer, more creative, healthier and more wonderful, and mothers who have experienced this joy first-hand understandably want to share it with their children, so they can experience it too. The desire to bring music to others, to improve the aesthetics and quality of life, is what makes mothers good. Music brings connection and gives joy and is a deeply human activity (Frith, 2008), but we need to release our Western ideals of exclusive perfectionism so that all can take part inclusively without reservation, and without judgement. This does not mean that we settle for second-best, or that actors should not strive to do their best, but rather have the freedom to do one's best without having to be perfect, as Frith suggests, where freedom enables us to be the best versions of ourselves.

Mothers nurture a 'family feeling' (Atkinson, 2014, p. 340; Bourdieu, 1998, p. 68) when they support children's musical development, select what music to listen to in the home or in the car, and share their love of music more generally. A sense of belonging is created by music and engages family members in an experience that is emotionally gratifying. Certain music becomes a soundtrack of family life and embodies that feeling of family, that "the taken-for-granted, unquestioned and shared sense of 'what is done' or 'to be done' in 'this family' manifest and sustained in all the elements of ordinary life acting as barriers to entry for outsiders" (Atkinson, 2014, p. 227); music is routine and embedded as family practice and culture. Music deepens ordinary family experience to a heightened and profound level of emotion and aesthetic exquisiteness. Specific musical activities symbolise what it is to be part of 'this family'. Atkinson (2011) states,

> This 'family sense' or 'family feeling', perpetuated through generations, has the effect of integrating agents, says Bourdieu, of making them feel and act like an exclusive unit, and, being maintained through narratives, maxims, celebratory occasions and photographic displays (cf. Finch, 2007), develops into a taken-for-granted sense of 'family tradition' or 'family spirit'; that is to say, a family-specific *doxa*. (original emphasis, p. 340)

Family get-togethers create a sense of belonging which is constructed and unique to particular families. Mothers initiate and perpetuate this family feeling over generations through activities such as music, and where specific songs and pieces of music capture meanings for individual families. In this way, forms of music become like an 'in' joke, shared only by close family members which serves to make their special bonds stronger and more united. Using Rosemary's analogy, music is the water flowing through an intergenerational stream, invigorating family life and "satisfying the thirst for family connection and human solidarity" (Savage, 2019, p. 181) and transferred through family habitus.

Aarshia's narrative tells how she fosters a family feeling with her young daughter. They love to dance to music, so together, they search YouTube to find music that suits their need whether that be Western music or Hindi music. Aarshia explains, *"music for me is not lyrics, like in songs. I go to the music part of it—like you have people who listen to the lyrics side and people who listen to the music, so I'm the music side"*. For Aarshia and her daughter, this activity forms part of their family bank of memories and family identity (De Nora, 1999), encapsulating their past, present and future. Mukherjee and Barn (2021) in their study of British Indian middle-class families note that it is common for parents to enrol their daughters in Indian cultural activities such as folk dances so children can learn about their ethnic heritage. Engagement in this family music and dance gives Aarshia a break from her research work and an opportunity to share another side of herself with her daughter. Aarshia usually worked long hours as she studied for her doctorate, and making time for daughter and herself is important for her mental health and their relationship. Drawing on her rich Indian heritage, this was also a chance to teach her daughter traditional dances from her culture:

> *You have this festival called Dandia where you dance with those sticks and everything. I try to take her to all those places, and so that she knows the culture, appreciates the different aspects of it and kind of enjoys it. She doesn't understand Hindi. She has forgotten our mother-tongue. When I am putting on Hindi music, I put on music that she would like and enjoy—Indian music I choose that way—she will instantly pick up and remember, it's a beautiful thing—it's a loss thing if people don't do it because they're turning modern. Indian classical music is beautiful, but people are like—"Nah, Justin Bieber" – but that's good, too. But do not lose what you have.*

The bonding experience is enhanced through collaborative music and dance, aiding the development of their collective family identity, which is enhancing the bonding and attachment that has already occurred in the family environment (Boer & Abubakar, 2014). Aarshia has deliberately chosen music that works for her and her daughter, where "music is part of this care of self, they are engaging in self-conscious articulation work, thinking ahead about the music that might 'work' for them" (De Nora, 2000, p. 53). It is interesting to note that Hindi music was the music that Aarshia's mother forbade her to listen to, stating *"Hindi music is basically those romantic songs. I didn't want to expose her [Aarshia] to that culture"*, yet Aarshia wants to share this with her daughter.

The affordances for Aarshia are that she can enhance that connection with her daughter to make it even stronger, replicating the close relationship she had with her mother—her 'anchor' as she is referred to—a relationship that was closer because her father worked away and there was often just the two of them. The transference of culture is a moral imperative for Aarshia because it connects the cultural contexts of her family's past, present and, hopefully, future. Aarshia actively resists the homogenisation of music in her family by including a variety of music. This is important mother work as it maintains culture and positions her as a 'good' mother. Aarshia embraces the notion of being 'modern' through the mixture of Western popular music and traditional Indian music. Embracing both cultures and appearing 'up with the times' was important to her mother, and as such, this melding of cultures also replicates the mothering that Aarshia received. Aarshia explains her musical mothering further:

I do a lot of Bollywood dancing. There's a south Indian form called Bharatnatayam and Kathakali which is a typically classical one. I love dancing, so we dance a lot at home.

Aarshia consolidates her relationship with her daughter, creating a bridge between the two cultures, embracing contemporary and traditional dance forms in a mutually enjoyable experience. Just like the bond with her own mother, Aarshia is becoming the 'anchor' for her child, through their informal music experiences as integral to family life.

Another example of family musical experiences is shown through a story from Kelele. She tells how singing is part of their everyday family life, and she speaks about the relaxed and casual nature of this engagement. Laughing, Kelele explains how her husband's voice is 'bad'; however, she still interprets his contribution to family life as a gift,

I like singing and then, 'cause at home, we make our own words, probably like not going in the notes but then put in the tones. Like my husband do that for my kids, too. He joins in—he makes his own singing words—probably someone hear, like ourneighbours hear, he's bad, but his singing ... he makes the kids sing and even my youngest one, when he's in [the] back [garden]... he just stands there singing his voice out loud and probably make up song. All of them, they love singing.

There is no pretention in Kelele's family's singing. It is something they do, and they do it with gusto. Everyone gets involved as Kelele demonstrates; music is spontaneous and joyful and forms a foundation of family memories that have deep significance (Smart, 2007). Kelele appreciates her husband's participation as a response to affirm music's importance for Kelele, showing his affective recognition of her. I acknowledge that fathers are active participants in family music (Scarlato, 2020) as seen in Kelele's vignette, but also reiterate that it is mothers who are the primary initiators and facilitators of this engagement in families (Savage, 2015a, 2019; Savage & Hall, 2017). This is made clear through Kelele's language when she says *"he joins in"*, suggesting that the musical event was already happening. Kelele had set up the musical play, yet her labour in doing this remains hidden as she valorises her husband and son's participation. This privileges the husband and son and masks the gendered nature of family life and mothers' work that is rendered invisible. Many of the mothers in this study commented how their husbands and/or fathers were 'tone deaf' and unable to maintain a tune. The mothers position themselves as the 'musical' members of the family, in an effort to attain recognition for the crucial role they play in transmitting family cultural capital, and to enhance their value and self-worth.

Musical Grandmothering

It is not only musical mothers who experience joy from their children's musical engagement, but great pleasure is felt by musical grandmothers as they interact with their grandchildren in musical ways. Singing was front and centre of Rosemary's narrative. Starting with her story of when she was a child, she speaks of singing around the piano with her family. Both Penelope and Rosemary told stories of how Rosemary would sing around the house when the children were young, and of family holidays where they would all sing and Penelope would accompany them all on her guitar. Now Rosemary sings with her grandchildren. It is something she does automatically, without conscious thought. She is musical (grand) mothering personified. It is important for Rosemary to maintain her status as a musical mother where in these family musical experiences, she gets to "recapture the aesthetic agency they possessed (or which possessed them) at the time" (De Nora, 1999, p. 47) and bolster her self-worth. Not only can Rosemary relive her musical memories experienced with her own mother, but she can pass on music to the youngest family members into family ways of being, family spirit and connectedness. She tells,

> *I never stopped singing, and I never stopped singing to my grandchildren. I walk in the door and I'm singing, and a thousand songs come back into my head. My daughter-in-law is stunned how that happens, but it just happens.*

Musicality is transferred to grandchildren as the musical grandmothers continue their work, as informal family interactions. There is growing acknowledgement that senior members of our society are often forgotten and isolated. Older people can feel devalued and can be left behind when their adult families' lives are busy, resulting in increased loneliness and social isolation. There is sometimes a disconnect between seniors and younger people to assume that their interests are too distinct, too different. There is often little tolerance, desire or time to make the effort to find that point of connection and realise our similarities, citing historical or cultural differences and resistance to change. Music is known for its ability to connect and be a community language and is therefore the perfect medium to make connections and forge positive relationships.

Reminiscences evoke memories and emotions of one's attachments to family and our subjectivities with them. Within memories, feelings are embedded and deeply social, guiding our perception of family. Music acts as a powerful reminder of past times and recollections of how we used to be and what has been created (De Nora, 1999). The '*thousand songs*' that instantly pop into Rosemary's head are an embodiment of this, and her joy she experiences in this is palpable. Her daughter-in-law continues the affective recognition to secure Rosemary's place as a worthy musical grandmother and the daughter-in-law learns Rosemary's family culture that is now hers too. The family doxa is perpetuated through their shared repertoire of songs.

Susan, like Rosemary, affirms her position as musical grandmother within her family. Susan's passing of her '*cultural inheritance*' is visible when she visits her grandchildren,

I did find with [eldest daughter's] four boys, mornings totally chaos, so I just started playing … I gave them one of my old pianos, so I just started playing 'Wimoweh'—you know it's just three chords. Next thing, the little boy number two comes out with the big bass drum and number one comes out with something else and, all of the kids had their instruments—and their dad's got a terrific voice—I gave him a harmony and [my daughter] just goes off like a firecracker—she can sing—gospelly type stuff—and just suddenly the whole family was doing his spontaneous combustion and yeah, I really like that sort of thing.

Susan reins in the perceived 'chaos' with music to entrain and engage. She has channelled the children's energy into an opportunity for musical connection. This is indicative of Susan's sensitive and perceptive mothering through music; "chaos is met with music, harmonising literally and metaphorically" (Savage, 2019, p. 185). Susan knows this is an impressive anecdote and is keen to share it because not only does it highlight her grandchildren's extraordinary musical abilities but also her 'good' grandmothering. The capturing of his family dynamic into a family memory shows good times together, and a demonstration of music habitus, transmitted intergenerationally.

Sangeeta and Hema articulate similar ideas when they talk about 'polishing' Aarshia's daughter. Hema used this term to denote the interplay between grandmother, mother and grandchild during the time spent together, full of gentle encouragement, active listening to the grandchild's songs and carefully watching her improvised dances, with each maternal figure nurturing her habitus in their own way. Hema reminisces, saying that she relives her own motherhood when she is with her granddaughter. She recalls those early times with her (only) son, full of nostalgia. Hema reflects,

I feel (as a) grandmother, ah, excit(ed) again. I (am) back to my son's childhood. I can just see that sometimes she sings, sometimes she dances and sometimes she speak … (the) same as my son was at his age, at her age, so I think that again I get his childhood … I enjoy it …

The complexities of maternal subjectivities are reflected in Hema's words. Woven into the mother's narratives are subjectivities that the mothers have occupied whether it be as grandmothers, mothers, daughters, and sometimes wives, highlighting the dynamic, relational and temporal nature of these relationships (Bueskens, 2018). Bueskens (2018) writes:

There is a temporal complexity to the maternal subject insofar as she is in the past, present and future dynamically. … The relation with her child also gives the mother an opportunity to rework her own past, to sift through and reinterpret it, to create new social practices and (new) meaning. In this sense, there is a dynamic quality to the mother-child relation, producing reworkings of self in the mother as she nurtures the self of the child. (p. 204)

Hema is able to relive her motherhood and change the narrative if she so chooses. This is, of course, dependent upon the opportunities to reconstruct this that are relationally shaped with her granddaughter (Bueskens, 2018). Memories are selectively stored and recalled when they have value or relevance and retrieved when prompted as Hema shows. Hema creates a family feeling through music via her encouragement of her grandchild, just as she had with her son. It is these interactions that give our lives meaning and richness. However, it is not only mothers and grandmothers who initiate and foster these important family relationships through music; children, as musical agents, also nurture musical connections and joy within the family.

CHILDREN'S MUSICAL INFLUENCE ON MOTHERS AND GRANDMOTHERS

Children are not just sponges soaking up what they are offered, but active agents in the family musical space. Musical influences are not one-directional. Children can have a profound influence on the listening repertoires of their mothers and grandmothers. I recall putting on my children's favourite CDs in the car and having them on repeat. Mothers have anecdotally mentioned how they have put on their children's music when the children were not even in the car with them! Aarshia commented, perhaps facetiously, that she was thankful to Disney for providing her family with a playlist of tunes—*"thanks to Disney we have so many songs (laughs)—Let it go—and everything"*. Aarshia's daughter has been the initiator of this listening repertoire, influenced no doubt by the mega marketing machine that Disney is and her peers who are also under the same spell. Jessica's daughter, too, mentions this song, *"You know she sings that Frozen song—like all the kids do—like a football anthem, 'Let it gooooo'. She's pretty hilarious"*. As an aside, this particular song has had outstanding accolades, reaching the number 5 spot in the Billboard Hot 100, and with the writers of the song receiving the award for Best Original Song at the

Oscars in 2014 and a Grammy award for Best Song Written for Visual Media in 2015 (Robbins, 2020). The story purports a feminist theme—based around girls who "fight to overcome childhood tragedy, find emotional freedom, (in Elsa's case) control of world altering powers, and bring about peace and happiness for themselves and their kingdom" (Robbins, 2020, p. 1). Disney songs have been heavily critiqued by some who view the Disney themes as being anti-feminist, using "a patriarchal lens and gendered shame" (Robbins, 2020, p. 1). Other scholars have suggested Elsa cannot have romance and power as the two seem mutually exclusive, for girls at least (Streiff & Dundes, 2017)—a dig at *Frozen* was also reiterated in the recent Barbie movie (Gerwig, 2023)—while others suggest *Let it go* is a 'coming out' ballad (Cocks, 2022). Robbins explores that rather than being a power couple, the sisters have a toxic relationship, highlighting the "the weaponisation of family responsibility that has been used to moderate female behaviour and defines a palatable representation of female power. Elsa can only be queen if she relinquishes or hides her magic. Meanwhile, she must also operate as a dutiful daughter and sister" (Robbins, 2020, p. 6; See Robbins for further critique). I wonder if the mothers I interviewed would be so keen for their daughters to sing this had they been aware of these perspectives. This notion returns to surveillance that was discussed in Chap. 6, when mothers restricted children's music listening repertoires because the themes were too sexualised, or the language deemed inappropriate.

Moving on from Disney songs, Jessica spoke of another song that her daughter had engaged with and how they now play it together,

> She kinda does it herself and we happily go with those moments. So, she wanted to learn how to do "Peppa Pig". (laughs) Oh lord! I know. (laughs) And so we worked out the series of notes that it would be based on the colour of the different keys on the glockenspiel, so we just drew circles with the different colours of the notes. So, she does that kind of thing … she engages in it in her own way.

Choosing her own repertoire, Jessica's daughter enlists the help of her mother to play the tune, and Jessica is happy to oblige. Jessica's daughter brings home music from kindergarten—"*she comes back, and she knows the words to all these amazing songs, and she really loves it, really heartfelt singing. They've got all these beautiful songs and the actions and so they all do this lovely stuff*", explains Jessica. Within the family unit of Susan, Jessica and Jessica's daughter's relationship is their interconnections and inter-influences—Jessica's influence on her mother, Susan, of Tibetan and Indian music, while Susan shares her recent finds of contemporary avant-garde music and her extensive knowledge of the classical repertory, and Jessica's daughter inculcates popular culture of her own. The three generations resource each other through their musical sharing, learning and meaning-making.

It is impossible to articulate the intensity of feeling that is experienced when family members connect through shared music-making. The mothers related many stories of musical assemblages, with friends and with others, which Susan labelled as '*sharing humanity*'. These words echo Frith's (2008) sentiments when he writes, "we are as humans, as feeling, empathetic beings, interested in and engaged with other people" (p. 178). Mere language is not enough to express the depth of emotion and spirituality embodied when participating in joyful and personally significant music. To find words that capture a close proximity of this experience is cultural capital itself (Hall, 2018).

INTERGENERATIONAL TRANSMISSION OF FAMILY CULTURE

Musical traditions, as family priorities, are means to social reproduction and 'something that we do' and are as diverse as what connects them. Mothers are the drivers of these traditions, upholding music as prized and valued. Through the mothers' narratives of intergenerational cultural transmission, stories of family memories and family connections have emerged. These rituals form ways to transmit family values and expressions of love. Mothers' labour maintains, monitors and replenishes that feeling of family as an expectation. Even when children have left the family home and are raising their own children, mothers still feel the need to build, support and negotiate family emotions, demonstrating that mothers' work continues relentlessly as a lifelong pursuit. We need to look beyond mothers' work through a lens of investments and exchange-mechanisms, looking at maternal labour only as capital accumulation for social reproduction, and instead recognise the dimensions of meaning-making and feeling for the mothers, as Frith (2008) advocates, as well as the depth of their emotional labour.

Musical mothering can be expensive, time-consuming and labour-intensive, but similarly, it need not be. It can compromise mothers' lives and influence mothering practices in multiple ways. The mothers in this book made deliberate decisions regarding their children's musical development with varying degrees of intensity in the ways they enact musical mothering. That is not to say that in some ways things could have been different or better. I am sure Linda feels that her decision to encourage Ashley to attend the conservatorium was not what she would do in retrospect. I perhaps would not have insisted my eldest daughter continue to pursue music to the extent she did in her later school years when I hear from her now what pressure she felt. As mothers, we are not perfect; we do the best we can at the time given the resources available to us. Mothers want the best for their children, and for their children to be safe, live good and loving lives, and to be healthy, happy and have what they need. It's a tough but ultimately rewarding gig.

For the women whom I interviewed, the meaning of music may be diverse; however, it is deeply personal and part of their very being, as embodied memories, emotion and belonging. Connections to heritage and culture, past and present, and musical futures are evident, as are expressions of love. Gratitude is another strong theme, with the mothers expressing sincere thankfulness for having music as part of their lives, grateful for those who gave them this gift. Some of these people were not mothers but 'significant others' as Atkinson (2016) reminds us. Music is an intense spiritual experience for these mothers. It is part of their history and present subjectivities and ways of being.

I have argued that involvement in music can be for advantage and gain, or to separate the social classes, but also to connect and build community. While in some ways I agree with Bourdieu (1998) that all action is interest, that we do things because it provides something for us in return. However, to posit that all action is for economic gain, or only a future-oriented pursuit for the purposes of class reproduction and the accrual of cultural capital, does not always ring true for music—not for me and not for the musical mothers who I interviewed. The gain is not always economic but psychological for managing self, social for connection and belonging, spiritual and aesthetic, creating something more valuable than anything money could buy. Linda attempts to articulate how observing her children's performance makes her feel,

> *Enjoyment from a mother's point of view ... I just enjoyed listening to them ... all the orchestras, you like to go and see your children perform ... when you've got somebody in it that you know they've practised, and you know they've enjoyed it. It just brings a bit of a ... you know ...*

Linda cannot find the words she needs, and the sentence remains incomplete. She suggests we might have shared subjectivities, as musical mothers who have travelled similar paths, in the understanding that I will know what she means. Various words were used by the mothers I spoke with to describe the feeling they get from engagement with music including: '*wonderful*', '*emotional*', '*gorgeous*' and '*deep joy*'. Penelope said, "*As a mother, [music] is one of the most important ways that my daughter can get joy from life … joy*".

What is more important than for a mother to show her child how music can offer meaningful and joyful lives? This is the role that musical mothers play as a contrast to the strategising and capital accumulation for exchange and economic advantage. Music consolidates that family feeling and builds connection, transmits family heritage and culture to future generations through musical habitus. Therein lies the rub.

Music connects to mothers' wellbeing and sense of self. Mothers see their success in their successful children where positive outcomes are translated as a validation of their mothering practices, affirming their self-worth and self-confidence. A sense of achievement and pride is expressed by the mothers in response to their efforts and labour of love.

REFERENCES

Atkinson, W. (2011). From sociological fictions to social fictions: Some Bourdieusian reflections on the concepts of 'institutional habitus' and 'family habitus'. *British Journal of Sociology of Education, 32*(3), 331–347. https://doi.org/10.1080/01425692.2011.559337

Atkinson, W. (2014). A sketch of 'family' as a field: From realized category to space of struggle. *Acta Sociologica, 57*(3), 223–235. https://doi.org/10.1177/0001699313513114

Atkinson, W. (2016). *Beyond Bourdieu*. Polity.

Boer, D., & Abubakar, A. (2014). Music listening in families and peer groups: Benefits for young people's social cohesion and emotional well-being across four cultures. *Frontiers in Psychology, 5*, 392–392. https://doi.org/10.3389/fpsyg.2014.00392

Bourdieu, P. (1998). *Practical reason*. Polity.

Bourdieu, P. (1999). The contradictions of inheritance. In P. Bourdieu, A. Accardo, & P. P. Ferguson (Eds.), *The weight of the world: Social suffering in contemporary society*. Polity.

Bueskens, P. (2018). From containing to creating. In C. Nelson & R. Robertson (Eds.), *Dangerous ideas about mothers* (pp. 197–210). UWAP Press.

Campbell, P. S. (2011). Musical enculturation: Sociocultural influences and meanings of children's experiences in and through music. In M. Barrett (Ed.), *A cultural psychology of music education press* (pp. 61–81). Oxford University.

Clement, F., & Dukes, D. (2017). Social appraisal and social referencing: Two components of affective social learning. *Emotion Review, 9*(3), 253–261. https://doi.org/10.1177/1754073916661634

Cocks, N. H. (2022). Letting go, coming out, and working through: Queer frozen. *Humanities (Basel), 11*(6), 146. https://doi.org/10.3390/h11060146

De Nora, T. (1999). Music as a technology of the self. *Poetics, 27*, 31–56. https://doi.org/10.1016/S0304-422X(99)00017-0

De Nora, T. (2000). *Music in everyday life.* Cambridge University Press.

Frith, S. (2008). Why music matters. *Critical Quarterly, 50*(1–2), 165–179. https://doi.org/10.1111/j.1467-8705.2008.00811.x

Gerwig, G. (2023). *The Barbie movie.* Warner Brothers.

Hall, C. (2018). *Masculinity, class and music education: Boys performing middle-class masculinities through music.* Palgrave Macmillan.

Ilari, B., Hafteck-Chen, L., & Crawford, L. (2013). Singing and cultural understanding: A music education perspective. *International Journal of Music Education, 31*(2), 202–216. https://doi.org/10.1080/1461380 8.2011.553277

Mukherjee, U., & Barn, R. (2021). Concerted cultivation as a racial parenting strategy: Race, ethnicity and middle-class Indian parents in Britain. *British Journal of Sociology of Education, 42*(4), 521–536. https://doi.org/10.108 0/01425692.2021.1872365

Robbins, H. (2020). "I Can't Be What You Expect of Me": Power, palatability, and shame in frozen: The broadway musical. *Arts (Basel), 9*(1), 39. https://doi.org/10.3390/arts9010039

Savage, S. (2015a). *Intensive mothering through music in early childhood education.* Unpublished Masters' Minor Thesis, Monash University.

Savage, S. (2015b). Understanding mothers' perspectives on early childhood music programmes. *Australian Journal of Music Education, 2*, 127–139.

Savage, S. (2019). *Musical mothering: Middle-class strategies and affect across generations.* Unpublished PhD thesis, Monash University.

Savage, S., & Hall, C. (2017). Thinking about and beyond the cultural contradictions of motherhood through musical mothering. In M. J. Rose, L. Ross, & J. Hartmann (Eds.), *The music of motherhood* (pp. 32–50). Demeter Press.

Sayer, A. (1999). Bourdieu, Smith and disinterested judgement. *Sociological Review, 47*(3), 403–431. https://doi.org/10.1111/1467-954X.00179

Sayer, A. (2005). Class, moral worth and recognition. *Sociology, 39*(5), 947–963. https://doi.org/10.1177/0038038505058376

Scarlato, M. K. M. (2020). Musical fatherhood: A phenomenological study. *Journal of Research in Childhood Education, 35*(3), 373–388. https://doi.org/10.1080/02568543.2020.1728445

Smart, C. (2007). *Personal life.* Polity.

Streiff, M., & Dundes, L. (2017). Frozen in time: How Disney gender-stereotypes its most powerful princess. *Social Sciences, 6*(2), 38. https://doi.org/10.3390/socsci6020038

Conclusion: Articulating the Relationship Between Music and Women's Mothering Practices

Conclusion

Mothers who have musical engagement in their lives were always more likely to make music part of their children's lives. Music was part of their family habitus, as something they do. Everyday musical experiences such as singing, learning an instrument or attending concerts were a usual occurrence and not sought to achieve any specific advantages, but rather an expected practice from intergenerational understandings of what musical families do, their family doxa, what their families do without question. Music might also be integrated with other practices like going to church and children become familiar with musical ways of being through osmosis, joining in with their family cultural practices. Involvement in formal music tuition can be expensive, time-consuming and labour intensive, and it is middle-class mothers who often have the resources to be able to support such activities over the long term.

For some middle-class women, involvement in music may be a deliberate strategy to procure particular skills and dispositions that they know are culturally valued and will provide advantages in institutions that value similar attributes. Middle-class mothers are well-read and well-versed in knowing what to do to be seen as 'good' mothers and to achieve the best outcomes for their children. Sometimes, they actively seek advantages for

© The Author(s), under exclusive license to Springer Nature Switzerland AG 2024
S. Savage, *Musical Mothering*, Palgrave Macmillan Studies in Family and Intimate Life,
https://doi.org/10.1007/978-3-031-65157-1_9

their children because they feel insecure about their children's futures; they want their children to live lives that are as good, if not better, than theirs. So, as the wider literature in this area attests, for many middle-class mothers, engagement with music is very much a future-oriented pursuit for the purposes of social reproduction and the accrual of cultural capital. The findings from my interviews substantiate this.

Intensive mothering and concerted cultivation were means to appear 'good'; however, this is varied according to the intentions and aspirations of the mothers. A definite continuum exists in the intensity that mothers engage in the concerted cultivation of their children through music. At one end of the continuum, intensive mothers spend phenomenal amounts of time finding suitable teachers, driving children to lessons, rehearsals, examinations and competitions, sitting in on practise, volunteering at musical organisations and scheduling these events. Additionally, musical mothers work at funding the expense of good quality instruments, expert teachers, and fees for examinations and orchestra membership and performing the emotional labour in making sure all this happens in a seamless way that fits in with family routines and timetables, all while making the whole process appear effortless. Middle-class mothers who are not working in paid employment but have the financial support of a significant other, have the greatest opportunity to enact this type of practice because they have the time and financial resources in which to do this. At the opposing end of the continuum are mothers who might choose musical activities but do not show the same intensity of involvement. Such mothers might be happy for their children to learn through opportunities afforded at school and may hire an instrument from the school, for example, and lessons may not extend beyond the time that such resources are available. Extensions for further opportunities may not be sought, such as joining an orchestra or doing music examinations or competitions.

'Good' mothers are those who are seen to make investments in their children and produce children who are growing to be worthy citizens. Mothers felt a moral responsibility to ensure their children developed attributes that would be useful in their future educational and work spheres and would develop to be productive citizens who are not a burden on society. These aspirations all fit neatly into the neoliberal ideals of our current social system where the responsibility of success lies with the individual and with mothers.

Mothers' work to develop such dispositions takes a great deal of intentionality; however, middle-class mothers work equally hard to make their efforts appear effortless. This presents with a paradox when mothers want to be acknowledged as 'good' and for their work to be recognised; however, they do not want that work to appear excessive and that it required substantial labour to achieve on their behalf. It was important for these women to make their children's musical proclivities seem natural rather than the result of extensive cultivation. This masking of the work involved in developing such abilities is a form of misrecognition, where mothers disavow the time and labour taken to curate such talents. Some of the mothers believed musical talent was genetic, something that was passed down through generations; however, others saw it as a 'cultural inheritance', acknowledging that such abilities were enculturated through family life. In doing this work to develop musical skills, mothers did not wish to appear 'pushy' or that they forced their children to engage in musical activities which would be antithetical to good mothering logic which is nurturing and child centred. The mothers openly demonised those mothers who forced their children to practice, for example, and yet they agreed there was a 'fine line' between forcing and knowing that practise was necessary for proficiency. A moral dilemma for mothers was created between nurturing dispositions and enforcing practise.

While wishing to appear child-centred and self-sacrificing for their children, mothers also gained respectability and social credibility through their children's musical practice. To maintain this, some of the mothers I interviewed carefully surveyed their children by restricting their friendship groups and managing their listening repertoires. Some mothers went so far as to home-school their children so they could control their social connections, but also enable them to practise their instruments for several hours each day. Home schooling offered flexibility which allowed children time to fit extended practise into their schedules. Children who were controlled in this way later showed resentment towards such practices and showed a determination to mother differently.

I showed that the cultivation of music in families was unequal and where some children received more support than others. Mothers sometimes made judgements on which of their children was considered musical and who to invest their time, resources and labour in. These decisions were often based upon the resources that were available. Children not selected by mothers to develop musically showed regret and sought other ways to gain their mothers' love and affective recognition. And for those children whose mothers did invest in but who later decided music was not for them, mothers remained hopeful that they would take up their interest in the future and that this time was not wasted.

It was the mothers who are now grandmothers that showed the more intensive mothering practices but that could be because the younger mothers' children are only very young. The young mothers said they were more casual in their approaches to their children's musical development, although they were all still looking out for signs of musicality and inculcating music into their lives in immersive ways. I wondered as children got older whether their practices would become more intensive as the children's musical skills developed. I am certain they would. Grandmothers would continue their musical cultivation too, still wanting to appear 'good'.

MUSICAL MOTHERING AS A CLASSED AND GENDERED PRACTICE

I have written about middle-class mothers and the additional resources they have readily available to seek extra-curricular activities such as music. I have shown that such investments can be financially expensive and require huge amounts of time and labour to enact. There were constant judgements around the best instruments to play and purchase, the right teachers to choose, and what technique to adopt. Boundaries of acceptability around activities such as classical music tuition are fiercely enforced. Middle-class mothers were cognisant of the 'right' ways to do things because they had a feel for the game, as they have been playing the game for generations.

Middle-class mothers sought to differentiate themselves from other mothers whom they deemed not to be 'good'. There was a constant inter-class adjudication from other middle-class mothers which added to the pressure felt to make the 'right' choices. Working-class mothers were already demonised for lacking in aspiration and not fostering their children's potential. Asian mothers, who learn to play the game to perfection and take up spaces in institutions usually reserved for white, middle-class families, are also subjected to racialised criticism and concerns over punitive parenting. Mothers who work are also stigmatised as not 'being there' for their children, a prominent concern among middle-class mothers that aligns with essentialist views on mothering that only the biological mother can properly care for their children.

Neoliberal notions around employment suggest that women can participate fully in the workforce and still raise successful children without the need for additional supports. The nonsensical idea that women can have-it-all and do-it-all is pervasive and yet impossible to achieve. However, middle-class mothers continue to set themselves unrealistic targets and perfectionist ideals which continue to drive mothers to more intensive practices, both in and outside of the field of music.

Mothers continue to do the bulk of the emotional labour and mental work involved in raising a family. I would argue that they also bolster communities through their unpaid work. Many schools and other organisations would cease to function or have to charge significantly higher fees if it were not for the generous time and labour donated by mothers. Mothers do benefit from such work in the form of accumulating cultural and social capital; however, such labour should be renumerated and acknowledged in more explicit ways.

INTERGENERATIONAL CULTURAL TRANSMISSION

Musical traditions are passed down through generations as a form of social reproduction and maintaining that feeling of 'who we are'. Mothers are the keepers of such practice. I have shown that through music, family traditions are continued, and family memories are made. This is not to say that these cultural practices do not evolve over time, because they do. Musical traditions in families are ways to transmit family values and expressions of love and acceptance. Mothers monitor these family feelings and mediate family emotions which is emotionally challenging work, especially when mothers need to keep their own emotions in check and appear to be in control. Even when children have become adults and left the family home, this emotional labour continues with their own children and their children. While Bourdieu maintains that all action is for investment and exchange, we also see the mothers' actions and intense desire to have music as part of their lives for the meaning it gives, as part of family love and a resource for the self.

The meaning of music for the mothers in this book is as different as they are. Engagement with music is imbued with deep memories and feelings and a sense of belonging. Connections to past, present and future offer a validation of the self and one's heritage and culture. To share music with their children was an aspiration expressed by some of the mothers and to not be able to do so would amount to a severe loss. Mothers expressed gratitude to their mothers for passing on the gift of music to them and shared their decision to do the same. Participation in music is visceral, a deeply embodied, spiritual and personal experience that becomes part of the very cells of our being. For these mothers, music is their life's work and an integral part of who they are and who they have been.

Engagement with music for the women in this book, myself included, has always been about regulating the self. Stories of challenging childhoods, separation from loved ones, feelings of not being quite good enough, or accepted have been told and retold, and yet music has always been the constant. It is there when times are hard, to calm, soothe and comfort.

A sense of achievement was felt by the mothers when their children were successful musically as an acknowledgement of their labour over many years. Their musical mothering was validated. Family life was enhanced through connections with music, yet it was misrecognised as an expected practice. Mothers understood music to enhance and enrich their lives, inside and outside of the family domain. The meaning of music in the mothers' lives cannot be overstated because they experienced deep joy when participating in music and when seeing their children involved in music. However, music's

> profound importance is not limited to the family home but weaves into the very fabric of society, where music becomes the interwoven threads of our human existence, without which culture would be threadbare. It is mothers who are the creative weavers of the vital tapestry. (Savage, 2019, p. 204)

In doing this book, I was afforded the opportunity to reflect upon my own upbringing and musical journey and reconcile my own musical mothering. I am grateful for the interest and encouragement given to me by many over the years towards my musical development which is still ongoing. I still feel immense joy when my children visit my home and get out of their old piano music and play. They sing in the car along to the radio or their soundtracks on Spotify, and I smile. I have never regretted investing in their music education although I do believe in hindsight I may have mothered differently. When you're in the thick of things, it is often hard to see the wood for the trees, or the music from the noise.

I offered a classed and gendered account of my upbringing and contexts within which I was raised and raised my children. In many ways, the experience has been cathartic but also profoundly emotional as I have realised, reconciled and gained far deeper understandings of my mothering and how I was mothered. The importance to me of having music in my life and the lives of my children has been articulated and brought to the fore, although, to be honest, there were times when I struggled to find words to keenly express the depth of meaning this had for me.

What I have been able to see is music's value for me and for the mothers who I interviewed. Music's ability to connect, soothe and heal is incredible and not acknowledged enough. Music's potential to support and engage can create communities of care that transcend class divides and offer inclusion, wellbeing and emotional resilience. What would life be without music, as famous 1970–1980s Swedish pop group ABBA once asked? Surely less rich, and less meaningful. I cannot imagine life without it.

REFERENCE

Savage, S. (2019). *Musical mothering: Middle-class strategies and affect across generations*. Unpublished PhD thesis, Monash University.

REFERENCES

Adkins, L. (2002). *Revisions: Gender and sexuality in late modernity.* Open University Press.

Adkins, L. (2005). Social capital: The anatomy of a troubled concept. *Feminist Theory, 6*(2), 195–211.

Aldredge, M. (2006). Negotiating and practicing performance: An ethnographic study of a musical Open Mic in Brooklyn, New York. *Symbolic Interaction, 29*(1), 109–117. https://doi.org/10.1525/si.2006.29.1.109

Allan, S., & Jackson, G. (2010). The what, whys and wherefores of home education and its regulation in Australia. *International Journal of Law & Education, 15*(1), 55–77.

Allatt, P. (1993). Becoming privileged: The role of family processes. In I. Bates & G. Risenborough (Eds.), *Youth and inequality* (pp. 139–159). Open University Press.

Amusicmom.com. (2023). https://amusicmom.com/changing-music-teachers/

Andrews, M. (2004). Memories of mother: Counter-narratives of early maternal influence. In M. Bamberg & M. Andrews (Eds.), *Considering counter narratives: Narrating, resisting, making sense* (pp. 7–26). John Benjamins Publishing.

Andrews, M. (2014). *Narrative imagination and everyday life.* Oxford University Press.

Andrews, M., Squire, C., & Tamboukou, M. (Eds.). (2008). *Doing narrative research.* Sage.

Ang, K., Panebianco, C., & Odendaal, A. (2021). Viewing the parent-teacher relationship in music education through the lens of role theory: A literature

© The Author(s), under exclusive license to Springer Nature Switzerland AG 2024
S. Savage, *Musical Mothering*, Palgrave Macmillan Studies in Family and Intimate Life,
https://doi.org/10.1007/978-3-031-65157-1

review. *Update: Applications of Research in Music Education, 39*(2), 25–33. https://doi.org/10.1177/8755123320951994

Appadurai, A. (2004). The capacity to aspire: Culture and the terms of recognition. In V. Rao & M. Walton (Eds.), *Culture and public action* (pp. 59–84). Stanford University Press.

Arnold, L. B. (2014). I don't know where I end and you begin: Challenging boundaries of the self and intensive mothering. In L. R. Ennis (Ed.), *Intensive mothering: The cultural contradictions of modern motherhood* (pp. 47–65). Demeter Press.

Atkinson, W. (2011). From sociological fictions to social fictions: Some Bourdieusian reflections on the concepts of 'institutional habitus' and 'family habitus'. *British Journal of Sociology of Education, 32*(3), 331–347. https://doi.org/10.1080/01425692.2011.559337

Atkinson, W. (2014). A sketch of 'family' as a field: From realized category to space of struggle. *Acta Sociologica, 57*(3), 223–235. https://doi.org/10.1177/0001699313115114

Atkinson, W. (2016). *Beyond Bourdieu.* Polity.

Australian Bureau of Statistics [ABS]. (2021). *Aboriginal and Torres Strait Islander Australians.* https://www.abs.gov.au/statistics/people/aboriginal-and-torres-strait-islander-peoples/estimates-aboriginal-and-torres-strait-islander-australians/latest-release

Australian Bureau of Statistics [ABS]. (2022). *Cultural diversity.* https://www.abs.gov.au/articles/cultural-diversity-australia

Australian Bureau of Statistics [ABS]. (2023). *Marriages and divorces.* https://www.abs.gov.au/statistics/people/people-and-communities/marriages-and-divorces-australia/latest-release

Australian Government Department of Education, Skills and Employment. (2020). *Increasing women's workforce participation with Career Revive.* https://www.employment.gov.au/newsroom/increasing-women-s-workforce-participation-career-revive

Australian Government Workplace Gender Equality Agency [WGEA]. (2021). *Parental leave and gender equality.* https://www.wgea.gove.au/sites/default/files/documents/Parental-leave-and-gender-equality.pdf

Australian Institute of Family Studies [AIFS]. (2020). *Families then and now: How we worked.* Research Report. https://aifs.gov.au/research/research-reports/families-then-now-how-we-worked

Australian Institute of Family Studies [AIFS]. (2021). *Work and family.* https://aifs.gov.au/facts-and-figures/work-and-family

Babcox, D., & Belkin, M. (1971). *Liberation now! Writings from the women's liberation movement.* Dell.

Ball, S. J. (2003). The risks of social reproduction: The middle class and educational markets. *London Review of Education, 1*(3), 163–175. https://doi.org/10.1080/1474846032000146730

Ballantyne, J., Kerchner, J. L., & Aróstegui, J. L. (2012). Developing music teacher identities: An international multi-site study. *International Journal of Music Education, 30*(3), 211–226. https://doi.org/10.1177/0255761411433720

Bamberg, M. (2004). Considering counter narratives. In M. Bamberg & M. Andrews (Eds.), *Considering counter narratives: Narrating, resisting, making sense* (pp. 351–372). John Benjamins Publishing.

Barrett, M. S. (2009). Sounding lives in and through music – A narrative inquiry of the everyday musical engagement of a young child. *Journal of Early Childhood Research, 7*(2), 115–134. https://doi.org/10.1177/1476718X09102645

Bartleet, B.-L., Bennett, D., Bridgestock, R., Draper, P., Harrison, S., & Schippers, H. (2012). Preparing for portfolio careers in Australian music: Setting a research agenda. *Australian Journal of Music Education, 1*, 32–41.

Bautista, A., & Ho, Y. L. (2021). Music and movement teacher professional development: An interview study with Hong Kong kindergarten teachers. *Australasian Journal of Early Childhood, 46*(3), 276–290. https://doi.org/10.1177/18369391211014759

Benhabib, S. (1992). *Situating the self*. Polity.

Bennett, T., Emmison, M., & Frow, J. (1999). Music tastes and music knowledge. In T. Bennett, M. Emmison, & J. Frow (Eds.), *Accounting for tastes: Australian everyday cultures* (pp. 170–200). Cambridge University Press.

Bennett, P. R., Lutz, A. C., & Jayaram, L. (2012). Beyond the schoolyard: The role of parenting logics, financial resources, and social institutions in the social class gap in structured activity participation. *Sociology of Education, 85*(2), 131–157. https://doi.org/10.1177/0038040711431585

Boer, D., & Abubakar, A. (2014). Music listening in families and peer groups: Benefits for young people's social cohesion and emotional well-being across four cultures. *Frontiers in Psychology, 5*, 392–392. https://doi.org/10.3389/fpsyg.2014.00392

Bogt, T. F. M., Delsing, M. J. M. H., van Zalk, M., Christenson, P. G., & Meeus, W. H. J. (2011). Intergenerational continuity of taste: Parental and adolescent music preferences. *Social Forces, 90*(1), 297–319. https://doi.org/10.1093/sf/90.1.297

Bok, J. (2010). The capacity to aspire to higher education: 'It's like making them do a play without a script'. *Critical Studies in Education, 51*(2), 163–178.

Bottrell, D. (2013). Responsibilised resilience? Reworking neoliberal social policy texts. *M/C Journal, 16*(5). https://doi.org/10.5204/mcj.708

Bourdieu, P. (1977). *Outline of a theory of practice*. Cambridge University Press.

Bourdieu, P. (1984). *Distinction: A social critique of the judgement of taste*. Routledge and Kegan Paul.

Bourdieu, P. (1986). The forms of capital. In J. Richardson (Ed.), *Handbook of theory and research for the sociology of education* (pp. 241–258). Greenwood.

Bourdieu, P. (1990). *The logic of practice*. Polity.

Bourdieu, P. (1998). *Practical reason*. Polity.

Bourdieu, P. (1999). The contradictions of inheritance. In P. Bourdieu, A. Accardo, & P. P. Ferguson (Eds.), *The weight of the world: Social suffering in contemporary society*. Polity.

Bourdieu, P. (2000). *Pascalian meditations*. Polity.

Bourdieu, P. (2007). *Sketch for a self-analysis*. Polity.

Bourdieu, P., & Passeron, J. C. (1977). *Reproduction in education, society and culture*. Sage.

Bourdieu, P., & Wacquant, L. (1992). *An invitation to reflexive sociology*. University of Chicago Press.

Boyd, E. R. (2002). "Being there": Mothers who stay at home, gender and time. *Women's Studies International Forum, 25*(4), 463–470. https://doi.org/10.1016/S0277-5395(02)00283-2

Bracknell, C. (2020a). The emotional business of Noongar song. *Journal of Australian Studies, 44*(2), 140–153. https://doi.org/10.1080/1444305 8.2020.1752284

Bracknell, C. (2020b). Rebuilding as research: Noongar song, language and ways of knowing. *Journal of Australian Studies, 44*(2), 210–223. https://doi.org/1 0.1080/14443058.2020.1746380

Brannen, J. (2019). *Social research matters: A life in family sociology*. Bristol University Press.

Brannen, J., Moss, P., & Mooney, A. (2004). *Work and caring over the twentieth century: Change and continuity in four-generation families*. Palgrave Macmillan.

Bueskens, P. (2018). From containing to creating. In C. Nelson & R. Robertson (Eds.), *Dangerous ideas about mothers* (pp. 197–210). UWAP Press.

Bull, A. (2014). *The musical body: How gender and class are reproduced among young people playing classical music in England*. Unpublished doctoral thesis, Goldsmiths University.

Burland, K., & Davidson, J. (2002). Training the talented. *Music Education Research, 4*(1), 121–139.

Calhoun, C. (2013). For the social history of the present: Bourdieu as historical sociologist. In P. S. Gorski (Ed.), *Bourdieu and historical analysis* (pp. 36–66). Duke University Press.

Campbell, P. S. (1998). The musical cultures of children. *Research Studies in Music Education, 11*(1), 42–51. https://doi.org/10.1177/1321103X9801100105

Campbell, P. S. (2011). Musical enculturation: Sociocultural influences and meanings of children's experiences in and through music. In M. Barrett (Ed.), *A cultural psychology of music education press* (pp. 61–81). Oxford University.

Castrillon, C. (2022). *Why soft skills are more in demand than ever.* https://www.forbes.com/sites/carolinecastrillon/2022/09/18/why-soft-skills-are-more-in-demand-than-ever/?sh=45e3efde5c6f

Chan, T. W., & Goldthorpe, J. H. (2007). Social stratification and cultural consumption: Music in England. *European Sociological Review, 23*(1), 1–19. https://doi.org/10.1093/esr/jcl016

Cheadle, J. E., & Amato, P. R. (2011). A quantitative assessment of Lareau's qualitative conclusions about class, race, and parenting. *Journal of Family Issues, 32*(5), 679–706. https://doi.org/10.1177/0192513X10386305

Chen, C. P., & Wong, J. (2013). Career counseling for gifted students. *Australian Journal of Career Development, 22*(3), 121–129. https://doi.org/10.1177/1038416213507909

Chin, T., & Phillips, M. (2004). Social reproduction and child-rearing practices: Social class, children's agency, and the summer activity gap. *Sociology of Education, 77*, 185–210. https://doi.org/10.1177/003804070407700301

Cho, E. (2015). What do mothers say? Korean mothers' perceptions of children's participation in extra-curricular musical activities. *Music Education Research, 17*(2), 162–178. https://doi.org/10.1080/14613808.2014.895313

Cho, E., & Ilari, B. S. (2021). Mothers as home DJs: Recorded music and young children's well-being during the COVID-18 pandemic. *Frontiers in Psychology, 12*. https://doi.org/10.3389/fpsyg.2021.637569

Choi, K. W. Y. (2015). On the fast track to a head start: A visual ethnographic study of parental consumption of children's play and learning activities in Hong Kong. *Childhood, 1*, 1–17. https://doi.org/10.1177/0907568215586838

Chua, A. (2011). *Battle hymn of the tiger mother.* Penguin.

Clement, F., & Dukes, D. (2017). Social appraisal and social referencing: Two components of affective social learning. *Emotion Review, 9*(3), 253–261. https://doi.org/10.1177/1754073916661634

Cocks, N. H. (2022). Letting go, coming out, and working through: Queer frozen. *Humanities (Basel), 11*(6), 146. https://doi.org/10.3390/h11060146

Colvin, E., & Knight, E. (2023). The development of career-related early intentions in the home. In I. E. Colvin & E. Knight (Eds.), *Young people and parenting obligations of the state: Implications for higher education in Australia* (1st ed., pp. 61–87). Springer International Publishing. https://doi.org/10.1007/978-3-031-38285-7

Commonwealth of Australia. (2016). *'A husband is not a retirement plan': Achieving economic security for women in retirement.* The Senate: Economics References Committee. https://www.aph.gove.au/Parliamentary_Business/Committees/Senate/Economics/Economic_security_for_women_in_retirement/Report

Conejeros-Solar, M. L., & Smith, S. R. (2021). Homeschooling gifted learners: An Australian experience. *Australasian Journal of Gifted Education, 30*(1), 23–48. https://doi.org/10.21505/AJGE.2021.0003

Conkling, S. W. (2018). Socialization in the family: Implications for music education. *Update, 36*(3), 29–37. https://doi.org/10.1177/8755123317732969

Cooper, K. (2021). Are poor parents poor parents? The relationship between poverty and parenting among mothers in the UK. *Sociology (Oxford), 55*(2), 349–383. https://doi.org/10.1177/0038038520939397

Coulangeon, P. (2015). Social mobility and musical tastes: A reappraisal of the social meaning of taste eclecticism. *Poetics, 51,* 54–68. https://doi.org/10.1016/j.poetic.2015.05.002

Crabb, A. (2014). *The wife drought.* Random House Australia.

Creech, A. (2010). Learning a musical instrument: The case for parental support. *Music Education Research, 12*(1), 13–32. https://doi.org/10.1080/14613800903569237

Crenshaw, K. (1991). Mapping the margins: Intersectionality, identity politics, and violence against women of color. *Stanford Law Review, 43,* 1241–1299. https://doi.org/10.2307/1229039

Crozier, G., Reay, D., & David James, D. (2011). Making it work for their children: White middle-class parents and working-class schools. *International Studies in Sociology of Education, 21*(3), 199–216. https://doi.org/10.1080/09620214.2011.616343

Custodero, L. A. (2006). Singing practices in 10 families with young children. *Journal of Research in Music Education, 54*(1), 37–56. https://doi.org/10.1177/002242940605400104

Davidson, J. W., & Borthwick, S. J. (2002). Family dynamics and family scripts: A case study of musical development. *Psychology of Music, 30,* 121–136. https://doi.org/10.1177/0305735602301009

Davidson, J. W., Howe, M. J. A., Moore, D. G., & Sloboda, J. A. (1996). The role of parental influences in the development of musical performance. *British Journal of Developmental Psychology, 14*(4), 399–412. https://doi.org/10.1111/j.2044-835X.1996.tb00714.x

De Nora, T. (1999). Music as a technology of the self. *Poetics, 27,* 31–56. https://doi.org/10.1016/S0304-422X(99)00017-0

De Nora, T. (2000). *Music in everyday life.* Cambridge University Press.

De Vault, M. L., & Gross, G. (2012). Feminist qualitative interviewing: Experience, talk, and knowledge. In S. N. Hesse-Biber (Ed.), *Handbook of feminist research: Theory and praxis* (pp. 188–206). Sage.

De Vries, P. (2007). I do music with my children because… Proceedings of the XXIXth Annual Conference: 2–4 July 2007. *Music Education Research, Values and Initiatives* (pp. 39–46).

Debs, M., Kafka, J., Makris, M. V., & Roda, A. (2023). Happiness-oriented parents: An alternative perspective on privilege and choosing schools. *American Journal of Education, 129*(2), 145–176. https://doi.org/10.1086/723066

DeGroot, J. M., & Vik, T. A. (2020). 'The Weight of our household rests on my shoulders': Inequity in family work. *Journal of Family Issues, 41*(8), 1258–1281. https://doi.org/10.1177/0192513X19887767

Dermott, E., & Pomati, M. (2016). "Good" parenting practices: How important are poverty, education and time pressure? *Sociology (Oxford), 50*(1), 125–142. https://doi.org/10.1177/0038038514560260

Doucet, A. (2006). 'Estrogen-filled worlds': Fathers as primary caregivers and embodiment. *The Sociological Review, 54*(4), 696–716. https://doi.org/10.1111/j.1467-954X.2006.00667.x

Dweck, C. (2006). *Mindset: The new psychology of success*. Random House.

Dwyer, R. (2016). *Music teachers' values and beliefs*. Routledge.

Dyndahl, P. (2013). Towards a cultural study of music in performance, education, and society? In P. Dyndahl (Ed.), *Intersection and interplay. Contributions to the cultural study of music in performance, education, and society* (pp. 7–20). Lund University.

Ennis, L. R. (2014). Intensive mothering: Revisting the issue today. In L. R. Ennis (Ed.), *Intensive mothering: The cultural contradictions of modern motherhood* (pp. 1–23). Demeter Press.

Enticott, J., Callander, E., Garad, R., & Teede, H. (2022). Women, work and the poverty trap: Time for a fair go to support health and wellbeing for Australian women. *Monash University: Lens*. https://lens.monash.edu/@medicine-health/2022/04/06/1384563/womens-reverse-wealth-trajectory-leads-to-poverty-in-older-age

Evans, S., Mikocka-Walus, A., Klas, A., Olive, L., Sciberras, E., Karantzas, G., & Westrupp, E. M. (2020). From 'It has stopped our lives' to 'Spending more time together has strengthened bonds': The varied experiences of Australian families during COVID-19. *Frontiers in Psychology, 11*, 588667. https://doi.org/10.3389/fpsyg.2020.588667

Fancourt, D., & Perkins, R. (2017). Associations between singing to babies and symptoms of postnatal depression, wellbeing, self-esteem and mother-infant bond. *Public Health, 145*, 149–152. https://doi.org/10.1016/j.puhe.2017.01.016

Few-Demo, A. L., Lloyd, S. A., & Allen, K. R. (2014). It's all about power: Integrating feminist family studies and family communication. *Journal of Family Communication, 14*(2), 85–94. https://doi.org/10.1080/15267431.2013.864295

Fleetwood, J. (2016). Narrative habitus: Thinking through structure/agency in the narratives of offenders. *Crime Media Culture, 12*(2), 173–192. https://doi.org/10.1177/1741659016653643

Fraser, A., & Hagedorn, J. M. (2016). Gangs and a global sociological imagination. *Theoretical Criminology*, 1–21.

Frith, S. (1996). Music and identity. In S. Hall & P. du Gay (Eds.), *Questions of cultural identity* (pp. 108–127). Sage.

Frith, S. (2008). Why music matters. *Critical Quarterly*, *50*(1–2), 165–179. https://doi.org/10.1111/j.1467-8705.2008.00811.x

Gale, T., & Parker, S. (2015). Calculating student aspiration: Bourdieu, spatiality and the politics of recognition. *Cambridge Journal of Education*, *45*(1), 81–96. https://doi.org/10.1080/0305764X.2014.988685

Geertz, C. (1973). *The interpretation of cultures: Selected essays*. Basic Books.

Germov, J. (2004). What class do you teach? Education and the reproduction of class inequality. In J. Allen (Ed.), *Sociology of education: Possibilities and practices* (pp. 250–269). Cengage Learning Australia.

Gerrard, J. (2014). All that is solid melts into work: Self-work, the 'learning ethic' and the work ethic. *The Sociological Review*, *62*, 862–879. https://doi.org/1 0.1111/1467-954X.12208

Gerwig, G. (2023). *The Barbie movie*. Warner Brothers.

Gillies, V. (2006). Working class mothers and school life: Exploring the role of emotional capital. *Gender and Education*, *18*(3), 281–293. https://doi.org/10.1080/09540250600667876

Gillies, V. (2007). *Marginalised mothers: Exploring working-class experiences of parenting*. Routledge.

Gillies, V. (2010). Is poor parenting a class issue? Contextualising anti-social behaviour and family life. In M. Klett-Davies (Ed.), *Is parenting a class issue?* (pp. 44–61). The Nuffield Press.

Glanville, J. L., Sikkink, D., & Hernández, E. I. (2008). Religious involvement and educational outcomes: The role of social capital and extracurricular participation. *The Sociological Quarterly*, *49*(1), 105–137. https://doi.org/10.1111/J.1533-8525.2007.00108.x

Golden, D., & Erdreich, L. (2014). Mothering and the work of educational care – An integrative approach. *British Journal of Sociology of Education*, *35*(2), 263–277. https://doi.org/10.1080/01425692.2012.747589

Golden, D., Erdreich, L., Stefansen, K., & Smette, I. (2021). Class, education and parenting: Cross-cultural perspectives. *British Journal of Sociology of Education*, *42*(4), 453–459. https://doi.org/10.1080/01425692.2021.1946301

Goodwin, S., & Huppatz, K. (2010). The good mother in theory and research: An overview. In S. Goodwin & K. Huppatz (Eds.), *The good mother: Contemporary motherhoods in Australia* (pp. 1–24). Sydney University Press.

Gracio, R. (2016). Daughters of rock and moms who rock: Rock music as a medium for family relationships in Portugal. *Revista Crítica de Ciências Sociais*, *109*, 83–104. https://doi.org/10.4000/rccs.6229

Gudmundsdottir, H. R., & Gudmundsdottir, D. G. (2010). Parent-infant music courses in Iceland: Perceived benefits and mental well-being of mothers. *Music*

Education Research, 12(3), 299–309. https://doi.org/10.1080/1461380 8.2010.505644

Guendouzi, J. (2006). "The guilt thing": Balancing domestic and professional roles. *Journal of Marriage and Family, 68*(4), 901–909. https://doi.org/10.1111/j.1741-3737.2006.00303.x

Hall, C. (2015). Singing gender and class: Understanding choirboys' musical habitus. In P. Burnard, Y. Hofvander Trulsson, & J. Söderman (Eds.), *Bourdieu and the sociology of music education* (pp. 43–59). Routledge.

Hall, C. (2018). *Masculinity, class and music education: Boys performing middle-class masculinities through music.* Palgrave Macmillan.

Hamer, L., & Tranter, K. (2021). Parents…Next: The ongoing neoliberalising of Australian social security. *Griffith Journal of Law and Human Dignity, 9*(1), 29–55.

Hand, K., Baxter, J., Carroll, M., & Budinski, M. (2020). *Families in Australia survey: Life during COVID-19 Report no. 1: Early findings.* Australian Institute of Family Studies.

Hanna, L. (2012). Homeschooling education: Longitudinal study of methods, materials, and curricula. *Education and Urban Society, 44*(5), 609–631. https://doi.org/10.1177/0013124511404886

Harrigan, M. M., & Miller-Ott, A. E. (2013). The multivocality of meaning making: An exploration of the discourses college-aged daughters voice in talk about their mothers. *Journal of Family Communication, 13*(2), 114–131. https://doi.org/10.1080/15267431.2013.768249

Hartas, D. (2016). Young people's educational aspirations: Psychosocial factors and the home environment. *Journal of Youth Studies, 19*(9), 1148–1163.

Hays, S. (1996). *The cultural contradictions of motherhood.* Yale University Press.

Ho, C., Hu, W., & Griffin, B. (2023). Cultures of success: How elite students develop and realise aspirations to study medicine. *Australian Educational Researcher, 50*(4), 1127–1147. https://doi.org/10.1007/s13384-022-00548-x

Hochschild, A. R. (1983). *The managed heart: The commercialization of human feeling.* University of California Press.

Hofman, A. (2015). Music (as) labour: Professional musicianship, affective labour and gender in socialist Yugoslavia. *Ethnomusicology Forum, 24*(1), 28–50. https://doi.org/10.1080/17411912.2015.1009479

Hofvander Trulsson, Y. (2013). Chasing children's fortunes. Cases of parents' strategies in Sweden, the UK and Korea. In P. Dyndahl (Ed.), *Intersection and interplay. Contributions to the cultural study of music in performance, education, and society* (pp. 125–140). Lund University.

Holochwost, S. J., Propper, C. B., Wolf, D. P., Willoughby, M. T., Fisher, K. R., Kolacz, J., Volpe, V. V., & Jaffee, S. R. (2017). Music education, academic achievement, and executive functions. *Psychology of Aesthetics, Creativity, and the Arts, 11*(2), 147–166. https://doi.org/10.1037/aca0000112

Housing for the Aged Action Group [HAAG], Social Ventures Group. (2022). https://www.oldertenants.org.au/resource-author/social-ventures-australia

Howe, M. J. A., Davidson, J. W., & Sloboda, J. A. (1998). Innate talents: Reality or myth? *Behavioural and Brain Sciences, 21*(3), 399–407. https://doi.org/10.1017/S0140525X9800123X

Ibarra, F. P. (2017). Transmission of Araquio music, songs and movement conventions: Learning, experience and meaning in devotional theatre. *The Qualitative Report, 22*(4), 1031–1049. https://doi.org/10.46743/2160-3715/2017.2699

Ignatow, G. (2009). Why the sociology of morality needs Bourdieu's habitus. *Sociological Inquiry, 79*(1), 98–114. https://doi.org/10.1111/j.1475-682X.2008.00273.x

Ilari, B. (2005). On musical parenting of young children: Musical beliefs and behaviors of mothers and infants. *Early Child Development and Care, 175*(7–8), 647–660. https://doi.org/10.1080/0300443042000302573

Ilari, B. (2013). Concerted cultivation and music learning. *Research Studies in Music Education, 35*(2), 179–196. https://doi.org/10.1177/1321103X13509348

Ilari, B. (2016). Middle-class musical childhoods: Autonomy, concerted cultivation, and consumer culture. In B. Ilari & S. Young (Eds.), *Children's home musical experiences: Across the world* (pp. 92–106). Indiana University Press.

Ilari, B., Moura, A., & Bourscheidt, L. (2011). Music education research between interactions and commodities: Musical parenting of infants and toddlers in Brazil. *Music Education Research, 13*(1), 51–67.

Ilari, B., Hafteck-Chen, L., & Crawford, L. (2013). Singing and cultural understanding: A music education perspective. *International Journal of Music Education, 31*(2), 202–216. https://doi.org/10.1080/14613808.2011.553277

Illouz, E. (1997). Who will care for the caretaker's daughter? Toward a sociology of happiness in the era of reflexive modernity. *Theory, Culture and Society, 14*(4), 31–66. https://doi.org/10.1177/026327697014004002

Ishizuka, P. (2019). Social class, gender, and contemporary parenting standards in the United States: Evidence from a National Survey Experiment. *Social Forces, 98*(1), 31–58. https://doi.org/10.1093/sf/soy107

Jackson, G., & Allan, S. (2010). Fundamental elements in examining a child's right to education: A study of home education, research, and regulation in Australia. *International Electronic Journal of Elementary Education, 2*(3), 349–364.

Jaeger, M. M. (2022). Cultural capital and educational inequality: An assessment of the state of the art. In K. Gërxhani, N. D. de Graaf, & W. Raub (Eds.), *Handbook of sociological science: Contributions to rigorous sociology.* Edward Elgar Publishing.

Jamal Al-deen, T. (2018). Class, honour and reputation: Gendered school choice practices in a migrant community. *Australian Educational Researcher, 45,* 401–417. https://doi.org/10.1007/s13384-017-0255-6

Jamal Al-deen, T., & Windle, J. (2017). 'I feel sometimes I am a bad mother': The affective dimension of immigrant mothers' involvement in their children's schooling. *Journal of Sociology, 53*(1), 110–126. https://doi.org/10.1177/1440783316632604

Juuti, S., & Littleton, K. (2010). Musical identities in transition: Solo-piano students' accounts of entering the academy. *Psychology of Music, 38*(4), 481–497. https://doi.org/10.1177/0305735609351915

Kamin, S., Richards, H., & Collins, D. (2007). Influences on the talent development process of non-classical musicians: Psychological, social and environmental influences. *Music Education Research, 9*(3), 449–468. https://doi.org/10.1080/14613800701587860

Kaufman, P. (2005). Middle-class social reproduction: The activation and negotiation of structural advantages. *Sociological Forum, 20*(2), 245–270. https://doi.org/10.1007/s11206-005-4099-x

Keeler, J. R., Roth, E. A., Neuser, B. L., Spitsbergen, J. M., Waters, D. J. M., & Vianney, J.-M. (2015). The neurochemistry and social flow of singing: Bonding and oxytocin. *Frontiers in Human Neuroscience, 9,* 518–518. https://doi.org/10.3389/fnhum.2015.00518

Kenway, J., & McLeod, J. (2004). Bourdieu's reflexive sociology and 'spaces of points of view': Whose reflexivity, which perspective? *British Journal of Sociology of Education, 25*(4), 525–544.

Kokas, K. (1970). Kodaly's concept of music education. *Bulletin of the Council for Research in Music Education, 22*(Fall), 49–56.

Kong, S. H. (2021). A study of students' perceptions of parental influence on students' musical instrument learning in Beijing, China. *Music Education Research, 23*(3), 287–299. https://doi.org/10.1080/14613808.2020.1832978

Koops, L. H. (2018). Musical tweens: Child and parent views on musical engagement in middle childhood. *Music Education Research, 20*(4), 412–426. https://doi.org/10.1080/14613808.2018.1491541

Koops, L. H., Kuebel, C., & Smith, S. S. A. (2017). Mama's turn: A mother's musical journey. *Research Studies in Music Education, 39*(2), 209–225. https://doi.org/10.1177/1321103X17711629

Koza, J. (2001). Multicultural approaches to music education. In C. A. Grant & M. L. Gomez (Eds.), *Campus and classroom: Making schooling multicultural.* Prentice-Hall.

Kristensen, G. K., & Ravn, M. N. (2015). The voices heard and the voices silenced: Recruitment processes in qualitative interview studies. *Qualitative Research, 15*(6), 722–737. https://doi.org/10.1177/1468794114567496

Lareau, A. (2000). *Home advantage: Social class and parental intervention in elementary education*. Rowman & Littlefield.

Lareau, A. (2003/2011). *Unequal childhoods: Class, race, and family life*. University of California Press.

Lawler, S. (2000). *Mothering the self: Mothers, daughters, subjects*. Routledge.

Lawler, S. (2004). Rules of engagement: Habitus, power and resistance. In L. Adkins & B. Skeggs (Eds.), *Feminism after Bourdieu* (pp. 110–128). Blackwell Publishing.

Lawler, S. (2005). Introduction: Class, culture and identity. *Sociology, 39*(5), 797–806. https://doi.org/10.1177/0038038505058365

Lewis-Beck, M. S., Bryman, A., & Futing Liao, T. (2004). *The SAGE encyclopaedia of social science research methods*. Sage.

Lilliedahl, J. (2021). Class, capital, and school culture: Parental involvement in public schools with specialised music programmes. *British Journal of Sociology of Education, 42*(2), 245–259. https://doi.org/10.1080/0142569 2.2021.1875198

Lois, J. (2012). *Home is where the school is: The logic of homeschooling and the emotional labor of mothering*. NYU Press.

Lois, J. (2017). Homeschooling motherhood. In M. Gaither (Ed.), *The Wiley handbook of home education* (1st ed., pp. 186–206). Wiley.

Lovell, T. (2000). Thinking feminism with and against Bourdieu. *Feminist Theory, 1*(1), 11–32. https://doi.org/10.1177/14647000022229047

Mackinlay, E. (2009). Singing maternity through autoethnography: Making visible the musical world of myself as a mother. *Early Child Development and Care, 179*(6), 717–731. https://doi.org/10.1080/03004430902944320

Mackinlay, E., & Baker, F. (2005). Nurturing herself, nurturing her baby: Creating positive experiences for first-time mothers through lullaby singing. *Women and Music: A Journal of Gender and Culture, 9*, 69–89. https://doi.org/10.1353/wam.2005.0010

Macvarish, J. (2016). *Neuroparenting: The expert invasion of family life*. Palgrave Macmillan. https://doi.org/10.1057/978-1-137-54733-0

Macvarish, J., & Martin, C. (2021). Towards a 'parenting regime': Globalising tendencies and localised variation. In A. M. Castrén et al. (Eds.), *The Palgrave handbook of family sociology in Europe*. Palgrave Macmillan. https://doi.org/10.1007/978-3-030-73306-3_22

Manne, A. (2018). Mothers and the quest for social justice. In C. Nelson & R. Robertson (Eds.), *Dangerous ideas about mothers* (pp. 17–34). UWA Publishing.

Mapana, K. (2011). The musical enculturation and education of Wagogo children. *British Journal of Music Education, 28*(3), 339–351. https://doi.org/10.1017/S0265051711000234

Maton, K. (2005). A question of autonomy: Bourdieu's field approach and higher education policy. *Journal of Education Policy, 20*(6), 687–704. https://doi.org/10.1080/02680930500238861

Maton, K. (2012). Habitus. In M. Grenfell (Ed.), *Pierre Bourdieu: Key concepts* (2nd ed., pp. 48–64). Acumen.

McLeod, J. (2005). Feminists re-reading Bourdieu. *Theory and Research in Education, 3*(1), 11–30.

McLeod, J., & Thomson, R. (2011). Generation. In J. McLeod & R. Thomson (Eds.), *Researching social change* (pp. 107–124). Sage.

McPherson, G. E. (2009). The role of parents in children's musical development. *Psychology of Music, 37*(1), 91–110. https://doi.org/10.1177/0305735607086049

McPherson, G. E., & Davidson, J. W. (2002). Musical practice: Mother and child interactions during the first year of learning an instrument. *Music Education Research, 4*(1), 141–156. https://doi.org/10.1080/14613800220119822

McRobbie, A. (2004). Notes on 'What not to wear' and post-feminist symbolic violence. In L. Adkins & B. Skeggs (Eds.), *Feminism after Bourdieu* (pp. 99–109). Blackwell.

Middleton, A. (2006). Mothering under duress: Examining the inclusiveness of feminist mothering theory. *Journal of the Association for Research on Mothering, 8*(1–2), 72–82.

Milkie, M., & Warner, C. H. (2014). Status safeguarding: Mothers' work to secure children's place in the social hierarchy. In L. R. Ennis (Ed.), *Intensive mothering: The cultural contradictions of modern motherhood* (pp. 66–85). Demeter Press.

Miller, T. (2005). *Making sense of motherhood: A narrative approach*. Cambridge University Press.

Miller, T. (2017). *Making sense of parenthood: Caring, gender and family lives*. Cambridge University Press.

Moore, R. (2012). Capital. In M. Grenfell (Ed.), *Pierre Bourdieu: Key concepts* (2nd ed., pp. 98–113). Acumen.

Morgan, J. P., MacDonald, R. A. R., & Pitts, S. E. (2015). "Caught between a scream and a hug": Women's perspectives on music listening and interaction with teenagers in the family unit. *Psychology of Music, 43*(5), 611–626. https://doi.org/10.1177/0305735613517411

Mukherjee, U., & Barn, R. (2021). Concerted cultivation as a racial parenting strategy: Race, ethnicity and middle-class Indian parents in Britain. *British Journal of Sociology of Education, 42*(4), 521–536. https://doi.org/10.1080/01425692.2021.1872365

Murakumi, K. (2004). Socially organised use of memories of mother in narrative re-construction of problematic pasts. In M. Bamberg & M. Andrews (Eds.), *Considering counter narratives: Narrating, resisting, making sense* (pp. 351–372). John Benjamins Publishing.

Nagel, I. (2010). Cultural participation between the ages of 14 and 24: Intergenerational transmission or cultural mobility? *European Sociological Review, 26*(5), 541–556. https://doi.org/10.1093/esr/jcp037

Neuman, A., & Guterman, O. (2019). How I started home schooling: Founding stories of mothers who home school their children. *Research Papers in Education, 34*(2), 192–207. https://doi.org/10.1080/0267152 2.2017.1420815

Nichols, J. (2005). Music education in homeschooling: A preliminary inquiry. *Bulletin of the Council for Research into Music Education, 166,* 27–42.

O'Reilly, A. (2004). *From motherhood to mothering: The legacy of Adrienne Rich's of woman born.* SUNY Press.

O'Reilly, A. (2008). Introduction. In A. O'Reilly (Ed.), *Feminist mothering* (pp. 1–24). SUNY Press.

O'Reilly, A. (2010). *Twenty-first-century motherhood: Experience, identity, policy, agency.* Columbia University Press.

O'Reilly, A. (2016). *Matricentric feminism: Theory, activism, practice.* Demeter Press.

Orgad, S. (2019). *Heading home: Motherhood, work, and the failed promise of equality.* Columbia University Press.

Oyarzún, J. d. D., Gerrard, J., & Savage, G. C. (2022). Ethics in neoliberalism?: Parental responsibility and education policy in Chile and Australia. *Journal of Sociology (Melbourne, Vic.), 58*(3), 285–303. https://doi.org/10.1177/ 14407833211029694

Parkin, F. (1979). *Marxism and class theory: A bourgeois critique.* Tavistock.

Pecen, E., Collins, D. J., & MacNamara, Á. (2018). "It's your problem. Deal with It." Performers' experiences of psychological challenges in music. *Frontiers in Psychology, 8,* 2374–2374. https://doi.org/10.3389/fpsyg.2017.02374

Perkins, R. (2013). Hierarchies and learning in the conservatoire: Exploring what students learn through the lens of Bourdieu. *Research Studies in Music Education, 35*(2), 197–212. https://doi.org/10.1177/1321103X13508060

Perrier, M. (2013). Middle-class mothers' moralities and concerted cultivation. *Sociology, 47*(4), 655–670. https://doi.org/10.1177/0038038512453789

Peterson, R. A., & Simkus, A. (1992). How musical tastes mark occupational status groups. In M. Lamont & M. Fournier (Eds.), *Cultivating differences: Symbolic boundaries and the making of inequality* (pp. 152–168). The University of Chicago Press.

Pettinger, L. (2015). Embodied labour in music work. *The British Journal of Sociology, 66*(2), 282–300. https://doi.org/10.1111/1468-4446.12123

Phoenix, A., & Brannen, J. (2014). Researching family practices in everyday life: Methodological reflections from two studies. *International Journal of Social Research Methodology, 17*(1), 11–26. https://doi.org/10.1080/1364557 9.2014.854001

Pianostreet.com. (2023). https://www.pianostreet.com/smf/index.php?topic= 37985.0

Pitts, S. (2012). *Chances and choices: Exploring the impact of music education.* Oxford University Press.

Pollock, D. C., & Van Reken, R. E. (2009). *Third culture kids: Growing up among worlds.* Nicholas Brealy Publishing.

Power, R. (2015). *Motherhood and creativity: The divided heart.* Affirm Press.

Prior, N. (2013). Bourdieu and the sociology of music consumption: A critical assessment of recent developments. *Sociology Compass, 7*(3), 181–193. https:// doi.org/10.1111/soc4.12020

Raith, L. (2015). Support, judgement, and marginality: The shifting terrains of the mother country. In L. Raith, J. Jones, & M. Porter (Eds.), *Mothers at the margins: Stories of challenge, resistance and love* (pp. 157–171). Cambridge Scholars.

Reay, D. (1995). A silent majority? Mothers in parental involvement. *Women's Studies International Forum, 18*(3), 337–348. https://doi.org/10.1016/ 0277-5395(95)00029-C

Reay, D. (1997). Feminist theory, habitus, and social class: Disrupting notions of classlessness. *Women's Studies International Forum, 20*(2), 225–233.

Reay, D. (1998). *Class work: Mothers' involvement in their children's primary schooling.* Routledge.

Reay, D. (2004). Gendering Bourdieu's concept of capitals? Emotional capital, women and social class. In L. Adkins & B. Skeggs (Eds.), *Feminism after Bourdieu* (pp. 57–74). Blackwell Publishing.

Reay, D. (2010). Class acts: Parental involvement in schooling. In M. Klett-Davies (Ed.), *Is parenting a class issue?* (pp. 31–43). The Nuffield Press.

Reay, D. (2015a). Foreword. In P. Burnard, Y. Hofvander Trulsson, & J. Söderman (Eds.), *Bourdieu and the sociology of music education* (pp. 43–59). Ashgate.

Reay, D. (2015b). Habitus and the psychosocial: Bourdieu with feelings. *Cambridge Journal of Education, 45*(1), 9–23. https://doi.org/10.108 0/0305764X.2014.990420

Reeves, A. (2015). 'Music's a family thing': Cultural socialisation and parental transference. *Cultural Sociology, 9*(4), 493–514. https://doi.org/10.1177/ 1749975515576941

Riessman, C. K. (2002). Analysis of personal narratives. In J. F. Gubrium & J. A. Holstein (Eds.), *Handbook of interview research: Context and method* (pp. 695–710). Sage.

Riessman, C. K. (2015). Ruptures and sutures: Time, audience and identity in an illness narrative. *Sociology of Health & Illness, 37*(7), 1055–1071.

Rivera, L. A. (2012). Hiring as cultural matching: The case of elite professional service firms. *American Sociological Review, 77*(6), 999–1022. https://doi. org/10.1177/0003122412463213

Robbins, H. (2020). "I Can't Be What You Expect of Me": Power, palatability, and shame in frozen: The broadway musical. *Arts (Basel), 9*(1), 39. https://doi.org/10.3390/arts9010039

Rose, J. (2017). Never enough hours in the day: Employed mothers' perceptions of time pressure. *Australian Journal of Social Issues, 52*(2), 116–130. https://doi.org/10.1002/ajs4.2

Sanders, R. (2020). The impact of capitalist-led neoliberal agendas on parents and their children. *Children Australia, 45*(2), 101–108. https://doi.org/10.1017/chn.2020.1

Sanghera, B. (2016). Charitable giving and lay morality: Understanding sympathy, moral evaluations and social positions. *The Sociological Review, 64*, 294–311. https://doi.org/10.1111/1467-954X.12332

Savage, S. (2015a). *Intensive mothering through music in early childhood education.* Unpublished Masters' Minor Thesis, Monash University.

Savage, S. (2015b). Understanding mothers' perspectives on early childhood music programmes. *Australian Journal of Music Education, 2*, 127–139.

Savage, S. (2019). *Musical mothering: Middle-class strategies and affect across generations.* Unpublished PhD thesis, Monash University.

Savage, S. (2021). The experience of mothers as university students and pre-service teachers during Covid-19: Recommendations for ongoing support. *Studies in Continuing Education, 45*(1), 71–85. https://doi.org/10.1080/0158037X.2021.1994938

Savage, S., & Hall, C. (2017). Thinking about and beyond the cultural contradictions of motherhood through musical mothering. In M. J. Rose, L. Ross, & J. Hartmann (Eds.), *The music of motherhood* (pp. 32–50). Demeter Press.

Sayer, A. (1999). Bourdieu, Smith and disinterested judgement. *Sociological Review, 47*(3), 403–431. https://doi.org/10.1111/1467-954X.00179

Sayer, A. (2005a). *The moral significance of class.* Cambridge University Press.

Sayer, A. (2005b). Class, moral worth and recognition. *Sociology, 39*(5), 947–963. https://doi.org/10.1177/0038038505058376

Scarlato, M. K. M. (2021). Musical fatherhood: A phenomenological study. *Journal of Research in Childhood Education, 35*(3), 373–388. https://doi.org/10.1080/02568543.2020.1728445

Scharff, C. (2017). *Gender, subjectivity, and cultural work: The classical music profession* (1st ed.). Taylor & Francis Group.

Scripp, L., Ulibarri, D., & Flax, R. (2013). Thinking beyond the myths and misconceptions of talent: Creating music education policy that advances music's essential contribution to twenty-first-century teaching and learning. *Arts Education Policy Review, 114*(2), 54–102. https://doi.org/10.1080/10632913.2013.769825

Sheppard, J., & Biddle, N. (2015). *ANU Poll 19 Social class.* [Computer file]. Australian Data Archive, The Australian National University.

Shirani, F., Henwood, K., & Coltart, C. (2012). Meeting the challenges of intensive parenting culture. *Sociology, 46*(1), 25–40. https://doi.org/10.1177/003 8038511416169

Silva, E. B. (2007). Gender, class, emotional capital and consumption in family life. In E. Casey & L. Martens (Eds.), *Gender and consumption: Domestic cultures and the commercialisation of everyday life* (pp. 141–162). Routledge.

Simpson, D., Lumsden, E., & Clark, R. M. (2015). Neoliberalism, global poverty policy and early childhood education and care: A critique of local uptake in England. *Early Years: An International Journal of Research and Development, 35*(1), 96–109. https://doi.org/10.1080/09575146.2014.969199

Sims, M., Calder, P., Moloney, M., Rothe, A., Rogers, M., Doan, L., Kakana, D., & Georgiadou, S. (2022). Neoliberalism and government responses to Covid-19: Ramifications for early childhood education and care. *Issues in Educational Research, 32*(3), 1174–1195.

Sjödin, D., & Roman, C. (2018). Family practises among Swedish parents: Extracurricular activities and social class. *European Societies, 20*(5), 764. https://doi.org/10.1080/14616696.2018.1473622

Skeggs, B. (1997). *Formations of class and gender.* Sage.

Skeggs, B. (2004a). *Class, self, culture.* Routledge.

Skeggs, B. (2004b). Exchange, value and affect: Bourdieu and the 'self'. In L. Adkins & B. Skeggs (Eds.), *Feminism after Bourdieu* (pp. 75–96). Blackwell.

Skeggs, B. (2011). Imagining personhood differently: Person value and autonomist working-class value practices. *The Sociological Review, 59*(3), 496–513. https://doi.org/10.1111/j.1467-954X.2011.02018.x

Small, C. (1998). *Musicking: The meanings of performing and listening.* The University Press of New England.

Smart, C. (2007). *Personal life.* Polity.

Smit, R. (2011). Maintaining family memories through symbolic action: Young adults' perceptions of family rituals in their families of origin. *Journal of Comparative Family Studies, 42*(3), 355–367. https://doi.org/10.3138/jcfs.42.3.355

Smith, A. (1759 [1984]). *The theory of moral sentiments.* Liberty Fund.

Sosniak, L. A. (1995). Learning to be a concert pianist. In B. S. Bloom (Ed.), *Developing talent in young people* (pp. 19–67). Ballantine.

Squire, C. (2008). Experience-centred to socioculturally-oriented approaches to narrative. In M. Andrews, C. Squire, & M. Tamboukou (Eds.), *Doing narrative research* (pp. 42–64). Sage.

Stahl, G. (2015). *Identity, neoliberalism and aspiration: Educating white working-class boys.* Routledge.

Stefansen, K., & Aarseth, H. (2011). Enriching intimacy: The role of the emotional in the 'resourcing' of middle-class children. *British Journal of Sociology of Education, 32*(3), 389–405. https://doi.org/10.1080/01425692.2011.559340

Stone, P. (2007). The rhetoric and reality of "opting out". *Contexts, 6*(4), 14–19. https://doi.org/10.1525/ctx.2007.6.4.14

Streiff, M., & Dundes, L. (2017). Frozen in time: How Disney gender-stereotypes its most powerful princess. *Social Sciences, 6*(2), 38. https://doi.org/10.3390/socsci6020038

Suzuki, S. (1978). *Nurtured by love*. Centre Publications.

Teague, A., & Smith, G. D. (2015). Portfolio careers and work-life balance among musicians: An initial study into implications for higher music education. *British Journal of Music Education, 32*(2), 177–193. https://doi.org/10.1017/S0265051715000121

Threadgold, S., & Gerrard, J. (Eds.). (2022). *Class in Australia*. Monash University Publishing.

Tierney, A. T., Krizman, J., & Kraus, N. (2015). Music training alters the course of adolescent auditory development. *Proceedings of the National Academy of Sciences, 112*(32), 10062–10067. https://doi.org/10.1073/pnas.1505114112

Tiggermann, M., & Anderberg, I. (2020). Social media is not real: The effect of 'Instagram vs reality' images on women's social comparison and body image. *New Media & Society, 22*(12), 2183–2199. https://doi.org/10.1177/1461444819888720

VanderValk, D. H. (2010). Sensitive mothering (Walkerdine and Lucey). In A. O'Reilly (Ed.), *Encyclopaedia of motherhood* (pp. 1112–1113). Sage.

Villalobos, A. (2015). Compensatory connection: Mothers' own stakes in an intensive mother-child relationship. *Journal of Family Issues, 36*(14), 1928–1956. https://doi.org/10.1177/0192513X13520157

Vincent, C., & Ball, S. J. (2007). 'Making up' the middle-class child: Families, activities and class dispositions. *Sociology, 41*(6), 1061–1077. https://doi.org/10.1177/0038038507082315

Vincent, C., & Maxwell, C. (2015). Parenting priorities and pressures: Furthering understanding of 'concerted cultivation'. *Discourse: Studies in the Cultural Politics of Education, 37*(2), 269–281. https://doi.org/10.1080/01596306.2015.1014880

Violinist.com. (2008a). https://www.violinist.com/discussion/archive/14196/

Violinist.com. (2008b). https://www.violinist.com/discussion/archive/13037/

Wacquant, L. (1989). Towards a reflexive sociology: A workshop with Pierre Bourdieu. *Sociological Theory, 7*(1), 26–63. https://doi.org/10.2307/202061

Walkerdine, V., & Lucey, H. (1989). *Democracy in the kitchen: Regulating mothers and socialising daughters*. Virago.

Wang, G. (2009). Interlopers in the realm of high culture: "Music Moms" and the performance of Asian and Asian American identities. *American Quarterly, 61*(4), 881–903. https://doi.org/10.1353/aq.0.0114

Wang, G. (2011). On tiger mothers and music moms. *Amerasia Journal, 37*(2), 130–136. https://doi.org/10.17953/amer.37.2.v5127j0371807341

Wang, G. (2015). *Soundtracks of Asian America: Navigating race through musical performance*. Duke University Press.

Wardman, N., Hutchesson, R., Gottschall, K., Drew, C., & Saltmarsh, S. (2010). Starry eyes and subservient selves: Portraits of "well-rounded" girlhood in the prospectuses of all-girl elite private schools. *The Australian Journal of Education,54*(3),249–261.https://doi.org/10.1177/000494411005400303

Warner, J. (2006). *Perfect madness: Motherhood in the age of anxiety*. Vermilion.

Warren, S., & Barnes, A. (2023). *"I've never seen it as bad as this": Community sector family homelessness research priorities in the current housing and homelessness crisis*. QUT, Centre for Justice Briefing Paper, 35.

Weeks, K. (2011). *The problem with work: Feminist, Marxist, antiwork politics, and postwork imaginaries*. Duke University Press.

Weinshenker, M., & Kim, S.-K. (2023). Concerted cultivation and parental satisfaction: A profile analysis via principal component analysis. *Journal of Family Studies, 29*(3), 1249–1269. https://doi.org/10.1080/13229400.2022.2040574

Wiemer, S., & Clarkson, L. (2023). "Spread too thin": Parents' experiences of burnout during COVID-19 in Australia. *Family Relations, 72*(1), 40–59. https://doi.org/10.1111/fare.12773

Williamon, A., & Thompson, S. (2006). Awareness and incidence of health problems among conservatoire students. *Psychology of Music, 34*(4), 411–430. https://doi.org/10.1177/0305735606067150

Williams, R. (1989). *Resources of hope: Culture, democracy, socialism*. Verso.

Williams, K. E., Bentley, L. A., Savage, S., Eager, R., & Nielson, C. (2023). Rhythm and movement delivered by teachers supports self-regulation skills of preschool-aged children in disadvantaged communities: A clustered RCT. *Early Childhood Research Quarterly, 65*, 115–128. https://doi.org/10.1016/j.ecresq.2023.05.008

Williamson, T., Wagstaff, D. L., Goodwin, J., & Smith, N. (2023). Mothering ideology: A qualitative exploration of mothers' perceptions of navigating motherhood pressures and partner relationships. *Sex Roles, 88*(1–2), 101–117. https://doi.org/10.1007/s11199-022-01345-7

Witte, A. L., Kiewra, K. A., Kasson, S. C., & Perry, K. R. (2015). Parenting talent: A qualitative investigation of the roles parents play in talent development. *Roeper Review, 37*(2), 84–96. https://doi.org/10.1080/02783193.2015.1008091

World Economic Forum. (2022). *Global gender gap report 2022*. Insight Report 2022. https://www3.weforum.org/docs/WEF_GGGR_2022.pdf

Zembylas, M. (2007). Emotional capital and education: Theoretical insights from Bourdieu. *British Journal of Educational Studies, 55*(4), 443–463. https://doi.org/10.1111/j.1467-8527.2007.00390.x

INDEX[1]

[1] Note: Page numbers followed by 'n' refer to notes.

© The Author(s), under exclusive license to Springer Nature
Switzerland AG 2024
S. Savage, *Musical Mothering*, Palgrave Macmillan Studies
in Family and Intimate Life,
https://doi.org/10.1007/978-3-031-65157-1

Printed by Printforce, the Netherlands